Richard Doyle lives in Oxford. His previous novels include *Imperial 109*, *Executive Action* and *Flood*.

Also available by Richard Doyle

Imperial 109
Executive Action
Flood

RICHARD DOYLE

VOLCANO

arrow books

Published in the United Kingdom by Arrow Books in 2006

3 5 7 9 10 8 6 4 2

Copyright © Richard Doyle, 2006

Arrow Books
The Random House Group Limited
20 Vauxhall Bridge Road, London, SW1V 2SA

Random House Australia (Pty) Limited
20 Alfred Street, Milsons Point, Sydney
New South Wales 2061, Australia

Random House New Zealand Limited
18 Poland Road, Glenfield
Auckland 10, New Zealand

Random House (Pty) Limited
Isle of Houghton, Corner of Boundary Road & Carse O'Gowrie
Houghton 2198, South Africa

Random House Publishers India Private Limited
301 World Trade Tower, Hotel Intercontinental Grand Complex
Barakhamba Lane, New Delhi 110 001, India

The Random House Group Limited Reg. No. 954009

www.randomhouse.co.uk

A CIP catalogue record for this book is available from the British Library

Papers used by Random House are natural, recyclable products
made from wood grown in sustainable forests. The manufacturing
processes conform to the environmental regulations of the country of origin

ISBN 9780099469353 (from Jan 2007)
ISBN 0 09 946935 9

Typeset by SX Composing DTP, Rayleigh, Essex
Printed and bound in Great Britain by
Cox & Wyman Ltd, Reading, Berkshire

Prologue

Goodwill, Maine. It began, as it would end, with the whales.

That summer the pods were back off the Maine coast in greater numbers than ever. The experts at the marine aquarium over in Portland put it down to a switch in the ocean currents, but Goodwill folk kept their own counsel; in Jean-Alice's diner on Bearskin Neck, where Rick Larsen played his sad guitar on winter evenings, locals touched the blackened iron harpoon behind the bar for luck. Rick's great-grandfather had captained the last whaler to set out from the Neck in the spring of 1885 and some instincts died hard.

Rick was a troubled boy. His mother died when he was fifteen. Then his father threw him out and he made his home on a catboat salvaged from Indian Creek that he had raised and patched up. Working with his hands came natural to Rick; he could fish, hunt, build a trap, and handle any kind of vessel. He put in a season as a river driver moving logs on the Machias before that was stopped, then for a couple of winters he shipped as crew on a deep-water lobster boat hauling pots 200 miles off the coast. He might have had a job anywhere except that he found it hard taking orders. Stubborn, he was, like all the Larsens.

Old Leif Larsen had sailed as a harpooner in the Southern Ocean before the ban. Back home he filled his children's heads with wild tales of whale hunts and adventure in the Roaring Forties. Whales were his passion; summers were spent working the tourist boats, expounding his lore to the passengers. As his drinking worsened, his moods gave way to periods of black depression punctuated by savage rages.

Rick was nineteen when he met the girl and Viking tall; she was half child still with hair as black as a crow's wing. He was checking Long Beach early one morning and there she was struggling to lift a piece of driftwood timber. The wood was heavy and jagged with rusted wire and it was automatic for Rick to move in, twist the wire off with his fingers and throw the timber in the back of his truck.

The girl spun round at him accusingly.

'You stole my driftwood!'

Rick could only stare. A gust of wind caught the gypsy hair and flung it against the sky in a ragged sheet. A summer kid, he thought. She was fourteen and like no one else in the world. In that moment he was lost and he knew it.

'What do you want with it anyway?' she challenged him.

He looked her in the face and said, 'I'm building a house.'

Poised for flight, she searched his eyes. She read grey seas and ice floes and men with bloody spears. She saw Eric the Red and long-hulled ships sailing up from the sunrise. 'I know about you,' she said.

'You think you do.' He parried her words like a blade, both working by instinct, feeling the way, blind against blind, wary of giving too much too soon.

He turned to go. 'Wait,' she said. 'This house,' she said, 'when can I see it?'

'When it's ready,' he told her.

Her name, he learned later, was Natalie, Natalie Maxwell and she lived in a cliff-top mansion.

And Rick was wary. Not that he was intimidated, just the feeling he had outgrown summer girls. They inhabited a different world and they were welcome to it. Also his battles with his father occupied most of his attention just then. That year he seemed always to be in trouble of one kind or another, so girls were an unnecessary distraction.

The next meeting came six months after. Someone plucked his arm in the diner and there she was at his side, in cut-off pants this time, pulling him towards the door.

It was after midnight and the Neck outside

was deserted. The night was fine, there was no moon, but the sky was lit by a thousand stars. They stood together under a lamp and the beams struck shadows in the hollows of her eyes. In one hand she clutched a heavy flashlight.

'There's a whale stranded out in the Sound.' They were the first words spoken between them all summer.

'Where?' It never occurred to him to ask why she should seek him out. It was as if everything had fallen into place. Of course she would ask and he would help.

'Off Curtain Bluff. I heard some people talking about it.' She spoke quickly, decisively, her head with its dark mane tilted to look him directly in the eye. 'There's a bunch of boats out there trying to help I guess. I couldn't see properly, but I think it's a calf.'

He checked his watch. The tide would soon be turning. There wasn't a lot of time left for arguing. Dad would be in the Pier Street bar drinking Cape Horners, Guinness in a pint pot stirred with a tumbler full of schnapps.

Dad's boat was moored at the factory wharf. She followed him down the ladder. Rick felt in the dark for the engine key in the cockpit from where his father never troubled to remove it. No one would dare to touch anything of his, he threatened, and he was right. Only now was an emergency.

His hand was ready on the starter button when he felt the boat tilt and sway as someone

4

else stepped down off the ladder from the wharf. Rick froze. He knew instantly it was his father, knew from his shape and bulk, from the deft way he ducked in under the cockpit cover, as much as by the beer- and spirit-laden breath. And he flinched inwardly waiting for the old man's fury.

'Hell's teeth! Trespassers is it?' The foghorn voice was thickened by liquor and rage. A huge hand lunged out to catch Rick by the shirt, hauling him bodily off the controls. 'Told you I'd whip your hide off if I ever caught you sneaking round my ship again, boy. And Leif Larsen never breaks his word!'

Rick flung himself backwards to break the hold. The sudden movement rocked the boat, pitching them both off balance. They crashed to the deck, kicking and gouging.

'Let him alone!' The girl sprang at the old man like a wild cat. Lofting the flashlight over her shoulder, she swung it in a furious backhand that rocked him back on his heels.

'Son of a bitch!' he swore, rounding menacingly on her. 'Who in blazes is that?'

'Natalie Maxwell is who.' There was not a trace of fear in her voice. She tossed her head and hefted the flash, poised for another blow. 'There's a whale calf trapped in the Sound.'

A trickle of blood dripped down Leif's face. He focused on her and rubbed his head, wincing. 'Hell's teeth, missy, you pack a punch,' he growled.

Rick snapped the cockpit light on. His father

stared at the girl, recognition dawning. 'The Maxwell brat, eh?' He looked her up and down. 'All grown up, ain't you?'

Rick interrupted. 'It was an emergency. We didn't know where to find you . . .'

'Shut your mouth,' his father snapped. Still addressing Natalie, he continued, 'You got some spirit in you, I'll say that much.'

She stood her ground. 'Please, we need your help; there's a whale stranded.'

'Yeah, I heard you before. Curtain Bluff? Anyone else know?'

She nodded. 'Chance Greene has taken his boat.'

'Greene,' the old man snorted. 'What does a builder know about whales?' He wiped his face and spat over the side. 'Well, what are you waiting for? Cast off the warps.'

Bewildered by the older man's sudden shift of mood, the two hesitated. 'Move, damn you, or I'll put you both ashore and sail alone!'

His bellow broke the spell. As one they leapt to do his bidding, the girl scrambling out onto the prow to free the bow rope, while Rick attended to the stern. His father punched the starter button and the diesel rumbled into life.

Outside the harbour, they crammed on speed. There was a moderate swell running. The radio was on and they listened to the chatter crackling over the airwaves.

'They think it's a right whale,' Natalie whispered to Rick.

6

The old man had ears like a bat though. 'How would they know? There's not two among them have seen a right, even in daylight.'

They motored on steadily into the starry night. Leif Larsen held the throttle open and the throb of the diesel made the boat shake. 'That damn cruiser of Greene's has two knots easy over us,' he sniffed sourly.

Rick joined Natalie staring out over the bow, trying to pick out a light. They passed the entrance to Maple Cove to the north, still hugging the coastline.

'Two Bush Island coming up,' Rick called back a minute later. He had spotted the pale gleam of waves breaking on the island's rocks in the moonlight. He waited for his father to put the wheel over, edging them onto a more southerly course that would put the island on their port side.

'Dad!' he called back. There was an answering growl, most of it lost in the wind, of which they caught the words '. . . tide running . . .'

'What's the matter? Didn't he hear you?' the girl said as the boat maintained its course, heading steadily towards the line of broken water.

'He heard okay,' Rick told her tersely. 'He's just not listening. The dumb bastard is set on beating Greene's boat and he's taking us through the Gurge.'

'At night?' She gripped his arm. 'Isn't that risky?'

Rick bit his lip. 'Normally I'd trust him if he takes it slowly, but tonight with the liquor he's drunk . . .'

Side by side they watched as the boat tore on with no sign of slackening pace and the breakers coming nearer. 'Crazy old coot,' he muttered savagely.

Her hand reached out for his in the darkness. 'It's me, isn't it?' she said into his ear.

'Yeah, he's showing off.'

'I guess it means he's human after all.'

The boat was batting along into the waves, headed east again with the lighthouse beam showing dead ahead. To their left, a quarter of a mile off, the cliffs of Curtain Bluff stood clear in the moonlight. 'Those lights over there by the shore, have they found the whale?'

Leif Larsen swore, 'That's Chance Greene and his merry men trying to drag the whale clear.' He spat over the side disgustedly, 'Trying to kill it more like.'

Rick was staring astern, cupping his hand to his ear to listen. 'Be quiet,' he said softly. 'You're both wrong. It's right here, close to us.'

The old man's head whipped round. 'What's that you're saying, boy?'

'The whale calf, it's here with us. I can smell it.'

'It's a right, poor dumb animal.'

The whale lay on the surface, half submerged, its back a smooth black hump that glistened slickly in the spotlight as waves washed against it. The creature breathed exhaustedly with long, ragged respirations. Tears spilled unrestrainedly down Natalie's cheeks as she watched. It was apparent that the whale was dying. Leif played the beam of the spot along its flank and tail. The great flukes drooped heavily. There was no reaction to the light; the calf was too weak to care any longer. Rick's heart sank; *Eubalaena glacialis*, the true ice whale, a North Atlantic right whale, the rarest of the rare. A ten-month-old female newly separated from its mother by the look of her and in dire straits.

The old man's breath hissed between his teeth in a thin whistling noise. 'She's finished,' he said flatly.

Natalie threw an agonised glance at Rick. 'It's not true! Say it isn't true!' she begged him in a whisper.

That was how he recalled the scene; the line of surf silver in the moonlight, the silhouette of the girl's face in the stern, the laboured breathing of the stricken beast, his father's brooding menace.

'Aye, take a good look.' His father scowled. 'It'll likely be the last you'll ever see.' He was searching round the flukes with the light. 'There's blood in the water there, see? Must have cut herself deep; severed the tendons.'

The long despairing breaths were the saddest sounds imaginable. 'We've got rope,' Natalie beseeched the two men. 'We could tow her back into harbour . . .'

'There's one thing we can do.' The old man's voice was granite harsh and Rick stiffened in every fibre at her side. A sense of dread filled him and he knew what was coming.

With a violent movement the old man jerked at a lashing, dropping the inflatable into the water astern.

'Get in,' he spat. 'And you, little missy, you've been playing whale watchers. Now I'll show you what whaling is really about. Go on' – he clawed his son's shoulder – 'a clean death or a lingering one. Dawn in two hours and the orcas will be here. They'll rip its tongue out and leave it to bleed.'

Rick's colour was bleached corpse-like in the glare of the spot. Natalie clung to him. 'No!' she cried in horror.

Leif Larsen rounded on her, the savagery showing in his face. 'This is nature, this is how the whales live – and die.'

Reaching out to the cockpit rim, he snatched up the long harpoon clipped there and thrust the shaft into his son's hand. 'Here, take this and show what you're made of! You know how, a long thrust and deep to find the heart.'

Rick paled. He stood, clutching the lance, staring across to where the whale floated heavily on the dark rollers.

'Go on!' his father bellowed. 'You heard me!'

'Rick, no!' Natalie shrieked.

He seemed not to hear. Like a man in a

trance he moved to the side of the boat. He stopped.

'Do you care about the whales or are you like them?' With a sweep of his huge arm Rick's father indicated the lights of the departing boats. 'Pious fools, who think they can interfere. You know it has to be. If you shirk this it'll be the calf that pays the price, not you.'

Slowly, stiffly, like a man going to his execution, Rick climbed down into the inflatable, the harpoon lance clamped in one hand. He laid it down and took up the paddles.

'Wait!' Natalie cried out to him. He looked back over his shoulder at her with dazed eyes like a sleepwalker still. She read the blankness in them as if darkness had touched him and covered her face. With a savage laugh the old man cast off the painter and setting his foot against the smaller craft thrust it clear.

They watched him work his way alongside with painful strokes, the whale inert, unmoving, waiting helplessly for the inevitable. The girl's gaze locked on the dying beast. There was a bond between man and animal here that she could only guess at. Something that the father had learned down in the Southern Ocean all those years ago and was passing on to his son. An atavistic throwback to a line of hunters that reached back to the dawn of humanity, of hunter and quarry. The old man was a link with that past and now his kind was done for just as the right whale was. Partners in extinction.

11

Casualties before the march of progress. She wept. How could one believe in mercy when life itself was merciless?

The rubber side of the inflatable bumped alongside the whale's flank. Water sloshed between them into the dinghy. His father was covering the scene with the spot; the beam picked out the light-coloured patches of calloused skin on the beast's head and upper jaw. A part of Rick's brain was numb, blanked out with horror; the other side still functioned smoothly, planning what had to be done, breaking the task down into a series of steps. That part of him was now visualising the whale's internal structure and directing the dinghy to the point closest to the calf's twin blowholes. The waves seemed to have moderated for the moment, making the task easier. He was aware of the bow sliding over the right flipper. The calf still seemed unconscious of his presence or too weak to offer resistance.

He shipped the oars and, standing up, reached for the lance.

A tremor ran through the flank and a feeble respiration vented from behind the head, bathing him in the creature's warm breath. Rick shuddered, balancing on the stiff thwart. The calf was so low in the water now that he looked down on it with ease. Horror filled him at the thought of meeting its eye. If that happened he knew he would not be able to go through with this. A mist seemed to have formed about him, shutting out the boat, Dad, Natalie. For now only the whale mattered and the lance in his hand. He didn't stop to think any longer. Any delay and the sea might get up. He lifted the twelve-foot lance over his head, measuring the spot with his eye, and struck with all his strength.

He struck and struck again, plunging the petal-shaped blade deep into the thick flesh to find a vital organ. More tremors ran through the huge body. It heaved and twisted, almost hurling Rick off into the water. Then abruptly on his fifth or sixth thrust, his lance found its mark. A river of bright blood twice his height spouted up. The tip of the lance had pierced the coiled arteries around the lungs. Rick fell back into the dinghy as the crimson rain fell about him. Around him the water churned into a bloody froth as the whale flailed in its death agony. Its fins beat the waves, slapping up and down, while all the time blood and gore spewed from the great head. Urgently Rick flung himself on the paddles, pulling the dinghy clear. He was witnessing what his father and the old-time whalers called 'the flurry', the death throes. It seemed to last for ever, but in reality was over in less than thirty seconds. With a last convulsive heave the calf rolled over, fin up, and lay motionless and silent, afloat in a spreading pool of its own blood.

Rick collapsed at the paddles, blood drenched from head to foot, the sweet sickly stench clinging to him like guilt. With a diesel growl the

13

boat surged alongside and a splash of cold water doused him, a pail chucked by his father. His raucous laughter echoed in his mind now, that and the horror on the girl's face.

He left town that same day. Sailed off into the blue-bright morning in his boat as his father had done before him.

That was ten years ago. Now Leif was dead and the boy had returned, a man.

14

Chapter 1

Thursday, mid-afternoon. Cumbre Vieja, La
Palma, Canary Islands. The ride over the
mountain had been hot and the dust on the road
descending the western slope caught in their
throats. 'How much longer?' the girl shouted
into the driver's helmet. She spoke in English,
which was their common language. Flavia her
name was, she was twenty, from the Rhineland,
bare-backed, with golden skin and hair streaked
silver by sun and sea. He was two years the
junior, Spanish with some French Arab mixed in
and a boy's insolent carriage. The Honda was his
older brother's, borrowed without permission
and the girl likewise.

He slid the bike into another hairpin and the
girl squealed as the wheels bounced over bare
stone. He braked and halted a moment. 'Look!'
He threw out an arm, pointing. 'Down there,
see?' Four hundred precipitous feet below the
road, a tiny cove fringed with black volcanic sand

15

was sculpted out of the cliff face as perfectly as a film set. 'No one comes here. Just us on the beach.' He felt her arms tighten around his waist and flushed under his helmet. He had had the hots for this one ever since Raul started going out with her. Two days ago, knowing his brother would be away on Tenerife, he had dropped a casual hint of a secret beach on the far side of the island, a hidden spot where dolphins came to play and where a couple could be alone and unobserved. He had seen her violet eyes narrow like a cat's and the tip of her tongue flick across her mouth. She had nodded, just once quickly, a twitch of the head, but enough.

Another ten minutes and they stopped the bike in the shade of a Canary palm. It was as the boy had promised, a perfect spot. The sand was unmarked, powder smooth, the water blue and inviting, protected from the Atlantic breakers by the enveloping arms of the cove. Samphire and juniper clung to the lower cliff face while the higher slopes of the mountains were crowded with stands of pine. Higher still, like an ever-present threat, loomed the volcanic crags of Cumbre Vieja.

'A good place to swim.' The boy grinned happily, waving his snorkel and mask. 'Many fish.'

The girl gazed out westwards over the smooth water, rocked by the gentlest ripples. The horizon was hazy in the heat with no sign of ship or land. 'What is out there?'

16

His teeth flashed in his brown face. 'America.' He grinned. 'Three thousand miles.'

She laughed back, 'And Africa?'

He jerked a thumb over his shoulder. 'That way; Morocco only sixty miles. Here is just us.'

'And dolphins,' she teased him.

'Yes, and whales.'

Her eyes went large. 'Whales?'

'Small whales only. They do not hurt people.'

The girl found her suntan lotion and began oiling her arms. 'My shoulders, please.' She turned her back to him. He squeezed the lotion into his palm and smoothed it on, marvelling at the silky skin, the soft firm flesh and slender bones beneath. He felt himself becoming aroused again.

She wrinkled her nose. 'Do you smell something?'

The boy straightened up. The air was hot and close in the cove, almost as if a storm was due except the sky was clear. Not a bird stirred and the only sound was an occasional click from the bike's engine block as it cooled. Mingled with the perfume of the tanning oil it seemed to him he caught a momentary whiff of rotten egg. Then it was gone. He shrugged. 'Maybe.' He had no time for niceties. He was sweating from the ride. He wanted to swim and then have sex. 'Come.' He started down the beach.

The girl replaced the cap on the bottle. She shaded her eyes, staring at the unbroken surface. 'Where are the dolphins?'

The dolphins would appear, the boy assured her. They liked to play in the clear water of the bay. He had often seen them.

With a deft movement the girl swept her hair up in a bunch at the back of her neck and fastened it with a band. She sniffed again. 'What is that smell? It hurts my nose.'

'Nothing. The sea. Ozone. Come and swim and be cool.'

Maybe, she thought, it was sweat from the ride running into her eyes. She would be okay when she was in the water. Another acrid waft caught in her throat, making her cough. A puff of smoke floated up into the sunlight nearby. Whatever was burning had stained the rock bright yellow. 'People have been here!' she called.

'What?'

'People, they have made a fire.'

The boy shook his head dismissively. 'No one comes here.' The nearest fishing village was almost a mile away. The single hotel there had its own beach. He reached the water and waded out. Ripples spread in front of him across the glassy surface. A dead parrot fish floated on its side in the shallows, the red and yellow markings unmistakable. Probably that was what was making the smell. He kicked it away out of sight. He was half conscious of a faint humming sound in the air or the ground, he could not be certain. It seemed to come to him through the soles of his feet, very low and distant like a truck high up the mountain.

When he was knee-deep he turned to face her and throwing out his arms let himself fall backwards with a splash. 'The water is beautiful,' he cried, surfacing.

The girl took a last glance at the smoke. Maybe after they had cooled off they could move to the other side of the bay. She settled her diving mask over her head and trotted out on the sand. 'Aiee, hot!' she yelped, startled.

'Are you okay? Did you hurt yourself?'

'No, the sand burned my feet.' She swam out to join him. The water was marvellously clear. Tucking up her tail neatly, she dived down to pick up a piece of dark volcanic glass. 'Look!' she showed the boy on her return.

He snatched it from her. 'Now we must find it again!' he shouted, throwing it. Laughing, they chased one another out into the bay.

'The water is warm down there,' she spluttered, emerging after another dive. 'And I see no fish, only, how do you say? Bubbles?'

He frowned at her, perplexed. 'Bubbles?'

'With air, yellow like balloons.'

He dived with her and together they observed the glistening streams rising past them towards the surface. 'What makes them, do you think?' she demanded when they returned for air.

He grinned. 'Fish?'

'Stupid!' She splashed water in his face and twisted away, diving down through the iridescent strings. He followed her down, swimming fast to catch up, gliding with her near the seabed. Fresh

19

columns of bubbles were bleeding from the sand over the bed of the cove. Some of the vents were stained yellow and green and the couple examined them curiously.

'Where are the fish?' she protested, when next they rested. 'I have seen not one fish. And you said there would be dolphins.'

'Dolphins will come,' he promised, taking her hand and leading her back towards the shallows. They found a hollow place among the rocks along the shoreline where they could stand shoulder deep on the firm dark sand.

'Oh,' she said again. 'It is warm here. But this water is too much salt; it makes my skin itch.' She rubbed her arms, but the boy was done with talking. Settling her back against a smooth piece of rock, he took her face between his hands.

'Raul?' she protested, hesitating, her hands against his chest.

'Raul is not here,' he reminded her.

'We do not tell him, okay?'

He nodded, kissing her again. This was between the two of them. His hand slipped round behind her back, reaching for the strings of her bra top.

'My eyes they are sore,' she complained, blinking. 'The salt here is bad for them.'

He kissed the thick lashes gently. 'Better?' he said.

'Mmm,' she responded, lifting the bikini top over her head and tossing it on the rock behind her. Underneath, her tan was perfect. After that neither noticed much of their surroundings, though it did seem to the boy at one point that he felt the seabed quiver underfoot again and this time more strongly.

Some little while later she stiffened suddenly. 'What was that?'

The boy grunted. He was too busy to care. 'What?' he panted.

'A big noise, loud, like a gun.'

'In your head. I hear nothing.'

Her nails dug into his back. 'I heard it,' she insisted.

He sighed, 'A rock cracking on the mountain. It happens all the time. Everything okay.' He caressed her smooth flanks under the water. She was everything he had dreamed and more. 'Everything okay,' he repeated.

She relaxed, feeling him move again inside her. He was so handsome this one, gentle and sensitive. Not like the brother, who went at her like a bull. Her lips nuzzled against his neck as he thrust, brushing the dark curls. One thing was curious: the silver ring he wore in his ear had turned black, she noticed, and was disturbed without knowing why.

Later, when they were spent, they swam slowly out into the middle of the bay, their clothes left behind on the rocks. The water felt clean against their naked bodies. Flavia still itched. There were red inflamed patches on her arms and chest where she had rubbed herself. Maybe it was the sun on the trip over, the boy

21

suggested. 'Look, more bubbles,' he pointed, trying to distract her. 'Many more.' It was true. The sandy bottom was hissing with streams of rising gas like the base of a boiling pan.

'What makes that?'

He shook his head. 'Steam from underground?' He reached behind her playfully and cupped her breasts as they trod water. She put her hands on his and saw with a flicker of concern that her own rings had turned black like his. As she looked a shiver seemed to shake the water, stirring up the surface into a maze of conflicting ripples as if whipped by discordant gusts of wind. Except that there was no wind. It lasted for perhaps a minute, then the ripples slowly died away and the cove settled back into an uneasy peace.

Dreamily they drifted across the cove, half swimming, half floating, caressing one another lazily. It did not strike either as odd that the water seemed to be growing warmer; it was still the hottest part of the day. Then abruptly the girl gave a squeak of disgust. They had drifted in among a shoal of dead fish, floating on the surface, glassy eyes staring.

As they struggled clear, an iridescent dome blossomed on the surface an arm's length away. It swelled and burst with a soft plop, releasing a pungent gas that set both gasping.

'Aiee, horrible!' the girl protested, splashing away out of range. 'We cannot stay here.' Barely had she finished speaking when a thudding sound, low but heavy as if a huge bass drum was being beaten up behind the mountain, rolled ominously round the cove.

'*Ist kommen ein sturm?*' she demanded bewildered.

The boy looked up at the clear sky and across at the mountain ridge, seeking an explanation. 'No, no storm, that was Cumbre Vieja.' He saw her brow crease. '*El volcán*,' he elaborated.

'Volcano?' A look of alarm came over the girl's face. She glanced back towards the shore. The palm trees where they had left the bike were half obscured by steam or smoke. The bubbling of gas from under the water became more urgent, sizzling around them like a spa bath. Already the temperature was growing measurably warmer.

The boy tried to recall what he knew of the volcano. Eruptions were a fact of life like the weather. For all his lifetime the mountain had lain dormant. Two years ago there had been minor tremors. Then this winter the activity resumed, but always confined to the summit; smoke plumes and spectacular spark displays at night, lava streams flowing in the craters. His brother made good money guiding tourists up to watch. Lately the mountain had gone quiet again. Was this noise a signal of a fresh outburst? They were a long way here from any danger surely? Unless the gas in the water, the fumes, the dead fish were somehow connected . . .

Another, louder rumble rolled among the upper slopes, setting the surface quivering again.

23

'This is not good.' The girl's voice sounded frightened. She coughed on the fumes spreading around them. 'I want to go back now.' She shook his arm. 'We get our clothes, okay?' she pleaded.

Without waiting for his answer she led off, swimming strongly. The boy followed in her wake. The gas eruptions were nauseating, staining the water with clouds of sulphurous yellow or poisonous green. Every breath was painful now. The boy's skin burned from the acid release and his eyes stung so that he could hardly bear to open them. This must have been what killed the fish, he thought, and drove away the dolphins.

They reached the rock where they had made love together minutes before and scooped up their bathing things. The beach was only a few yards further. It seemed to have become steeper than before. The beach was burning hot. Beyond the water line, patches of sand smoked and steamed as if the ground below was on fire. But there was the bike under the trees. Yelping, they sprinted across the burning sand.

Steam was hissing from a vent under the Honda's front wheel. Tossing the girl the bits of her bikini, he grabbed the handles and hastily moved the machine out of danger.

There was a shriek from the girl. He looked back. She was struggling with her pants, dismay on her face. 'What's wrong?' he called. 'Hurry, get dressed.'

'It's broken!' she wailed.

He stared uncomprehendingly. She pulled at the string, trying to tie a knot. A gap opened up across her rump as the cloth tore across the hips like a rotten sack. The girl shrieked as the remains dropped away.

The boy examined his own shorts. The colour was different, bleached out and there were small holes that he hadn't noticed before. When he stretched the waistband to put them on, the fabric shredded in his hands.

He gaped at the remains and then at the naked girl. 'Acid, acid in the water.'

The girl stamped her foot. 'Do something! I cannot go back like this!' she stormed, tears welling.

The boy looked around helplessly. He couldn't think of anything to suggest. Neither of them had thought to bring a towel. The girl was sobbing with rage and humiliation. The boy hung his head; their little escapade had ended in disaster. The news would spread all round the island; they would be laughing stocks. Raul would kill him for sure. His mother would box his ears, and as for Flavia's father . . . Wild thoughts ran through his brain. What if they made him marry her? They would have to live in Germany together. No, surely they couldn't do that.

Without warning a tremendous detonation split the air overhead. The earth shuddered. He knew what that was, everyone on the island recognised an earthquake. Showers of rocks cascaded off the cliffs, pelting the two with dust and debris. Grabbing the girl, he pulled her under the shelter of the trees and they cowered there shaking while stones crashed down around them. More concussions shook the cove and the ground vibrated with sharp snapping sounds as if it was being stretched apart by unendurable pressures.

A vast column of smoke as thick and solid as a wall was boiling straight up from behind the mountain ridge. Torrents of ash streamed down out of the sky, turning day to night. Out in the cove waves smashed against the rocks and the once green water was stained with filthy discharges that steamed and bubbled like some nightmare cauldron. Thirty yards out in the middle of the bay, a roaring geyser erupted, hurling a column of boiling mud skywards. Black rain lashed their bare skin, searing unbearably with every drop.

'We can't stay here!' he screamed in the girl's ear above the cacophony. Grabbing her by the hand, he ran with her to where the bike lay on its side. Wrenching it upright, he leapt naked into the saddle and pumped the starter, praying it would catch. To his relief the motor burst into life. The girl was clambering on behind, her arms locked around his waist, screaming at him to hurry. Gunning the throttle, he bounced forward over the blackening sand. A fragment of rock pinged off the speedo. They had forgotten their helmets, but there was no time to go back for them. The ground was still shaking at intervals, threatening at any moment to spill them off.

They wobbled along the track leading to the road, steering a path between fallen boulders. Overhead the volcano was panting like a giant animal, squirting ash shot through with streaks of fire from an unseen vent. Both were terrified that at any moment they would meet the greedy red tongue of a lava flow spilling down the mountainside to trap them. The boy had constantly to slow to avoid obstacles and to wipe the ash and mud from his eyes.

Blackened from head to foot, they finally reached the road, the bike's wheels churning through a rapidly deepening carpet of hot ash. What had started out as a harmless affair had ended up a terrifying nightmare. At least, the boy reflected wearily, in this state nobody could possibly recognise them.

Chapter 2

Goodwill, Maine. Six p.m.

'Did you ever see a sunset like that?' a woman sighed from the terrace. 'Such colours! Like the whole sky is on fire.'

It had been a perfect day. Now at last the heat was beginning to fade, leaving the evening air soft and damp, scented by jack pines. Beyond the lawn, the woods ran down to the shore where the last sailboats crept home across the mirrored surface of the Sound while away to the west the sun went down in a blaze of glory that seemed like the end of the world.

The party at the Maxwell house on Indian Point had been going since five. The bottles sat in iced tubs under the century-old beech trees shading the deck and there were two barbecue pits serving up lobsters to the hundred or so guests.

Rick Larsen's new shirt stuck to his back as he threaded his way through the boisterous vacation crowd. The champagne he had drunk had left him light-headed, euphoric. Relief surged inside him; that the ordeal of the announcement was over, the future settled finally.

He looked around for Natalie. She had been at his side for the toasts. Now she had disappeared, swallowed up in a posse of girlfriends. People everywhere were slapping him on the shoulder, congratulating him. Rick grinned back mechanically, trying to recall names. He was a local boy who had sailed around the world, served a hitch in the navy and come home to settle. Now he stood out in this gathering of affluent kids in designer sportswear, their parents fresh from yachts and tennis parties. Natalie's people, not his own.

Across a sea of heads he spotted Don Egan signalling to him. Don looked worried and out of place, as well he might. His broad red face was sweaty and his uniform shirt rumpled. He must have driven here straight from his office downtown. For a moment it crossed Rick's mind that something could be wrong, though that was hardly likely in Goodwill. Excusing himself, he set a course up the steps towards the terrace doors where Don was standing.

A sunburned matron in a monogrammed silk shirt blocked his path. Mindy Drexler McNeil, Harvey McNeil's wife, whose family controlled Boston's Drexler Bank. 'Rick.' Her teeth flashed a double-edged smile. 'I hope you know you are the luckiest man in Goodwill.' Rick mouthed some platitude and slid past. Her son, Cole, had been squiring Natalie before Rick came back on the scene. Natalie was wealthy as well as beautiful. Rick's good fortune was the keynote of the evening. The people wringing his hand were most likely covertly speculating how she would cope sharing his apartment downtown, to say nothing of the yet-to-be-completed house.

Another woman in a billowing red dress with ethnic bracelets jangling at her wrists enveloped him in a warmly scented embrace. 'Tell me, dear,' she heaved, hanging on to both his hands, 'what sign were you born under?'

'Capricorn, I think.' With an effort Rick placed her: Mrs Smith Tyrell, an incomer who lived in Goodwill all year round now and produced plays with the Repertory Company.

'Ah, and sweet Natalie is a Pisces. A water sign makes the perfect partnership with the earth, but beware' – her manner grew stern – 'the ocean can be fickle.'

'I'll bear it in mind.' Rick never read his horoscope though Natalie dabbled. 'Excuse me now.' Freeing himself, he escaped into the crowd.

Out in the gardens lamps had been switched on among the trees. Natalie's parents threw a big get-together every year on the family's arrival for the summer season. Traditionally it marked the kick-off for the town's Founders' Day celebrations that would climax in three days' time with a public holiday and a parade with floats and a band. Rick had never been included in the invitation list. Only sometimes, back in the heady days when he and Natalie had first started going together, he used to sneak up here to the boathouse when her parents were out.

'My *dear*,' the swooping accents of Elise Maxwell cut through the babble, 'you know Natalie, once she decides she wants something!' Rick winced. Natalie's mother could be charming and funny or spoiled and demanding according to her whim of the moment. She was a talented artist whose works were exhibited locally. Natalie had inherited her gift – and her temper.

His older sister, Rebecca, looked to have chickened out but his mother's sister, his aunt Anne Peck, who did the catering for Maxwell parties, had come through from the kitchen to drink their health. And a number of locals had turned out in support. Hike Davis, former football coach at the high school, was here, glass in hand as ever, along with Larry Smollett, owner of the lobster pound on the Causeway. Over by the rail three different breeds of doctors were locking heads: Dr Southwell from the Medical Center, Dr Potter, the high school principal, who had suspended Rick for fighting in his senior year, and Reverend Dr Jean Gosling of St Andrew's Episcopal Church who had brought along her pop-eyed twin daughters, the Gosling Girls, one of whom was slipping round behind the family's back with a married fisherman from Ellsworthy.

31

Don had been intercepted by a silver-haired man in plaid pants and was stammering apologies for his presence. 'Not at all. You're most welcome. Everyone is invited,' Rick heard his future father-in-law assure him. Of course, everyone who had received an invitation, that was. Elliott Maxwell managed to make it sound as though he had thrown his doors open to the entire population of Goodwill.

Rick pushed through to join them. 'Elliott, you know Don, our Chief of Police?'

'Of course I know Don. Very well in fact. Don and I are old friends. We have had many interesting conversations, haven't we, Don?' There was an edge to Elliott's tone. The Maxwells had always made a particular point of getting to know the locals. Mixing in, they called it.

'Have a drink, Don.' Rick grabbed a glass off a tray carried by Izzy Jenks, his cousin Beth's girl, who had been hired for the event along with half a dozen other classmates. Izzy gave him a huge wink and moved off, her tongue caught between her teeth as she concentrated on not spilling the Maxwell champagne.

'Elliott,' boomed a voice behind. Turning, Rick recognised another local but a prosperous one this time: Chance Greene, builder and property magnate. He and Elliott Maxwell were old cronies.

At that moment he caught a glimpse of Natalie across the deck. She was reaching up to kiss the mouth of a handsome summer guy. A boy who probably rowed crew for some Ivy League college. The sort of boy her parents must have imagined she would pick one day instead of him. The look on her face was so radiant that his heart turned over with sheer jealousy. The line of eye and cheek, of jaw and throat, so achingly perfect.

Taking Don's arm, Rick guided him down off the deck onto the close-clipped turf. They stood under the flagpole, looking back at the lighted house and listening to the click of crickets in the dusk. The dying sun stained the landscape with flaming hues of vermilion and mauve. Don wiped a hand across his face. 'Sure is warm still. Figured I'd stop by, keep an old buddy company on the big day.' He surveyed the party scene, puffing. 'Helluva turnout. Guess I don't know too many people here, Rick.'

This was embarrassing for Rick. He and Don saw each other every day. They had been to the same school. In the way of small towns their mothers were distantly related. Don was a loyal friend who had seen Rick through some of the bad times; he had every right to be present to celebrate his engagement, but this was the Maxwells' party.

'Relax,' Rick told him. 'Enjoy yourself. Natalie will be glad you're here. Everything okay downtown?'

Don tasted his drink and smacked his lips. 'This has to be real imported, not domestic, huh?

I didn't mean to butt in on you guys. Yeah, pretty much what you'd expect. Lot of tourist traffic, which is good, I guess. Cars and trucks backed up all the way to the bridge. Had to use the siren to get past. I reckoned coming out here qualified as an emergency, huh?' He chuckled nervously. 'Plus we have a bunch of surfers took it into their heads to pay a visit.'

'Surfers?' Rick had to bend to catch his words.

Don nodded. 'A whole bunch just drove in off Route One around five, camper vans, SUVs, pick-ups, thirty or forty at least.'

Rick was puzzled. Goodwill was mainly famous for its tides. The harbour lay at the end of an inlet at the mouth of the Bay of Fundy, which had the highest tidal range in the world. It made for good fishing grounds but the coastline was all rocks. No one in their right mind would dream of surfboarding here.

'And Founders' Day coming up,' Don added. Two days from now it would be the tercentennial of the First Landing in Goodwill in 1708. With a local force of six, Goodwill PD was stretched anyway in summer. Founders' Day was the township's big event of the year, drawing crowds from Bangor and Bar Harbor as well as from across the Canadian border.

'Surfers go all over. Maybe they're on their way to some beach party up in Nova Scotia.'

'Yeah, most like.'

Don was a poor liar. Rick could tell he was holding something back, but there was too much on his mind. Already Natalie's mother was throwing him hard glances to signal he wasn't pulling his weight socially. 'Don, have another drink. Forget about the surfers. They can't do any harm tonight.'

Don looked away. 'Maybe so,' he agreed. 'One guy wanted to know had we had any big waves yet? When I told him three to four foot is tops round here for the time of year, he laughed in my face.'

Bursts of laughter from the deck rang out overhead. Izzy Jenks came by again and Rick asked her to bring him down a beer. He was tired of champagne. More guests were arriving, some spilling down onto the lawns. Up on the deck by the doors leading into the house Rick made out the tall figure of Sarah Hunter who acted as Elliott Maxwell's secretary when he was in town for the summer. There had been a time back in high school when he and Sarah had gone around together. Another of those details that was awkward now he was engaged.

Don was speaking again. 'I sort of figured you should be the first to know, Rick. You being a Selectman and all.'

'Know what, Don?'

'We had this fax from State. They are putting out an advisory warning for possible high waves. Something to do with tectonic activity across the ocean.'

'Tectonic activity?' Rick was concentrating now. A connection triggered. 'Is this connected with that volcano that featured on TV a while back? Some island off the coast of Africa?'

'Sounds like the one. Right part of the ocean anyhow.'

'But that's been rumbling on for weeks now, months even.'

'Yeah, well,' Don shrugged, 'seems like it's gotten bigger or something. Else maybe just the media talking the thing up again. Like I said, they put out this advisory.'

'Who did, Coastguard?'

'Uh uh.' Don shook his head. 'MEMA, that's Maine Emergency Management Agency and the Department of Homeland Security both. Looks like everybody wants to get in on the act.'

Rick stared at him. 'Jesus, Don,' he said softly. 'High waves? If it is the one, then we're talking goddam tsunami here, aren't we?'

Don glanced around, afraid of being over-heard. 'I dunno, Rick. They didn't specify. That's why I came straight out. I thought you'd want to get the word first before anyone else.'

'You did right, Don.' Shit, Rick was thinking, now of all times. Sunday's yacht regatta was the climax of the Founders' Day celebrations. Cancellation didn't bear thinking about. But a tsunami! Images from the aftermath of the Indian Ocean quake and the devastation in New Orleans crowded his mind. If anything similar were to impact on the New England coast the consequences would be unimaginable.

Don was still speaking in an undertone.

'Officially the threat is categorised as low to medium risk. Further updates as conditions warrant. Other agencies have had the same. Warnings will be given on radio and TV. I'm instructed to post notices on the beaches advising the public if they notice the ocean running out then to hightail it for the nearest high ground.'

'Great,' Rick muttered sourly. 'With our tidal range that should guarantee panic at least twice daily.' With the approach of the full moon, every low tide at Goodwill could be expected to expose a half-mile of shingle and rocks.

'It's just an advisory this far,' Don reminded him. 'According to what they say there are warning systems in place that should give around six hours' notice. Time to get everybody well back inland. Most of them anyway,' he added soberly.

That was the trouble, Rick told himself. With a coastline dotted with bays and inlets and thousands of vacationers, many of them camping out where the spirit took them, it would be next to impossible even with helicopters to locate everybody.

He was conscious of Don watching his reactions to all of this. Rick was a Selectman, as town councillors were called in Goodwill, and nominally Don's boss. There were five on the board of selection, but Seb Elkins, the Mayor, was taking time out recovering from surgery and the others had asked Rick to stand in for him.

Don scratched his ear. 'Hell, these emergency people, they have to cover their asses. I mean it doesn't seem like there's a storm brewing, huh?' He gestured out towards the rose-flushed bay.

Rick relaxed slightly. Don was right; he was overreacting. After all, Africa was thousands of miles away. 'We'd better have Annie draft a warning notice that we can distribute to motels and camp sites if needed.' Annie Pellew was Don's secretary at the Police Department.

'Might be an idea to put out a statement for local radio too,' Don suggested. 'Something low key advising people to be alert near the water.'

'I'll have a word with Sheena.' Sheena Dubois edited the *Monitor*, the town newspaper. 'She's sensible.'

'Who's sensible?'

Fingers brushed Rick's neck. A waft of 'Air du Temps. Natalie had joined them. 'Don.' She kissed the officer merrily on the cheek. 'Thank you for coming out.' In the dusk she seemed glowing, the wine sweet on her breath, her eyes wide, bright with mischief. 'Give me a swig, darling,' she said to Rick. 'I've set my glass down somewhere.' She raised the bottle to her lips and the men watched the arch of her throat as she put her head back to drink and the way her breasts lifted under the thin fabric of her dress.

'So what's the big secret?' She tweaked Don.

Don glanced at Rick. 'Uh, nothing, we were just, you know, talking town stuff.'

38

'Surfers,' Rick answered for him. 'We're being invaded.'

Natalie's eyes widened. 'Wow, in little old Goodwill? That's funny.'

'You think so, huh?'

'You bet. Some of those good-looking California beach dudes, they're cute.'

Both men laughed. Don's phone beeped with a message. He dug it out and flipped open the screen. 'Uh oh,' he grunted. 'Gotta leave you, folks.'

'Something wrong?' Rick flashed him a sharp look.

'Fire call. Bush alight out behind the dump.'

'Another?' Rick's eyes narrowed. 'That makes the second in two days.'

'I'll be on my way,' Don said. 'I just stopped by to wish you guys well.' He punched Rick's shoulder and gave Natalie a squeeze. 'Look after my old buddy and you can tell him from me he picked the best one.'

'Oh you go on, Donald Egan,' she chuckled. 'Thanks for your support. See you tomorrow.'

'Wait.' Rick tossed his beer in a nearby bin. 'I'm coming with you.'

'Rick!' Natalie's fingernails sank into his arm. 'Don't you dare!' she hissed furiously. 'Don't even think about running out on me this evening.'

'It's an emergency call-out. I have to respond.'

'You heard Don; it's a dump fire. And you signed out tonight, remember?'

'Okay, okay.' Rick heaved a sigh. 'Force of habit.'

'God, but you can be so selfish! How do you think it makes me look in front of all our guests?'

'You made your point. I'm staying.'

She shook him again. 'Don't act like it's a punishment. This is supposed to be a celebration.' She made an exasperated sound. 'Come on, act like you're enjoying yourself before Mom sees us fighting.'

He pulled his arm free. 'I have to place some calls.'

Chapter 3

Maple Cove, Goodwill Sound. Afterwards they worked out that Tab Southwell, Bailey's son by his first wife that spent summers with him and Donna, was the last person to have seen the missing tourist couple. Tab was a gangly thirteen-year-old, a lonesome boy since the divorce, who spent most of his day cruising around on the new bike his dad had given him. He took the track down from the cliff road at a sharp clip that sent the gravel spurting under his new tyres and slewed to a halt by the old wooden shed in the parking lot.

A quick look around in the dusk showed the beach was deserted. He dismounted and propped the bike up against a rail. For a minute he forced himself to stand listening, his backpack held loosely in one hand. His heart was still thumping in his chest from excitement and he took several deep breaths to steady his nerves. That had been a close call up behind the dump.

The flames had taken hold fast in the tinder-dry brush and the smoke had brought the fire crews racing. He had only just managed to slip away in time before the first trucks arrived on the scene.

A light breeze ruffled the water in the cove. The tide was flowing in. He skipped from rock to rock filled with wild exhilaration at his own daring. This would shake the old town up and teach certain people a lesson too.

For several minutes he patrolled the beach, striving to look natural, all the while scanning up and down along the shore, checking again that no one was watching. One evening last week he had spotted his dad's car down here and marked the spot out as a target in his campaign of retribution. Now was the time to strike back again.

Satisfied finally that everything was safe, Tab crept up on the shed from the seaward side. His pulse drummed in his ears, every nerve tense. Crouching down in the lee of the shed, hidden from anyone up on the road, he unzipped the pack and pulled out a handful of loose rags and a bottle of gasoline.

The shed had been built here twenty years ago as a store for fishermen using the cove. The bottom edge of the planking was worn away in places. Stuffing the rags into a handy-sized gap, Tab doused them with fuel, splashing more against the wooden planking. He screwed the top back on the bottle and stowed it carefully away in his pack again and felt in his pocket for the lighter. The breeze had dropped away for a moment and the cove was utterly still and quiet.

Tab was on the point of flicking the flame when the quiet crunch of gravel made him start. He leapt up and sneaked a look round the corner of the shed in time to catch a pair of mountain bikes skimming down the track from the cliff road. There was just time to stuff the lighter back in his pocket and sling the pack over his shoulder. There was no place to hide and his own bike was still out front; the only thing to do was feign innocence.

His heart racing, he stepped out into view, doing his best to act natural. His knees trembled as he stooped over the bike, pretending to fiddle with the gears while watching the newcomers out of the corner of his eye. A man and a woman in their early thirties, got up like tourists. The man in the lead halted at the edge of the beach and sat a moment staring out at the ocean. His companion pulled up beside him, stretching her legs to balance on her toes. She arched her back and inhaled the still warm air. 'Mmm, smells sweet. This has to be the place.'

'You better believe it.' The guy was off his machine and leaning it against the rail. He was mid-thirties, big shoulders, confident, professional. Both bikes, Tab noted enviously, were expensive designer numbers fitted with the latest high-tech gears and suspension. The girlfriend matched, cute blonde hair, tight shorts, slim legs. She looked up as Tab straightened up and gave him a friendly grin. 'Hey, how you doing?'

Tab's mouth was dry. He had to swallow to clear his tongue. 'I'm good. You people on vacation?' His voice sounded odd to his own ears and his legs were shaking more than ever.

The woman didn't seem to notice anything out of the ordinary.

'That's us. We're staying in town, the Seafarers. I'm Kim, he's Randall. We're from New York. And you?'

'Tab Southwell from New Jersey, but my dad lives in Goodwill. He's a paediatrician at the hospital.' Great, he thought, now I've told them my name. How much dumber can anyone get? 'You guys here for some fishing?'

The woman laughed. 'No way!' She pointed to the man, who was busy unpacking a camera from a pannier on his bike and checking it over. 'Photography is our thing. We're looking to take shots of this sunset.'

They both gazed out across the wide strip of sand running down to the smooth cove. Dusk was falling fast and a faint phosphorescence clung to the surface of the water. Black against the violet sky where the afterglow lingered, a V-shaped flight of cormorants that earlier had been diving for sand lance flapped slowly away eastwards towards their nesting ground on Curtain Bluff. Everywhere was quiet. Not a leaf stirred in the woods behind. Only the faint wash from the water broke the stillness. 'Man, it's glass out there,' she breathed. 'This place is just beautiful.'

'Perfect,' the man agreed. He swivelled his gaze to the south-east up the Sound. His expression brooded. 'I'd like to capture the shape of this bay, the way it angles to the ocean. See how those offshore islands crowd the channel?' He pointed. 'Great silhouettes there.'

'Yeah, but the sun is dropping down behind the headland. If we shoot from here we lose the light.'

Tab eyed them wonderingly, trying to follow what they were talking about. The woman had also produced a camera. 'Smile!' she commanded. She showed him the result on the screen. Tab experienced a bolt of sheer panic. Were they some kind of cops gathering evidence? He was sweating profusely. He must look guilty as hell.

'The headland there is called Indian Point,' he said hoarsely, hoping to distract them.

The man glanced at him briefly, incuriously, and sucked his lip. His eyes went back to the ocean again. 'It's a flat calm. What say we take our kit and wade out to that island?' He pointed to a rocky outcrop.

Tab was being careful to keep downwind in case one of them smelt the gasoline on him. 'That's Two Bush Island,' he volunteered. 'Nothing much growing there now though.'

'Two Bush?' The girl laughed. 'Cute name. Any seals?'

'No, no seals,' Tab told her. He thought the reason was the rocks there were sheer so it was hard for a seal to haul out. The channel between the island and the shore was known as the Gurge. 'It gets real deep in one place, the Mudhole, lobstermen call it.' There was a strong current there sometimes, he added, but with the tide running in that shouldn't be a problem this time of year. 'When the tide is low like it is now you can make it across easy.' He was babbling now in his attempt to sound natural.

'Bummer, I really get off on seals. Guess we'll go take a look anyway. Catch you later, buddy.'

Tab watched as they locked the bikes up and trotted down across the sand to the water's edge. The beach was deserted now and the two waded straight out. The girl squealed at the cold. Like her partner said, the waves were scarcely more than ripples. 'The island looks kind of small,' he suggested. 'If we could get around to the far side that would be neat.'

They waded on, cleaving the slick swell before them. The bottom was firm and sandy, easy walking. Fifty yards out they were still only thigh deep. The water was chilly but the effort kept them warm. After they had gone perhaps a hundred and fifty yards the channel became deeper.

'I don't want to get my shorts all wet!' the girl protested. They were almost at the mouth of the cove where it opened out into the main bay. She glanced back over her shoulder. The sun was sinking fast. Along the shoreline a few lights twinkled.

'Come over this way, it's shallower.' The man reached out a hand in support.

They picked their way on for a while. 'Not far now,' he said.

They paused a moment to take their bearings. 'Listen to the silence,' she marvelled. 'We've got this whole cove to ourselves.'

'Yeah, spooky, huh?' He pinched her through her shorts, making her yelp. 'Don't! You'll make me drop the camera.'

They waded on. 'I feel a current,' she said after another few yards. 'It's tugging out into the bay.'

'I feel it too. Place your feet firmly and hold on to me. We're almost there.'

A minute later there came more squeals of dismay. 'Boy, this water has gotten real cold suddenly!'

'It's getting shallower. We'll be okay now.'

'Can we climb out here?'

'I don't think so. The rocks ahead look difficult. We'll have to try further round.'

'Gee, Randy, I'm not sure this is sensible. It's getting dark and my legs are numb. Maybe we should think about going back.'

'Aw, c'mon, honey. We're almost there. Hang on to me.'

Their voices carried faintly shoreward to where Tab stood watching from the parking lot. He was still shaking from the nearness of his escape. If those two had shown up just a minute or two later they would have caught him red-handed. An urge to be off seized him, but first he must somehow retrieve the incriminating rags from under the shed. But not yet, they might look back and spot him. Better to wait a few minutes longer till it got really dark. He crouched beside the bike again, acting like he was trying to fix it. Out along the beach the two figures slowly diminished into the distance. He was still staring after them when his attention was distracted.

Something strange was taking place. The ocean was flowing out. The tide had not long turned and should be starting to rise and yet the ocean was receding. The light was starting to fail but in spite of that Tab could clearly see that the water was retreating from the shallows, exposing wide expanses of sand and weed-covered rock. Stranded fish were flopping in pools and crabs scuttled for shelter. He screwed up his eyes, searching for the couple, but they were too far out to spot now.

For what seemed a long time but could really only have been two or three minutes at most the sea continued to suck back. To Tab it seemed as if the whole cove was being drained out into the Sound, leaving a path across to the island. His chest heaved as he stared at the changed seascape, wondering what was going to happen next. For the first time he felt afraid. The cove, a place which had always seemed so familiar and safe, seemed suddenly to have become strange and charged with menace.

For an indeterminate time nothing happened. Then imperceptibly and without a sound there came a change. Rivulets of movement broke out on the denuded bottom. The tide had reversed itself. The ocean was flowing in again. Smoothly but with increasing speed it was running in over the mud, submerging the rocks. A line of leaping surf appeared as a huge breaker swept in around the side of the island. In the silence of the cove the sound was a long rumble like approaching thunder. Broken water crashed against the rocks where the current was driving the ocean back through the narrow gap of the Gurge.

The rumbling continued, growing louder and deeper, changing into a grinding noise as if immense boulders were being rolled along the stony seabed. It boomed in the cove, a sound like nothing Tab had ever heard before. He sure hoped the two visitors were safe. The surge swept on back up the beach. It frothed up the foot of the sand-dune in front of the parking area. Tab stared awestruck as the water level mounted, two feet, three. The dark tide slapped at the crest of the slope, splashing him with spray, and he retreated back in alarm. This was like winter-storm height except it was the middle of summer.

And still the grinding sound rolled across the water. Tab knew where it was coming from now; it was coming from the Gurge.

At last the surge ceased. The swirling waters eased and stayed, lapping the ground, swirling against the edge of the shed right where Tab stood. A cold sweat pricked his skin and made his T-shirt clammy. There was something ominous about such a swollen mass of ocean filling the cove and pressing against the land. He felt unaccountably nervous. The dreadful noise from the Gurge had ceased. In the stillness that followed there was only the slap of the waves on the rocks and once a thin wailing sound, a kind of bubbling cry carried on the air, very faint. He listened for a moment, trying to locate the source but it wasn't repeated. Most probably a seabird, he told himself, disturbed from its perch. He waited another minute to see what would happen.

Dusk was closing in, lengthening the shadows under the trees. A few stars appeared. A breeze got up, ruffling the water's surface. It chilled the cove and set the woods rustling. Tab shivered. Then the ocean started to recede again. It sank slowly back down the beach till it attained its normal depth and stopped, slopping to and fro like the aftermath of a boat's wake.

Tab gradually relaxed. Weird stuff certainly happened. He squinted into the dusk for a sight of the two photographers, but it was too dark now to distinguish much. When last he had glimpsed them they had been way out near the mouth of the cove. Maybe they had climbed on the rocks around the far side of the island. A spike of memory tugged at him, something bad about the Gurge, a danger signal in the recess of his mind, a warning he must have overheard from back when he was small. A shadow of unease, nothing more.

He remembered the man's shoulders. Shit though, he was one big dude. He could take care of himself okay. The lady too. Guys like that were used to the outdoors. And their equipment was awesome. Tomorrow if they were back here again he would see if he could get them to demonstrate some of it.

The urge to be gone overwhelmed him. Clutching his pack he grabbed the bike and started up the lane to his dad's house.

Indian Creek was the largest of several water-courses flowing into the Sound, joining the ocean to the south of the town below the promontory of Indian Point. At one time the creek had lost itself among a salt marsh fringing the Sound, but the marsh had long ago been drained and the channel left to run clear. It was tidal for a good way inland and popular with kayak parties exploring the interior.

A few hundred yards west of the bridge leading into town stood a clapboard house perched on the far bank. Known as Indian Patch, it had been bought for a fancy price last year by a couple from Philadelphia as an investment. It had three bedrooms and two hundred feet of river frontage and the weekly rental for June was

$1,500. The price was steep, but the location was attractive and two families from the Boston suburbs were sharing the rental. The Gardiners, Ted and Jessica, had a boy and a girl, six and eight. The Van Burens, Julie and Brook, one daughter, Paula, also eight. The three children shared the third bedroom. They had been warned to take care near the creek.

A pair of canoes came with the house. The adults sat at either end paddling with the kids in the centre. Life jackets were provided and used. Both pairs of parents were anxious to set a responsible example. They also went bicycling and took a boat trip on the ocean to see the whales. But the river was the favourite.

The youngest of the three children, the Gardiner boy, was named Lloyd. He was small for his age, but made up for it by daring and agility. He had climbed all the trees in the yard and his father had strung a line up with an old car tyre and made a swing for him and the girls. There was no TV in the house so the kids played outside most evenings till they dropped.

On the fifth day of the vacation the families arrived back late. They had picnicked upriver, then gone for a hike, and on the way back downstream one of the canoes had run aground on a sandbar and the excitement and hilarity of working it free delayed them so that the light was fading by the time they saw the shingle roof of the house coming into view round the bend.

They were in a hurry because it was Paula's

birthday and the plan was to take in a movie at the Cinema on the Green. The mothers collected the paddles and called to the children to bring their stuff and hurry inside to get washed. The men lifted the canoes out of the water and carried them up the bank. The boy Lloyd trailed after them to the boathouse. 'Shucks, I lost my cap!' he exclaimed.

'You probably dropped it down by the bank when you were getting out,' his father said. 'Run back and take a look. Quickly or we'll miss the start of the movie.'

The boy shot off across the grass. The ground sloped quite steeply down to the creek. When he reached the crude landing stage where they put the canoes in, he saw his cap lying there and snatched it up and crammed it on his head. He glanced at the creek and frowned. Something was different. It was hard to tell in the dusk, but the bank appeared steeper than before and there were black streaks of mud showing beneath the timbers of the dock. Surely he hadn't scrambled up that height from the boat? The water level must have gone down then. Did rivers do that and why? He would have to ask Dad.

There was a rushing noise from the direction of the Sound. A frothing wave swept into view round the bend in the creek, moving swiftly upstream towards him. Rooted to the spot, Lloyd watched open-mouthed. He hadn't seen a wave on the creek before. The ridge of broken water stretched from bank to bank and appeared

53

at least as high as him. Behind it the creek was swarming back up the banks, covering the mud again and submerging the reedbeds till only their tips showed above the swirling ripples. Lloyd skipped back hastily off the dock as the crest surged over the wooden planking. Without slackening pace the surge swept on upstream and out of sight. The turbulence eased, but the creek remained swollen way beyond its usual level. He stared fascinated, waiting to see what would happen next. He wasn't frightened, only curious.

'Lloyd!' his mother's voice floated down from the house. 'C'mon or we'll lose our seats!'

Reluctantly, he turned away. Halfway up the slope he looked back. The water was still high, gleaming like a silver-red sheet in the dusk. He had the impression that it was flowing back the other way now, out towards the Sound like before. Strange. His mother called again. The movie! He broke into a run.

On the ride into town, he said to the others, 'The creek sure looked mighty full tonight.'

'That'll be the tide coming in,' his father answered. He launched on an explanation about the moon and ocean rhythms, but they were nearing the Green and he had to break off to look for a parking space.

In the excitement of the movie, Lloyd forgot about what he had seen. Later, though, after the girls were asleep, he remembered. He sat up and, kneeling by the window, gazed out at the tide-turning moonlight. The line of the creek was faintly discernible winding away under the trees, glimmering and mysterious. He longed to see a repeat of the wave foaming upstream. Perhaps if he woke up early he could sneak down and catch one.

'. . . *In a worst-case scenario scientists estimate a total collapse of the volcano flank might generate a splash up to half a mile high, sending a series of tsunami racing across the ocean at speeds of five hundred miles per hour. Taking approximately six hours to reach the United States, these would devastate the eastern seaboard from Florida to Maine with a succession of giant waves on a scale similar to the disaster in the Indian Ocean earthquake which claimed two hundred and fifty thousand lives* . . .'

In her small apartment on School Street, Sheena Dubois sat at her laptop, scribbling notes on a legal pad, listening with half an ear to the TV. She had been working flat out since a phone call from Rick Larsen alerted her to the first newsflash an hour ago. Now she was alarmed to discover that Atlantic tsunamis were more frequent that she had supposed, with more than thirty registered in the past century and a half, the most recent in 1964.

Her cellphone warbled. She flipped it open. 'This is Sheena. Oh hi, Rick. I was just going to call you. First up, the eruption does seem to be a minor one, so far. Cumbre Vieja is officially listed as "active but not dangerous", and the current event described as "minor venting with some solid matter ejected". In other words a lot of noise and smoke. A volcanologist I spoke to in Cambridge said it was the latest in a series of similar eruptions which take place along the spine of the mountain every twenty years or so. Basically the volcano is a seamount sitting on a destructive plate margin. If this one follows the previous pattern eruptions could continue intermittently for several months before dying out again.'

'This friend of yours, did you ask him about the tsunami risk?' Rick said. Sheena picked up the noise of clinking glasses. He must still be at the party.

'Of course, and you know, he laughed. Everybody, he said, is asking about that. It's just dumb, he says. The claim is that the spine of the island has been weakened by erosion and a big enough eruption could cause it to break up and slide into the sea. Some scientist calculated that if this happened the displacement would generate a tsunami half a mile high. Most responsible geologists think this is just wild. It would take one almighty explosion to bring that about, way bigger than the current series. Not only that, but the mountain would have to slide in one single chunk and the odds against that happening are simply huge. Lewis, my friend, says forget about La Palma, if you want a truly scary situation look no further than Yellowstone.

When the caldera there blows it'll take out half the Midwest.'

Rick spoke next to the Coastguard down at the harbour. Conrad Wolfowitz, the duty officer, took his call. From the outset Rick sensed a chill.

'First up, Rick, inshore safety is a Coastguard area of responsibility. Period. Our service did not initiate this advisory. I'm not saying we don't accept some of the details, but it didn't emanate from this chain of command.

'Second point, as far back as May second, Coastguard, in conjunction with the US Geological Survey, issued a formal notice to all Atlantic and Caribbean coastal states, including the Florida Keys and Gulf of Mexico and Puerto Rico advising of the possibility of extreme wave conditions. US Coastguard has the situation under continual review liaising with the relevant departments and will issue updates as appropriate commensurate with its zones of responsibility.'

It sounded like he was reading from a prepared statement. Great, Rick thought, a turf war. Just what was needed. 'That's why I called you, Con. This thing has sprung at the council out of the blue. Just how serious is the situation?'

'Yeah, well that's what comes from other departments horning in on areas that don't properly concern them. Our phones have been ringing ever since that damn notice went out with people thinking they are about to get hit with a tsunami in the next five minutes. Next thing we're going to have a bunch of idiots phoning the radio stations saying they can see a giant wave coming and we'll have a panic on our hands. I call it downright irresponsible to be honest.'

'You may have a point there, Con.'

'Too damn right, I do. A few false alarms and then when the big one does finally come nobody pays attention.'

Clearly feelings at Coastguard were running high. Rick cut in. 'Founders' Day falls day after tomorrow. There's the parade, yacht races in the Sound and the whole harbour fair thing. If the last couple of years are any guide there could be five thousand visitors down by the waterfront. We can't afford to take risks with that many lives.'

'Which is our responsibility as Coastguard. We take our job seriously and I won't have anybody try to tell me different. This risk has been known about for quite a while. Coastguard in conjunction with NOAA and other agencies is participating in the National Tsunami Hazard Mitigation Program, an ongoing effort to improve our capability for early detection and reporting of tsunamis in open ocean.'

Con was off reading from a prepared text again. Rick interrupted. 'Is that the warning buoy network I've heard about?'

'Correct. There is a whole new warning system being deployed with pressure buoys out

58

in deep water to protect against exactly this kind of incident. The network is in place, but how many buoys are functioning at this exact moment in time and what the warning period is, they haven't told me yet. I did hear on TV it is of the order of five hours. That may be correct, I wouldn't know.'

'So what you're saying is, this system is not operational right now?'

'Don't go putting words in my mouth, dammit. As far as my knowledge goes the buoys are in place, but the system still has to be tested and any bugs ironed out. We are talking here about sensitive equipment emplaced on the ocean bed at five thousand metres depth. There have to be checks run, base parameters established. It's not like a burglar alarm where you throw a switch. There is an announcement due on this final phase of the project any day now and if you ask me that says a whole lot about the timing of this advisory.'

'So it is safe in your opinion, Con, for the parade to go ahead as planned?'

'I hear what you say, Rick. Obviously you have to consider all the factors and we have our responsibilities too, especially where the sailing is concerned. I'll make some calls and try to get you some answers. What I will say though is as at the moment we have been told this is no more than a heads-up notice. People should be aware, but there is no reason as we speak to close the beaches. That could change.'

59

Perfect, Rick thought wearily. The agencies were fighting each other and the alarm systems were turned off.

Chapter 4

Across town at his two-storey home on Ditch Street, Jack Pearl sat down at the table in the kitchen with a grunt of relief. It had been a long day down at the dock. 'What's for supper?'

'Meat loaf,' his wife answered. 'With butternut squash and blueberry cake for dessert.' She fetched out a jug of cold milk from the fridge and as she set it beside him the phone rang. 'Oh no,' she protested. 'Can't they leave you in peace just a while?'

'Better see who it is,' Jack sighed, pushing back his chair. Summer season was always one thing after another. He stepped across to the dresser and picked up the phone: 'Harbourmaster.' He was a short, hard-fibred man with a nearly lipless mouth who spoke mostly in monosyllables. Later he would say he guessed right away it was not a social call. He had a sense, a premonition almost, only it was not as strong as that, more an instinct that this was the start of something.

'Jack?' He recognised the voice right away. It was Jean-Alice Penny who ran the diner on Bearskin Neck down by the harbour and who often fielded enquiries from the public outside of regular hours. 'Jack?' she said and he knew she was speaking quietly so as not to alarm the customers. 'I think maybe you should come back down here.'

'We're about to eat. Can't it wait, Jeannie?'

'I don't know that it can, Jack.' The strain was apparent in her tone. 'Something's come up that I think you should see right away.'

Jack twisted round to look where his wife was standing holding the meat loaf on its plate and gave a helpless shrug. Jean-Alice wasn't one to panic unnecessarily. He sighed again. 'Okay, Jeannie,' he said wearily with a last regretful glance at the meat loaf. 'I'm on my way.'

'Keep it hot for me,' he told his wife. 'Ten to one it's nothing at all.'

Jack drove a pick-up paid for by the township. He had had this one for six years now and the transmission was about to go. It tried to climb out of low ratio and had to be held down. He had spoken to the council but money for a replacement came from three different sources and it was hard to get everyone signed up. The darkness was nearly complete with the street-lights on and a full moon rising. Traffic was heavy heading into town. The sidewalks were jammed with tourists checking out the bars and restaurants. He drove down Sugarshack Road, made a right into Bay Road then turned left onto Bearskin Neck. The Neck was a spike of ground jutting out between the old fishing harbour where the lobster boats moored and Lincoln Bay, which now contained the marina. Clustered here were a number of small businesses including the Lobsterman, Jean-Alice's diner, which functioned as the unofficial meeting place for harbour types, and the Larsen Chandlery that Rick and Rebecca opened after they sold up the old Ice Factory that their dad owned. Jack's office was at the far end.

Wire lobster cages were stacked four and five high along the side of the dock, each with a coloured plastic float. Summer was the slack season when the lobsters came inshore to breed. A light breeze stirred the water, rocking the sailboats in the new marina and rattling their wire riggings. More than thirty craft were moored there tonight; one of Chance Greene's successful enterprises. The largest vessel in the harbour was the all-white *Pequod*, the eighty-foot former Coastguard cutter converted for whale watching that Rick Larsen had mortgaged his share in the Chandlery to buy into. She was tied up against the main pier at the far end of the Neck. Rick was taking a risk in Jack's opinion. If not enough tourists showed up to buy tickets then Rick and his backers would be hard put to meet the payments on the boat. But then Rick always walked his own way.

Outside the diner there was a knot of people

gathered under the streetlight. When Jack pulled up they all moved over to meet him.

'Okay,' he growled, stepping down from the truck. 'So you got me out here. Now what?' He recognised several of them: Cal Burrows, a lobsterman from the town with his own boat; Shaun Sullivan, a carpenter in the boatyard in his faded coveralls; and skinny Sheena Dubois who wrote for the *Monitor*. With them were a number of boat owners from the marina. Jack's jaw tightened when he saw Sheena, who knew everything that went on in town, scribbling busily in the spiral-bound notepad she carried everywhere. If Sheena smelled a story it meant there was trouble. There was no sign of Jean-Alice; she must be back inside attending to her customers.

Then he noticed that one of the yacht owners was dripping water on the sidewalk. Jack cocked his head, eyeing the man's soaked clothing. 'What happened to you, mister?' he asked curtly.

'This here is Dan Shoemaker. He has a boat down at the marina.' It was Shaun Sullivan who answered. 'His dinghy got swamped in a wash and he lost some property.'

'Yeah? Suppose you let Mr Shoemaker tell me about it,' Jack said politely, taking out his own notepad and flipping it open.

Mr Shoemaker had short reddish hair and a trimmed beard and the thickening about the waist that came with middle age. He had the look of a professional person, a doctor perhaps or a lawyer or something similar, who was very angry for being wet through and frozen. It might be a balmy 70 degrees on the dock but the ocean temperature cooled by the Labrador Current hovered around 50. When he spoke his accent showed he was from the Boston region but it was hard for Jack to make out exactly what he was saying at first because he couldn't speak straight he was so outraged and his teeth were chattering, besides which his friends constantly interrupted with complaints of their own.

'Some people out there got a problem of attitude, by God. They are so damned selfish they don't stop to think about the consequences of what they do. Just on account of they have more money and a bigger boat they imagine they have some God-given right to ignore speed restrictions . . . !'

'Did you recognise the offending vessel?' Jack asked, cutting off the flow.

'It was dark. I couldn't see a damn thing out there, but it was a boat okay and a big one. Had to be.'

'Happens all the time,' put in another owner.

'Too f-ing right, it does!'

'My galley is wrecked!'

'So what you're telling me is, Mr Shoemaker,' Jack summarised eventually, 'an unseen vessel disregarded the speed limit in the Sound and its wash swamped your dinghy as you were tying up in the marina. As a result of which you lost valuable personal possessions. Have I got that correct?'

'Selfish bastard had so much speed on the water sucked right out from under the dinghy leaving me stranded on the mud. Before I could get clear the return wave flipped the boat and washed me out with all my gear. I lost a cellphone, a PDA . . .'

Jack listened patiently to the list and wondered if Sheena was writing all this down to save him the trouble. Why in heck people had to take so much electronic gadgetry with them on the water was something he would never know. It was asking for trouble. 'Okay, now where is the dinghy as of this minute, Mr Shoemaker?'

The other boat owner, who was evidently a friend, spoke up. 'Tied up in the marina alongside my boat, *Indigo Kali*. When the wash hit I came on deck and saw Dan's dinghy drifting and managed to catch a hold of the painter. Then I went to look for Dan but by then he had managed to swim over to the steps.'

'That wake must've been all of five feet when it hit me. Some people don't care a damn what they do. They should have more respect for other people on the water. Whoever was responsible should be prosecuted and I want damages to make good my loss, by God.'

'Well, I have the details now, Mr Shoemaker. I'm sorry for what happened.'

'Yeah, well your being sorry isn't going to buy me a new cellular phone. Your job is to prevent this kind of irresponsible behaviour from happening.'

Jack sighed again. 'We do our best. What I want you to do now is go home, get out of those wet things. You can make out a list of all the items you lost together with valuations and bring it into the harbourmaster's office right over there any time between eight and six tomorrow. Then we'll issue a report of the incident, which you can use to claim off your insurance.'

'How come we're so sure it was a boat wash?' someone in back of the crowd demanded. 'They just said on the radio there's a tsunami headed this way.'

The word triggered a babble of excitement. 'No kidding,' the man insisted. 'It's official from Maine Emergency. All boats and residents of coastal areas on the eastern seaboard are warned to be on alert for exceptional waves resulting from seismic activity off Africa.'

'Tsunami! No shit!'

'They come in sets,' someone called. 'In Thailand the first wave was shallow with a long suck back.'

'Same as tonight's!'

'Local people went out on the beach after stranded fish. Then came the big one and drowned them all.'

'A hundred thousand dead. That was just in Indonesia.'

'Two hundred thousand, I heard.'

'Darn things travel fast as a jetliner.'

Jack raised his voice, cutting through the rising chorus of voices. 'Now everybody hold your horses. I already spoke with Coastguard about this. That notice was an advisory only, drawing attention to the possibility of exceptional waves occurring in the event of earthquakes or whatever. So far as I'm aware there have been no such events yet. If one does occur there will be several hours' warning, time enough to get everybody back from the water.'

'In a tsunami the best place to be is out on the ocean,' someone said.

'The waves that hit Thailand were higher than thirty feet.'

Jack Pearl interrupted. 'Quieten down. If there was a tsunami due we'd have had advance notice. No such warning was received. No damage has been reported anywhere along the coast that I've heard.'

The hubbub subsided, the men exchanging sheepish glances. 'Aren't you going to get after the guy responsible then?' a boat owner wanted to know.

'What I am going to do now is make some calls to try to establish what vessel it was that caused this mess. Mr Shoemaker, go home and get yourself warmed up before you catch cold. I'll see you in the morning. The same goes for anyone else who has suffered loss. See me with the details tomorrow.' Jack studied the notes he had made. Time of incident, he had written, approx. 1830 hours. Magnitude of displacement five feet. And it struck him then as unusual that any vessel big enough to make a wash that large would have been speeding at low tide.

Mr Shoemaker squelched away accompanied by a couple of his buddies and Jack turned to the others. 'That's one problem dealt with. Now what's troubling the rest of you good people?'

Sheena Dubois tossed her frizzy hair and turned over a fresh sheet in her notebook. She poised her pen, her dark eyes glowing in her narrow face. 'Cal here found something in the water—' she got in, but Cal Burrows gripped her by the elbow, checking her in mid-sentence. He was a big man, slow of speech, the father of nine children.

'Best see for yourself, Jack,' he said heavily.

They climbed down the steps into Cal Burrows's *Jason 28* that he used for inshore work, Jack and Cal and Bud Stevens, Cal's stern man this season, who was just out of school and who, when he wasn't on the boats, delivered firewood. Shaun had taken himself off and Sheena Dubois came last with her notebook. Cal offered her a life jacket but she shook her head. She wore a long-sleeved T-shirt and seemed at home on the water. It seemed to Jack she must be twenty-six maybe or twenty-seven, perhaps older. She had been working on the *Monitor* for the past couple of years that he recalled. Other than that he knew nothing about her, if she was married or had a boyfriend or even where she lived.

'So where is this thing?' Jack bawled above the thump of the diesel motor.

'Over against the raft.' Cal jerked his head out to starboard. The raft was a kind of pontoon in which he and the other lobstermen stored their catches before selling them on. Jack didn't ask what the thing they were going to take a look at was and Cal didn't say. Unspoken between them was the word 'floater'. A floater would be bad. Jack told himself no one had been reported lost but that didn't signify. With sailboats and powerboats and kayaks and windsurfers out all hours this time of year and half the owners living inland or in RVs or camping in the woods, it could be days, weeks even, before a person was missed.

It was cooler out on the water in the moving boat. Jack tried to gauge the swell. Was it a little uneven still? 'Did you feel the ship wash that city guy was talking about?' he asked Cal.

Cal unwrapped a stick of gum and popped it in his mouth before replying. 'Bud and I was off Rock Island,' he said thoughtfully. 'Had some trouble with a line wrapped round the prop so we was late getting back. Flat calm one minute then bang.'

'Any sign of a vessel speeding?'

The raft was coming up. Jack could distinguish its low hulk in the beam of the forward spot. Cal eased off the throttle before he spoke again. 'Pretty near on dusk by then. Bud and me was concentrating on clearing the screw. Heck of a suck back though, really dragged at the boat. Then *whoomp*, up she went. Big slow old devil but plenty of lift on it.'

'Sounds like a rogue wave then?'

There was a grunt from the lobsterman as he shifted the gum in his mouth. The beat of the engine slowed again. Cal threw her astern a moment to take the way off and switched on the big working roof light pointing aft. Bud stood by with the boat hook. Sheena had a camera out. One of those tiny digital models; she must have been carrying it in a pocket. The boat was drifting very close now. Cal idled the engine and Bud leaned out with the pole to hook onto the raft and hold them steady. 'You want this, Jack?' He proffered a heavy-duty plastic lantern.

'Thanks.' Jack snapped it on and leaned over the stern. The smell hit him at once, a sickening putrescent stench. His throat constricted instinctively.

'Stinks, don't it?' Cal called unnecessarily. 'Thought maybe it was a dead whale when I smelled it first. They can catch you real heavy if you come up on one in a fog.'

'I smell it.' Sweet Jesus, Jack thought to himself. This was worse than he had imagined. 'Looks to be in a bad way.'

'Yeah, I figured that too. Didn't want to tell them on the dock without you taking a look first.'

Sheena's camera flashed. She was clutching Bud's shoulder for support, snapping away one-handed, and the breeze was blowing her hair back from her face, flattening her T-shirt against her chest. The camera flashed again, freezing the scene in Jack's memory. The boat, the patch of water held in the light from the deckhouse, the girl leaning into the wind and that ghastly thing down there in the gurgling swell rubbing against the lobster cages.

Over at Maple Cove, Tab Southwell was in his room playing on his Xbox when the front door banged and he heard Donna call up. 'I'm in here,' he yelled back.

'Did you eat already? If you're hungry I could heat up a pizza or we could send out if you prefer.'

Tab paused his game and wandered downstairs. Donna was in the kitchen bustling about. Tad watched her deft movements. He liked his father's partner, her sunny temper and pretty ways. She treated him as if she was the big sister he never had. 'How was your party?' he asked.

'It was fun.' She flashed him a bright smile. 'Lots of people, champagne, Natalie looking happy.'

'Dad stayed on?'

'No, he had a call-out, poor lamb. An accident in the Sound they think.'

'In the Sound?' Tab stood very still. 'What kind of accident? Whereabouts in the Sound?'

Donna looked at him quickly. 'He didn't say.

They were sending the Coastguard launch out, I think. Why, do you know something?'

His mouth felt dry suddenly. He dropped his eyes. 'It's nothing,' he mumbled, 'just something I thought I heard on the radio.'

'Could it be somebody you know?' Concern showed in her face. 'A friend?'

'No,' he told her, still looking at the ground. 'I told you, I don't know anything.'

'Do you want me to call your dad for you?'

Tab shook his head. 'I'm fine.' Turning away, he slouched through into the lounge. The windows there faced out over the cove and the treeless hump of the island stark under the bright moon. The water stared back at him silent and hateful.

'You want to eat now or wait till Dad gets back?' she called after him.

A lump rose in his throat. He tried to speak but no words came.

'Tab?' she called anxiously. 'Are you feeling okay? Did you get too much sun?'

'Guess I'll wait,' he croaked. He slumped on the settee and reached for the TV remote, staring blankly at the screen. A newscast channel was showing images of a mountain spewing fire.

Chapter 5

Eight p.m. The full moon hung huge above the Sound, gilding the water with its unusual red cast. Out at Indian Point the woods were alive with fireflies. Shutting up his phone, Rick rejoined the party. A barefoot youth in baggies and a headband bumped against him. 'Hey there, Captain Ahab!' he called drunkenly. There was a snigger from his companions. The nickname was a favourite joke among the summer crowd, rarely made to his face.

Rick gave him the stare. 'What did you call me?' he said in an iron voice from behind his teeth. The kid's smile froze; he looked so scared that for a moment Rick felt almost sorry for the sucker. He meant well, like all the others. That was their problem.

'I'm sorry. I guess that didn't come out right.'

'Too right, friend.'

'I said I'm sorry.'

Rick got a hold of himself. This was a party

after all. 'Forget it,' he muttered, pushing past.

Natalie came up on his other side. Her fingers dug into his arm. 'This is our engagement. At least try to look as though you're enjoying yourself. These are our friends come to wish us well.'

'Your parents' friends maybe,' Rick snapped. 'I don't see many locals, do you? Anyway, I have to go. There are things that need seeing to.'

Natalie stared at him, her jaw set. Hot tears stood in her eyes. Then she bolted back into the throng.

Moving towards the house, Rick was button-holed by Sarah Hunter. 'You're driving back into town.' It was a statement, not a question. He was too choked up to speak so he gave her a curt shrug to which she made no answer but followed him with long strides. She was wearing a full skirt that added to her height and her back was very straight, her hair caught up in a coil behind. The inner hall and staircase were dark panelled and eclectically furnished with items acquired over the passage of time.

'If this was my place,' Sarah muttered, 'I'd lighten it up.'

He said nothing. She was asking him without saying it if he could really see himself fitting in here? She was conveying what many people in the town probably thought, that it wouldn't work out. That Natalie was a city girl at heart. That she would want him to leave eventually and

75

settle in Boston or Washington or some other place.

They walked out together into the warmth of the summer night. His pick-up was parked under the trees. Sarah slid in the far side. They might have been back ten years ago when they used to ride out together to the beach on summer evenings. That was before he had gone away and she had hitched up with guy who ran trips on the Kennebec River.

In silence he started up and swung the truck out. The headlamps shone on the trees and he glanced at her profile. She was sitting very straight and pale with her lips pressed tight, staring ahead. He felt she was angry and it worried him that he could read her moods so well still after all this time.

'Jesus, I hate these parties,' he said sourly as they turned out of the driveway.

Sarah made no response but continued to stare in front of her at the dusty road unfolding in the beams. He remembered how proud she always was. Breaking up and starting over must have been hard for her.

'You and Natalie have a fight?' Her tone was distant.

Rick shrugged again. 'There's been a fire call downtown. I need to check.'

'And she said stay?'

The white tail of a deer darted across the road as they rounded the first bend. 'Her mother gives her a hard time,' Rick said shortly.

'Mothers and daughters.' Points of light from the dash reflected in Sarah's eyes.

'Elise is something else though.'

It was strange talking about the Maxwells with Sarah. It made Rick feel uneasy. 'Natalie thinks I don't try hard enough to get along.'

'Seems to me sometimes that Natalie wants the world.' Sarah reached in her purse, took out a pack of cigarettes and lit one. 'Sorry, I shouldn't have said that,' she added, inhaling.

They had emerged from the woods and the bridge over Indian Creek was coming up. The water of the creek gleamed under the moon as they rattled across. The lights of the town showed ahead. Rick slowed to take the turn. The truck swayed. Sarah relaxed; she twisted round in her seat, leaning her head against the door pillar to face him with her knees pulled up beneath her. Reaching up, she tugged at the knot in her hair and it fell loose in a pale cascade about her shoulders. The glow of the cigarette cast pools of shadow under her cheekbones. He was disturbed again. 'I didn't know you smoked.'

A throaty chuckle echoed in the darkness of the cab. 'I smoke. I'm a divorcee. I'm a bad girl now, Rick.'

'I have to stop by Seafarers on the way in to drop off some flags,' Rick told her as they reached the edge of town. Seafarers Motel on Pier Street had belonged to the Cotton family for two generations. There were thirty-two units on two storeys with parking either side for guests' vehicles; and Abby Cotton and her sister-in-law, Beth Robbins, who now ran it together, had put in a pool at the rear last year. Rick parked the pick-up in the forecourt and left Sarah to wait while he carried the bundles of red, white and blue flags inside the office.

Abby was at the computer when he pushed open the screen door. 'Hi,' she said turning round. 'Oh, it's you, Rick. Be with you in a minute. Just got to finish entering this in.'

'Take your time. I'll just bring the rest.' The flags were to be strung along the street as part of the Founders' Day decorations. Joe, the handyman employed to do odd jobs around the motel, would do the stringing, supervised by Abby and Beth.

'Looks like you got a full house,' he observed as he dropped the last of the bundles on the floor. Nearly all the parking spaces in front of the units were taken up.

'All bar one no-show couple.' Abby pushed back her chair and got up from the desk. A crisp bustling woman, she kept the motel's accounts as well as running a home with a husband and four grown children, helping with the church and lending a hand with town affairs whenever needed. She was unfailingly cheerful and Rick had never seen her when she wasn't busy.

'It happens.' No-shows were the bane of the motel trade.

'Yup, and when it does I charge them for it. Always take a credit card number for a reservation.' She shook her head. 'Nice-sounding young man on the phone too. Said they were coming from New York State.'

'You never can tell,' Rick laughed. Abby was hard to fool. So was Beth come to that. 'Don't forget Friday's final meeting before the big day. Seven p.m. at the Chamber of Commerce.'

'Swell, I'll be there. Beth can mind the office. And congratulations to you too, young man, by the way,' Abby added. 'Natalie's a fine girl.' She glanced out the window as she spoke to where Rick's pick-up stood. 'Is that her out there? Oh, no.'

Rick smiled wryly as he caught her eye. 'Sarah was at the party. I'm dropping her off at her place.' By tomorrow that would be all over town.

Sarah was still curled up with her cigarette as he climbed back into the pick-up and backed it round. 'That Abby Cotton is watching us from the office window,' she observed. 'I slapped her man's face when he stuck his hand up my skirt on my sixteenth birthday and he said I led him on. She's had it in for me ever since.'

Rick said nothing. Ted Cotton hadn't been the only one to make a fool of himself over Sarah Hunter. Perhaps she hadn't led men on deliberately, but her taut body and insolent carriage were a challenge that seemed to lead to trouble.

They drove along West Street to the Green.

The first showing of the cinema had just emptied, groups of teenagers were hanging out round the memorial to the Great Storm of 1812 and there was a line forming outside Pam's Dairy for ices. Downtown was humming. Stores and businesses stayed open all hours in the season. Many premises had hung out flags and streamers in anticipation of Saturday's parade. The night was bright and warm and the crowds were having a good time.

Goodwill – 300 years of American history! proudly proclaimed a huge banner on Main Street. Rick had helped to hang that himself this afternoon before the party. Now it looked good up there. A lot of people were putting their backs into getting the town ready for the big day.

'You can drop me off at the Shady Tree,' Sarah told him, stubbing out her cigarette in the ashtray. 'There's an attic there they let me have. It's not much, just a couple of rooms, but it's cheap and private.'

When Rick pulled over outside the restaurant it looked like every seat was filled and customers were waiting at the bar. In back, under the famous oak, were a dozen more tables, people dining under the stars. Groups of passers-by were clustered round the menus pinned up at the entrance, wondering whether to join the line. 'Mat's doing good business. Must be a hundred mouths in there.' Two sittings, he was calculating, maybe three on some tables. A night like this a restaurant could clear a thousand dollars profit. And those same customers would be staying at motels and inns, bringing in yet more revenue. The town was growing right here in front of their eyes.

'He sure does. I help them out evenings on the till.' Sarah snapped her purse shut. 'So long, Rick. Thanks for the ride.' Leaning over, she put up a hand to his face. Their mouths touched. Music thumped outside as an open-backed red SUV went past with a couple of tangle-haired boys up front. The kiss lasted longer than he intended. Sarah broke away first. 'You should never have left town, Rick. Life's all mixed up now.' Patting his cheek, she jumped out and ran quickly into the restaurant. He had a glimpse of her tall figure disappearing among the tables and then she was gone.

Rick swore to himself. How had he managed to get bounced into that? If anyone had seen, it would make a juicy bit of gossip, him kissing Sarah Hunter on the night of his engagement to Natalie. Damn!

Pulling out into the traffic again, he drove on down the street onto Bearskin Neck. Moonlight was pouring down on the harbour and shining on the hulls of yachts in the marina. The Lobsterman looked bursting. Further up, swatches of red, white and blue decorated the front of the Chandlery, the family store. His sister must still be there because the lights were burning.

The red SUV that had passed by a moment

ago was stopped outside the old trap shed opposite, its rear loaded with surfboards and a trailer with a powerful jet ski hooked on behind. Rick parked in front of it and switched off the engine. As he stepped out a figure emerged from the shadow of the building moving rapidly down towards him. Some kid on a skateboard. No, not a kid, a husky youth in baggy shorts Rick didn't recognise calling out to a companion further down the dock as he rattled past.

The chandlery had changed since his father's day and Rick wasn't completely used to it yet. His sister, Rebecca, was managing now. She had installed new lighting and banished all the low-tech staples, the reels of nylon rope, the anchor chains and mooring buoys, out to the rear. To reach them customers had to pass racks of the latest in waterproof clothing and brand-name leisurewear on which margins were higher. At the ends of the aisles were bins containing impulse bargains like designer sunglasses, pocket knives and light sticks. There were harnesses to stop you falling overboard and life vests to keep you afloat if you did.

Rebecca was behind the counter. She was four years his senior, fair like him and strong boned. Married to a lobster fisherman, Mike Caine, with two sons, she had a no-nonsense air about her that made other people, Rick included, wary.

The two surfers from downtown were peering over a chart Reb had spread out for them. Rick recognised it as the nautical chart of the bay and islands with depth soundings in feet. One was talking into his cellular, apparently taking instructions.

Rick studied them curiously. Hoodies and board shorts; flat West Coast vowels spiked with cult language. Fit, confident, comfortable in themselves and their world.

The one with the phone ended his conversation. He was in his teens, Rick guessed, but the other, named Gimp apparently, looked older, thirty maybe. 'Thanks, lady, guess this will do us.' Gimp paid and rolling the chart up moved away from the counter. Rick saw for the first time that he had a twisted right leg that left him with a limping gait.

'Nice PWC you got out there,' Rick remarked as they passed him.

The Gimp turned to look at him. His eyes were dark as pebbles. 'Is that going to be a problem here?'

'Shouldn't be. Some beaches are restricted and like all boat users we ask that you give seals their space, otherwise you're welcome. I take it you're surfers?'

'He surfs.' The Gimp jerked a head in his friend's direction. 'A wave busted my leg last year. Now I ride the jet.' He said it with bitterness.

'I'm sorry,' Rick said. 'Where was that?'

The Gimp turned away with a shake of his shaggy head. Lurching to the door, he wrenched it open and limped out.

'Thailand,' the younger man answered as he made to follow. 'A thirty-footer wiped him out. Now he does tow-outs for other dudes. It gets to him sometimes. Don't take it personal.'

The door swung to behind them. Rick turned back to Rebecca. She made him a rueful half-smile. 'Sorry I couldn't make the party.' Rick didn't comment. They both knew why she had stayed away. 'Everything go off okay?' she said.

'Pretty much. Don showed up and Coach Davis. And Sarah Hunter was there.'

'Ha. How's she taking it? The engagement, I mean.'

Rick sniffed. 'Okay I guess. She had me bring her back into town after.'

Rebecca's eyebrow flicked upwards. 'Now, this evening? Natalie know about that?'

'Natalie's a big girl, Reb.'

Rebecca gave him her older sister look. 'So is Sarah,' she said tartly, 'and she's on the prowl again from what I hear.'

On the prowl about summed up Sarah's feline intensity, Rick felt. It was on the tip of his tongue to say that she had been coming on strong to him tonight but he stopped himself in time. Reb was usually tight-mouthed but the less said the better.

'How's it been tonight?'

'Pretty quiet mostly. Just those two fellows in.'

'I saw them in town earlier. What are they after?'

Rebecca shrugged. 'The younger guy wanted

to know how long to repair a torn wetsuit. Then his partner with the limp wanted a chart of the Sound. I sold him one.'

'I mean what are they after in Goodwill? We don't have any surfing here.'

'I guess that's their business.'

Rick had switched his phone on while they were speaking and was checking for messages. There was one from Don confirming that the blaze was nothing serious, another from Rebecca apologising for not making the party, other congratulations from friends and family. He was listening to these when the phone *chirruped* signalling a fresh call. Chance Greene's voice this time, sharp and urgent. 'Rick, pick up will you and get your ass down to the Neck pronto. We have a bad situation here.'

Chapter 6

Indian Point. Nine-thirty p.m. The night was still warm. The last guests were gone. Natalie let herself out by the garden door and ran across the now deserted lawns onto the gravel path leading through the woods. A dusty red veil hung over the full moon and the boles of the trees gleamed straight and mysterious on either side. There was no wind. The path ran steeply downward towards the shore, dry and dusty underfoot. It had been weeks since any rain had fallen.

'*Darling*,' her mother's voice still rang in her ears, 'I feel so *sorry* for you. Your big day spoiled! Was Rick drunk? He tried to pick a stupid fight with Victor Harrington over some perfectly *innocent* remark . . .'

'Vic started it. He was trying to wind Rick up. It would have served him right if Rick had hit him.'

'That's no excuse. Rick behaved disgracefully in front of all our guests.'

'Mom, please. I don't want to talk about it any more right now,' Natalie had snapped, biting back the tears.

At the far end of the woods she halted, looking down over the western tip of the Point. Ten thousand years ago a retreating glacier had scooped out a shallow bay in the coast, now fringed by boulders, leaving a strip of pale sand, a private place where she came when she wanted to be alone. Scrambling down the rocks, she reached the beach and stood a moment, breathing in the silence. Damn, Rick and that stupid pride of his that made him so touchy. Why did he have to let her down tonight of all nights? Maybe her mother was right and their relationship was doomed to fail.

She gazed at the ocean, her emotions churning. Away to the north she picked out the flash of the light on Curtain Bluff where Rick had slain the whale all those years ago. He had run out on her then; would he do so again now? She sighed; sometimes it seemed the burden of the past was too great to carry.

Her anger faded and in its place came a black despair. The tears began to flow and she hugged herself for comfort. The tide was still flowing in and she paced the shallows, the chill water lapping at her bare feet. The beach was cool and firm, rinsed clean by the tide. Once she paused in mid-step, thinking for a moment she heard a voice. Her head twisted, searching to track it down. A fragment of song? She could not be sure; it must have been her imagination.

She was almost up to the rocks at the far end when she checked again, her nostrils twitching. A scent of wood smoke hung in the still air of the cove. Peering into the shadows she caught a momentary flicker of sparks, the dying remnants of a small fire smouldering on the sand. For several moments she stood watching, scanning the moonlit beach. The steady lapping of the ocean came and went. The red glow of the embers flickered in the shadows. Nothing else moved. Perhaps whoever set the fire had departed, leaving it to burn out. Most likely it was kids from one of the neighbouring summer-houses on the Point.

She padded up the beach for a closer look. The wood had all but burned out in the centre leaving a ring of smouldering ash. Kneeling, she pushed some larger bits into the middle, making a heap, and blew on the sparks to coax them back to life. In a minute she had a flame. There was spare wood lying nearby. She added some and soon had a small blaze going.

Comforted, she sat back on her heels, watching the warm light throw dancing shadows across the sand. The soft air and quiet rhythm of the water brought a magical sense of calm. The strains of the party seemed far away. She threw another branch on the fire. The smoke had a resinous tang that tickled her nose. Lifting her head, she glanced towards the woods and stiffened suddenly. Up in the shadows she had caught an unmistakable gleam of eyes watching her. A dozen feet away, just beyond the circle cast by the blaze, a man was sitting.

'Figured you'd notice me sooner or later,' the quiet voice floated out of the half-light. He made no movement. That must have been why she hadn't spotted him from the first. His stillness was absolute. She narrowed her eyes warily but detected no threat. And the house was near. She let herself relax.

'I thought I heard music a moment ago.'

There was a dry chuckle in the gloom. 'Bob Marley and Metallica *St Anger*. The surfers' choice.'

She squinted through the moonlight. The stranger was bare-chested with a stubble beard and a handkerchief tied round his head pirate fashion. From his accent he was West Coast. 'You're one of the gang just blew in tonight?'

'That's me. And you, you're from the big house?'

'Yes, we . . . this is our beach.'

'So I'm trespassing?' He sounded amused at the thought.

She shrugged. 'This place is pretty hidden. No one comes here much except me when . . .' Her voice tailed off.

'Except when you want to be alone,' he finished for her. 'I figured you looked kind of down when first I saw you.'

She dropped her head. 'Well, you know how it is sometimes.'

'Sure, we all get that way. Me, I come down to the ocean, listen to the song of the waves. Never fails.'

Straightening his legs he stood and came to join her, kneeling by the fire, his movements fluid as a cat's and as soundless. He was tall, taller even than Rick, with a muscular power that stirred her. He stoked the embers with a stick. In the ruddy light his hands were beautiful, his features at once mysterious and potent. A gold ring gleamed in one ear.

'I'm Natalie,' she said.

'Glad to meet you, Natalie.'

There was a pause. 'What do they call you?' she asked.

He flashed her a sideways look, crinkling up his eyes, and shrugged. 'I don't have a name.'

'You what?'

He stared into the fire absently, watching the end of the stick smouldering. 'Sure, I did have of course. Different names, different places. None of them seemed to fit. Like I hadn't earned one, you know?'

'But your parents . . .?'

'Well, nobody stuck around me much,' he said. 'There were foster homes. I kept changing schools. Each new school there'd be another name. In the end I kind of lost track, I guess.'

He was being quite serious but Natalie found herself laughing at the absurdity of it. He chuckled too. 'Kinda weird, ain't it? Around ten years back, I must have been twelve, I think, I stopped answering to names.'

The glowing tip of the stick traced patterns in the darkness. 'Ages, names, they pin you down. Without a name you don't figure on any of their lists or files. You're free to wander.' Softly he chanted to himself, 'A dude with no name, a girl without shame.'

There was another silence. Neither felt a need to say anything. It was enough to sit together beside the fire. The light flickered on the stone in Rick's ring and feeling shy suddenly she turned it inward to her palm.

'So what brings you guys to Goodwill?' she asked tentatively after a while.

'Same as most places, surf our brains out, crash a few parties, ride the perfect wave.'

'Anyone tell you waves are scarce round here in summer?'

His mouth stretched in a wide grin. Strong teeth. 'I don't listen to people much. Maybe there's a few surprises in store.'

'Winter is different. In a big storm seas will rip full-size trees out from the woods up there.'

They sat without talking for a minute, staring into the fire. Finally he spoke again. 'There was a wave earlier that I saw. It came right up to where we are now.'

She frowned. 'When was this?'

He shrugged. 'I don't carry a watch. Half-six, seven maybe. I built this fire to mark the spot.'

She measured the distance with her eyes. 'Seven p.m., the tide was only just starting to run in. It's unusual for a wave to reach this far up the beach.' Her tone was doubtful.

He nodded, acknowledging her remark without replying, apparently unconcerned about what she thought. He seemed comfortable with silence. Before she could think of something clever to follow up with though there came a cry from up in the woods behind, a shrill sound that pierced the darkness, startling her with its suddenness. Her companion listened a moment, his head cocked attentively. Then he stuck a finger in the side of his mouth and produced a series of piercing whistles. He paused and listened again. At once the call was answered from up on the cliff with a pattern of alternating notes. The exchange continued for less than a minute, then both fell silent.

Natalie stared at him in wonder. 'Wow, what was all that about? I thought it was an owl maybe, but you sounded like you were holding a conversation with someone.'

'Spanish, the whistle code. I stayed on this island they have out there where the villagers use it to speak to each other across the valleys. The *silbo*, they call it. A crowd of us picked it up and it's cool. We use it all the time.'

'Neat!' She laughed delightedly. Everything about this man was strange and engaging. 'How far does it range?'

'Depends, a mile, two miles sometimes.'

'That's so funny! Like a cellular only free. So that was a friend of yours up the hill calling?'

'Yeah, he was asking where I was. I whistled back I'm down on the beach. Are you alone? he asks. No, I'm with somebody.'

He wasn't coming on to her at all like guys usually did and it piqued her a little. 'You have anywhere to stay?' she asked and was surprised at her own daring.

'Oh, I'll shack up with my buddies.' She flushed. He had turned her down without waiting for her to offer. He stuck the stick back in the ashes and they both scrambled to their feet. Erect, face to face, his physical presence was awesome. She felt a child again. His features were shadowed, his eyes dark with secrets. 'Guess I'll let you have your beach back,' he said.

'Any time you want to come again,' she said.

'It's been nice talking.' A hand reached out to rest briefly on her shoulder and her skin tingled at his touch. Without a word he turned and moved towards the shadowy trees.

'Hey!' she called after him, 'how do I find you again?' and immediately felt foolish.

His voice floated back from the darkness. 'If it's meant to happen we'll meet. Be sure of it.'

She blinked and looked again, but he was gone.

Chapter 7

At the eastern end of the Neck where the *Pequod* lay moored alongside the pier there were lights showing, including the flashing beacons of at least two emergency vehicles.

The end of the pier had been taped off and a police cruiser was drawn up across the entrance, holding back a small crowd of tourists with a scattering of locals and boat owners. The driver's door was open and there was a cop slumped in the front seat. Rick recognised Lenny Duke, a veteran who often worked the late shift.

'Evening, Len, what gives?'

'Who's that? Oh, it's you, Rick. Couldn't see your face a moment.' Lenny heaved himself up in the seat with a grunt. 'Got ourselves a drowning.' He jerked his head in the direction of the steps where a small crowd had gathered beside an ambulance and a truck with 'Coast-guard' markings. 'Jack Pearl and Cal Burrows radioed in, oh, must be a couple of hours ago.

Coastguard sent the launch out. Don is up there but he said not to bother you on account of you were getting hitched up tonight. They're bringing the remains in now if you want to go see.'

It was the very last thing Rick wanted but he knew he had to do it. 'Do we have a name yet?' he asked to delay the moment. 'Anyone been reported missing?'

'Nope.' Len shook his head emphatically. 'Nothing so far. From what I hear establishing identity is going to be a problem. They're saying over the radio that the body is in real bad condition.' His fingers drummed the steering wheel and he made a sucking sound with his teeth.

'Have the press gotten onto this yet?'

'Sheena Dubois from the *Monitor* is up there and a photographer with her. I forget his name but he's local. *Ellsworthy Courier* guy that covered last year's parade, he's showed up, and WGBC are sending a TV crew but looks like they are going to miss the fun unless they get here in the next couple of minutes.'

It didn't matter if the crew made it in time or not. With every second tourist nowadays clutching a video camera the networks would find it easy to buy any footage they wanted. Rick ducked under the tape and walked tight-lipped towards the ambulance waiting next to Don Egan's official car. It was coming up for a spring tide in a couple of hours and *Pequod* was riding high in the water already with a Coastguard launch next to her. Underneath a floodlight, Jack Pearl and a bunch of other people who had made it through the police line were mingled with coastguards and paramedics round a hoist.

'Make way, please.' Doc Southwell, who had been at the Maxwell party earlier and who acted as police medical advisor in such cases, shouldered through importantly.

'Get back there,' Don was ordering. 'Give the man room.'

Rick pushed through the throng to where the ambulance was drawn up. The tailgate was open and Southwell was stepping into white disposable coveralls, a youthful-looking man who took care of his appearance with workouts and tanning sessions.

'Doctor, looks like they're ready for you,' Don told him.

'I'm coming.' Southwell zipped the suit up.

The winch whined again and the crowd pressed forward to see the gurney sway up from the launch with its shapeless bundle covered in a yellow plastic sheet. Rapid bursts of camera flashes blazed out. Dribbles of water glittered blackly in the lights. Don was standing close. Rick saw him reach out a hand to steady the sling as it swung inwards and the body was lowered onto the dock with a wet flopping sound that set Rick's teeth on edge.

Doc Southwell pulled on surgical gloves, snapping the cuffs. 'Do you have your pictures?'

he asked Sheena and her colleagues. The photographers obliged with another volley. Southwell tied on a facemask and nodded. At a signal from Don two of the coastguards removed the yellow sheet, exposing a dark blue body bag. A collective sigh went up from the onlookers.

Southwell squatted down on his heels to take a closer look. 'Move back some more. Move back, you people,' Don ordered again as the spectators, Rick among them, pressed forward, craning their necks in horrified fascination. Sheena was holding out her voice recorder to catch what was said. Southwell pulled the zipper back and lifted his head away with a cough. There were gagging sounds from the watchers as the stench hit them. People pushed back from the scene clutching their noses.

'Sorry, Doc, should've warned you,' Jack Pearl grunted.

The doctor's breath hissed between his teeth as he peered inside the bag. 'Hold that flash closer,' he said thickly to one of the paramedics. He was using some metal instrument, a probe or a scalpel, Rick couldn't see from where he stood, to investigate whatever was inside. There was a tense pause while everyone waited for the doctor's verdict. He seemed to be taking a long time to make up his mind. Rick could hear the whirr of camcorders sucking in the scene. A white-haired tourist lady yelped as somebody trod on her foot.

Finally Southwell waved the flashlight away

and stood up. He peeled off his mask. Underneath, his face appeared strained in the lights. His shoulders drooped with tiredness. Standing there on the dock he seemed determined to extract the last ounce of drama from the event. Mutely he signed to the paramedics to close up the bag again.

A voice broke the lull, Sheena's. 'What can you tell us, doctor?'

Southwell gestured towards the gurney at his feet. 'The remains are . . . extensively decomposed,' he said heavily and paused. 'Tests will be necessary to establish identity.'

Sheena was waving her voice recorder. 'Doctor, can you give us any idea how the person died?'

There was something wrong, Rick sensed, badly wrong. Southwell was passing a hand across his face. Clearly he was holding something back.

Chapter 8

The hospital was new; a two-storey building put up by a consortium from Ellsworthy and located on the far side of the Causeway on a piece of ground belonging to Chance Greene. It handled paediatrics and minor trauma and Dr May, the surgeon, also attended there for some cases. Anything more serious was sent up to Bangor, a trip that took an hour even with the siren and if you went that far you might as well keep right on going along Highway 95 to Portland where the standard of care was better.

At least though the local hospital had a morgue for when people passed away and for autopsies, which was convenient. Sheena Dubois followed the ambulance out over the Causeway in her car and smoked a cigarette outside under the porch. She had a problem with hospitals; it was the smell. The ambulance that had brought the body from the harbour stood parked nearby, its engine ticking as it cooled down. Ellsworthy lay two miles west on Route One. From time to time cars hummed through the night travelling along the Causeway, their headlight beams reflecting on the water.

In her head she worked on the piece she needed to write for the paper. First the tsunami threat and now a body washed up. Down at the Neck they were all spooked. Sailors were a superstitious lot. A drowning brought bad luck.

On cue her phone went. 'Sheena?' Chance Greene again, wanting to know what she was going to print.

'Give me a break, Chance. You saw the state the remains were in. You're talking dental records and DNA tests here. At present they'll be hard put to establish the sex let alone identity.'

'So what's the betting? Fallen off a boat then?'

'That would be my guess too.'

'Could have happened anywhere, off the Banks, a passing freighter.'

'Listen, it could have come off the *Titanic* for all we know right now. There's no story. Without an ID the TV stations won't run it. Get some sleep. You've enough to worry about with Founders' Day coming up.'

'I don't need you to remind me,' he snapped, cutting the connection.

Sheena sighed wearily and lit another cigarette. She had been waiting twenty minutes more when Doc Southwell emerged carrying his jacket.

'Oh, it's you,' he said. The corners of his mouth were turned down, a sign he was tired. She trailed after him to where their cars were parked. 'You're not going to believe what we've learned,' he said without looking at her as he felt in his pocket for his keys.

'Try me.'

'Let's go somewhere.'

She followed the tail lights of his Landcruiser back along the Causeway. There was almost no traffic on the road now. Half a mile before the town he turned off. The track wound between silent trees to a hidden clearing. He stopped and switched off his lights. Sheena pulled up alongside. Together they climbed into the back seat of her Toyota.

'So what's this hot gossip?' she asked as he started tugging at her shirt.

'Later,' he grunted, reaching underneath.

'Let me get the belt undone first.' She pulled the shirt off over her head and leaned back, wriggling out of her jeans. He liked her to get naked always. He got off on the risk. He shed his own clothes and plunged into her.

'I thought you were whacked,' she said as his thrusts subsided.

'I'm never too tired,' he boasted.

They shared a cigarette, the glowing end casting shadows on their bodies. One day they were going to be caught out. In a small town nothing stayed secret for long. She would have to leave town and he, would he lose his pretty wife?

And if he did would he marry her? She laughed to herself silently. No chance. That was one thing: with a bastard like Southwell at least your expectations were low. No danger of disappointment. Why did she let him use her then? Sex, love, loneliness, boredom? They were just words.

He was talking again. 'What we found is just weird.'

'Weird in what way? Like two heads or something?'

'Way beyond that. We get the remains on the table and what do you think we find? A shroud no less.'

'A shroud?'

He made an impatient sound. 'You know what I mean. A winding sheet, a thing they used to wrap bodies in for burial. You see them in paintings.'

'I know what a shroud is, but no one uses them nowadays surely?'

He inhaled deeply. 'Down here who knows what goes on? Some of these backwoods parishes they probably cling to all manner of old ways.'

'I'm trying to work this out.' Sheena took the cigarette from him. 'You're telling me what got washed up on Cal Burrows's lobster raft was a body that had a sea burial? Yuck!'

He was still chuckling. 'Way off, honey. They don't do sea burials off this coast. Marine sanctuary. And where they do they drop them off in deep water beyond the continental shelf. Also from the state of decomposition with this one you can tell it was in the ground a long time, like twenty years, before it got into the ocean.'

'Someone digs up, exhumes a body that's been in the ground and disposes of it at sea? Why do that?'

'Short on space maybe. The only other explanation I can think of is a burying ground right near the ocean became eroded.'

Sheena was silent a minute. 'The sea giving up its dead,' she said, pushing herself up and feeling around for her top. 'It sounds biblical. Like a portent.'

'Yeah, but of what?'

Bearskin Neck. It was nearing eleven. The paramedics and police vehicles had departed. Chance Greene had gone home. Rick and Rebecca were sitting in the Lobsterman nursing coffees and doughnuts. Jean-Alice's ponytailed manager Mitch was behind the counter reading a newspaper. Country and western music from a radio request show played low in the background. The only other busy table was the big one in the front window where half a dozen of the newly arrived surfers were gathered.

The man nicknamed the Gimp appeared from the rear where Jean-Alice had internet. His gaze met Rick's for a moment. Dark eyes, unfriendly still. Realising he was being impolite, Rick looked away. The man limped over to the group, which parted to make space for him. Evidently some kind of leader.

Rebecca pushed her plate with a half-finished doughnut away. 'I shouldn't eat these things. Calorie bombs! What do you think Southwell was holding back?'

Rick turned his attention back. 'We'll know soon enough when the tests are done,' he said flatly.

Reb touched his hand. 'I'm sorry. It spoilt your big day. Are you going to tell Natalie?'

He moved his hand away. 'What's to tell?'

'Yeah, you're right.' Rebecca stood up, reaching for her shoulder bag. 'Time I hit the hay. Mike will be wondering where I am. See you down the store tomorrow.'

Rick wandered over to the counter for a refill of coffee. Unsettling images persisted in his mind: the body bag being pulled from the water; Southwell's strained face; Sarah Hunter's mouth against his own; the crippled surfer's hostile stare; the pain in Natalie's eyes as he left the party. The day, which had started out simple, had turned complicated. Something important was missing from the picture and he couldn't figure what it was.

The soft music trickling from the radio paused to be followed by the announcer's voice. 'Five minutes before midnight on WGBC on the *Easy Listening Hour*. This next song is for a lucky guy down in Goodwill, Rick Larsen. Rick, the caller sends her love and says you'll know who this is from: Celine Dion singing "It's All Coming Back to Me Now".'

'Hey, Rick!' Mitch called. 'Here's one for you.'

'*There were nights when the wind was so cold . . .*' the opening words spilled out into the room.

Rebecca paused in the doorway to listen. 'Somebody certainly loves you, huh, little brother?'

Rick forced a smile. He remembered the song – all too well; it had been popular back when he was running around in high school. It had also been Sarah Hunter's favourite.

A figure flashed past outside the window. A burst of cheering from the other table drowned the music as the surfers applauded the antics of their buddy clowning on the skateboard. In a moment they had all leapt up and surged outside to join in the fun. As Rick followed them out to the door his eye fell on a scrap of paper on the recently vacated table. Glancing down, he saw it was a copy of an e-mail torn off a printer. *La Palma – long tremor 5.2 magnitude approx. 1 p.m. local time. Reports of landslides on west coast. Sea state confused for several hours waves 5 metres plus.* It was unsigned.

Underneath was another message: *Bermuda 4 p.m. Heavy seas reported on outer reefs. Wave heights 2 metres.*

What was all that about? He couldn't tell.

'. . . *There were nights when the wind was so cold . . .*'

Natalie tossed her head impatiently and the

105

lamplight caught the sheen of her hair. 'There, they've done it again.'

'Done what?' her mother asked. They were in the family room at the Point. The phones had been going all evening.

'They keep playing that song on the radio, but I never catch the title. I can't place it and it's driving me crazy.'

'I wish you would *concentrate*, my dear. We need *decisions*.'

Natalie made a face. 'I told Rick we have to set a date, but he says first he has to finish that stupid house of his.'

The Man with No Name, who was known in the surfing world as the King of the Mountain, had called a meeting of his chieftains. These were his most trusted followers, his closest buds, the fearless warriors of the water. Together they had charged the weird realms of the deep ocean. And survived with scars to prove it. There was Kiwa, the Polynesian enforcer with the tattooed chest, Earless, who had been dragged over a reef and come up less than whole, Greg the Namibian, Pico from Brazil, the Brisbane Bandits, reef riders from the North Shore and Southern Cal. No grommets or adolescent hangers-on here, but hard men, professionals, the tow-in veterans of Jaws, Tahiti, Mavericks and a hundred secret spots in six oceans and unnumbered seas.

Out on the headland at Curtain Bluff they made a fire at the edge of the trees facing out

over the Sound, yards from the ancient graveyard and where the only sounds were the surf
crashing on the cliffs below and the owls crying
in the woods. They were comfortable in the
darkness. The outdoors was their spiritual home,
nature's way the surfer's path. Now they had
come to listen to their undisputed leader, the
Pope, the unnamed King of the Mountain,
crowned more times than most could remember.
This was to be his wildest, most testing challenge
yet. A solemn moment.

So they built their fire and sat round in the
whispering darkness. They had answered the
summons, now they waited to hear the reason
why.

The Gimp spoke first, standing out, his
crippled leg braced against a board for support.
He needed no introduction. His story was
known, the wipeout that all but destroyed him
and the long quest that had brought meaning to
a shattered life. This was his discovery; he had
done the research, now he made the presenta-
tion, unveiling his secret while sparks flew
upward into the warm sweet night.

His tale was familiar in parts; when he spoke
of the great swells, the reefs and the giants they
spawned his audience nodded wisely. These
were challenges they had faced and within
measure overcome. He talked of Jaws, of
Mavericks, of Tasmania and Teahupoo and
these were nothing new. When he moved on to
Cortes Bank there was more interest. '. . . the

107

wave hits the reef and just unloads . . . Parsons caught a ride of sixty-six feet there in 2001 to take the XXL prize . . . but it could go higher . . . potential for one hundred feet . . .' – and here the Gimp paused for effect – '. . . even talk of one twenty . . .'

They sat up at that. 'One hundred twenty, that was Garrett McNamara said that,' Coughlin grunted, the silver stitching of his shark-torn shoulders shifting in the moonlight as he stirred. 'Sean Collins reckons a hundred easy.'

'Hell, Cortes has been photographed at ninety!' someone else spat scornfully.

'So Cortes it might be if anywhere,' the Gimp allowed smoothly. 'So what do we know of this legendary bank then? A seventeen-mile-long undersea mountain one hundred miles off San Diego, eighty foot of water on the continental shelf, great abalone incidentally, capping off at just three feet. What distinguishes it from Jaws or Mavericks or Shipstern's Bluff or Teahupoo or any of the other legends?'

'The sucker is bigger!' another dude shouted to laughter.

The Gimp shrugged. Anyone, he implied, could be stupid if they wanted. This was serious business. 'They are all wind-driven waves,' he said. 'They are dependent on three factors: wind strength and duration, water depth and fetch. Two of those factors, water depth and fetch, the distance the wind is blowing over water, are subject to physical constraints. Wind strength on the other hand is a variable as all of us know. Now hundred-foot waves are a relatively common phenomenon in severe storms. Oceanographers tell us it takes a force twelve gale, eighty plus miles per hour, blowing over a thousand miles of ocean for something like twelve hours. The biggest wave ever officially recorded topped out at a hundred and twelve feet. Okay' – he raised a hand – 'I know what you're thinking, truly huge waves wipe out the recording gauges. My point is there are physical limits to the storm-driven wave and those limits lie within one hundred to one hundred and twenty feet – even at Cortes Bank.'

'Hell, we didn't come out here to have you tell us stuff we already know,' Mack the big biker growled. 'Cut to the chase, man. How big of a sucker are you selling us here?'

The words hung on the air. The surfers waited. The Gimp's gaze was impossible to read. 'This wave, our wave' – he glanced back at the King who squatted behind him staring at the heart of the fire as if none of this touched him – 'the Goodwill wave will top . . .' he paused and his voice softened to become a deadly whisper, '. . . will top fifty metres!'

The silence that followed was absolute. They could do the math. The Gimp was promising a wave 160 feet high, almost three times the tallest wave ever surfed. It was epic. It was glory. It was death.

The King rose and stepped forward into the

firelight, his shadow reaching behind him like the shrouded wings of an archangel and his head touched the stars. 'This is my dream,' he told them and his voice was whisper soft yet throbbed with base power as if it came to them through the ground. 'All my life has been lived in preparation for this moment. The wave will be born. It will cross the ocean here to this Sound and I will fly it to the moon.'

'To the moon!' echoed the Gimp.

'To the moon!' the others took up the response. 'To the moon!'

Big Mack stood up. His body language was sullen as he faced the King. 'And what about us? Do we get to share in your glory?' A bird cried in the woods. The sky darkened as a wisp of cloud passed over.

The King gave him back look for look. He feared nothing, neither man nor beast nor the ocean's fury. 'Anyone is welcome to fly with me,' he said and his tone was chill. 'All it takes is *cojones*.'

Chapter 9

Friday. La Palma, Canary Islands. Carlos from the hotel provided the explosive. Ten kilograms purchased from a quarry north of Taburiente and brought down in Carlos's pick-up using the back roads to avoid the cordons. The soldiers were under orders to turn back all vehicles at El Paso. Since the new vent opened up the ash had been so bad there was talk of evacuating the southern half of the island. Ridiculous when the mountains were crawling with scientists and press crews. Thank God for them though. With the tourists shut out by the craven island council, the hotel would be empty otherwise.

Shaped like a stone axe head, La Palma was the largest of the western Canary Islands. An oceanic mountain sixty miles off the coast of north-west Africa, it rose 21,000 feet above the surrounding ocean floor, three-quarters the height of Mt Everest. The Cumbre Vieja volcano, along whose ridge Carlos was now driving, was one of the fastest-growing volcanoes in the world and highly active. In the past century it had erupted on three occasions. Black lava fields, cinder cones and red volcanic ash had blasted the lush greenery on the island's steep-sided slopes. Ash and debris were not the only hazards; twice on the trip Carlos had been forced to turn back and detour around gaping fractures in the road, torn by repeated earthquakes.

The pick-up lurched over a pothole buried under dust as he took the right-hand fork descending towards the coast. From here the flares of the two ash plumes were both visible, the old one far down towards the south at San Antonio where the eruption first began and the new vent which had opened up almost at the midpoint of the west coast not half a mile from the hotel. It was this last one that threatened to destroy his livelihood and that of his friends.

The vent had appeared three days ago, early in the afternoon. Carlos was behind the bar, preparing drinks for the American TV crew that had flown in from Madrid the previous day, two cameramen and the blonde presenter with the loud voice who had just returned from filming in San Antonio and the two assistants who carried their equipment. They were inside sheltering from the heat and looking out across the ocean towards the USA. Behind the hotel reared the near-vertical thousand-metre ridge that was the first shelf of the volcano, off which, before the eruption, adventurous parasailors would launch their gaily coloured chutes.

Carlos was just setting the beers on a tray when the ground began to shake and he grabbed the edge of the counter, for support. There was a cry from the woman, and Carlos turned to call to them to get out on the terrace because the tremor felt close, too close, and the roof might go any moment. Before he could speak there came a noise like a thunderclap, followed a moment later by the ringing crack of the earth's crust snapping. The shaking eased and in its place came a screech of high-pressure steam escaping interspersed with the rumble of falling rocks. And a smell. Carlos knew that smell. Every islander did.

Carlos ran out through the lobby to the main entrance. Smoke and steam were belching from behind the rocky ridge jutting into the ocean just north of the village. That could only be a fresh vent opened up, but that was impossible surely, it would mean an eruption in the ocean itself. And he set off at a run along the beach, others from the village following in his wake.

The ridge was a thirty-metre-high spur of jagged black basalt formed by an ancient lava flow. The sharp rock was steep and painful to climb and cut off a small cove that was seldom visited. As Carlos and his neighbours neared the end of the beach, they became enveloped in a rain of steaming black mud spouting over the spine of the ridge. Beyond, the cove had

113

vanished, swallowed up by a scalding geyser fifty metres or more across now vomiting its stinking contents over their village and harbour.

And as they continued to gape in horror and dismay, crouching under the bombardment of boiling mud, a white-hot semi-solid lump of plastic lava oozed from the belching vent and slid steaming down the mud cone already building round the geyser's monstrous throat. More followed in a thickly moving stream that changed from white to fiery red as it crawled outward. Lava! A waft of powerful acidic gas sweeping across the slope caught Carlos's throat and dropped him gasping to his knees.

Now that lava flow had to be stopped. Stopped somehow, anyhow, before it ruined Carlos and the whole village with him. Which was why he was driving through the ash clouds with a load of explosives.

Friday. Two thousand miles east of Bermuda out in mid-Atlantic, the USS *Tarp*, a T-AGS-60 class ocean survey vessel, steamed at eight knots on a south-easterly course in the direction of North Africa. Three hundred and thirty feet overall, with a displacement of 5,000 tons, her operating crew of twenty-five was outnumbered by the scientific personnel aboard. Hull and laboratories were packed with the latest commercial ocean survey equipment including multi-beam echo sounders and side scan sonars, married to state-of-the-art military underwater positioning systems and acoustic sensors. For the past month the *Tarp* had been conducting a seismic survey of the north-eastern boundary of the Mid-Atlantic Ridge, a submarine mountain chain extending from Jan Mayen Island on the Arctic Circle a thousand miles north of Iceland topped by the mighty Beerenberg volcano, all the way to the smoking glacier-covered peak of Bouvet standing sentinel at the approach to the southern Antarctic ice cap.

Deployed beneath *Tarp*'s stern on a chain-block assembly was a 500-kilogram acoustic transceiver pole that transmitted a seismic pulse to the seabed 3,000 metres down where it was reflected back to be captured by receivers and processed on-board to generate a 3-D sonograph image of the ocean floor.

Two years ago NOAA, on the orders of the president, had initiated a programme designed to provide both the Pacific and Atlantic coasts of the United States with a comprehensive early warning system against the tsunami threat. The plan called for a quadrupling of the existing warning network in the Pacific and erecting similar coverage for the eastern seaboard as well as for the Gulf and Caribbean coastlines. Known as DART for Deep Ocean Assessment and Reporting of Tsunamis, the project called for the deployment of thirty-eight bottom pressure recorders anchored to the seafloor. Linked by an acoustic coupling to a companion surface buoy, these would calculate the height of the overhead water column and transmit the data to a ground station via a GOES satellite signal.

The first twenty-five of these buoy systems were earmarked for the Pacific to supplement a smaller six-buoy network already in place. By the end of last year all thirty-one had been successfully installed and the network declared operational. Now it was the turn of the Atlantic. Already four out of five DART systems had been positioned along the ridge. Tomorrow morning the last remaining buoy would be lowered into position from *Tarp*'s winch, extending coverage over the northern sector of the arc around the Canaries. Then at a signal from NOAA the full network would go live for the first time and residents of the eastern seaboard could sleep easier in their beds.

Alongside the DART project the voyage had another objective. Two years ago, one of the *Tarp*'s sister ships, the USS *Maven*, had chanced upon a previously unmapped canyon running east–west through the axis of the MAR. A further survey confirmed not only that the canyon was deeper than first appeared, but also that it connected to a chain of fissures in the ocean bed extending right back as far as the continental shelf of the US eastern seaboard.

The discovery was potentially significant for the US Navy since it appeared to offer a covert route for submarines to transit the Atlantic undetected. *Tarp*'s secondary mission therefore was to map the eastern sector of the canyon to see where it led.

In the data-processing centre aboard, Dr Mary Sennett studied the latest imagery on her workstation in awed silence. On a twenty-inch flat screen the scale of the fissure was vast, comparable to the great African Rift Valley. Towering escarpments with sheer cliffs plunging 500 feet into a ravine 10 miles across cleaving the ocean bed like a lightning stroke. And as yet there was no end in sight. The betting was that the feature extended all the way to the West African littoral.

As to how it had been formed there were differing theories. Some figured it for a transform fault line created by a stretching of the earth's crust as the African plate and the North American plate were forced apart, releasing molten rock from the interior mantle. Mary's preference was asteroid impact. Collision with a supra-meteorite body on the far side of the globe would, she argued, have generated immense tidal forces in the earth's crust, ripping and tearing the crust opposite the impact site.

A nearby plotter sprang into life as fresh data was released, spewing out paper. Derek Wanless, professor at NOAA's University of Connecticut Underwater Research Center and deputy in charge of the project, came up behind her and tore off the printout to examine under the light. He grunted.

'More spikes?'

117

'Yup, seismic from the Canary Islands eruption. It's a nuisance.'

Mary's gaze went to the big Atlantic wall chart. A yellow line etched in marker pen showed *Tarp*'s track to date and current position out in mid-ocean. Cumbre Vieja on La Palma, the volcano responsible for the disturbance, lay approximately 300 nautical miles due east. Less than a day's steaming at this speed. The sonar equipment trailing from the ship was so sensitive it registered the faintest tremors. Mary had tried tweaking the computer program to filter out the interference, but noise from the eruption persisted in degrading the imagery. This irritated a perfectionist like Wanless.

'It puzzles me,' she said to him, 'why the signals should be so strong. We're some way from the seat of the eruption. Only reason I can think of is maybe the fissure itself could be magnifying the sonar effect.'

'I wondered about that too,' Wanless agreed, sucking his lip. 'Interesting to stick a seismograph in the water off the East Coast to see if the shock waves propagate right along the fissure.'

Mary tapped a key, bringing up a smaller-scale image of the entire canyon structure as mapped. It weaved back through the peaks of the MAR, narrowing on the far side as it reached for the New England coastline. Both scientists studied the screen for several moments.

'Remarkable topography there,' Wanless observed. 'See how the fissure slices deep into

118

the continental shelf almost to the Bay of Fundy itself.'

'Hagmar has a theory that whales may be using the canyon as a migratory route up to Nova Scotia,' she said. Felix Hagmar, another Woods Hole graduate, was a specialist in cetaceans. 'So did you submit a request for the seismographs?' Mary asked, twisting round to look at him.

'Uh huh.' He nodded.

'And?'

Wanless shrugged. He ran a hand over his scalp. His hair was thinning; he smoothed what was left carefully. 'Usual story. The budget for this year is overspent, so ask the navy they said. Navy is interested, but we have to make a case for how it would impact on national defence. We might slide it into our projection for the next financial year.'

'By which time the eruption will be over so there'll be no point.'

'But that won't stop the committee including it,' Wanless added with a faint smile.

'No, they'll place the seismos anyway, record nothing and blame us for wasting money on a flawed experiment,' Mary laughed.

Wanless was looking out the window at the empty ocean. 'A few more hours and we should spot Cumbre Vieja's smoke plume. I won't be sorry when the last buoy is dropped and we can head back,' he confessed.

'You really think the volcano is going to blow soon?'

He shook his head. 'God knows, but I lost a good friend on Mount St Helens in 1980. Volcanoes are unpredictable brutes. Remember that film about Krakatoa? The people in the ship sailing unsuspecting towards the island about to erupt. That could be us.'

In spite of the warmth in the cabin, Mary shivered.

Chapter 10

Friday. La Palma, Canary Islands. Two hundred metres from the lip of the crater, Dr Malcolm Mackenzie of the US Geological Survey paused for a drink of water. He had been hiking all morning in full sun at an altitude of 6,000 feet across a landscape of solidified lava, grey volcanic rock and copper-coloured sand. Behind him three more geologists, two men and a woman, picked their way up the rough track along the mountain crest that split the island north to south. Five miles to their rear the ash plume blasting from the first eruption at Fuencaliente on the island's southern tip rose thousands of feet into the air. It was not that which concerned them now, it was the one ahead, the eruption they couldn't see thanks to the rock wall rising in front of them, they could only hear it, a screeching roar of gas and steam coming from fumaroles high in the crater.

Malc screwed the top back on his flask and

stowed it away on his belt. As he did so he felt a tremor run through the ground. It lasted only a few seconds then died away only to be followed by another of similar intensity. Half a dozen metres behind him on the trail, Felipe stopped. 'Two point five!' he called. 'Maybe more, point six or seven.'

Malc waved back. 'And shallow like the others, around five kilometres.' He waited for Felipe to catch up. The Spaniard was an older man, fifty against Malc's thirty-nine, fit and wiry with the beaked nose of pirate ancestors. Thirty years of scrambling among these rocks had left him tanned almost black and given him an unparalleled insight into the volcano's workings. 'Seismic swarm,' he said to Malc and both men frowned. It was a serious matter. A sudden increase in shallow earth tremors like they were now experiencing was a strong indicator of an imminent eruption.

A Spanish army helicopter had flown the party and their equipment onto the mountain. Since then they had been walking for more than four hours along the rugged summit ridge of Cumbre Vieja, stopping at intervals to check clusters of instruments en route. Now they were on their way to Hoyo Negro, a crater that had lain dormant for over fifty years. Data from GPS receivers positioned on the crater rim indicated that the distance between the eastern and western rims of the crater had widened by almost two centimetres in the past twenty-four hours.

Ground levels over the central ridge were deforming under pressure from below, literally tearing the island apart. The geologists wanted to view the process at first hand.

The shocks had begun two hours ago and continued at irregular intervals since. Taken with the GPS readings they indicated a magma plume intruding through the mountain towards the surface, shouldering the rock apart. Where it broke through to the surface would mark a fresh eruption.

Malc scrambled on with the cone of the volcano rising ahead. Stands of ash-covered Canary pines, largely burned out now, gave way to shale and cinder streaked glittering red and ochre with dark outcrops of hardened lava. The wind carried fumes with it, making their eyes smart. At the top of the rim he and Felipe paused thankfully by the charred skeleton of a last tree, chests heaving from their exertions in the thin air. They were looking down into an uneven pit half a kilometre across and a hundred metres deep at the centre. It was choked with grey cinder and gravel interspersed with larger boulders, the products of former eruptions. Jets of steam, fumaroles, spouted piercingly from the earth at several points, staining the rock around vivid shades of green, yellow and cyan blue and giving off a throat-searing chemical stench.

They waited for the rest of the party. First to join them was Viktor, a bearded Russian specialist in volcanic gases, shouldering a pack filled with temperature gauges and sample bottles. He scrambled up the crest, his nose working vigorously. 'Ah!' he exclaimed with delight, inhaling the fumes. 'Good. Excellent. This is what I come for.'

Malc saw Felipe check his watch and glance up at the sun, now partially obscured by smoke and drifting clouds of steam. He switched on the radio to contact La Palma authorities and report their position. It was two p.m., leaving two hours at most for work before setting off for the landing site where the helicopter was due to pick them up at five. Anxious not to lose a moment, Viktor was already struggling into his orange heat-resistant overalls.

Felipe's student assistant, Concha, the youngest on the team, picked her way up lightly in spite of her heavy pack. Below her shorts her sturdy legs were caked with ochre dust. Her helmet bore a surfing logo, incongruous in this barren moonscape. She was a pretty girl and brave, but sullen. Malc had never been able to work her out. He gave her a quick smile now but she ignored him and turned away to say something to Viktor.

Felipe shut off the radio. 'Observatory estimates possibility of an eruption in the next twelve hours at twenty per cent.'

There was now a one-in-five chance of the mountain exploding in the very near future, just as they were about to descend into its throbbing heart. Volcanoes were the last mythical monsters, unpredictable and deadly. The only way they could be studied was by getting in close; taking instrument readings from inside the crater itself. 'Sniffing the dragon's breath', volcanologists called it. The peril was very real. Scientists died every year attempting what they were about to do now.

'Stay alert,' Felipe warned them all. English was the common language. This was his mountain; he was the leader. 'If I shout, leave your equipment, run for the lip of the crater. Wear protection at all times.' He tapped his helmet. 'Okay?'

They started down the slope together, Viktor leading. The crater lip was loose scree and Malc's boots sank ankle-deep in places. Dotted about were heavy lumps of solidified magma, lava bombs ejected from the volcano during previous eruptions.

Viktor hurried over to his fumarole and crouched near the spouting steam jets, thrusting heatproof glass tubes into the vent to draw off vapour for sampling. A dangerous and unpleasant job. The steam shot from the ground at 1,000 degrees and the fumes were often toxic. By rights he should be wearing a breathing mask as well as a helmet, but Viktor was immensely experienced; he had worked on scores of volcanoes around the world and scorned the risks. Felipe and Concha were busy checking the GPS devices and taking temperature readings. Felipe was also making a photographic record of the site.

Malc's speciality was the gravity meters. A rise in magma towards the surface brought about changes in the density of the rock at that point. This could be measured. The meters had to be located as widely spaced as possible around the crater and adjusted. Then the transmitters that relayed the data back to the observatory needed to be tuned and the reception tested. This took time. He worked as quickly as he could, conscious every now and then of a faint quiver underfoot as the monster in the mountain's entrails stirred restlessly. Already he could feel the heat penetrating through his heavy boots. The heat, the suffocating fumes and the constant deafening shriek from the fumaroles inside the crater made him feel queasy. He tried to put out of his mind the knowledge that they were treading on a thin crust resting on a column of superheated liquid basalt that at this moment was gathering energy for the final burst of pressure that would blow the crater open and fry them to a crisp.

It took him more than an hour to complete the last of his instrument readings and satisfy himself all systems were working properly. Drained and dizzy from the noise and smoke, he looked round for the others. Felipe was on the radio again. Viktor was still crouched over his collection bottles. He seemed unaffected by the mountain's toxic exhalations. On site he became completely absorbed in what he was doing, oblivious to time.

The girl Concha came hurrying across from the other side of the crater, her face pale beneath its coating of dirt. 'Felipe wants you to be ready to leave in five minutes,' she told him. 'La Palma is warning that the GPS data shows vertical movement and ground temperature is up to seventy degrees.'

'I can come right away.' Relieved, Malc scooped the remaining items into his pack. Laser measuring instruments on a satellite overhead had detected that the crater cap was starting to bulge outward, swelling under the intensity of pressure building below. It was time to be gone. As if in confirmation a fresh tremor ran through the crater floor, dislodging particles of rock from the lip.

He stood up. The girl was biting her lip. He remembered Felipe saying she had a surfer boyfriend. She was probably wishing she was safe back down on the beach. Well, he was right with her there. 'Better make sure Viktor understands,' he told her. 'He probably won't notice anything so trivial as an eruption.'

The girl quivered. She made an angry movement with a fist, batting his words aside.

'Marco says,' she snorted fiercely. Marco he guessed must be the boyfriend. 'Marco says when Cumbre Vieja explodes the shock will be felt in America!'

Chapter 11

Friday. Bearskin Neck, Goodwill. The siren went off again at six-thirty, which was Rick's usual waking time. He was instantly awake, heard the second wail, thought, Shit, not again, and rolled out of bed, grabbing for his clothes. He was alone in his apartment above the store; Natalie had spent the night with her parents.

Two minutes later he was out on the dock. The night had been stifling hot, but now the wind had shifted round to the east and the greyness was damp and cool, heavy with sea salt. No smell of smoke down by the harbour, but as he headed up Main in the pick-up he saw a thick plume belching skywards south-west of the town this time. The big pump truck was pulling out from the fire station doors, horn blasting, and he followed it out to the edge of town. Sammy Lewis, who owned the launderettes here and in Ellsworthy, was hanging on to the rear platform for dear life as the heavy vehicle took the corners.

Fred Tarr met them at the junction of Forest Road and the Loop Road, his yellow jacket dirty with soot and ash. Behind him the former Sawyers lumber yard was burning fiercely and the flames were threatening the overspill camping ground. RVs and motor homes were charging to and fro in the smoke looking for an exit, and people were running in every direction with a good deal of panic.

Fred was volleying orders to the fire crew. 'Rick, we need to get those idiots out of there before they injure someone!' he yelled above the noise.

'Give them a lead with your vehicle,' Rick told him. 'They'll follow the emergency beacon through the smoke.'

'Some of them need tows. They won't leave their dumb trailers.'

'I'll come behind you and straighten them out.'

As they drove into the campsite a huge and obviously brand-new Winnebago came plunging towards them on a collision course, a woman in night attire clenched to the wheel. Rick blocked her path and jumped down from the pick-up, grabbing his hard hat.

The lady wound down the window. 'Get outta my way!' she screamed. Rick could count three kids at least in the cab, all of them plainly terrified they were about to be burned alive.

'Ma'am, you can't drive through this way. It's not safe. Please back up and follow the fire vehicle with the beacon.'

'Clear the way or I'll drive right over you!' she yelled, beyond listening. She jammed her thumb on the horn and kept it there. The noise at close range was deafening, adding to the chaos. Even without that the kids inside were screaming so loud she probably couldn't hear him anyway.

Rick reached for the handle and wrenched the door open. As the woman gaped at him, still yelling insanely, he put a foot on the step and sprang up beside her. 'Bunch over,' he told her, at the same time giving her a firm shove. Before she could resist, he bundled her out of the driving seat and grabbed the controls, pulling the door shut after him. 'Okay, everyone,' he bellowed above the screams. 'My name is Rick, I'm with the emergency services and I'm going to get you out of here. Just sit tight and do as you're told.'

The woman's response was to dive for the passenger door, dragging the nearest child after her. Rick caught her by the seat of her pants and hauled her back. 'Stay put!' he commanded with all the fierceness he could put into his voice. He slammed the shift into reverse, trying vainly to check the mirrors. The smoke rolling across the site made it almost impossible to see. 'Go back and tell me if I'm going to run anyone down,' he ordered the mother. She gaped at him wordlessly and subsided into helpless sobs.

'I'll go,' a boy who looked about ten told him. He disappeared through the hatch door. A moment later an even younger child appeared in his place. 'Joey says it's okay.'

Praying Joey was right, Rick backed the massive wagon up and succeeded in turning it around. The smoke was getting thicker, some of it entering the cabin. The girl began making retching sounds, but Rick had no time to spare for her. Other vehicles were blundering about in the murk. He wound down his window and shouted at the drivers to follow them. A frantic man surrounded by family clutching at him waved them down. 'We're blocked in. I can't move the truck!'

'Get your people in behind. We'll take you out.'

'What about my trailer?'

'The fire crews are here. They'll stop the flames spreading. The important thing is to get your family out now.'

'You'd better be telling the truth, mister. That trailer cost me sixty thousand. If it goes up I'll be suing somebody.'

Just great, Rick thought. You rescued a man's family and he thanked you by threatening to file suit.

Up ahead he could make out Fred Tarr's beacon flashing through drifts of smoke. Somewhere up there lay the Forest Road exit. Once on that the campers would have a safe route through the woods to the bridge over Indian Creek. The woman had ceased her wailing at last and was wiping her face. 'I don't know who you are, but you saved our lives,' she cried hugging him. She was quite young, Rick saw now, and quite largely

131

nude where he had grabbed her clothing to prevent her abandoning ship. He hoped that wasn't going to lead to a lawsuit as well.

He marshalled the campers on an area of hard standing well away from any trees, where they could feel secure. Fred Tarr had returned to the scene of the fire and reported that once again the blaze was under control. 'You've all had a scare,' Rick told the visitors. 'I don't blame some of you for being sore. But these things happen out here in summer. Woods get dried up without rain and catch light. As you saw we have the equipment and we have the trained personnel and they respond fast. Nobody's been hurt.' That was mostly true. A twelve-year-old had been knocked over in the smoke by a confused driver, but miraculously had scrambled clear without a scratch.

'A fire truck with crew will remain on watch throughout the weekend,' he promised. Fred Tarr was going to love that, Rick thought, but it was vital to reassure these people. 'We're just checking to see everything is safe, then you will all be able to return. Our fire chief has just confirmed that no vehicles have been damaged. The firebreaks kept the flames well away as they were designed to. Of course if anyone chooses not to remain the town will try to find you an alternative site or else refund your money.'

'Where are we supposed to go to then?' a man grumbled. 'Every place is booked up solid this week even if we did want to move.'

'Our vacation has been spoiled,' complained another woman sourly. 'My kids won't sleep tonight.'

They will if you run some energy off them, Rick thought. In his experience children bounced back quickly after a fright. It was the adults that whimpered on.

'Well, we are going back to camp for sure,' announced the woman Rick had rescued. 'So long as this hero here drives us back personally,' she giggled and her children clapped and squealed. Rick could have kissed her. After that there was no more trouble.

'So how did this one start?' he asked Fred Tarr later. They were standing in the smouldering remains of the lumber yard. One of the tenders had been sent back, the other crew was dousing any embers that might reignite. Sheena Dubois had shown up. Rick could make her out talking to the campers, snapping pictures and recording impressions.

'You tell me.' Fred rolled his eyes. 'We're a long way from any known dump and I guess we can rule out lightning strike, which leaves human intervention as most likely.'

Rick glanced across at the campsite. 'Kids playing with matches? It happens. We can speak to the parents, make sure they understand the risk. If they haven't grasped it already by now.'

'I'm not necessarily thinking of anyone from the camp.'

'You saying this was deliberate?'

'Two fires in different locations in twelve hours? I'd say we definitely have to be looking at the possibility, don't you?'

Rick drove back to town. The barriers were going up on Bay Road, closing it off to non-essential traffic. The air was cool, but with a metallic foretaste of heat to come. For the moment a breeze was still coming off the ocean. There was some mist but it was lifting fast. The sun climbed ringed by a blue corona which changed to a greenish hue, giving way in turn to a red haze that lasted only a brief period before fading out as it lifted above a rim of cloud on the eastern horizon.

Today was his turn to take out the boat. *Pequod* was a family operation owned and run by Rick with his Olsen cousins, Magnus and Paul. There was a strong strain of Scandinavian blood in the town from forebears who came over in the nineteenth century to work the granite quarries along the coast. The quarries were uneconomic now but they had left a legacy of fine stone buildings along Main Street and Bay.

Back in the apartment he showered off the smoke and soot. Weather forecast for the day was fine, high pressure, light swell. Perfect conditions for a trip. He switched the TV to CNN. Yesterday's excitement over the tsunami threat appeared to have abated. This morning

134

the volcano only rated third spot after a multiple slaying in Atlanta and a movie star wedding. More shots of the vents pouring smoke. A team of international experts had flown to the island to make an assessment.

His first calls were all to fish boat captains. He needed to know where the whales were so the boat could locate them directly and not waste precious time and fuel in searching. He also spoke to the airfield. Pilots there called in whale sightings too. Nothing doing as yet, was the general report, but it was still early and he wasn't concerned.

His phone rang again. 'Rick!' Chance Greene had heard about the fire.

'Have you spoken with Don yet? This is serious, Rick. If word gets out we have a firebug in town it could wreck the entire season and set us back years.'

For a man with his experience and resources the developer was strangely given to panic.

'Chance, it's only a possibility. Fred Tarr is liaising with Don's people, but there's no history of fire-raising in Goodwill.'

'When did we last have a fire call? Not for months and suddenly there are two in two days. We have to catch this maniac before someone gets killed!'

Rick pointed out that all they had to go on was Freddy Tarr's gut instinct that the blaze at the campsite was suspicious. 'But it could have been an accident, someone getting careless with a barbecue. There was no dew last night; an ember could have smouldered away for hours.'

'It's bad enough there's this tsunami scare. Suppose one of those waves hits in the middle of the parade with the streets packed. There'd be carnage.'

'Sure and the world could come to an end tomorrow. Listen, Chance, you want my opinion, that's all a lot of media hype. Scare tactics make news headlines. At the very least we should have five to six hours' warning of trouble. Time enough to get everyone on the mainland if we have to.'

'I hope to God you're right, Rick. If we have to call this thing off at the last minute we're going to look a bunch of idiots.'

'Not half as much as we will if we cry off now and nothing happens. I'll catch up with you later.'

Out on the dock gulls were squalling overhead as the lobster boats put out to check their traps. The first of the big fair trailers was manoeuvring onto its pitch across by the old Ice Factory. Others would follow until the entire harbour front was lined with rides and sideshows. There were flags out in front of the Lobsterman.

'Coffee, black and hot,' Rick told Jean-Alice inside.

'Guess you earned it. That blaze could have turned ugly.'

The coffee was good. Rick gulped it down and wiped his mouth. 'Yeah, well it's done with now.'

'Until the next time,' she muttered as she swabbed the counter. The TV on the wall was tuned to a sports channel and the place was humming. Jean-Alice did good business down here on the waterfront, fishermen and tourists both. 'Chance Greene was in earlier. He reckons some tourist has turned firebug.'

Rick made a face. He changed the subject. 'That was a messy business in the harbour last night.'

'Don't talk about it.' Jean-Alice scowled. She was superstitious about dead bodies.

'Hear that?' boomed a voice behind. Shannon 'Whale' Morrissey whomped into a neighbouring seat. 'Old Cal Burrows can't find a buyer for those lobsters of his. Wonder why? Ha, ha.' The diner rocked to his laugh. The Whale lived up to his name, not so much in height as in girth.

'Hi, Whale, thought you'd be out in the boat,' Rick greeted him.

'Darn pot hoist went on me yesterday. Couldn't find a part anywhere. Dan finally came up with something and he's fitting it now. Reckoned I'd leave him to it and mosey over here for a bite of breakfast.' Dan Pedhoe was a local mechanic and boat repairer. 'Hey, Jeannie.' The Whale thumped the counter. 'Give us a kiss and don't look so glum. Nobody's died, ha, ha!' and he roared again.

'You mind your manners, Whale Morrissey,' Jean-Alice scolded him. 'At least it was nobody from round here, poor soul. Now I said no more

137

talk about it. Are you eating or are you just taking up space?'

'Well, what d'you think I'm doing here, Jeannie? Just bring me doubles on everything you got, okay.'

The dock worker on Rick's right finished up and a young woman with bouncy blonde hair and a deep-water tan grabbed the seat. It was Patsy Easton, the graduate research student who rode with them on the *Pequod* to talk the tourists through the experience. 'Hi, Rick.' She punched his arm. 'Great day for it, huh?' Whales were Patsy's passion. When she was not in Goodwill she was down in the South Atlantic following the great pods on their migrations, bringing back videos of her travels to show the tourists. Upbeat, frank and funny, she was handy about the boat too, which made an extra crew in an emergency. This was her second season and Rick and his cousins were lucky to have her.

'There was a whole bunch of trippers in the booking office as I came by,' she said.

That was a good sign. The boat would be full for the morning run and afternoons were busier still as a rule. Days like these boat owners made the money to carry them through the slack times. Whale-watching season was March through September but high summer was the make or break period. If only this tsunami scare would hold off.

'I spoke with a couple of the boats. No sightings yet, but it's early.'

138

'Yup, I bumped into Saul Harris on the dock. His brother went out first light, said the same. But he did report a big swarm of *Physalia* around eight miles out.'

'*Physalia*? That's bluebottles?'

'Uh huh, also known as Portuguese man-of-war. Unusual for them to make it this far north. Must be this steady east wind we're having.'

Rick felt a twinge of exasperation. It was one thing after another today. 'If any of those wash up on the beaches they could give a nasty sting.'

'You said it,' Patsy agreed. 'Coastguard are getting set to post a warning.'

Jean-Alice had overheard. 'Boy, soon there'll be more warning notices than people,' she observed caustically. 'Just what we need for the big day tomorrow.'

Patsy was nodding to a couple of the surfers. She went running out at Deep Bay each morning and had gotten to know some of them already. She and Rick talked about waves and what the newcomers could expect. Rick reckoned two to three feet, tops. Patsy shook her head. 'You saw their jets. These guys are giant killers. They'll be out off the bank looking for the big ones.'

Jean-Alice passed over Rick's order of eggs with ham and fetched him coffee. Patsy asked for cranberry juice, yoghurt and an English muffin.

They discussed the tsunami scare. 'What's the buzz down at Woods Hole?' Rick asked.

'They've got guys on a navy ship standing off

La Palma. That's one of the Canaries group, off Africa for your information,' she added.

'Here you go, Whale. Tuck into that.' There were cheers as Jean-Alice plonked the lobster-man's mountainous plate in front of him.

'I served in the navy, remember?' Rick said. 'We got to travel. Also the Canaries are three thousand miles from here, give or take.'

'Three thousand miles is nothing to a tsunami.' Patsy launched into a technical lecture about how the volcano could collapse and slide into the ocean, kicking up a wave that would propagate across the ocean to the US east coast. 'Relax,' she finished. 'It's not going to happen this thousand years.'

'But when it does, we could get swamped here in Goodwill?'

'Maybe not swamped. According to the reports I hear such a wave would be noticeable, but not damaging.'

'How big is noticeable?'

'Well, they were saying it could start out as high as thirty to forty metres but by the time it reached the continental shelf it would drop down to three or four.'

'Three or four metres? Ten, twelve feet?'

'According to the experts. With the tidal range we get here I guess you'd call it a ripple.'

'And the surfers? What do they make of a tsunami?'

Patsy shrugged. Whatever it was the surfers believed, she was not telling.

Natalie Maxwell drove into town. She took the Jaguar, the red XK convertible her parents had given her last birthday.

The top was down and the wind blew her hair. It was a glorious day. She flicked on the radio.

'*There were nights when the wind was so cold* . . . Yes, folks, Celine Dion, "It's All Coming Back to Me Now". That was a request for Rick Larsen in Goodwill. Rick, the caller sends her special love and says, "Do you remember the game we played?"'

Natalie was still trying to figure out in her head what that meant, when her phone went off.

'I know, I just heard.' It was Cindy Thompson calling, another summer resident her own age. 'You thought it was me? Celine Dion! Please. Well, how should I know who she is, one of his excs I presume? Ask him yourself, why don't you?'

Natalie listened a minute more to her friend's breathless views on former girlfriends and the propriety of one's fiancé being bombarded with record requests in gross-out taste. Finally she cut in, 'What am I doing? I'm off downtown to hang out with some cool surfer dudes. No, you can't tag along, bye!'

She flipped the phone shut and gunned the throttle, sending the sportster howling into the next corner in a cloud of dust and squealing tyres.

'Bitch!' she yelled into the slipstream, hammering the wheel. 'Bitch! Bitch! Bitch!'

Down on the Neck, Rick was leaving the diner when the Jag's long red snout rounded the dock. Bay Street was supposed to be off-limits to traffic, but Natalie had gotten past the barriers.

'Hi.' He leaned in to kiss her. She looked disturbingly young.

'Hi there yourself, sailor.'

'Everything okay out at the Point?' How were her parents taking the engagement in the cold light of day? was the subtext. Elise especially could be tricky and Natalie's dad had always harboured grand dreams for his only girl.

'Standard parent behaviour, mostly in denial, but nothing overt said. Dad acts cool. Mom's talking dates.'

'Already?'

'You know how she is.' Natalie made quotation marks with her raised fingers, mimicking her mother's voice. 'She's like, "You should really pick a day and stick with it. That's what your father and I did." As if she thinks we should get married tomorrow or something.'

Rick knew. Secretly he suspected Elise of talking up the wedding as inevitable in the hope of making her daughter feel trapped. 'What are you telling her?' he asked, aware of delicate ground.

Natalie's eyes met his steadily. 'Oh, that we have to wait till your damn house is built first,' she said. Her smile was light, but the glint in her eye warned him the joke was wearing thin.

'Right,' he agreed, careful to keep the emphasis neutral. They both laughed. Her hand rested on the Jaguar's wood rim wheel and the ring, his ring, was turned inwards as if it embarrassed her.

'No regrets yet?' he asked her.

'A few,' she told him with a hint of chill now.

'Such as?'

'I heard you ran Sarah home last night?'

He shrugged a shoulder, deliberately casual. 'She had no transport.'

'Must have been like old times, huh? You and her?'

Rick said nothing. He saw the angry glint in her eye, the white line of her jaw, and waited to hear her out.

He shrugged. 'It was a kid thing. Back when we were in high school.'

'And now you're not kids any more.' Natalie's mouth was tight.

'No,' he agreed, 'and neither are you.'

They glared at one another in stubborn face-off.

'And how do you think I feel when I hear requests over the radio for you? When my friends call up laughing, what am I supposed to answer? That it's your ex boasting about the tricks you got up to?'

There was no mistaking her fury now. She felt betrayed, humiliated. Rick didn't blame her. 'Sarah is messed up. She split from the guy she

143

was living with and now she's back where she started scrabbling for waitress work and running errands for your dad. Of course she's jealous. It's made her a little crazy in the head. I'll straighten her out.'

'More than a little, I'd say,' Natalie retaliated. 'Tell Sarah from me, lay off, you hear? And no more rides in the pick-up. God, men can be so dumb! It should have been obvious to anyone who wasn't an idiot she was trying to nail you. Next time tell her to start walking.'

If Sarah was trying to drive a wedge between the two of them she was getting her money's worth, Rick decided, but Natalie wasn't done yet.

'And what's with the game she was talking about? What does that mean? What's the big secret, huh? Let's hear it. If there's a game you and I haven't played yet I want to know what it is.'

Rick flushed. 'There's no secret, as you call it. I don't know what she's talking about. The only games are inside her head and the ones she's playing with us.'

He tried to make his voice convincing, but it was hard and he knew she didn't believe him.

He put a hand in to touch her shoulder, but she shrugged him off. Her jaw was clenched as she threw the car into gear, spun it around, tyres squealing, and roared off back up the dock in the direction of town.

★ ★ ★

Rick trailed Patsy up the dock, heading for the *Pequod*, a pretty sight on the water. Steel hulled, with the rakish lines of an ocean-going yacht, she was one of the best whale-watching boats on the coast. Tourists in bright clothes with video cameras and rucksacks hanging off them crowded the gangway. Magnus and Paul were both aboard, making ready with the rest of the crew. Neither spoke much beyond a casual greeting. Your typical taciturn Swedes. It was left to Patsy and Rick to sweet-talk the passengers, stop the kids running wild.

The crew moved among the passengers, passing out flotation aids, and Rick called everyone together to begin the safety lecture. 'We'll be travelling out to the mouth of the Bay of Fundy,' he explained. 'It takes about an hour at twenty knots to reach where the whales are feeding. We'll spend approximately two hours observing them before putting back to Goodwill again. We adhere strictly to federal whale-watching guidelines regarding operation of vessels near cetaceans, including dolphins and porpoises.'

Someone asked what were the chances of seeing whales. 'Around ninety to ninety-five per cent at this time of year,' was Patsy's answer. 'Expect to see fin whales or humpbacks most probably. Also pods of dolphins and porpoises frequent the bay area. As a bonus today you may also catch a sight of bluebottles otherwise called Portuguese man-of-war, which are among the

145

world's largest stinging jellyfish. So make sure you have plenty of memory and spare batteries with you. Also sunscreen because it looks like today is going to be another scorcher.'

A little old lady in a red squall jacket put up her hand. 'Please, will it be rough?'

'It can be choppy out on the ocean even in summer, ma'am,' Rick responded. 'We have medication if you are prone to motion sickness.'

A man chipped in, 'I saw on the TV in the hotel that the waves could be extra strong.'

Patsy fielded this one. 'Sir, I saw that too. The kind of waves the report was referring to are extremely unlikely and if they ever did occur would be hardly noticeable out on the ocean. The effects only become apparent when they break on shore.'

'I guess that's why they're called breakers,' someone else laughed.

Everybody was in a good mood and most headed up on deck to line the sides as the crew cast off. Patsy moved among them, pointing out different types of bird life and answering questions. Her passion and energy were infectious and she soon had the whole deck buzzing.

Rick took the wheel as they headed out past the mole with Indian Point ahead and the dark brick hulk of the old Ice Factory, where Natalie had her studio, momentarily to starboard. The wheelhouse was fitted out with radar and state-of-the-art sonar for picking up the whales plus the usual suite of communications gear. The engines were running sweet, the sun was getting hot, and it had all the makings of a great day on the ocean. Patsy took a break from the passengers to go forward. She was anxious to have the latest data on whale sightings. The tide was running in strongly to the bay right now and should be bringing in plenty of food so the omens were good.

'Yesterday we had a load of sightings,' Rick observed. 'Now it seems to have gone quiet.'

'Happens. Could be a big shoal has moved off and the whales are following.'

Rick checked his Loran bearing to locate their position on the chart. The radar was on, reaching out fifteen miles or thereabouts. The screen registered reflectors from several sailboats and a couple of other vessels further out, most likely lobster boats. The depth gauge showed around 200 feet. The international borderline actually ran quite close here; they would cross it in a few minutes. And still the video plotter showed no sign of life below the keel.

'Okay, folks, listen up if you will,' came Patsy's voice cheerily over the PA system. 'Now I'm sure you've all heard of the continental shelf, which normally extends twenty to thirty miles off the coast with a depth of around four to five hundred feet, marking the shoreline some twenty thousand years ago when ocean levels were lower than they are today. Separating the continental shelf from the deep ocean floor we generally find

147

a steep slope with a gradient of from two to twenty degrees for a similar distance down to two to three thousand feet. Thereafter Atlantic margins are generally marked by further gradual sloping over the next four hundred miles or so down to the abyssal plain, which is the deep ocean floor lying at about twelve thousand feet.'

She paused to grin at them. 'All following so far? Sorry for being techy, but it will help you to grasp what makes Goodwill Sound so special.'

In the first place, she continued, we have to consider the topography of the coast, the way the ocean is semi-enclosed by the southward-reaching arm of Nova Scotia. 'This, as I'm sure you're aware by now, generates the highest tidal range in the world on this stretch of the coast and in the Bay of Fundy to the immediate north.'

But there was another feature that was unique to Goodwill, she added. 'We spoke about the continental shelf which extends beneath us. The water here is quite shallow; we are actually passing over what is called the Goodwill Bank. But it is not really a bank as such, it's an underwater cliff and on the far edge, about half a mile from here, the depth drops suddenly from two hundred feet to over four thousand.'

She paused again to allow the predictable murmurs of surprise. Rick always enjoyed the way Patsy handled this. The passengers certainly did.

'What we have here is a valley or rift in the continental shelf that cuts through the shallows, bringing the ocean bed right to the entrance of the Sound.'

And this had immense significance for fishing, Patsy explained. 'What you get is deep cold water flowing in from the ocean, hitting the end of the valley and rising towards the surface. This upwelling is important because it brings plankton to the surface. Plankton feed in cold waters. It is a myth that warm seas are fertile. In fact it is cold seas that are full of life. The reason warm Caribbean water is so clear is because it is empty of plankton, no food for the fish. Fish cluster round the coral reefs, not in the open sea. The cold water from the deep ocean comes to the surface right here in the Sound, bringing a huge harvest of life-sustaining plankton. That is why we have so many fine fishing grounds on this stretch of coast and that is what attracts the whales back here every summer, year after year, to feed.'

The breeze picked up. It was cool out on the ocean. The high pressure zone to the north over the Canadian shield was holding steady and the wind was light from the south-east, but as Patsy said, the water was chill, barely 50 degrees. Overhead the sky was a milky blue with a trace of haze. The waves were smooth, no hint of choppiness. Patsy went back out to schmooze with the passengers lining the rails. It felt good to be out on the boat. *Pequod* ducked her bow into a roller, sending spray bursting over the fore-peak. Kids scattered screeching with delight.

'Just keep watching,' she promised a family from the Midwest. 'Any moment a pod of minkes could breach right alongside. Make sure you have your cameras ready, lens caps off.' This drew a predictable laugh. She was puzzled though. Normally they would at least have met dolphins by now.

Five miles out Paul gave a hail from the wheelhouse roof. Everyone pushed to the rail, gazing eastward, but it was only a slick of blue-bottles. Patsy was enthusiastic. 'We're fortunate to see a bloom on this scale, generally we only find these creatures singly and in warmer waters. Not so deadly as the Pacific sea wasp, but the thread-like tentacles reach out thirty feet and deliver painful stings. Be warned, if you meet one in the water, keep your distance.'

Pequod's bows cut through the swarm, the tourists happy to have something to shoot. Up in the wheelhouse Rick regarded the floating sacs with disgust. If any wound up on the beaches they would be an added nuisance just when resources for a clean-up were fully stretched.

He put the wheel over, bringing *Pequod* round onto a north-easterly course, tracking the northern rim of the undersea canyon. If the whales were out there this was most likely where they would be found.

The radio was tuned to Channel 16, the emergency frequency, and the single sideband similarly to 2,182 megahertz. He switched over to one of the working channels to see what was happening. There was a crackle of static and a voice came over. He recognised the call sign of *Cat's Eye*, one of the two other whale boats working out of Goodwill. Her skipper, Steve Moreno, was asking had anyone seen any whales. Rick's heart sank. Whale watching was a competitive business. Skippers guarded any sightings close to their chests. And Steve was a good skipper with an almost uncanny ability to find whales whatever the weather. Rivals joked he could smell them out. He must be desperate. 'Negative,' he replied. 'Where are you?'

Way up in the mouth of the bay, came back the answer. The whole place was dead. Nothing on the plotter. 'There was a long burst of vocalising around an hour ago and since then nothing. No noise, no sightings. It's as if they've all taken off somewhere. And me with forty-three passengers aboard wanting refunds.'

Rick signed off and called Patsy in with a grim feeling in his bones. Bad days happened, most passengers understood that, but almost always there were a few sightings at least, a distant spouting, a dolphin or two. This emptiness was uncanny, disturbing. 'Maybe something's spooked them,' he suggested.

Patsy made a face. 'I don't get it. This is where they come every year at this time. It's where the food is. It would have to be something major to drive them away suddenly.'

Chapter 12

Maple Cove, Goodwill Sound. Ten a.m. Out in the garage, Tab Southwell was messing with his bike.

'Oh, Tab honey,' he heard Donna call.

'Be right with you,' he yelled back, jumping up guiltily.

She appeared in the doorway in a pink house-coat. 'That was Bruno's mom on the phone. He has a tennis lesson booked at the club this morning. She wondered if you'd like to go over. The other coach has a cancellation so you could take it and afterwards have a game with Bruno. I'll play a set with Bruno's mom and we'll all have lunch there and maybe a swim. What d'you say?'

Tab thought. Bruno's parents were summer people, friends of his dad's. The boy was his own age. 'Sounds okay,' he agreed cautiously.

'Fine. I'll tell Sue then. The courts are booked for eleven-thirty so we need to leave at eleven, I guess.'

Tab was silent, looking at his stepmother. 'What's the matter? Is something wrong?' she asked.

He hesitated. 'Dad was home kinda late last night,' he said reluctantly.

'I know, poor lamb, he had to do an autopsy on the body they pulled out of the Sound.' She saw his expression and her voice changed to a quick concern. 'Is that what's worrying you? The person had been dead a long time, he said. A real long time. It was nobody you could have known.'

Tab looked relieved. 'If we're not leaving till eleven I might take my bike down to the beach, see how the fish are doing.'

'Say, I just heard on the radio there are jellyfish in the Sound, so you will be careful, won't you?'

'Jellyfish! What kind of jellyfish?'

'I didn't catch what kind, but they're real stingers so you watch out, okay.'

Ocean Drive, Goodwill. Doc Southwell was on duty again at the hospital. Sheena recognised the Toyota parked in its usual space as she drove past on her way back from the fire. He must have had an early call. Poor guy, he couldn't have had much time for sleep. Had Donna kept him up last night after he left her, questioning him about where he had been?

She imagined him with his patients. Did he have affairs with any of them too? Quite possibly, probably even. He was an intelligent man, enjoyed his work and was good at it, loved his son and maybe his pretty wife too, but fundamentally he was flawed. A serial adulterer.

The hospital diminished in her rear mirror and she put him from her mind as she had done before. Compartmentalisation. Southwell undoubtedly did the same. How else could he survive?

One thing, Southwell had promised her an exclusive on the origins of last night's corpse and so far he seemed to have kept his word.

The intersection came up and she made a left onto the coast road out towards Curtain Bluff. Southwell's speculations on the body in the water were a long shot, but in Sheena's experience they were often the ones that paid off.

The church on the Point loomed up on the skyline between the trees. It was picturesque with its clapboard steeple and arched porchway but too small and too far from town to be used much nowadays.

The track ended in a flattened-out turning circle. Sheena parked and locked the car, taking the camera with her. The path was dry and well worn. The place was a favourite with courting couples from town. Southwell had brought her out here once, but there had been another car and they had had to go elsewhere.

The burying ground was out back, close to the cliffs. The day was heating up, but still with a faint haze. The wind had shifted round to an on-shore breeze that often brought a mist with it.

Sheena quickened her pace. All she needed was a quick look to confirm Southwell's theory.

She came in sight of the low wall. And then she recoiled.

Even though she had been expecting something of the sort, the spectacle was still shocking.

She tried to recall where the cliff edge had been originally. On her last trip out, the time with Southwell, they hadn't even gotten as far as the church. So her memory must be a year old at least, eighteen months probably. The image in her mind had been of a good thirty feet between the end wall and the cliff edge. Of course there could have been erosion since then.

But not this much! The far wall was gone, vanished, obliterated. Where she had pictured eight or ten irregular rows of weathered stones leaning peacefully in a rough-cut pasture, in their place was now a hideous gaping wound. Overnight, the cliff had been hacked back with a ruthless savagery that had torn half or more of the graves from their resting places, sweeping them at a stroke over the edge into the water a hundred feet below. Clumps of freshly torn earth clung to the edges of an almost perpendicular crevasse like clots of dried blood round the socket of an extracted tooth.

Maple Cove. The beach was deserted when Tab came skimming down the slope from the cliff. The first thing he noticed was the mountain bikes belonging to the couple from last evening.

They were leaning up against the wooden rail in the same place as before. Shading his eyes, he scanned the cove. No people around, but the cormorants were back, diving off Two Bush Island. Maybe the guy and his wife had swum across to photograph them.

Avoiding the shed, he kicked off his shoes and trotted down to the water. The tide was high. He hunted around for jellies, but could find nothing. Disappointed, he clambered out on the rocks opposite the island, hoping to find them washed up there. Something in a small pool caught his eye. Not a jellyfish, something white, a shoe.

He had to jump a gap to get there. Balancing carefully, he picked it up, held it upside down to drain out. It was a trainer with a Nike flash, a woman's from the size and the coloured laces. He thought back to yesterday evening. What had the couple been wearing? Her top had been pink, he recalled. He could picture the way it fitted her chest and the tanned legs, but had the shoes matched? Maybe, he couldn't be certain.

Carrying his find, he returned to the beach and went to take another look at the parked bikes. The saddles were dry, but the sun was warm, any dew would have dried off by now. He glanced back at the sand. No footprints that he could see bar his own, but there was a line of weed and debris left from where yesterday's record swell had reached the car-park.

The sound of a motor startled him. A police vehicle was coming down the track, a heavy four-wheel drive that bounced over the potholes. It pulled into the car-park and stopped. A middle-aged cop got out. He carried a bunch of leaflets in his hand and a staple gun. 'Hi, son.' He nodded to Tab. 'Fishing?'

Tab shook his head mutely. His throat was dry and he felt scared.

'See any jellyfish around?'

'No,' Tab answered this time. 'My stepmom told me about them though.'

'Well now, you see any, you stay clear. These are bad guys to mess with. Got a sting could kill you just like that.' He was stapling notices to the wooden rail as he spoke. Tab studied one.

'Wow, Portuguese man-of-war. I'd like to see one of those.'

'You would?' the cop grunted. 'Well, just remember look, but don't touch, especially the stingers, that's where the poison is.' He glanced curiously at the shoe. 'You find that here on the beach?'

'No, over there by the island, among the rocks,' Tab told him. 'I guess somebody lost it.'

'Here. Let's stick it on the rail. Maybe the person will come looking,' the cop suggested. His eye strayed to the bikes.

'They were here last night,' Tab said.

'What, all night?'

'I think so. I mean it doesn't look like anybody moved them.'

The cop strolled over to take a closer look. 'Nice,' he observed.

'Those frames are titanium.'

'You don't say. Cost a lot, I reckon.'

'A thousand bucks easy. Those are custom gears, Japanese. Photographers, the guy said they were.'

'You saw them then?'

Tab recounted their meeting. 'The woman said they were staying at Seafarers.'

'Get a name?'

'I think she said her name was Kim. I don't remember about the guy though.'

The cop looked around. 'Dusk, you said. What were you doing down here?' he asked curiously.

Tab mumbled something about riding around. The cop nodded. 'Maybe they came back to shoot some more pictures,' he hazarded.

Tab was almost sure the bikes hadn't been moved. He stared at the shoe, wondering. Perhaps he ought to tell about the strange swell he had seen, but he was afraid of more questioning.

The cop took the shoe from him and weighed it in his hand thoughtfully. 'Seafarers, huh? I'll stop by there on the way back into town. See if anyone knows anything.'

The main entrance of the old Ice Factory was chained and the ground-floor windows facing onto Bay Road shuttered and barred.

Natalie unhitched the padlock. It was cool inside the building. The warmth of the sun outside could not penetrate the thick timber-lined walls. Which was how it was designed to be. For three generations it had been in the Larsen family till the fishing fleet abandoned Goodwill for Portland and Gloucester. They had struggled on for a while, selling the machinery and renting out space; Natalie had leased her atelier from Rick's father originally but after his death maintenance and taxes had eaten up the place. Now it had fallen into the hands of Chance Greene.

The heavy door closed behind her with a noise that boomed and echoed under the cavernous central chamber. At the far end the rear wall gaped open where the ice chutes had been removed, leaving a view of the harbour beyond and sounds of gulls crying. Water covered the concrete floor and she wondered where that had come from, for the roof was still intact more or less and anyway there had been no rain. This would make such a great space for an exhibition if only it were cleaned up.

She picked her way over to the stairs leading to the upper floor. Rick's dad had kept a room up here in the old days, a den to retreat to with a bottle and his memories. His old harpoon had hung on the wall next to the black iron stove that he used in wintertime. Up here on stormy nights, with the wind howling in the chimney pipe and rattling the shutters, it had been easy for Leif Larsen to imagine himself back in the Southern Ocean, hunting the great whales again.

She could hear now the roars as he exploded from his lair like a drunken bear, cursing intruders to hell and damnation.

Her workroom opened off the top stairs. When the old man first showed her up she had gasped; a hundred-foot attic space floored in maple with a pitched roof of pine beams and long windows admitting light from either end. 'This is just perfect,' she had cried. 'I can't believe it's been here all this time.' And old Leif had grinned wolfishly. He had an eye for girls, but he had never troubled her in that way, she had to grant him.

Lashed against an upright beam by the far wall, a pale triangle reached into the shadow of the roof space. A giant baleen wishbone fused at the height of a tall man into a solid mass studded either side with teeth, 18 feet from tip to tip. A sperm whale's jaw; the bull it came from had measured 83 feet overall. Rick's grandfather had brought it back from one of his voyages. Natalie had rescued it from the salvagers and Rick had installed it up here for her. She touched a fingertip to the pointed teeth and smoothed the greasy surface of the baleen. Even after a hundred years in the open air the bone still exuded oil.

Natalie forced herself to focus. Urged on by her mother she was preparing for an exhibition at a local gallery. A retrospective, they were titling it – a fancy term for looking back, which with Natalie's mercurial output could mean just about anything. The driftwood sculpture from her beach-combing teens, early seascapes, the sketches and portraits as she'd come to know the townsfolk and now the intricate shell photography that was her current obsession.

She surveyed the walls. Canvases three or four high, hang carelessly from floor to pine ceiling. The seascapes were towards the top, glimpses of an earlier phase that now existed only in memory. At eye level the portraits stared back at her. These, she judged, showed where her talent lay. Lobstermen, deckhands, women with grit and hardship written in the lines on their faces. Her favourite was of Rick's father caught against an ocean background, his unshaven chin showing silver in the slanting light, eyes narrowed in fierce contempt for the world. She had dressed the old man in oilskins; his right hand gripped a long flensing knife, the other missing two fingers torn off by a line fired from a catcher's harpoon gun, looking for all the world as if he had just stepped off the deck of an Argentine factory ship stinking of whale blubber and schnapps.

A sound on the stair made her start. Turning, she saw a figure in the doorway.

Chapter 13

'You said we'd meet if it was meant to be.'

He grinned. 'There's a poster on the street with your face on it. I recognised you from the beach.'

'It was dark,' she said warily.

'Firelight, real romantic.'

His charm masked a vulnerability, she sensed.

He looked round at the pictures. 'You did these?'

She nodded, embarrassed suddenly for what he would think.

He stopped before the portrait of Leif Larsen. 'That's one tough-looking hombre.'

'An old-time whaler.' She folded her arms across her chest defensively. 'And yes, he was tough. Toughest man I ever knew.'

He glanced at the jawbone and laughed. His mood was infectious. 'Hey, you want to have some fun?'

She was cautious again. 'What kind of fun?'

'Come down to the dock and take a look.'

Natalie pushed open the door to the Chandlery. Rebecca was inside serving customers. 'Be with you in a minute, Nats.'

'I'll be okay. I need a wetsuit is all.'

'Over against the wall on the far side. Any idea what weight you need?'

'Summer, I guess. Some friends are taking me for a spin up the Sound.'

'You might do better with a medium thick. That's the green tag. If you want a rash vest there are seconds in the bin at the end of the row.'

Natalie passed between the lines of hanging suits. She picked out a light blue number with yellow side panels. From a rack of swimwear she added a bikini bottom, then threw in the rash vest and headed for the changing room.

'Hey,' Reb called from the counter where she was swiping a man's credit card. 'You'll need this.' She waved a plastic bag.

'Oh yeah, I forgot.' Inside the booth, Natalie stripped swiftly and reached down the wetsuit. Worn like a sock, the plastic wrapping helped slide each foot down the clinging neoprene leg.

'Sorry I didn't make it over last night,' Rick's sister called through the door.

'You didn't miss much.' Natalie pulled up the back zipper. 'Rick walked out and I got into a fight with Mom.' She emerged from the changing booth. 'Fits real snug. What d'you think?'

'Body Glove, that's a hot label. Looks good on you too. How's it feel?'

'Tight, but that's how it should be, I guess.'

'You need boots? Some neat split-toe numbers in the bin. Supposed to give better grip. Here you go.'

'Thanks, that's it, I think. Is it okay if I leave my clothes here with you?'

'Sure. Better let me have your purse. I'll put it in back with mine. You want me to ring all this up?'

'Sure, pick any card.'

'There were nights when the wind was so cold . . .' The well-remembered words trickled from the radio on the shelf behind the counter.

The women's eyes met for an instant. 'That darn song, they're always playing it.' Reb looked away.

'Yeah, I keep hearing it everywhere too.' Natalie kept her voice light.

'So you're going out on a jet?'

'That's the promise. Out to the reef to check on the breaks.'

'So have fun.'

'Thanks. Catch you later.'

But Reb's eyes were watchful as her brother's fiancée went out the door.

There were two jets and they were something else, massive machines with mean exhaust outlets and stripped-down chassis for speed and outsize-range extender tanks.

'Heavy,' Natalie said, impressed. 'Kawasaki?'

'And some,' he told her. 'Rebored and rebuilt

164

by a specialist I know. Sixty knots in open water. They'll take anything the ocean can throw at them.'

'Must be quite a handful.'

'You could say. Hit a wave at the wrong angle at that speed and you break every bone in your body.'

'I can't wait.'

'You don't have to. We're going out now.'

His own wetsuit fit like a second skin. Every muscle stood out. His physique was awesome. In his shadow she felt elfin.

The trailers were backed down into the water. The King dragged his machine clear and sprang aboard. It roared into life, spurting water. 'Climb on!' he shouted. She obeyed, locking her arms around his waist. With a jerk they were off.

The speed of the jets was terrifying and exhilarating. Both surfers drove their machines to the limits in open water, powering up the faces of approaching rollers and storming down the back slopes in mad swoops. Avalanches of white foam burst over their heads as they shot the crests. The King seemed to revel in throwing his steed into the path of every breaking roller.

They raced past Green Island where Rick's Folly, as she termed it, the half-built house, stood with its back tucked into the hillside, snugged out of reach of the autumn gales. The first time Rick had taken her out to see it, after weeks of teasing and prevaricating, she had thought it the most romantic spot in the world.

Now it was gone in a flash. They powered on past the lighthouse on Long Island, heading out for the reef, Goodwill Bank, the ice-pop cold of the Labrador Current spraying their faces. Blinded and frozen, Natalie dug her fingers into the King's back as the jet slammed into the troughs, thinking this was the way to go. You're too young to settle down yet, girl.

And in the back of her mind that song played like a nagging ache, '. . . *nights when the wind was so cold* . . .'

Bay of Fundy. SS *Pequod*. The video plotter was still showing zilch. Even the sharks and swordfish were making themselves scarce. It was an empty ocean down there. Patsy switched on the hydrophones. On good days the crew broadcast the eerie music of humpbacks calling to each other through the ocean deeps. The clicks and whistles of dolphins and orcas. Low-frequency sounds travelled across enormous distances underwater. There was some noise there but it was distant and confused. To Patsy it sounded like the whales were moving away from them.

'Up the bay maybe?' Rick asked hopefully.

'It's possible but if you want my guess this is coming from the open ocean. And it's sparse. They're moving fast, saving energy, not wasting breath on chatter.'

They motored on but the seas were empty except for the ship's wake. Passengers focused their lenses disconsolately on diving birds, more swarms of the ubiquitous jellyfish. Over the radio other boats were calling the same lament. It was as if all of a sudden every whale and dolphin inshore had taken off for the deep ocean. One of the crew voiced everyone's thoughts: 'What do they know that we don't?'

Patsy went down and out onto the forepeak. The ship was doing almost twenty knots and the wind buffeted her ears. Normally this was her favourite place out here away from the diesel fumes, with the salt breeze stinging her cheeks as the waves burst under the bow. A bunch of passengers gripped the rails, scanning the sea despondently. Bored kids played with the mooring ropes and Paul scowled at them. He was getting edgy and small wonder.

She called the passengers together. Important to keep their spirits up. 'Only yesterday we were out in this very spot and a family of four right whales breached off the port bow less than fifty feet away. Rights are rare; they were hunted almost to extinction. The spray from their spoutings reached where I'm standing. We were drenched.' In detail she described the vast flanks heaving up to part the waves, half the length of the boat. The whack of great tails smacking the surface, sending spray flying. 'Killer whales do that to stun shoals of smaller fish and make them easier to catch. It is awesome to find anything living can be that big and close and real.'

She continued in this vein awhile before she realised she was striking the wrong note. These people had seen the pictures and heard the stories before. Now they wanted the real thing. They had paid their money and nothing else would do. Her efforts were only making things worse.

They reached the mouth of the Bay of Fundy and tacked back and forth in an empty search. These were some of the richest feeding grounds on the coast; plankton and krill were so thick here that they stained the water green. Petrels and shearwaters circled the boat uttering rasping cries. Patsy remembered seeing a pod of eleven killer whales hunting for blue shark right on this spot. Today though the ocean was deserted. In the distance they could make out other vessels on the same fruitless quest.

A swell got up and the water turned lumpy. Several passengers began to exhibit signs of distress. Time was passing. Patsy went up to the wheelhouse. The ship was on autopilot, Rick standing by the window looking out over the bow, shoulders slumped. The trip, which had started out so well, had turned into a disaster.

Magnus appeared in the wheelhouse. After a brief consultation between the three of them, Rick took the decision to head back in. Over the public address system he announced that all tickets would be refunded. There was silence in the cabins now, a glum resignation. Rick and his cousins had just taken an $800 bath. Double that if the afternoon was a washout. By rights Patsy should still get her 100 bucks but she told them no, she would share the pain today.

Patsy felt deserted, betrayed. The whales were her friends. Many of them she could recognise by sight just like she could people back ashore. Now it was as if they had run out on her. What had gone wrong? 'Animals conform to patterns,' she said to Rick, 'and they seldom act capriciously. If they have altered their behaviour dramatically like this it has to be for a compelling reason.'

'Could it be environmental?' he hazarded. 'A change in water temperature or salinity? Something to do with whatever brought those damn jellies up from the tropics?'

She shrugged. 'Whales are complex animals. They differ widely, even among social groups of the same species. It's hard to imagine a single factor that would send different species running suddenly at the same moment.'

Whatever it was had to be something pretty darn big, she added to herself.

The barometer was still high. Rick tuned in to the NOAA broadcast but there was nothing on the plot. Nothing to give a clue as to what had made the whales take off. Magnus took the wheel, cramming on all speed even though it would cost them fuel. Might as well get the misery over.

North Head Island came in view again. It was still a perfect summer day. Patsy clung to the hope that something would show before they reached port. Dolphins and sharks had been known to enter the harbour and whales to venture within sight of the beaches. Suddenly there was shouting from the port-side rail. The passengers had spotted something. She had her binoculars up in a flash and saw it too, a white streak in the water moving fast. For a second her spirits soared. Then in another moment the image resolved itself in her field of view. A familiar shape, machine-like not mammal. A jet ski, and behind it another.

They were two miles offshore still and the swells were big enough to make *Pequod* pitch, yet the riders were skimming along without a care, powering up the sides of breakers, riding the crests with careless elan.

Magnus spat over his shoulder into the water. 'Those surfers! Now we know what is driving the whales off.'

He eased off the throttle momentarily as they approached. Patsy watched enviously at the freedom with which these guys treated the water. They seemed completely without fear. Rick trained the powerful bridge binoculars on them. As the boat drew closer some of the passengers waved, glad of anything to break the monotony. The riders returned the salutes, turning to plough through the waves in *Pequod*'s wake. 'No boards with them. Looks like they're checking out the breaks for later,' Patsy observed.

'This far out?' Rick's tone was curt. He was angry too and looking for someone to blame.

She shrugged. In Hawaii some of the biggest rides in the world were to be found four miles out where the waves broke on an ocean reef. Sixty-five footers. Waves so massive only the bravest and the best would think of riding them. The most ferocious of those breaks had a name: Jaws, they called it.

Patsy put a restraining hand on Magnus's arm. To his mind it was the jet skis with their high-revving engines that had scared away the whales. He was demanding that Rick as a Selectman make an order banning their use off the beaches. Impossible, Rick snapped, and even if they did they could never make it stick. Patsy shook her head. The surfers weren't to blame, of that she was certain. Whales seemed unbothered by boatloads of tourists. Over the Grand Banks they even sought out fishing vessels deliberately as good indicators of feeding zones. No, whatever it was that had frightened the pods off, it had to be something much more serious than a water-bike.

Surfers and whales. There was a connection, Patsy was certain. The surfers arrived and simultaneously the whales disappeared. But what was the linking thread?

Rick's mouth was grim. He was saying nothing. He was trying to tell himself that he must have been mistaken. That the passenger he had seen in the binoculars clinging to the back of the jet ski rider and waving at them could not have been Natalie.

Chapter 14

Cumbre Vieja, La Palma, Canary Islands. 'You're way off beam!' Malc shouted to Concha. Her brand of irresponsible exaggeration never failed to make him mad. 'That's exactly the kind of wild talk we don't need right now.' With the whole island community on edge anticipating another eruption any time panic was only a step away.

She continued to glare at him, fists bunched, her face hostile. 'America!' she spat. 'When the mountain splits and falls into the sea it will make the biggest wave that ever was. A wave that will cross the ocean and fall on the East Coast of your country.' As if the idea of havoc being wrecked on a defenceless New England was somehow justified in her eyes. He tried to imagine how he would feel if his own homeland were being devastated while smug scientists from rich nations far away studied the misery with detached curiosity. Perhaps he would be angry too and want to strike out at the foreigners.

A sharp jolt underfoot checked further argument. Felipe shouted to the others. The pressure of magma rising up the pipe below was increasing and the thin crust holding it in check like a stopper in a bottle was in danger of breaking up. Any moment now it would shatter with catastrophic consequences for anyone trapped in the crater. Shouldering his pack and pushing the girl ahead of him, Malc made for the crater lip.

They had gone a dozen steps, Viktor in the lead with his long swing stride, when a hideous vibration and drumming started up right beneath them. Terrified, they clutched at one another for support as the vibration swelled unendurably, the mountain thumping and quivering as if huge hammers were pounding it below. Malc and the girl were flung apart like toys. Staggering like a drunkard, he fought himself upright. He grabbed the girl by her overalls and dragged her up too. At all costs they must keep moving.

A crackle as of gunfire echoed around the crater. Puffs of dust and splintered rock exploded about them like shell bursts. Snapping and popping, fissures forked across the crater floor. As if cloven by an axe stroke, a metre-wide crevasse sprang open right at Concha's feet and a roaring geyser of sulphurous water erupted from the crack, drenching the crater in boiling

174

rain, and sending torrents of steam soaring into the sky.

Malc held Concha's arm, guiding her on. Corrosive gases venting from fumaroles and the scalding fall-out from the geyser seared exposed skin like acid. They groped their way forward, choking on fumes and gas, sweating in their heavy protective overalls and helmets, the mountain shuddering under them at every step. They reached the start of the crater slope and started to climb. The loose surface was fast turning into liquid mud that dragged at their boots.

They were halfway up to the lip when the volcano blew. Malc never consciously heard the blast; he was already deaf from the cacophony of noise, the shrieking of the fumaroles, the rumbling and cracking of the rock. A giant fist smacked him from behind, slamming him and the girl face-down against the scree slope. Bloodied and gasping, eyes, mouth, throat filled with acrid mud, he struggled to pull himself up again. To stay where they were meant certain death.

He glanced behind through the eddying smoke. A lurid glow lit a scene from hell. Plumes of liquid fire vomited up from the main vent, filling the air with sparks and gobbets of burning magma that seared everything they touched. Smoke, roiling and dark or shot through with toxic green and blue, boiled furiously overhead, darkening the sun. There came a whizzing sound and a reverberating concussion as something huge thudded into the slope close by and his heart went cold. Another blast shook the crater and a half-ton lump of white-hot rock scorched out of the smoke and crashed into an outcrop, shattering into a lethal hail of razor-edged shrapnel that sliced through fabric and flesh, igniting everything it hit.

Lava bombs! Cumbre Vieja was exploding and the scientists were caught up in the crater.

Chapter 15

Goodwill Sound. The jet with the King up front and Natalie digging her nails into his back to hang on made a wide sweep past the Long Island lighthouse in under the cliffs of Curtain Bluff. They slackened speed a little and Natalie shook the spray out of her eyes. From the way they were wallowing among the rollers she judged they were over the reef, otherwise known as Goodwill Bank, where the ocean bed dropped away. Other surfers were intermittently visible among the wave tops, mostly like themselves on PWCs waiting for action.

The King was calling across to his buddy with the twisted leg. The Gimp was pointing inshore. Evidently that was where he anticipated finding rideable breaks. The King nodded and they roared off together, bouncing along the troughs. They slowed again and this time it looked as if the Gimp was using a handheld radio. Natalie could see him stretching up to see further. He must have a lookout posted up on the cliffs somewhere, spotting rollers moving in.

They had drifted close to the other riders. The nearest jet had just dropped a board in the water and a girl with blonde hair whipping around her wetsuit shoulders was crouching on it holding a rope. The jet moved off, building speed, and the girl rose gracefully, leaning back against the tow, arms stretched. The board skimmed across the surface, leaping from crest to crest. She must have foot straps, Natalie realised, marvelling at her strength and agility.

The King twisted round, calling to her over his shoulder. The Gimp was off again, moving fast in the wake of the girl surfer. With a jerk the King accelerated up to full speed, tearing in pursuit, both looking for an entry spot. They clawed up the face of a heavy roller, reached the crest and Natalie's heart skipped a beat as the nose pitched down and she saw the ocean drop away into a yawning abyss opening before them. At a breakneck angle they skimmed down the back. A shadow darkened the surface as a wall of water reared overhead.

The girl on the board was fifty yards ahead. The wave was breaking from the left and her driver was angling up the face, aiming to put her on the crest at the highest point. The break was solid, twice the girl's crouching height or so it seemed to Natalie. They saw her drop the tow and drive forward graceful as a bird, powered by nothing but the wave's own energy. The King cranked the throttle, leaning to meet the crest. They made it just as it broke over them. Natalie gasped as a blast of water hit her like a bomb.

The jet spun on the crest, powering along in the wake of the tow craft, riding the breaker in towards the cliffs. Natalie lost sight of the board and its long-haired rider. The cliffs were close now, she could see the spray spewing up from the rocks at their feet, but then suddenly the girl shot into view again, bursting out of the foaming barrel right at the end of the break to skim out to safety at the side. Her tow darted in to pick her up.

'Hey, that was terrific!' Natalie shouted in her driver's ear. For some minutes they rode along parallel to the coast, the Gimp at their side. Natalie felt exhilarated and free. The ocean was calmer now and she was growing accustomed to the machine's motion.

The King was pointing again. She looked and saw a ship quite close heading in the direction of the Sound, a white hull that could only be *Pequod*. From here she looked swift and lovely. Rick would be up in the wheelhouse. As they neared, she made out people on deck and waved wildly, defiantly.

Pequod pulled away and they turned back towards the cliffs again, hoping for more breaks. The Gimp moved up close, exchanging comments about what they had witnessed.

The King shook his head dismissively. 'Eight feet tops. Ripples!'

The Gimp waved at the sky, shouting back, but his words were lost in the wind. He put his fingers to his mouth and suddenly she heard again the strange shrill whistling sounds from last night. The Spanish whistle code. The King responded, answering in short, harsh bursts that sounded angry.

The Gimp broke off the exchange and began talking on his radio. Suddenly they were springing into action again. Revving up to full speed, both machines hurtled shoreward in a mad dash back into the cliffs.

Someone was hurt.

Bearskin Neck, Goodwill. Sheena Dubois was still chasing up accounts of last night's events. She ran into Jack Pearl outside Jean-Alice's. They talked about the current that must have washed the body down the Sound and Ray Burns's name came up.

'White-haired guy lives on Pigeon Cove?'

Yeah, well, Jack drawled, old Ray was some kind of engineer originally. 'He moved up here twenty odd years ago. Eccentric old boy; won't drive a car, goes about everywhere on a bike. He has these theories about currents in the Gulf of Maine, figured the experts had the circulation mapped out wrong. Conservation Society got after him one time for dropping Coke bottles in the water off Curtain Bluff.'

Sheena registered the name. 'Tell me more.'

'Ray has this website. Anyone comes across

one of his bottles washed up somewhere there's a note inside asks you to let him know, where and when, all that stuff.'

'Does he get any replies?'

Jack Pearl scratched his head with a rasping sound. 'You wouldn't think it, would you, but according to Ray he gets hits on the site from all over, Africa, Portugal, Spain, the Caribbean, you name it. Like people living in those places got nothing better to do than check the tide line on a daily basis. Another thing,' he added, 'old Ray, he says now he's started receiving bottles back again. People write their details on the card inside and toss them back in the ocean.'

'The same current brings them right back all the way to the Sound?' Sheena's tone was doubtful.

Jack sucked his cheeks in. 'Ray showed me a couple of the bottles. Some kind of circulatory system with the currents he reckons.' He chuckled. 'One of the finders was a Danish woman living on some island or other, I forget which. I told Ray he should ask to be her pen pal. Only trouble is takes two years to get an answer. Ha, ha.'

This town was full of surprises, Sheena thought, returning to her car.

As she drove off she heard the wail of the ambulance siren.

Indian Point. Midday. Natalie's mother was cutting flowers to the side of the house when the

181

battered pick-up came up the drive. It was the amateur archaeologist and dowser who was conducting a dig on the estate. Part of her husband's idea to encourage a respect for local history. He was waving to her and now she would have to talk to him. Just when she was busy.

'Why, Mr *Seymour*,' she exclaimed with an effort of memory.

'Good morning, Mrs Maxwell,' he greeted her warmly. 'Yes, I'm fine. You know that was an interesting conversation I had with your husband yesterday evening. I had no idea there was such a history to this promontory.'

'You certainly sound to be making some *unusual* discoveries, Mr Seymour.'

'Yes, it's really most curious', his spectacled face was lit up with excitement, 'the latest set of trenches dug behind the house, well in front of the house, I suppose, if you are looking from the driveway.' He paused for a moment. 'On the far side of the house and higher up the hill if you are standing with your back to the ocean as we are,' he added pedantically. 'In this latest set of trenches we've uncovered a series of low ridges composed entirely of shells and gravel.'

'Shells?' Elise said politely, wondering where all this was leading.

'And gravel. Well, rounded pebbles, what I call ocean-washed pebbles, to be exact.'

'How . . . interesting.'

'Yes, it's most curious. I haven't quite made

out their origin yet. It's almost as if this part of the promontory was under water at some recent date, well relatively recent, within the last five hundred years or so. Which is ridiculous of course because we're over a hundred feet above the shoreline.'

'Could they be connected somehow with our native Indian culture?'

Mr Seymour wobbled his head on his long thin neck. 'A possibility, yes, except that so far, as you know, we've uncovered not a single other trace of native tribal culture on the Point. And that's unusual. There is not only the name itself, but the Point is such an obvious site for a look-out. But then the Goodwill area is particularly poor in Indian remains close to the shore. Further back inland there are numerous traces of settlements. It's almost as though the entire coastal zone has been scoured clean at some time in the recent past. It's quite extraordinary.'

'*Extraordinary*,' Elise Maxwell agreed.

Officer Logan Clancy pulled over into the forecourt of the Seafarers Motel. Abby's odd-job man was up a ladder stringing flags across the entrance and the office was humming with visitors. Posters on the walls, a sign on the desk – LEAVE KEYS HERE. Abby was firing instructions to a preppy couple checking in. 'You cross the parking lot, through the walkway to the far side. Number eight is on the upper level. Park right out front. Vending machines in the walkthroughs; ice is free, just fill the bucket in the room. Supermarket and launderette right across the street. Towels for the pool we issue here at the desk. Anything else you need, let us know. We're here to help.'

'Do you have a map of the town?'

'Over on the table behind you. Maps, guides, leaflets, places to visit, activities, eateries, money-off vouchers. Enjoy your stay with us.' Abby turned to Clancy. 'Yes, young man?'

'Morning, Mrs Cotton. How you keeping?'

'I'm fine, Logan, thank you. What can I do for you?'

Clancy started to explain about the bikes.

'Excuse me a minute.' Abby broke off to attend to two young women. 'Checking out? Beth, dear,' she sang out to her sister-in-law, 'could you run off the bill for twenty-one, please.'

'Coming up!' Beth's fingers rattled over her keyboard.

'So,' Abby continued to the clients, 'did you guys finally get to go rafting yesterday?'

'We did too, on the Kennebec like you advised us. It was wild! Janis got tossed out in the rapids.'

'Yup, when they release the outflow on the hydroelectric station upstream the river rises real quick. And those guides like to see people go over the side, makes for plenty of excitement. They take good care of you though. Here's Beth with your account. Have a good trip and hope to see you back again sometime.

'Sorry about that, Logan.' Abby turned back. 'You were telling me about bikes?'

Clancy went back to the beginning, how he had noticed the bikes and spoken with the boy.

'And they definitely said they were staying here at Seafarers?'

'That's what Tab claims they told him.'

'And no names to go on?'

'She was Kim, he thinks.'

Abby frowned. 'We get our share of cyclists staying, but nobody's complained of a missing machine that I know of.'

She glanced out the window where a van was nosing into the forecourt. 'That's the laundry pick-up. I'll have to go see to it.'

'Two machines,' Clancy corrected. 'Custom built, not rentals.'

'Pardon me, ma'am,' a sandy-haired man with a wife and two kids in tow interrupted from behind, 'what time does the festival here kick off?'

'Founders' Day is tomorrow, sir. The big parade forms up at two p.m. outside the fire station on the Green and this year there will be a firework display in the evening. Sunday we have yacht racing and stuff on the water. Things will start to warm up tonight with streets closed off from seven and a fair on the recreation ground with rides for the kids. Lots of fun for all the family.

'Sorry again,' she apologised to Clancy. 'It's just hectic today. These bikes of yours, offhand I

185

can't think of anything we can do unless maybe put up a notice in here.'

Clancy shook his head. 'Forget it. If people can't look after their property that's their problem. We got too much on our hands as of now to go chasing after them.'

'Okay, Logan. Thanks for stopping by. Take care now.'

Chapter 16

La Palma, Canary Islands. On hands and knees
Malc and Concha staggered up the crater slope
towards the crest of the lip, while below them the
volcano mouth roared and thundered like the
opening of hell itself. With each blast the
mountain shook and blocks of magma soared up
hundreds of feet into the air to scream
murderously down again through the smoke,
slamming into the soft scree. Each time one
landed near, the impact hurled the climbers off
their feet, half burying them in dirt and rubble.

Spouts of fire filled the sky with each explosion, showering the scientists with incandescent
sparks. The heat and the stench were unendurable. Even the sand and shale underfoot
seemed to be burning and the air scorched their
lungs at every agonising breath. Another quake
shook the mountain, dislodging an avalanche of
scree down the crest. Caught in the onrush,
Malc was swept off his feet and carried down the

slope in a cascade of stones and choking dust to fetch up, dazed and gasping, pinned against a lava outcrop, while the ground underneath quivered and bounced as if the volcano was on springs.

The noise switched to a deep-throated chugging that vibrated right through him till it felt as if the bones in his body were being shaken to pieces. Fear lent him strength to struggle free. Concha was nowhere in sight and for a moment he thought they had lost her, then he picked out her helmet higher up near the crest, still moving slowly amid the smoke. Felipe was nearby. Malc saw him stop and look back down to Viktor crawling among the boulders below, lumbered by his pack. The Russian had been the last of the party to quit the crater floor. Felipe was shouting to him, probably telling him to abandon his pack. He would have done better to save his breath. Malc knew Viktor; it would be unthinkable for the Russian to jettison his kit.

Malc scraped away the crusted sweat and dust that caked his mouth, nose and eyes and turned to fight his own way back up, out from the crater. The heat was close to unbearable. His gloves were gone, leaving his unprotected hands torn by tephra shards, blistered and scorched. Without his fireproofs he would be in a bad way. Felipe scorned them and so did Viktor. The Russian claimed protective clothing was dangerous; it gave a false sense of security and slowed you up. A hard hat sure, it might save you from having your brains knocked out by a lava bomb maybe, but fireproofs were exhausting to wear and if you were trapped in a magma flow, which, please God, would never happen, then they were utterly useless.

Flaming boulders were still being spat out from the central cone, accompanied by a blinding hail of sand and stones that hissed and banged around them like iron rain. Felipe was starting to edge his way back down the slope to help Viktor. Malc waved up to him, signalling that he was closer and would go. He jabbed his hand in the direction of Concha to indicate that Felipe should take care of the girl, leaving Viktor to him. The Russian was up to his knees in loose shale and struggling to free himself. Malc slithered back downwards, endeavouring to work his way transversely across the slope to a point where he could reach down a hand. Viktor saw him coming and his teeth gleamed white in his soot-blackened face as he waved the American back. 'I'll be okay,' he was gesturing. 'I can manage. Look after yourself.'

Twenty yards separated them. Malc was halfway across when the volcano shuddered afresh and a hot red glare bathed the crater as explosions tore into the sky. Yellow sulphur clouds vomited upward amid the ash plumes, shot through with forty-foot jets of flame belching from vents in the rock. Out of the smoke and ash came hideous snapping sounds as the crater floor bulged and split apart under the relentless pressure below spewing out tongues of greedy magma. The air was thick with steam and gas and flying sparks so that every inhalation seared the lungs and it was agony to breathe.

Malc never saw the lethal bomb. All his attention was on Viktor, crawling up the slope, weighed down by his instrument pack. The huge glowing blob of molten rock from the earth's core dropped murderously out of the smoking sky onto the Russian, obliterating him, grinding him into the shale, smearing the life out of him with its hideous weight.

Cumbre Vieja had claimed its first victim.

Chapter 17

Well before *Pequod* was inside the Sound, Rick's phone began beeping. Munroe called up from *Cat's Eye* to ask was he taking *Pequod* out again for the late afternoon run? No, Rick told him, he had already made up his mind. The only result would be a load of fuel burned to no purpose and more upset passengers.

Patsy agreed. 'The whales will return in their own good time. They always do.'

Rick's call minder showed Natalie had tried to reach him, but had left no message, and when he called back there was no response.

Then the phone went again. Don's number this time. The police chief's voice was sharp. 'Rick, problems. First off, there's been an accident. Some surfer girl hurt off the Bluff. Her pals brought her in and she's been taken to the hospital. No word on how she's doing yet.'

'Have her people been told?'

'We're onto it. And to cap it there's more bad

191

news on the ocean front. It looks like the situation on that island has turned ugly. Another eruption, a big one this time and now rumours are flying.'

'How serious is it?' Rick tried to keep his voice low. Paul at the wheel was straining to overhear.

'Confused. I can't get a straight answer from Augusta. I'd say a definite upgrade in the threat level though. There's stuff coming over the TV as we speak. Looks like one heck of an eruption, smoke, flames, fire going up into the sky. Glad as hell I'm not there. They're talking casualties, but no numbers yet.'

'Listen, Don, I should be tying up in the next twenty minutes. Get onto the state emergency people. Find out exactly what's happening and how it affects us. When you get the information put out a statement on local radio and TV. Make clear where your information is coming from. Add that updates will be posted every hour on the hour. Warn people to stay tuned to their local station and be ready to react promptly to any instructions given. It's vital we keep control of the situation.'

'Okay, Rick, you're the boss.'

Rick cut the connection. There was another call waiting. Chance Greene. 'I've just spoken to Don,' he jumped in before the developer could speak. 'He's going to nail down the emergency centre at Augusta to a definite situation report. There are too many rumours going round.'

'I've got the TV on here, Rick, and I'm telling you it doesn't look good.' Chance's voice was jumpy. Under pressure he was quick to crack. 'Rivers of burning lava flowing into the ocean. Talk of earthquakes.'

'How big of a quake are they saying?'

'I didn't catch the scale. CNN have a camera team on the island and the anchorwoman said a big jolt, the ground was jumping underfoot while she was talking. She sounded scared.'

Not the only one, Rick thought. At this rate they wouldn't have to cancel the tercentenary; there wouldn't be a tourist left in town.

'There's been panic on Bermuda. Calls to evacuate the Florida Keys. People are worried. I'm worried. I think we should call a meeting to decide what to do.'

'Fine, Chance, let's do that just as soon as Don comes up with a response from the capital. From what they were telling us last night we should get at least five hours' warning of any tsunami coming. Time enough to move everybody inland if we have to.'

His brain was racing as he spoke. There were two bridges off the island, Indian Point and the Causeway. Indian Point led on to higher ground. To the west the land was flat as far as the highway. The medical centre would be at risk. The patients would have to be evacuated. Doc Southwell could be trusted to deal with that side. The municipal office held a list of disabled and housebound who would need assistance, but in

193

emergencies neighbourly spirit could still be counted on in a place like Goodwill. One big problem would be reaching people off camping along the shore.

Chance was talking again. Some of his properties were uninsured. Surely the government would pay compensation? Rick had no answer. He and Reb carried some insurance on the Chandlery, but was it enough? Some of those towns hit by the Indian Ocean tsunami had been erased from the map.

Could that happen here to Goodwill?

Beth Robbin's phone rang.

'Seafarers Motel.'

'Hi, do you have a Kim Schaffer staying with you?'

'Just a minute, I'll check for you. What was the name again?'

'Schaffer, Kimberly Schaffer from upstate New York – she's my daughter.'

Swivelling round in her chair, Beth Robbins ran a finger down the whiteboard where guests' names were scribbled against room numbers. 'Nope, sorry, ma'am, no Schaffer with us.'

'Could she be registered under her partner's name, Baines, Randy Baines?'

'Baines? I'll look. No, 'fraid not.'

'They couldn't have checked out already? A young couple with trail bikes arrived yesterday.'

'Bikes.' Beth's brow furrowed. 'Now who said something about a bike earlier? No, it's gone.

194

Listen, neither name is registered with us. Have you tried the Admiral's Inn?'

'I already checked with them, also Ocean View, Baytop and Captain Briggs.'

'There's the Aurora too, and the Landing as well as the Cape Inn. You could give those a try. There are a couple of motels out on the Ellsworthy Road, the Chieftain is one. And then there are the camping grounds, but they don't always list names.'

'Okay, I'll keep trying. Thank you for your time. Can I leave a number with you in case?'

'No problem. Sorry we couldn't help.'

'Everything okay over there?' Beth said as Abby returned to the office. The morning rush had eased off. Most guests were out sight seeing.

'No, but that Tracy didn't show up for work again so I had to help the little French Canadian girl fix the rooms on south side. She is such a pain; didn't even bother to phone. I called her mother at the bakery, told her to tell Tracy I'd had it with her.'

'What did she say?'

'She said Tracy is absent-minded. I said we knew that and we only took her on as a favour, but this is Founders' Week and we just can't be doing with someone who shirks. It isn't fair on the other employees.'

'I agree. I'm sorry for her mother, but we can't carry Tracy for her.'

'Anyway Marie-Crystal and I made up the

beds and cleaned the rooms. Now there is one good little worker. Never complains if she's asked to do extra and always has a smile for guests.'

Abby was straightening her desk. 'Any messages?' She reached for the diary in which calls were logged. 'Who is Schaffer?' she said, running a finger down the entries.

'Schaffer? Oh, some people from New York trying to reach their daughter.'

'Is she a guest? What did you tell them?' Requests of this nature were a difficult area for hoteliers; clients had a right to their privacy.

Beth shook her head. 'Not listed with us. They said she is travelling with a partner name of Baines. I checked, but we have no registration under either.'

'Baines.' Abby was thoughtful. 'Have we heard that name somewhere?'

'Not stopping here that I could see. They're on a cycling tour, I think the woman said. Bikes came into it somewhere.'

'Maybe that's it? Wait, no. Logan Clancy was in here earlier asking did we know anything about some bicycles abandoned down at Maple Cove.'

'Logan Clancy,' Beth said frowning. 'I don't get it. You're saying these bikes belong to the Schaffer woman and her partner?'

'I don't know, but Baines, Baines, it rings a bell.'

'They're not on the board or on the computer, I checked both.'

'Wait . . .' Abby was flicking back the pages of

the phone log containing brief details of every incoming call. Her finger skimmed down the entries. 'Nothing, nothing . . .' She searched further back. 'Yes!' she exclaimed triumphantly. 'I knew the name rang familiar. Here it is, Baines from New York, booked last month for the weekend. They were our no-shows yesterday. We took his credit card, remember?'

'I didn't think of going back. I just looked on the board and checked the computer.'

'They weren't on the computer any longer because I wiped them off last night when we relet the room.'

There was a loud splash from the direction of the pool and an outburst of children shrieking. A teenager in a halter top came in asking for the key to room 11. Beth passed it over.

'Those shoulders look painful,' Abby warned the girl as she turned to leave. 'You want to watch the sun out there. Easy to get burned with your fair skin.'

'Yeah, we went out on this friend's boat and now I'm like fried. I'm off to the room to shower and put on some cream.'

'Might be an idea to stay in the shade this afternoon.'

'Right, I feel zonked anyway. Guess I'll catch a couple of hours' sleep.' She trailed out.

'Hope the kid's okay,' Beth said. 'She looked dazed.'

'It's the glare off the water. She'll be fine after a rest.'

Beth was looking concerned again. 'So what's this about bikes and Logan Clancy?' she asked her sister-in-law.

Abby shook her head quickly. 'There may be no link, but Clancy found two trail bikes abandoned down at Maple Cove. Been out there all night, he reckoned, and now you say the Kimball couple were coming here on a cycling trip.'

The two women stared at one another. 'They would have checked in here first, surely?'

Abby's jaw set hard the way it did whenever there was trouble to be faced. 'Either way we have to let the family know right away. Speak to them again and this time try to find out everything you can. They made reservations for two nights only; maybe they were moving on somewheres else. Ask what was their intended route? It's possible they decided to skip this town for whatever reason.'

'I'll get onto it. Who are you calling up now?'

'Logan Clancy. I think it's time the police department brought those mountain bikes in from the Cove.'

Larry Hageman was on traffic patrol. This time with a tow-truck behind, picking up vehicles that had ignored warnings to clear Bay Road by eight. Orders were if possible to locate owners to give them a last chance to comply, particularly if they were visitors. 'No sense welcoming people to town, then seizing their cars,' as Don Egan put it. And certainly there always seemed to be a number who either couldn't read the signs or else somehow figured the restrictions didn't apply to them personally.

'What I'm doing, sir,' Larry explained patiently to the owner of a Mercedes coupé that looked like it cost more than Larry's house, 'is giving you a last chance to get this thing off the street. Otherwise that man there in the yellow truck is going to jack up your jalopy and drag it off to the pound. From where it will cost you a hundred dollars and a certain amount of time to fetch it out again. Now why don't you save us all a lot of aggravation by moving it a hundred yards up to the parking lot on Sugarshack, where I happen to know they still have space.'

Whereupon the Merc owner had looked round and observed Gus in his truck with the big hook dangling and promptly decided that he really didn't want his expensive car dragged through the town like a lump of scrap and hurriedly complied.

Larry got back into his blue and white, shaking his head. Some people.

It was down on the corner of Eden that he spotted the Explorer with the cycle rack. There was a note tucked under the wipers from last night advising the owner that it was liable for towing if not moved. There was a chance it might belong to a guest at the Eden Inn opposite. Larry asked Gus to wait while he checked.

'Nope,' he said on his return. 'Andy says he now has parking for all residents in back.'

'It's a rental, for sure.' Gus pointed to a hire company folder visible in a side pocket in the front. 'Boston plates, probably hired at the airport.'

Larry drummed his fingers on the roof, hoping the driver might materialise. Nothing happened so he nodded to Gus. 'Tow it away,' he sighed, reaching for his ticket pad.

Chapter 18

The bluebottles started coming ashore at mid-day. An onshore breeze had sprung up and between ten and eleven o'clock yachtsmen encountered the swarm's outliers at the entrance to the Sound, then all at once every cove and inlet had its blue-jellied rim bobbing on the swell. Word spread rapidly, bringing sightseers hurrying down to the beaches.

'Saint John says they are experiencing similar problems,' Con Wolfowitz from the Coastguard informed Rick. Saint John was on the Canadian side of the border up the Bay of Fundy. 'Winter Harbour to the south also report sightings. Nowhere as bad as us though.'

'Just great, Con. Don't you have any good news? The TV is talking of another big eruption in the Canaries.'

'I heard that too. Our people still say there is no increased threat to the USA as of yet.'

'How much longer do we go on believing them?'

Attempts to establish what had become of the missing tourists from New York were persisting. Beth spoke to the family twice, but beyond confirming that the pair had never checked in there was little more she could do to help.

Logan Clancy was despatched back to Maple Cove. The tide was flowing, bringing more jellyfish into the Sound. Several had been washed up along the beach and people were prodding them with sticks, ignoring his notices. The bikes were still chained to the rail in the parking lot. One had slipped or been knocked over; kids probably, Logan figured. Still, it gave him an excuse to bring the machines in 'for protection'.

'Which is fine so far as it goes,' Don Egan reported to Rick later that afternoon. 'Except that we got no identification marks on either machine. No one in the family ever set eyes on them, it seems.'

'What about a vehicle?' Rick suggested. 'I'm assuming they didn't cycle all the way up to Maine.'

'Yeah, well that's another blank wall at present. I spoke to the woman's brother. According to him the couple had given up owning a car in the city. Too much hassle parking and stuff. When they went out of town on trips they'd hire as they needed. As of right now it seems half the vehicles in town have out-of-state plates.'

Rick sighed into the phone. He was at his desk in the Chamber of Commerce building on the Green. Founders' Day was cranking up into high gear. Changes to the final order for tomorrow's parade still had to be agreed and he had a list of calls to make a yard long. Visitors were packing the town. So far in spite of fires and doomster predictions there had been only a handful of cancellations. That could change all too easily, as Rick was aware.

Now on top of everything, with Don and his force already fully stretched, they had a double disappearance to cope with.

'We're in contact with the phone companies. It might help to know when the last calls were made from their cellulars.'

'Or if they're still in use,' Rick pointed out. He still clung to the hope that there was some kind of simple explanation behind all this.

'That too,' Don agreed. Anyway there were administrative and legal difficulties to be overcome first. 'The relatives have to file a formal missing persons and we have to fax it over to get the companies to release the logs.'

'Are we positive the bikes Logan found do belong to this couple? For all we know they never even made it to Goodwill. They could have changed their minds about staying at the motel or gotten their dates wrong, anything.'

'You're forgetting the Southwell kid saw both

203

missing parties. His description tallies pretty good. Also he says they told him they were camera buffs and that fits.'

Don's intonation and the heavy pause after were part of what Rick had come to recognise as the police chief's 'bad news' signal. His gloom deepened. Was Don trying to tell him they had a murder on their hands? It seemed impossible in Goodwill. 'These people, they must have been driving a vehicle of some kind because otherwise where's their baggage?'

'That's what I asked myself. We're still checking with other places they could have gone to, but so far nothing. Like they stepped off the planet somewhere between here and Maple Cove.'

Don Egan hung up and punched the buttons for Patrolman Haden Booth's home number. While the phone rang he sat staring out the window at the tourists on Eden Avenue. Adding to his problems, now so many gawpers were trailing out to Curtain Bluff to take pictures of the collapsed cliff face that the town council had ordered the track closed off for safety reasons.

The phone was picked up at last. 'Haden, I need you back in again. Yeah, I know you only went off an hour ago, but this missing persons case is looking ugly and the way things are there's no one else. That'll be swell. Thanks, Haden. I knew I could count on you.'

That was something in favour of a small town:

204

people came through in a clinch. Everyone pulled their weight. He heard Annie Pellew's dry cough behind. 'Yes, what is it, Annie?'

'I spoke with Mr Baines's phone company,' she said in her clipped manner. 'His cellphone is not responding. I asked them what does that mean exactly? Is it the same as not answering? They said no, they sent out a test signal and got no answer back. Which could have three possible causes: either the phone is switched off or the battery is flat, which is the most usual, or it could be out of coverage, like out in the woods somewhere.'

'Yeah, and what's the third option?' Don asked.

'Or the phone is damaged or destroyed and no longer working,' Annie said. 'Off the record, they told me the last call placed from that number was ten-seventeen a.m. Thursday.'

'That's yesterday morning. From which we can assume what, that the phones haven't been stolen?'

Annie shrugged.

'Okay, I'm trying to figure out where we go from here, but thanks anyway,' Don told her.

Annie remained in the doorway. She spoke again. 'Donna Reid that married Doc Southwell was in earlier.'

Don waited for more. 'She would be Tab's stepmom, right?' Annie nodded. 'And?' Don said.

'Tab told her about meeting the missing

couple. Donna wants to know if we think he's done something wrong. She's fond of the boy and doesn't like to see him upset.'

'Why would Tab be upset? Unless there's something he's keeping back?'

Annie pursed her lips.

'We don't know for sure what happened,' Chance Greene protested. 'These two could be anywhere. Maybe they met up with friends, decided to stay at their place.'

'And the cycles?' Rick asked. 'They just abandoned three thousand dollars' worth of sports equipment in a car-park? That doesn't sound likely.'

'So maybe they forgot. The machines were chained up, didn't Don say? Insured probably. Maybe they intended to come back to pick them up and got delayed. Probably figured they'd be safer overnight in Maple Cove than tied on the back of a station wagon on the street.'

'He has a point there, Rick,' Don Egan agreed. The three of them were in Don's office in the police department building on Eden Avenue.

'The point I'm trying to make,' Chance emphasised, 'is that you are overlooking the background to all this. Have you forgotten we had a body washed up in the harbour last night? Or that there have been two fires, for God's sake? If now we start plastering the town with missing notices it is going to cause a lot of anxiety. This is a small town; what are visitors expected to

206

think? That we have a serial killer on the loose? That our beaches are unsafe?'

'We can't put out notices till we have photos and we still haven't received any,' Don told him. 'Same goes for TV. Which leaves an appeal over local radio. Please phone home, that kind of thing.'

It wasn't much, but it was the most they could do for the present.

Chapter 19

Goodwill. Natalie's red car was sitting empty at the barrier across Main Street. Rick looked around and spotted her coming towards him, her hair tousled and damp.

He waited to hear what she had to say, but she was all smiles. 'Reb says you had a bummer trip out. Sorry.'

He nodded. 'No sightings if that's what you mean.'

'Yeah, too bad. Happens sometimes, huh?'

He noted her hair, but she said nothing, just stood looking beautiful and aloof.

'You been in the water?' he asked finally.

She nodded dreamily. 'I went out on the ocean with friends.'

'Looks like you fell in.'

'I was fine.' She flicked the hair off her face. 'It's drying now. I treated myself to a wetsuit from the store.'

'These friends, anyone I know?'

'Just guys,' she told him, deliberately enigmatic. 'Just guys I met.'

He tried another tack.

'Apparently a girl got herself injured out on the ocean. One of the surfers.'

'Yeah, there was a kid had to be brought out off Curtain Bluff.'

'And?'

She shrugged. 'Surfing, all kinds of stuff happens.'

It seemed to him she was being deliberately uncommunicative. 'Well, was she?'

'Was she what?'

He was angry now. 'Was the girl hurt?'

Her slim shoulders stiffened under the sweater. 'She wiped out and got pounded.'

'You don't sound that bothered.'

Now it was her turn to tighten up. He saw the eyes narrow and colour flush along the cheekbones. He had scored.

'It was one of those things. She crashed out and got hit by the board. Luckily we were close by. The boys got to her fast and brought her in to Maple Cove.'

It cost him an effort not to rise to the bait and ask who were these guys with her, the driver of the jet for one.

'Sounds like it could have been nasty.'

Still she feigned indifference. 'Surfing has its risks. As injuries go this was minor. I mean it's not like she got attacked by a shark or anything.'

'I heard the girl wound up in hospital.'

'She was shocked, yeah. Banged her head and had a nasty cut. They ran her into the clinic and Doc Southwell stitched her up.'

'She needed sutures?'

'Apparently.' Natalie eyed him stonily. 'What is this, an inquisition? You act like I was to blame.'

She slid behind the Jaguar's wheel and reached for her sunglasses. 'Catch you later, Rick.' The car burst into throaty life.

Rick watched her out of sight. She wasn't wearing his ring today, he had noticed. Maybe she had taken it off to go in the water.

Outside Jean-Alice's on the Neck, Rick bumped into Mike Caine, his sister Reb's husband, loading pots into the back of his pick-up. 'Hi, stranger,' he greeted Rick.

'I know, I haven't been around to see the boys,' Rick apologised. 'Tough week.'

'It figures.'

Mike produced a match from the pocket of his coveralls and picked his teeth thoughtfully. 'Matter of fact, I was looking to run into you. I need a favour. Remember your dad's work boat?'

'Is it still ours? I thought it was sold off with the rest?'

Mike turned his head from side to side the once. 'Nope. Fellow from Lewisport made an offer finally and Rebecca accepted, but he pulled out. She's lying alongside the mole as of now. Problem is we got the gas tanker docking day after tomorrow and she'll need to berth up there.'

'Gas tanker? But that's not due in harbour till Monday.' Two years ago the utility company that supplied the town had installed a new generator that ran off liquefied gas. A tanker from Halifax, Nova Scotia, put in every three months to top up the storage. The fuel was more expensive, but there were grants available to offset the capital cost of the new plant and the federal government picked up the difference under some kind of environmental programme.

Mike shrugged. 'Jack Pearl stopped me five minutes ago and told me. Something about the company wanting to offload on account of all these rumours flying around. You know, this typhoon stuff.'

'Tsunami.'

'That's the one. Anyway I'd do it, only I promised Reb I'd run the twins up to Ellsworthy for an orthodontic check-up. I know you're kind of busy right now.'

'Sure, I can do it,' Rick told him. It would only take him ten minutes. 'Who has the keys?'

'Back home.'

'I'll stop by.'

Rick found Jack Pearl in his office. He was on the phone. 'Goddammit, Jack,' Rick said as soon as he had finished, 'what's this about the gas tanker docking Sunday?'

211

'Sunday heck, that was them on the line just now. They're talking tomorrow a.m.'

'You're kidding! Did you tell them it's Founders' Day, the regatta and all?'

'Sure I told them. The Sound is full of yachts and sailboats, I told them. You're asking us to let you bring that floating bomb in here. It's the stupidest dumb proposal I ever heard.'

'And they won't listen?'

Jack unwrapped a stick of gum and stuck it in his mouth. He had quit smoking and it was supposed to be a substitute. He chewed a minute and shrugged. 'I said I'd complain to Coast-guard, grounds of public safety.'

'And what did they answer to that?'

'They've already cleared it with them. It's all to do with this dumb tsunami alert thing. The tanker stops here, then goes on to Camden and Portland. Last stop is Boston where she empties out. They want to get the run through and out of the way before the situation deteriorates according to Con Wolfowitz.'

'Con said that?'

'His words.'

'If the authorities believe the situation is going to deteriorate, how does docking a twenty-thousand-ton tanker full of high-explosive LPG make it better?'

'You think I like it any better than you? I guess you and the Board of Selectmen can try complaining to the utility company, but you don't have a lot of time. She's due in first light

212

tomorrow. Only way I figure to stop her is set another fire. Ha, ha.' Jack laughed mirthlessly.

'Very funny,' Rick told him. He knew what had happened. The port authorities up in Halifax where the vessel was berthed didn't want a floating bomb around any more than Goodwill did and had ordered it out to sea.

Now it was Goodwill's turn. All they could do was cross their fingers and pray nothing would go wrong.

Meanwhile there had been further developments in the missing persons case. Instructions were issued by Don for the cycling community to be consulted in the hope someone might have met or noticed the pair. Anyone driving a vehicle with a bike rack was stopped and asked if they recognised the names. Eventually this reached the ears of Larry Hageman.

'Got one in the pound right now,' he informed Annie Pellew.

She eyed him doubtfully. 'One what, Larry?'

'Ford Explorer sport-utility, maroon, current year model with a cycle rack,' he explained as Annie continued scowling at him. 'He's been asking about them, hasn't he? Well, Gus and I towed one in this morning.'

'Towed it from where, Larry?' Annie was suddenly interested.

'Corner of Eden and Bay. Been there all night. Massachusetts plates, looked like a rental job. I checked with the pound as I came by and it's still in there. Nobody has come forward yet.'

'Chief!' Annie called. 'I think you should hear this!'

'Read me over the number again,' Don said to his man at the pound.

It took fifteen minutes only to establish that the Ford Explorer and been rented to a Randy Baines at Logan Airport the previous day. From there it was easy to reconstruct what must have happened.

'Three hundred and eight miles from Boston to the Causeway crossroad,' Don said. 'Six hours' driving, give or take depending on traffic conditions.'

'Thursday afternoon roads were busy, but Route One was moving well,' Larry put in.

'The rental was timed at twelve-oh-five p.m. They'd have reached the town around six then, half past perhaps allowing for a stop along the way. Question is, why don't they go straight to Seafarers where they have reservations made?'

'Because,' Rick reminded them, 'they are photographers. It was a glorious evening, remember? Everybody remarked on it. They had just made it to town and they really wanted to catch those colours. It was getting late, the light failing, they were in a hurry. The room could wait. Beth Robbins promised to hold it till, when was it, nine?'

'Eight,' Annie said. 'Seafarers hold rooms open till eight p.m.'

'Makes no sense,' Don objected. 'Seafarers is only four blocks along. Why not leave the Ford in the yard there?'

'You're thinking like someone who lives in the town. This couple are tourists on vacation. They were more concerned about missing a chance to snap some memorable pictures,' Rick told him. 'So they dumped the vehicle on Eden Avenue and pedalled off along Ocean Drive down to Maple Cove. Which was as far as they ever got.'

The interview with Tab Southwell finally took place in Rick's office. Don was present with Annie Pellew to take notes, Tab and his father, and Donna, because the boy had asked for her. Rick was present as as independent witness. He had suggested Tab should have a lawyer, but all agreed that Tab had done nothing wrong. All everyone wanted was to hear the facts. Don even stressed that notes were not strictly necessary. They were only for an aid during the search for these people and would be destroyed immediately afterwards. 'I'm happy to do this in Tab's own home if he'd prefer,' he offered.

'Hell, we're all here now,' Southwell snapped. 'Let's get on with it.'

No one knew how to begin. Questioning a boy like Tab, desperately worried he might have contributed to the deaths of two innocent strangers. In the end it was Donna who stepped in.

'Tab, honey,' she said softly, patting his hand. 'Why don't you tell these people what you told me? Everyone understands there's no blame on you. You did nothing wrong, nothing at all. None of it was your fault, okay?'

'Amen to that,' Don affirmed.

And slowly, haltingly, Tab recounted what he had seen.

'A suck back.'

'But not a big one from the sound of it.'

Donna had taken Tab home. The others were discussing his testimony.

'No, he was clear about that. He thought it was maybe a boat.'

'That's what Jack Pearl says people in the marina reckoned. Cal Burrows too.'

'He warned them to be careful trying to reach Two Bush Island. He stressed that. He feels guilty that he didn't go for help after he saw the water run back in again.'

'If what I guess happened,' Rick said grimly, 'by the time he saw the water rise up again nothing he could have done would have made any difference. The speed of the incoming current running between the island and the cove would have dragged them both through the Gurge and down into the Mudhole. They wouldn't have stood a chance. Probably never realised what was happening until they were pulled under.'

Southwell wiped his face. He was looking shaken. 'I never knew that business with the current was for real. I always figured it was a tale sailors told.'

'Poor bastards, no wonder we haven't found the bodies,' Don said.

'Cancel the Founders' Day parade? No way, do you hear? Out of the question!' Chance Greene smacked the flat of his hand on the table, his big face swollen up with anger. 'There is positively no evidence of anybody, anybody being drowned.'

'Jeez, Mr Greene,' Don protested. 'How can you say that?'

They were in Don's office with the door shut. Annie Pellew was outside at her desk probably listening to every word. The missing woman's brother had e-mailed photos of the couple across and copies were lying out in front of them.

Chance Greene was ranting on. 'You boys are supposed to have the best interests of the town at heart. Instead here you are making out that Goodwill is some kind of unsafe place for a family vacation.'

Rick tried again. 'Chance, two people are missing. Their hire car was found on Eden Avenue with their bags inside and their bikes down at Maple Cove, plus we have a witness saw them try to cross the Gurge to Two Bush Island minutes before a freak wave flooded the beach. Neither has been seen or heard from since. The woman's brother is flying into Portland tonight; what are we supposed to tell him? That his sister and her partner took a walk in the ocean last night, but not to worry? Suppose another person drowns because we haven't posted a warning? How are we going to feel then? Of course we have to act. If we don't we will be failing in our responsibility to the public.'

Chance scowled at Don. 'You're Chief of Police. It's your call as much as his. What do you have to say?'

'What do you want me to say? Rick's right, we can't keep a thing like this a secret. The *Monitor* has the story. Ray Burns is saying it's all down to the tsunami business. But the parade is something else. That's a decision for the Selectmen.'

Don was sitting on the fence as usual.

Chance sat fuming, mouth clenched in a lipless line. 'The parade goes ahead as usual. Period. The others will support me, no question.' He jabbed a stubby finger in Rick's direction. 'First the whales disappear, now this. I'll not forget, Rick Larsen.' Cramming his hat on his head, he stumped out.

Don looked worriedly at his friend. 'You shouldn't cross him, Rick. He can turn ugly. And it's not just you; a lot of people in this town are on his payroll.'

But Rick wasn't listening. 'Don, was that true about Ray Burns?'

Chance Greene had left the door open. Don dropped his voice. 'Sheena was in here. According to her, Ray reckons these freak surges and breakers are just a foretaste of what's to come.'

Chapter 20

Six p.m. Rick took the boat out afterwards. He had promised Mike he would move it and it was an excuse to take a look up the Gurge for himself.

The name on the bow was *Chimay* – iceberg in Norwegian. She was a thirty-two-foot Cape dory, cold-moulded with a Perkins diesel unit and a roomy cockpit. She looked shabby and unloved tied up alongside the mole. Dad never bothered much with maintenance. That was the joy of fibreglass, he would say.

The engine started reluctantly. When he had it running, he cast off and put the wheel over, edging her out into the Sound. She handled cleanly, riding the swell without pitching. The Perkins sounded ragged like Mike said, but it was a sturdy design and with a bit of work would be good for a while yet. A strip-down and new ignition might help.

It took no more than fifteen minutes to bring

Maple Cove in sight. The land to the north of the Sound was steeper and most houses took advantage of the view from the higher ground, leaving the shore uncluttered. Properties there were smaller and less pretentious than in the summer colony on Indian Point, but it was a nice place to live.

Several boats and sailing yachts were in view inbound for moorings. A helicopter with Coast-guard markings clattered overhead, stooping low over Indian Point. Don Egan had sent out three of his officers and a bunch of volunteers to scour the beach and cliffs on foot. A Coastguard launch was out checking the coastline on both arms of the Sound. If nothing was found the crew would move on to search the outer islands in case the bodies had been swept out to sea on the ebb-tide. Jack Pearl had lent the harbourmaster's boat to assist in the hunt and other craft in the vicinity had been asked to keep their eyes open and report anything unusual.

Rick passed a few clumps of jellies, sinister looking with their puffy blue hoods, but nothing like as bad as he had feared. There were several sailing craft in the area and three young guys showing off in what looked like a brand-new twenty-foot whaler with a big Mercury outboard and a full set of rods. As he neared the shore he made out figures on the beach walking in a spread-out search line. They stared at him, shading their eyes against the glare as he brought the boat close in under the lee of Two Bush Island.

The fish-finder depth gauge was showing eight feet as he approached the entrance to the channel. He was trusting it was calibrated right, but the brand was reliable as a rule and eight foot of water was about right for the state of the tide. The deepest part of the channel lay tight in against the north line of the island. There was a line of pot buoys off the western tip; Ethan Taylor's if he recalled the colour markings correctly. He took the way off the boat as much as he dared and fetched out the glasses to check the shoreline. A few cormorants regarded him sleepily from their perches, no seals. And no bodies or significant debris that he could see. He hadn't really been expecting much; Con had been through ahead of him already with the Coastguard launch, but you never knew.

He was keeping an eye on the depth gauge and sure enough halfway into the channel the indicator suddenly dropped off the scale almost. The reading fell away from seven and a half right down to forty-nine feet. The Mudhole. In times of spate, when the tide was running hard backed by winter swells driving up from the Atlantic, currents sweeping around the island from both directions caused a whirlpool to develop at this point, scouring out the channel bed into a deep pit. When the Gurge was running hard it was sometimes accompanied by a terrifying grinding sound, said by old hands to be caused by boulders on the floor of the Mudhole clashing together underwater.

If the missing photographers had attempted to cross the channel against the tide, then God help them.

Leaving the channel, he pushed open the throttle and the boat surged forward under him. Plenty of power there, they must be making ten knots against the tide. The fuel gauge was healthy. He looked up at the sky, still some daylight left. Just enough time to take a look at the mouth of the Sound.

Would there be whales there again?

Greenstone Island lay ahead to the south of his present course. The name derived from the veins of green marble found in one small bay facing onto the Sound. So far as anyone knew this was the only place in New England where such rock formation occurred. The veins were largely under-water, but fragments were washed up quite often on the beach. Legend had it that a piece of Goodwill greenstone was a powerful protection against drowning and old-time mariners like Rick's father never ventured out on the water without a piece. The old man had once been caught in a hurricane off Cape Hatteras. The ship was foundering and only a last-minute miracle shift in the wind saved the crew. Afterwards Leif discovered that his greenstone had gone from his pocket, although he was certain it had been there earlier. The storm had taken the stone in payment for a life. Superstition ran deep.

Rick had chosen a site overlooking Greenstone Bay as the place to build his house. There had been a house there years before, a cottage shared by twin sisters, but the last of them died when Rick was small and the house stood empty and eventually tumbled down.

Greenstone Island itself now belonged to the town, purchased by public subscription to protect it against development. A small legacy from his mother enabled Rick to acquire the lease on the old house site and the town fathers reluctantly ceded permission to build. The work had progressed slowly. Planning restrictions had been strict and besides that he had set some of his own, chief among them that all wood used must be driftwood washed up in the Sound.

He put the wheel over to starboard, taking *Chimay* round the point into the bay. The house stood tucked down in a fold, two-storey with a sun porch giving views back over Indian Point and the harbour right round to Curtain Bluff to the north. From here the house looked pretty much complete. Spurred on by Natalie he had finished the roof last fall. The shell was now complete along with the internal walls and floors. Only the fitting out remained and progress had slowed again. As Natalie had remarked more than once, it was a house that seemed designed never to be completed.

The little boat smacked her bows into the waves, cutting cleanly through the crests with a warm land breeze at Rick's back. A group of storm petrels were pattering on the surface of the water near by. Close into the bay, he raked the beach with the binoculars, but the sand was pristine, not even a jellyfish that he could make out. Definitely no corpses either. Raising the glasses he caught the red flash of the dying sun reflected from the windows of the house.

The light was failing, it was time to think of putting back. He spun the wheel, taking the boat out to sea again. He would pass Curtain Bluff on the way in and check the rocks there.

That was when the engine quit.

Rick wasn't concerned. He had had engines go down on him plenty of times before and way offshore at that. He was confident he could locate the problem and fix it. Most probably more dirt got into the fuel line. There was plenty of gas in the tank, he had checked before starting out, and in his experience most engine trouble stemmed from fuel feed blockage. He let her come up into the wind, left the wheel and started opening up hatches. There seemed to be a lot of oil spillage generally, which was to be expected, also a fair amount of water in the bilge, which might just be lack of maintenance or more probably the leak from the prop shaft that Mike had mentioned.

In the weak light it took some minutes to narrow down the problem. For a while he feared it was an ignition failure, which would have been worrying since he was fairly confident there were no spares on board. In the end it was only by checking the entire length of the fuel line with his fingertips that he discovered a split on the inside of a bend a few inches from where it joined the bottom of the tank. He found some duct-tape in a locker and strapped it up as tight as he could, working mostly by feel after the batteries in the flashlight gave out.

The first stars were out by the time he straightened up wearily from the engine. Fortunately he had the radar to see him home. He was wiping the oil off his hands with a rag when something made him glance back over his shoulder and what he saw made him freeze suddenly.

Dead astern of the boat, no more than a hundred yards off, a monster had risen silently from the depths. Dark against the sky, a massive roller was bearing down on *Chimay*. At least fifteen feet from trough to crest, its face towered over the boat, steep as a cliff. Instinctively, Rick rammed the throttle open to its fullest extent, gunning the engine to build up speed as the wall of water swept inexorably nearer. The best position to tackle a heavy sea like this one was to meet it bow on, but there wasn't time to bring her head round; he would have to run before it and trust she didn't broach. He knew now what the guys in the harbour had meant by freak waves. This one had appeared out of nowhere and as he gripped the wheel and felt the stern start to lift, as it slid into the trough, he was searching all the while in his head for an explanation.

The foot of the wave swept under the dory, tilting the bow down, pitching her so steeply it felt like surfing a break. Rick resisted the temptation to attempt to escape out the edge. If he once put the wheel over she would lose way, slide sideways on and risk being swamped as the crest broke over them. When faced with a big one you had to ride it out, hanging on in till the trough went by underneath. Rick had faced bigger seas in his time; he had battled through winter storms and a typhoon in the Pacific, but there was something strange and sinister about this one, the way it had materialised without warning out of a calm ocean, the way a bear could come at you suddenly out of the woods, dangerous and unpredictable.

And at the back of his mind was the thought that twenty-four hours back this same coldwater mountain had taken two lives.

Chapter 21

The King had standards. He could sleep on the beach under the stars if he had to; he had done so often enough. Hotel or shack, it was all the same to him, he said, but these days he had a reputation to keep up. He would do this thing, but he would do it the right way. That meant proper equipment, state-of-the-art that he could count on, and back-up, plenty of it. He needed film crews, two at least plus another in the air, cameramen with guts prepared to take risks to get in close.

It was a manager's nightmare, but the Gimp was prepared for that. All stars were the same; they thought money fell out of the air.

There were editors he was in contact with confidentially; in so far as anyone in that world could be trusted. It was hard. Some doors the King's reputation opened easily, others less so. The media company that had put out his last film was fighting shy.

'We're looking for new faces. I know he did the movie, but that was three years back. And then there was that business with the girl . . .'

'That's all in the past. The kids don't care about that stuff anyway.'

'Sponsors care. The sport is turning mainstream; image counts.'

The Gimp knew of another studio whose last feature had bombed and was as hungry as they were. He worked on the producer: 'This thing is hot like you wouldn't believe.'

'There's a new crowd now, wild riders, their stuff is unreal.'

'You don't know wild till you see this. We're talking epic, once in a lifetime. You'll blast the opposition out of the water, no contest.'

'Yeah, yeah, we believe you, but to convince the money-men we need a proposal, man. You got a script? You got a storyboard?'

'I got the King and I got a wave.' The Gimp's voice sank to an ominous growl. 'The biggest break that will ever be ridden. The biggest goddam monster this side of a hundred thousand years.'

A pause, a long one. They were biting, the Gimp knew, but would the hook sink?

'If you're talking about what I'm thinking, we already sent a crew to Bermuda to cover the action there.'

'They'll be wasting their time. Bermuda will be nowhere. The waves will top out at thirty, forty max, smaller than Jaws, smaller than

Mavericks even. Your guys might as well stay home.'

'Yeah? So what are you offering?'

'The big one, the mother of all breaks, goddammit.'

'Specifically on height?'

The Gimp let him hang a full half-minute.

'Well?'

'Three times Bermuda.'

'Three times Berm— A hundred and twenty! Shit, that's a joke, right?'

'I don't do jokes! A hundred and twenty feet and climbing.'

'I don't believe you, man. You're fucking crazy.'

'I'm not crazy and I'll tell you something else: as we speak this thing has started. The clock is running. *Two guys are dead already!*'

'Jesus! Now you are crazy.'

'You'd better believe it and this time it's for real. I've got the place and I've got the man.'

'Okay, we'll send someone. Where are you?'

'Maine.'

'Maine? What in hell happens in Maine?'

'The end of the world happens here is what. Tell your guy to bring a suitcase of dough.'

Sheena Dubois sipped a glass of cranberry juice on the screened porch of Ray Burns's place on Pigeon Cove. From all the stuff about Coke bottles and currents she'd been expecting someone wackier, but there was a grey-eyed intensity about Ray. She was asking him about the cliff at Curtain Bluff. 'Would the waves that caused this latest fall have been especially large?'

'Not necessarily, not necessarily at all in fact. Coast erosion is a continual process. It happens all the time. The boulders at the foot of cliffs everywhere are the product of this process. For a while the freshly fallen debris provides a degree of protection for the cliff foot, acts like a breakwater, but it is soon eroded away too and the cycle recommences.'

So, Sheena said, the cliff fall was pretty much an everyday occurrence and unconnected to the tsunami scare?

Ray shook his head. The question of whether so-called 'freak' waves had played any part in recent events was one for oceanographers. 'I did ask to see Jack Pearl's tide log for the evening in question however.'

'And what did you discover?' Sheena wanted very much to know.

'That the physical characteristics of the Sound can combine to magnify and distort wave action.'

Sheena waited, but he did not expand. 'According to Jack Pearl you're something of an expert on the Sound and the way the ocean currents operate.'

'Yes, I became interested after my wife died. I had time on my hands and used to take walks along the beaches. I picked up fragments of what I realised was pumice in the cove down here. It made me curious.'

'Pumice is lava, isn't it?'

'Porous volcanic rock, yes. It is light enough to float on water due to cavities formed by expanding gases in the magma.'

'So that came from where, Iceland?'

'Conceivably, although the samples I sent for analysis proved to originate from the African margin volcanoes, meaning the Azores or Canary Islands, probably the latter.'

'Would you call that significant,' Sheena asked him, 'in view of the current threat situation?'

'I'd certainly call it interesting,' Ray chuckled.

Sheena looked at her notes. She checked another item. 'The Office of Homeland Security talks about a new warning system that is supposed to give us warning of an approaching tsunami. Do you have any thoughts on that?'

Ray Burns stopped chuckling and his grey eyes met hers. 'I can tell you that it isn't working.'

The fairground rides were up and running by the time Rick nursed *Chimay* into her new berth. He was soaked through. The Neck was thronged with sightseers chattering and the throb of music reach out across the water. Jack Pearl was waiting for him to help him tie up.

Rick said, 'A big breaker ran me down out on the reef.'

'It did? How big of a wave?'

231

'Ten, twelve foot.'

Jack Pearl looked thoughtful. 'We had some more choppiness in the harbour. Makes the third time in two days.'

'Any damage?'

'Nope.' Jack shook his head. 'Not many on the water thanks to those damn bluebottles. Lucky, I guess.'

Rick finished tying up the boat. Then Jack said, 'Rick, something came up while you were up the Sound.'

'What's that, Jack?'

'A couple of those surfing kids want to talk to you. Well, not so much kids, these are older. Guy with the limp and the big fellow. They were wondering if you would be interested in a charter for *Pequod*.'

Rick was amazed. 'What do they want her for? Fishing?'

Jack was unclear on this. 'The way they were talking they want a bigger vessel to lie off the reef as a base for surfing. They're prepared to pay good money too.'

'Hell,' Rick told him, 'I can't do that. The whale trips pull in a lot of business. They're our bread and butter. I can't dump all those people for the sake of a bunch of surfers.'

'They know that, Rick. They appreciate your position. What they are offering is a retainer giving them a hire option at four to five hours' notice. They are checking out the forecast each day and if it looks like surf's up, then they

232

pay you an hourly rental. I figured it might be useful for you after you lucked out this morning.'

Rick made a face. 'Even so, *Pequod* isn't cheap to run.'

'They appreciate that. These guys understand the economics, Rick. They have done this before and seems they have a pretty good idea of the rates. Think about it. I mean if you're not pulling in any dough from tourist rides . . .' Jack left the sentence unfinished.

That was true. Another couple of trips like this morning's run and the syndicate would be seriously out of pocket. Looked at that way a surfer charter would be a godsend. 'I'll talk to them.' He nodded. 'But I'll need to see their money before I commit.'

'From the way they were talking that's not a problem. Seems they have a film company lined up to shoot a movie.' Jack shook his head in disbelief. 'Surfers, movies, it's a whole different world out there. Guess we just have to get used to it.'

Rick pushed through the crowds to the store and caught Rebecca just shutting up.

'That young lady of yours was in here this morning. She splashed three hundred dollars on a designer wetsuit.'

'Not for my benefit.'

'Running around with her new friends on their jet skis, huh?'

Rick shrugged. 'She needs a little space just

now. Getting engaged seems to have spooked her or something.'

Rebecca looked him in the eye. 'You ask me, what she wants is her bottom paddling.'

'Okay, okay,' Rick said. 'I get the message.'

His phone went. 'Rick, it's Elise. Where are you?'

'Hi, Elise, I'm down on the Neck. What can I do for you?'

'Is Natalie with you?'

'No, I haven't seen her since midday. Why, have you lost her?'

'She was supposed to be joining us here for dinner, but she's not answering her phone.'

'She's most probably out of range somewhere.' Cellular phone coverage in this part of Maine was notoriously patchy. 'Or out of battery. If I run into her I'll say you called,' Rick promised.

He hung up. Rebecca looked at him darkly. 'And what's Miss Scatterbrain gotten up to now?'

The Indian Patch party had exhausted themselves on the fair rides. Tired and happy they strolled up Main Street to the Shady Tree, but there was a line waiting for tables in the garden. Sarah Hunter took pity on them because of the children. 'Have you kids been for a ride on the Whale Train yet?' she asked them. 'You haven't? Well look, she's just pulling into the Green over there now. Run and grab seats on board. You

234

can rest your feet and watch the action and Pat will bring you right back here in forty minutes. I'll have a table under the tree waiting for you. It's a promise.'

Shrieking with excitement the children rushed across the Green and piled into one of the carriages. Pat Stevens climbed back aboard the loco in front and rang the bell and everyone squealed delightedly as the train pulled out. 'Hey, is this fun or what?' Ted Gardiner chuckled, leaning back on the open bench with his arm around his daughter as they rolled soundlessly down the street in the warm evening.

Lloyd sniffed the air. 'I smell smoke.'

'Dumbo,' his sister scoffed. 'It's a man in front with a cigarette.'

Chapter 22

Rick shut the door of the Chandlery behind him and strode off up the Neck. The fairground lining Bay Road was pulsating with noise and lights, hundreds of people, locals as well as tourists, crowding round the rides and sideshows. Smells of hotdogs cooking and popcorn greased the air. The event grew more successful every year, drawing in visitors from Boston and from as far away as Halifax and Montreal across the border.

The tail lights of the Whale Train were vanishing up Main Street as he plunged through the crowds, making for the Shady Tree. The restaurant was humming, every table filled and the waiters hopping. Out in the courtyard garden lights shimmered in the famous tree. On the far side of the tree he spotted Sarah Hunter's tall figure, her head bent over the maître d's station. She saw him threading his way between the tables and her face lit up, then

236

she read his expression and her mouth turned sullen.

He grabbed her arm.

'What do you want? Let go of me!' she hissed.

'Come with me, unless you want me to chew you out in front of all these customers.'

'Damn you, Rick, you're embarrassing me!'

They were speaking in furious undertones, but the nearer tables were all within earshot and heads were turning in their direction. Most were tourists, but there would be a scattering of locals or summer types, who might recognise one or other of them. To hell with it, Rick thought. He meant to have this out.

'I'm embarrassing you? What do you think you're hoping to do with your damn radio requests?'

'I don't know what you mean,' she said, looking away.

'Don't play dumb with me. I mean that stupid song you have them play over the radio six times a day, that's what!'

'Oh that.' She managed a bitter little laugh. 'That was my present to you. A little reminder of times past.' Her eyes narrowed teasingly. 'It was our song; they used to play it all the time. You do remember don't you, Rick?' Her voice sank to a husky whisper. 'That night on the highway in my dad's convertible. It was your birthday. You asked what I'd got you for a present and I said anything you want, darling. And you bet me I wouldn't drive naked from the Goodwill

237

Causeway to Portland with the top down. They played it then, do you remember?' Her tongue moved over her lips. 'God, it was so cold. You had to—'

His mouth tightened. 'Shut up, Sarah. That was all a long time ago.'

She laughed again, low and dangerous. 'Not so long, darling. Have you told sweet Natalie about our games yet, I wonder?'

'Damn you! If you breathe a word to Nats, I'll—'

'You'll what, Rick? I don't scare easy; you should know that by now. You haven't seen the half of it yet. Just wait.'

'Damn you, Sarah, leave it alone, can't you? Whatever we had once it's over.'

Her eyes softened. 'You're a fool, Rick. I'm doing you a favour. Do you think she really cares for you? It's all a game with her. She's playing you for a sucker behind your back with the surfer guys. She's got the whole town laughing at you.'

The taunt struck him like a knife. He gritted his teeth. 'What's between Natalie and me is our business. Stay out of it.'

She looked him straight in the eye. 'I can't do that, Rick. You and I go back for ever. I'm not giving you up without a fight.'

His ears were flaming as he left the garden.

Where was Natalie?

The Cinema on the Green was screening a special showing by popular request of a cult

238

feature. The sell-out audience had a median age of sixteen; the name of the movie was *Gigantor*; the only star the King of the Mountain. And the King himself was present among his adoring fans, sprawled front and centre on the big settee with beers on the table and fresh seafood pizza steaming.

Wave after extreme wave: Mavericks, Shipstern's, Teahupoo and Jaws, always Jaws, Jaws, Jaws. Sixty-footers, even a seventy once, though that was disputed and an ever-present grievance. There were the sequences from the big movies, the box office hits, feats so risky that no stunt artist could be found to attempt them till in desperation the producers had turned to him, the King, the greatest of them all and he had dared and there he was for all the world to see, storming down the vertical face of a charging mountain, holding the crest like a rail, leaping, jumping, turning, defying death.

Again and again the applause of the audience crashed in his ears. Great days, great waves. Now he needed one more challenge, a conquest that would make him immortal, put him at a single leap beyond the reach of all competition for ever. The ultimate extreme wave. It was a mirage, a dream that had been with him all his life; and now if the Gimp was to be believed it was within his grasp almost . . . almost . . .

Natalie lay against his arm. Watching him up there on the big screen, standing proud on his board, defying the ocean's fury, he might have stepped straight from some epic. A hero fated always to seek out fresh challenges, driven by an insatiable urge to attempt ever more impossible feats. Seemingly without fear, always choosing the hardest, most dangerous way, hurling himself against awesome odds, again and again.

'You're good for him, you know that?' the Gimp had whispered to her. 'He believes in himself, sure, but sometimes he needs someone there for him too. Don't let him down.'

The film rolled on; another set of waves, each larger than the one preceding, supersuck barrels borne of a hulking open ocean swell. A black-clad figure streaking for the mouth of a barrel even as the roof avalanched in behind him.

The feature ended and the lights went up. The Gimp heaved himself up. 'Got some calls to make,' he growled. A bunch of kids came up wanting the King's autograph. The King grinned at them. 'How you doing, guys?' They hung around awestruck. Natalie wished they would go away. A young, dark-haired girl in a crop top snapped a shot of the pair of them with her cellular.

The Gimp shut up his phone. 'That's settled,' he said with relief. 'We have the backing.'

'Wild Reef?' the King questioned.

'And Surf Chaser, they both signed up along with Waves West. Righteous Features . . .'

'The outfit that made *WaveKiller 2*, right?'

'That's them. They're contributing a camera

240

crew. K. Zamos is involved. He's flying in tomorrow on a private jet. It's all starting to happen.'

'Tomorrow? Yes!' The King punched the air triumphantly. 'I knew it. Yes! Yes! Yes!'

'They have a working title – *Wall of Death*.'

'Listen, I have a story for you, I think,' Doc Southwell said.

'Tell me.' Sheena blew smoke at the roof of the Landcruiser. She was lying up against him in the back seat. They were sharing a cigarette.

'Yeah, well I was talking with Tab. He's still cut up over that couple who went missing. Blames himself for not going back to help them.' Southwell inhaled and went on, 'Anyway we were talking and he started telling me about the surfers he had met. Turns out one of them is famous, a real big-time star.'

Sheena felt a stir of interest. 'How big a star are we talking about?'

'C'mon,' he chided her, 'like you can afford to be picky? This guy is famous, among the kids anyway. Doesn't have a name, or not one that he admits to; the others call him the King, short for King of the Mountain. That's a title held by the guy who rides the gnarliest wave in the world.'

'Gnarliest? Where'd you learn to talk that stuff?' she scoffed.

'Off Tab, who else? The kids all talk the language. Waves are gnarly or solid and some-times crushing. The point is the King of the

Mountain is here in Goodwill. There, that should be worth a thank you.'

'He's on a visit?'

Southwell shook his head. 'Nobody seems to know. Rumour is that he threw over some big competition, World Qualifying Series, whatever that is, to be here though.'

'And this is news?'

'Tab claims to surfers he's a god. He does movies, dates rock chicks.'

'Sounds like quite a guy.'

'So Tab says. Having him here is like the Pope dropping by apparently.'

'So what's the draw for a surfing star in these parts?'

Doc shrugged. 'You'd better ask him that.'

'Guess I might. Any ideas where to start looking?'

'Sure.' Doc laughed briefly. 'That's another thing: Tab says he's been seen running around with Natalie Maxwell.'

Rick was eating at Reb's with Mike and the boys. They had ordered in pizzas. Mike had the fridge stocked with beer and Rick was wrestling his nephews for control of the TV remote.

'Easy on that thing!' Reb yelled from the kitchen.

'I just want to check the headlines. Now hold still a second, you sea rats!' Pinning his nephews to the couch and ignoring their shrieks of protests, he flipped channels.

'. . . *and now over to Washington, where the Office of Homeland Security earlier issued a statement on the situation in the Canary Islands describing the threat to the United States as "remote".*' The image cut away to a studio shot. The news anchor flashed her guest a bright smile. '*Professor Jean Ballister, you have immense experience in this field. Summarise for us the risk as you see it.*'

'*Good evening.*' Professor Ballister tilted her profile to the camera, her expression composed. '*As I said earlier to Director Manning and repeated a little while ago to the president at the White House, both of whom thanked me for my advice, we should be aware; we should not be frightened; we are not on La Palma.*'

'*But the eruption is serious, surely, Professor? And according to many scientists could send a tsunami smashing into the Atlantic seaboard?*'

Jean Ballister made a dismissive gesture. '*That scenario is a fantasy cooked up by catastrophists bent on self-promotion. The current scale of volcanic activity is far too low level to pose a threat to anyone barring the unfortunate inhabitants of La Palma. If the volcano flank were to collapse, which is a very remote possibility, it would not generate a giant tsunami as claimed. By the time any waves it set up made it across to this side of the pond they would be no bigger than ripples.*'

'*Yet we have just heard tonight the authorities on La Palma have ordered the evacuation of a further ten thousand people from the affected area, resorts are being closed—*'

243

'Exactly. From the affected area,' Ballister interrupted cuttingly. 'We are talking about a small island, less than five hundred square miles in extent. The chief danger is to people in the immediate vicinity, who are at risk from ash fallout, lava bombs, landslips and forest fires. None of which equates to a giant killing tsunami. Let's have a little reality here, please.'

The news anchor had one more question. 'Even so, Professor, the government has seen fit to install a multi-million-dollar tsunami warning system out in mid-Atlantic with precisely this scenario in mind and hurried forward its deployment to cope with the current emergency, so they at least seem to be taking the threat seriously.'

'The government has deployed a warning system. The network went live for the first time today, I understand. The timing is coincidental. While we are on the subject it's worth pointing out that all significant tsunami of the past hundred years have resulted from earthquakes and not one from volcanic eruption.'

'Boring!' Mike Junior screamed, wriggling free of Rick's grip. 'We want to see a tsunami, a real biggy!'

'Yeah, a hundred-foot gnarly barrelling up the Sound!' Leif his younger brother echoed.

'Okay, enough TV everybody,' their mother called. 'We're all of us going to sit down to a family meal for once. Kids, any more fighting and no supper. Rick, same goes for you. Mike, bring on those beers. Now sit at the table.'

244

'Sounded like that professor lady knew her stuff.' Rick's brother-in-law cracked a can and set it in front of Reb. 'I guess we can sleep easy, huh, Rick?'

Rick stared at the screen, lost in thought. 'Seems to me it's hard to know what to believe these days.'

Mike's brow furrowed. 'What's that supposed to mean?'

'It's easy for that lady to sit in Washington and tell us not to worry. She's not got the ocean on her doorstep.'

'Didn't figure you for a doom-monger, Rick.' Mike looked sharply at his brother-in-law.

Rick shrugged irritably. He and Mike were good friends, but Mike had a way of riling people. 'I call it being a realist,' he responded.

Mike's colour darkened. His emotions could always be read in his face. 'And I suppose you know better than a professor called in by the president?'

'Boys!' Rebecca's voice rang from the kitchen. 'Come and get your pizzas!'

'Why don't you just say it?' Mike demanded. 'You're right and she's wrong.'

'For God's sake, Mike,' Rick snapped at him. 'What do you want me to think?'

'I don't know. But to me you sound like one of those scientists she was talking about, the ones who try to make out the end of the world is just around the corner and it just seems kind of disloyal, that's all.'

245

Rick looked at him a moment. 'Maybe so,' he said grimly, 'but a lot of odd stuff is happening round here these last few days. And it wasn't a ripple knocked down the cliff at Curtain Bluff and maybe drowned two visitors.'

Rebecca appeared. 'Now stop arguing, the both of you,' she told them. 'It's Founders' Weekend and—' She broke off. 'What was that?'

But the others had heard it too; there could be no mistaking that sound. Everyone in Goodwill knew and dreaded it: the fire siren.

Chapter 23

Doc was done finally. Sheena felt the sweat drying on her skin while they slowly recovered their breath. Doc had thoughtfully left the aircon running. 'That was good,' she gasped.

'Wild,' he grunted.

She stroked his back. For a man of his age he was in good physical shape. 'Is it like this with you and Donna?'

He twitched irritably. 'Leave my wife out of this, okay? What's between us stays that way.'

'Don't freak on me. I'm just curious, that's all.'

'Christ, you're as bad as Tab.'

'What's he got to do with it?'

'Last night after I got home I asked him did he like Donna and he snaps back, "Sure, do you?"'

'What did he mean?'

'It didn't mean anything. It's just one of those dumb things kids ask, that's all.'

'Do you think he knows about us?'

'Of course he doesn't! How could he, for God's sake? He's never even seen us together. You're being as dumb as he is.'

They were silent again. 'What's that noise?' Sheena asked after a minute.

'I didn't hear anything.'

She reached behind her for the electric window button. A gust of warm air wafted in as it whirred down. She wrinkled her nose. 'Smells like smoke.'

A low moan sounded in the distance, rising and falling. 'Is that an ambulance?' Doc stuck his head over the seat. He froze. 'Shit!'

'What's wrong?'

'Lights, lots of them! A whole bunch coming down this way.'

'Let me see!'

'Get your head down!' Southwell pulled her roughly away from the window. 'Shit, those are sirens. They must be fire tenders.'

'A fire? Out here? Jesus!'

'They're on the highway, not turning off. Oh, yes, they are. Shit, they're headed right this way!'

Something caught in Sheena's throat. 'Oh my God,' she coughed, 'there is smoke! We need to get out of here!'

'Get dressed! Hurry! We can't be found like this.' I can't be found like this, he meant.

Frantically they pulled on pants and shirts. Sheena zipped up her jeans, stuffing her underwear into the pockets. Doc pushed her out the way and scrambled over into the driver's seat. He threw the Toyota in gear and they bounced off down the track.

'It looks like they've turned off,' Sheena gasped. 'Oh my God, you can see the fire now!'

'Must be up near the power station,' Doc said tersely. 'Any closer and we'd have been trapped.'

'Don't.' She shivered.

They reached the highway and he jerked to a stop. 'You and I part here,' he snapped, reaching past her to open the door and pushing her out before she realised what was happening.

'What d'you mean? You can't dump me here!'

'There'll be roadblocks out. If they find you in my car it will get back to Donna. I'll be finished in this town.'

She hammered on the door. 'What about me, for Christ's sake?' she shouted. 'I left my car in town.'

'Hang around and catch the action. You're a reporter. It's your job to report fires.'

His tail lights disappeared up the road. 'Bastard!' she screamed after him.

Freddy Tarr had been as good as his word. He had left a tender and crew out by the camping ground. In fact it was the owner of an RV who first called in to report smoke and sparks while driving back across the Causeway from Ellsworthy after a meal at the Lobster Pound restaurant – '. . . a real blow-out, all you can eat for twenty-five bucks a head'. This man, his name was Carlsberg, 'that's right, like the beer', spotted a ruddy glow sprouting among the trees away to the right, 'so close up to the town we figured at first it had to be someone's barbecue gotten a little bright, you know, out of control. Then we got closer and I said, "Hey, that's a tree on fire over there!" Anyway, after our experience this morning I guess you'd call us a little over-sensitive so we didn't waste any time, just dialled nine-eleven right away.'

Freddy's rescue unit had only just been stood down following the Curtain Bluff incident. Due to the crowds downtown the stand-by station tender had to detour south across Indian Point Bridge and swing around on the highway to approach via the Causeway, so Blue crew up at the camping site were first at the scene. Willy Stevens, the crew chief, radioed back. 'Must be half an acre alight and the breeze is fanning the flames towards the power company sheds,' he reported, adding, 'We're going to want help on this one, Freddy.'

The second tender was on its way already. Freddy Tarr hesitated a moment, debating whether to call on Ellsworthy for back-up a second time in twenty-four hours or go see for himself if his boys could cope. He chose to place the call right away without delay based on Willy's estimate of half an acre burning, the wind freshening and the proximity to the power station, but largely because of some quality in Willy's tone of voice. One thing about working together with the same set of guys, you learned to read their voices like your own. So he dialled Sam Jones, Ellsworthy's chief. 'The forest is burning. Send me what you can across the Causeway.' Freddy knew the request wouldn't be well received or easy to fill, Friday nights were the same all over. That was why it was better to get the call in right at the start. Sam said the boys would be on their way soon as they could. He didn't add, 'Better damn well not be another false alarm this time,' or anything along those lines because fire chiefs had to back each other up no matter what. You could never tell when it would be your turn to ask a neighbour to pitch in and the Goodwill crews had never once let Ellsworthy down in the past.

By the time Freddy and Red crew reached the scene, the blaze had a good hold. Willy had said half an acre and he hadn't exaggerated. The wind was whipping the flames up and several good-sized trees were crackling away like torches. There was a lot of smoke at ground level and what worried Freddy most was the fire had no obvious shape to it. There seemed to be a number of hot spots as if flames had broken out in different places.

Willy had seen straight off that there wasn't much to be done with the trees except leave them to burn out. He was putting all his effort into getting around ahead of the crackling brush and scrub, trying to contain it from spreading. His guys were in there with shovels, beating out the flame front, reserving their water for the

251

bigger blazes. It was gruelling work in the heat and smoke and dangerous. If the wind sprang up suddenly they could find themselves trapped by a wall of flame.

What was needed was more men and machines. The reserve crew was suiting up now back at the station and at least one machine from Ellsworthy could be expected within the next fifteen minutes. Freddy used his phone to get a hold of Stu Baker. Stu owned a backhoe that he hired out to work on construction projects. He was a hard-driving, hard-drinking son of a gun, just the kind to come through in a pinch.

'Stu, we have a situation out here by the power shed. What we need right now is your big bucket to cut us a break, give my boys somewhere to fall back on.'

'My machine is down by the school.' Judging by the background noise Stu was in a bar, which was only to be expected. 'Be with you in twenty minutes, Fred.'

'Sooner if you can.'

'I'll do my best.'

'Knew we could count on you, Stu.'

One good thing, the breeze was off the ocean, carrying the smoke and sparks away from the town. But there were half a dozen homes that Freddy could picture at risk if the fire got a hold. The occupants would have to be warned. He spoke to Don Egan. Don said leave it to him. He would get word to the householders and send vehicles out to move anyone trapped. 'How you guys doing up there?' he asked. 'You want me to put out an appeal for volunteers?'

Freddy thought for a moment. He was tempted but with three maybe soon four appliances plus Stu's earthmover he figured he could cope. Besides which this was a night operation with all the hazards that entailed. Get a bunch of willing civilians out stumbling around in the darkness and if anything goes wrong, wind gets up, changes direction, you'll be asking for trouble, he told himself. Best leave it to the professionals.

'No,' he said. 'Thanks, we can handle this. Just have your officers tell those good people to be ready to move out. If the flames jump Bridge Road they may not have a whole lot of time.'

Don said afterwards he could hear the fire crackling and popping in the background all the while they were talking. It gave him a bad feeling. Two fires in one day was two too many. He would dearly like to have asked Freddy what he thought had started this one, but it was not the moment. Freddy had enough on his hands bringing the damn thing under control.

Annie Pellew had come back in without him asking and was making the calls to the threatened homes. She always appeared when she was needed. She lived on her own in a small apartment two streets away; the job was her whole life.

She looked up at him primly. 'I'm getting no response from the Glens or the Rabys. The

253

Glens are definitely in residence because I saw Mrs Glen in Bob's Market Thursday. The Raby house is usually let for the early part of summer. Could be there are tenants not picking up.'

'Tell the car to stop by anyway. We can't afford to miss anyone.'

'I already did. Logan Clancy is on his way.'

'God bless you, Annie.'

Don's next call was to Andy Orwell, manager of the power company. Andy had gotten the news already and was coming in. Don reached him on his cellphone. Andy had spoken to his night man who reported hearing a thump like a low explosion shortly before the sirens started. 'We put in a good wide firebreak back around the time when we made the switchover to gas. A maintenance crew goes through every spring cutting back the new growth and clearing the trash. All part of safety regulations. Have to be one hell of a firewall to jump that, but I guess you never know. Worse that could happen would be if the storage tank caught. It's well protected though with water sprays and relief valves.'

Don tried not to think about gas tanks going up.

Logan Clancy, driving out to check the addresses Annie had given him, ran into several home-owners tearing back to protect their property. He passed on Freddy Tarr's warning. 'Get your valuables together and be ready to move out if the flames get close. Don't leave it too late.

Better you leave and have to come back than stay and get burned up.'

One woman was burning already with outrage. 'You want to know who's behind this?' she stormed. 'Those surfers is who. They were up in the woods back there early this evening, playing music, doing drugs and stuff. You don't believe me? Go see. My husband and I were walking just before six and there was a bunch of them in there making a bonfire. A pile of firewood like you never saw.'

The next person Logan met was Rick Larsen driving his pick-up. 'It's serious,' Logan told him. 'I got instructions to clear this whole section.'

'Any word on how it started?'

Logan shrugged. 'There's a witness says he saw an SUV taking off at a hell of a rate right around the time the blaze was first reported. Don's ordered all vehicles stopped on the Causeway.'

Logan had one radio tuned to the emergency frequency and while they were talking there came an urgent crackle over the air. 'Car Three requesting back-up. Two male suspects detained in vehicle Parson's Corner. Repeat Car Three requesting back-up Parson's Corner.'

'Sounds like someone made a catch,' Rick said. 'I'll get out of your way.'

Rick drove on. Half a mile up he heard the wail of sirens behind, saw the lights in his mirror and pulled over. It was the appliance from Ellsworthy, fully crewed and steaming up the grade. He let them pass and followed on after. They swung through the big shallow loop around the power station and there was the fire in front of them; roiling clouds of incandescent smoke belching skywards, whole trees burning with a roaring noise like a runaway furnace and against this hellish background, dimly visible among showers of sparks, the figures of men battling to contain the blaze.

The Ellsworthy tender slewed to a halt alongside the two machines from the town, the crew piling out in the same instant, dragging out hoses, slamming in connections. In under a minute they had a pressure on and the first water jet arcing into the flames.

Rick had turned out to help at past fires. Like most locals he knew what had to be done. He grabbed a shovel from the back of his truck and pitched in, working round the edge of the blaze, beating out the flames spreading through the undergrowth and trash beneath the trees.

Minutes later there was another roar of heavy machinery. Stu Baker was thundering up the road, pushing his big front-loader to the limit. Soon he was in the thick of the smoke, cutting a firebreak to windward of the flame front just where it was most needed. Near where Rick was working, a tall pine on the edge of the blaze had caught alight. Stu saw and swung his bucket around. A single heave of the hydraulics ripped the shallow-rooted trunk from the soil, toppled the whole tree backwards into the fire, saving the others nearby.

'We're getting on top of it!' Freddy Tarr bellowed in Rick's ear twenty minutes later. More volunteers had pitched up to help and with four appliances concentrating their pumps on the flames plus help from Stu's mighty machine the spread of the blaze had been checked. Now it was a case of standing by while the flames burned themselves out.

Rick wiped a sleeve across his soot-blackened face. 'How do you reckon it started then, Fred?'

Fred cleared his throat and spat into the carpet of ash. 'Rick, I'll tell you straight, with the others we've had I couldn't be certain, but this one' – he shook his grizzled head – 'no way could it have been anything except deliberate.'

'See this.' He led Rick back to the edge of the clearing. 'The flames kicked off in this small hollow here. You can see from what's left that the vegetation was actually quite green at this point, but the fire took a hold on a wide band of four or five yards. Pretty much what you'd expect from someone with a can of gasoline sprinkling the stuff around. When he's done he throws the container in the brush and lights a match. Whoomp, he's got himself a blaze. Some of these firebugs are dumb enough to stand downwind. This one had more sense unfortunately.'

'Freddy, are you positive on this?'

Tarr snorted. 'You don't take my word? Here, look at this.' He marched over to the far side of the hollow. 'I said he wasn't dumb. Well, in a way he was because he threw the container behind him so it survived, what's left of it.' He crouched over a patch of grass and scratched with his fingers. 'Here, smell.' He handed Rick a sliver of glass.

Rick took it and sniffed. 'Gasoline.'

'Bingo. Give the man a prize. Don's getting a forensics team out in the morning and we'll see if they can find a print. Word is one of the patrol cars pulled a truck over. Maybe we'll nail the bastard yet.'

The drama had drawn the usual small crowd of spectators standing around in the dusk. Rick spotted Tab Southwell with his bike under the trees and waved to him, but the boy turned away. Sheena Dubois had showed up too. She saw Rick and came over. 'Are you heading into town? Can I catch a ride with you? My car wouldn't start.'

The moon was large and clear as they left the woods. Sheena leaned her elbow on the sill and yawned. 'Mind if I smoke?'

He laughed. 'You didn't have enough of a lungful back there?'

They drove on a minute in silence. Sheena spoke again. 'That makes the third fire in two days. Kind of a record, don't you think?'

He threw her a quick sideways glance. 'I can do the math too.'

'They're saying this one was deliberate.'

'Evidence certainly looks strong,' he agreed. There was no point trying to bullshit Sheena.

'In which case the same most probably goes for the other fires,' Sheena commented. 'Meaning we have a firebug on our hands, an arsonist.'

'Hard to fault the deduction,' Rick said drily.

'Coincidentally, Don Egan is holding two surfers on suspicion, were you aware of that?'

The lights of the town showed ahead. Rick kept his eyes on the road and took his time responding. 'I heard the cops stopped a vehicle. I didn't know it was surfers.'

They entered Sugarshack Road. Many of the houses here had a light on. A fire in the forest kept people awake. Sheena trailed a hand out the window to catch the air. 'One of the guys the cops are holding is called the Gimp,' she said.

'Guy with the limp? I know him.'

'Quite likely. He's been around a while off and on. The other blew in Thursday; big guy with tattoos from California.'

'That description would fit most of them. Does he have a name?' He was deliberately prevaricating and he could tell she knew it.

'He refuses to give a name; the rest of the gang call him "the King" though.'

* * *

259

Maple Cove. Tab Southwell woke with a start. He listened, the house was still. He switched on the light and took a drink of water. His watch said two a.m. He must have been dreaming again. Lying back on the pillow he tried to recall what it had been about. He was out on Bay Road; it was daytime, he could see ships in the harbour and there were people about. He tried to remember if there was anyone he recognised but the faces kept slipping away just as they came into focus. Dad was lost somewhere among the crowd and he was searching for him. That was a recurring theme in dreams just now.

His hair still smelled of smoke from the fire. It had been past eleven when he made it home. Donna had been waiting up for him. 'You promised you'd be home by ten!' she chided him. 'We were worried for you.'

'I heard the sirens and went to watch the fire.'

She ruffled his hair affectionately. 'I guessed that. Is everything okay?'

He shrugged. 'Where's Dad?'

'Still at the hospital, poor lamb. A fireman breathing too much smoke. He phoned to say he's on his way. You'd better go up and take a shower. Your hands and face are black. I'll fix you something to eat.'

'It would be neat if you could stay on a few more days,' she said to him later in the kitchen. It would please your dad a lot. Me too.' She gave him her sunny smile.

'I'm thinking about it,' he muttered.

'It's not bothering you, that business with the people in the cove?' She laid a sisterly hand on his arm. 'It really wasn't your fault, you know? They were adults; they had no business going into the water the way they did.'

He hung his head. 'It's nothing to do with any of that.'

Something pattered on the porch roof outside his window, a racoon probably after the kitchen garbage. Tab shut off the light and settled down to sleep.

Chapter 24

Saturday, five a.m. Mid-Atlantic. It was dawn, but not a dawn that anyone aboard the USS *Tarp* recognised. The ship was stopped a hundred miles west of La Palma in the Canaries group and dust and ash from the eruption cloud darkened the sky. A menacing sunrise greeted them, a sky shot through with vivid streaks of purple and green, through which the disc of the sun itself glowed like a bloodshot eye. Backlit by the dawn, the immense plume from the volcano, rising a mile or more into the atmosphere, reached a long shadow over the waves. The decks were grey with ash and an iridescent dust coated the swell. At intervals shoals of dead and dying fish drifted past.

Two hours earlier, the *Tarp*'s red-eyed crew had commenced deployment of the remaining buoy in the DART tsunami warning network. The process was elaborate and time-consuming. First the remote-controlled submersible ATMOS was hoisted up from the belly of the ship by *Tarp*'s big crane and poised over the stern. Checks were run and these took two hours. Meanwhile engineers were completing final tests on the bottom pressure recorder, the BPR, attaching the anchors and fitting the mooring link that would connect to the surface transmitting buoy.

Once these preliminaries were completed, the delicate business of lowering the BPR pack could start. The pack was placed in the water and the hoist slackened off to lower it to a depth of 20 metres. Divers went down to make a final inspection and check that the cables were running freely. The submersible followed into the water and its systems were tested. A last-minute glitch in communications with the mother ship was rectified and at eight a.m. the order was given for lowering to commence. The big cable reels in the stern began their steady turning and the submersible sank out of sight. At a rate of 16 metres a minute the package would take four hours to reach the seabed.

Below decks in the laboratory section, the seismic recorders were jumping as they traced the progress of the eruption, small tremors and larger. 'I'll be glad when this one is wrapped up,' Mary Sennett admitted to her boss Derek Wanless. 'The way these quakes keep coming it's a wonder the whole island doesn't slide into the ocean.'

Wanless shook his head dismissively. 'It's not going to happen.'

'You sound very sure.'

'I am sure. Massive flank failures of island strato-volcanoes are rare to the point of not happening. Do the math: the lateral sheer stress required to overcome the mass inertia of a five-hundred-cubic-kilometre block could only be generated by a massive caldera-type magmatic chamber collapse.'

'How about deep-magma dyke intrusion exerting lateral pressure at the base of the fault? Isn't that now accepted as the trigger for just such a massive flank collapse on Gran Canaria? That was a strato-volcano.'

'You don't get that type of eruption in the Canaries group. And anyway La Palma hasn't gone critical yet.'

Yet, Mary thought. Involuntarily, she glanced at the clock. Wanless noticed. He patted her shoulder. 'Another couple hours and we can cut the buoy free and be out of here,' he said. 'I guess we'll all feel happy to put some distance between us and Cumbre Vieja.'

Mary repressed a shudder. She didn't like to think about it. Last year her parents had moved down to live on the Keys.

Two thousand feet below the surface and 300 miles south on the edge of the Cape Verde Basin, the USS *Thresher*, a nuclear-powered hunter-killer submarine of the Los Angeles class, was homeward bound from patrol. In the attack centre, her commanding officer, Captain Butch Krauss, and executive officer Commander Leo Martin were concerned that a rattle in one of the main reactor cooling pumps was betraying their presence to a Kilo-class Russian sub loitering in the region of the Mid-Atlantic Ridge.

'The obvious choice,' Martin was saying, 'would be to point the nose into the westerly Canaries Current, reduce power to a minimum and let the current tow us along as near damn silent as possible.'

Captain Krauss studied the chart. 'I agree that's what the Russki is expecting us to do, which is why he's holding a position to seaward over the ridge. He's hoping that if he can keep close enough even at minimum revolutions he'll be able to pick up our pump squealing on his sonar and track us all the way to Norfolk.'

'The alternative is to blast off up the ridge and hope to lose him in the deep-water thermocline somehow.'

Captain Krauss made his decision. 'No, that's what he wants from us and I'm not going to give it him. Lay us off to the east.' He tapped the chart. 'We'll head for the shallows close in to the Canaries.'

'That's where the volcano is doing its stuff. The tremors are showing up on the screens all the time.'

'Good.' Krauss smiled. 'That's what I'm counting on. The volcano will mask the noise of that confounded pump. Give us a chance to lose the Kilo, head north into the Iberian Abyssal, go deep there, then look for a route through the ridge home.'

'Sounds neat.' The executive officer was making notes. 'How close do you want to approach the islands?'

'There's deep water there. We can hug the coast as close as we like.'

'Yeah, but don't forget the eruption. We don't want a rock on us.'

The captain grinned. 'Twenty miles should suffice. Far enough to duck anything the volcano can throw at us, I should think. Adjust our course accordingly.'

'Aye, aye, skipper.'

'And drop our speed down to ten knots. We'll do this slowly.'

'Ten knots it is, sir. That should put our closest approach to La Palma at around ten a.m. local time tomorrow.'

'Good, we'll make it an excuse for a communications check. Give us an opportunity to take some photographs of the fireworks.'

The executive officer chuckled. Captain Krauss enjoyed a joke.

USS *Tarp*. At midday the pressure array touched bottom 6,500 metres down. The submersible moved in for a close inspection and adjusted the position of the sensor with its remote-control arm while the technicians aboard the mother ship observed on their screens. When everybody was satisfied, the pressure gauges were switched to active and communications tested. Mary Sennett and Derek Wanless studied the readings and Derek pronounced them satisfactory. Everything seemed in order, always allowing for interference from the ongoing tremors from the eruption on La Palma a mere hundred miles distant.

Mary, watching the needles on the seismographs jump and skitter, could only hope Derek was right. The ominous shadow rising above the eastern horizon seemed to have grown in extent during the morning, rearing up to 20,000 feet and blocking out the sun.

When all sections had signed off, Woods Hole gave permission by radio for the submersible to commence its ascent. Meanwhile the surface array was powered up and the satellite relay tested. There were delays while every circuit was checked and pronounced robust. Finally at three o'clock, the surface buoy was set free. The entire network was now in place. All that remained was to integrate the new data stream and that was a software issue which would be addressed back at Woods Hole.

At last the submersible's humpback broke the surface fifty yards off the port quarter. It was immediately hoisted aboard and made fast below. 'Okay, everybody,' the skipper announced over the PA system to cheers from all aboard, 'time to hightail it out of here.'

Mary felt she wanted to cry with relief.

Saturday, three p.m. Charco Verde, La Palma, Canary Islands. The new vent down by the shoreline, which had begun life as an angry boil on the flank of Cumbre Vieja, had grown alarmingly. Aerial photographs showed a black lava cone 100 metres across surrounded by an outer ring of compacted ash and scoria. Estimates put the cone's growth at 10 metres in the past forty-eight hours. Estimates however were not enough; real-time measurements were needed. That meant installing instruments which required a field trip. Human exposure, in short.

Felipe would lead; that was a given. This was his mountain. *'Yo también!* Me too!' Concha declared and no one challenged her right as his assistant. As for Malc, he had come this far so he would see the thing through. 'If you'll have me along,' he said wryly, drawing grins from the others. At the last minute a journalist added himself to the party. No one knew how.

They went in by road. A helicopter had been promised but was cancelled at the last minute. Technical problems. So Felipe drove them skidding and sliding on drifts of newly fallen ash. Twice they had to turn back, once to avoid a landslip and the second time to find a way around a deep crevasse torn in the road surface. All traffic they encountered was travelling in the opposite direction east and north. Los Llanos was a ghost town, red-roofed houses grey beneath a covering of dust. Ahead of them in the distance the pine woods were burning and out along the ridge the three cones were pumping smoke and filth into the air.

The road to the western coast descended the mountain flank in long sweeping bends between vineyards and banana plantations. When finally they reached the village it seemed deserted, the outlines of the buildings blurred under heavy loads of ash. Along the seafront the palm trees stood lifeless, the shade parasols bent and twisted. It must have been an attractive little place before. As they passed the hotel a dog whined and a man gazed at them stonily from what had once been a terrace.

'I thought this place had all been cleared,' Malc said.

Concha shrugged. 'They cannot make people leave. All they have is here.'

'Poor bastards,' said the journalist. As if he cared.

Felipe drove the jeep as close to the cove as he could get. When they stepped out ash crunched under their boots with a sound like fresh snow. Felipe crumbled some in his fingers. The particles were very fine. 'Could be phreatic,' he said.

A prolonged detonation rumbled ahead. Flames and smoke spouted from the cone in vivid black clouds streaked with bright white vapour trails. Malc pointed silently. Felipe nodded in grim agreement. The fine ash being ejected and steam trails among the smoke were indicators of water vapour being vented. He glanced at his boots, half sunk in the layer of red dust blanketing the crest. 'There could be a lake of water trapped right underneath us.'

'The well water levels are static though, aren't they?' the American responded.

'Yes, but that signifies little. Many will have been fractured or choked with debris.'

Malc looked him in the eye. He trusted the older man and respected his judgement; he had greater experience of this volcano system than anyone else alive. And he wasn't a man to panic. 'You have a bad feeling about this, don't you?'

The Spaniard nodded slowly, his mouth compressed. 'Yes, I do.' But he would not elaborate.

Through a steady drizzle of warm ash they worked their way along the outcrop of the old lava flow, each bent double beneath a heavy equipment pack. Everyone sweated inside full protective suits, gloves, goggles, and helmets. The new crater was fresh and highly active. They were almost as close to the cone as Malc wanted to be.

At last to everyone's relief Felipe called a halt. They had crossed the old lava ridge and reached the outer ash ring where the instruments were to be positioned. 'Fifteen minutes only,' Felipe warned. They were less than 500 metres from the crater and the cone was now spouting bursts of fiery lava blobs every few minutes.

The geologists set to work, digging in the gravimeters and GPS receivers, protecting them against damage where possible behind boulders. The most vital item was the transmitting dish that would relay the data via satellite to the LPO station. Malc and Concha had brought it up between them and at Felipe's direction they erected a clumsy wall of piled rocks to shield it against a direct hit.

Felipe tested their communications over the sat phone and held a hasty exchange with the observatory. 'We should finish up quickly,' he told Malc and the girl. 'LPO say the GPS readings are even higher than we thought.'

'What does that signify?' Scott, the journalist, asked. 'What's he saying?' he repeated, worriedly.

'It's the GPS we've just installed,' Malcolm explained. 'The receivers signal their position to the satellite system. It enables us to monitor their positions in real time to a high degree of accuracy.'

'Yes, go on,' Scott demanded.

'If the calibrations are correct the upward movement is continuing faster than we expected, half a centimetre since we've been out here.'

'Is that serious?' Scott blinked at him foolishly, the sweat making rivulets in the dust that caked his features. 'Translate into plain language for me, someone.'

Malcolm did so. 'We've set up three receivers in a triangle around the crater. The separation between them has measurably increased. It indicates a swelling of the cone base.'

'Yes, yes, but what does that mean to a layman like me?'

'It means something is pushing up from below.'

And to echo his words the ground began to dance beneath their feet.

USS *Tarp*. Three-forty p.m. Mary Sennett had gone up on deck for some air. The ship was steaming at a brisk 20 knots on a north-westerly heading and she was standing in the bows watching the sun beginning its slide down the sky, leaving Wanless to monitor transmissions from the new baby as they called it. Then came the call.

'Come on down. You need to see this.'

'There's been another jolt,' he told her, when she reached the lab. 'A big one this time. Looks like the epicentre is right underneath the mountain. USGS is evaluating it as we speak.'

Mary gazed anxiously at the seismograph chart. It was easily the heaviest tremor of the current episode. More than ever she was glad they were quitting the area.

Wanless had returned to the pressure buoy workstation. All at once he whistled softly. 'Son of a gun, Mary, check this. Looks like our first positive reading!'

Mary hurried over. One glance at the screen

was enough to make her feel ill. 'Oh my goodness,' she whispered. 'It can't be, can it? It's not possible, not so soon.'

A couple of technicians, who had been listening, came over to see what was going on. 'Jesus,' one of them muttered, 'is that what a tsunami looks like?'

'I guess' – Wanless stared in awe – 'the citizens of La Palma will be able to answer that for you right about now.'

Santa Cruz de la Palma. Four p.m. Poised on the east-facing slope of an old volcanic crater, the island's capital was just returning to work from the afternoon siesta. Along the Avenida Marítima the bars and cafes were just reopening. Thanks to the steady pressure of the north-east trade winds the city had been largely spared the indignity of the ash falls. Even so fully a fifth of the population had flown out since the start of the emergency or taken the ferry across to Tenerife. For those remaining the tremors were perceived as two distinct sharp shocks that rattled window frames and cracked roof tiles. There were no serious injuries but a great deal of alarm and uncertainty. Bells pealed, emergency sirens blared and car horns honked and beeped. Avenues and squares filled with frightened inhabitants. Others fled the danger of high buildings onto the wide seafront where they waited, trembling and praying, for the earth to become still again.

Approximately twenty minutes after the initial jolt, those closest to the ocean observed that the waves, which regularly slapped against the sea wall, were growing larger, drenching them with spray. Alarmed, they attempted to push back towards the avenue, but the crowds prevented their escape. The sea state then eased somewhat for a time and calm returned. The waves diminished and some said that the tide was running out.

A second smaller tremor persisting for less than forty seconds only inflamed anxiety further. More people swarmed to the seafront seeking safety. The ocean had now run out far enough for those close to the sea wall to have no doubt as to what was about to happen next. A terrific screaming and crying erupted as the bay frothed furiously and an ominous line of surf was seen moving rapidly towards the shore. At last perceiving the danger in which they stood, people began running across the avenue into the safety of the side streets. Fortunately for many the city climbs steeply. There was time enough, just. Those who foolishly elected to remain in their cars were not so lucky.

An interesting fact was that the tsunami generated by the first tremor caused almost no damage anywhere else on the island. Ocean-ographers later theorised that shock waves radiated out from the western side of the island, spreading out north and south until both sets collided off La Palma. Here they were concentrated by the confines of the gulf on which the port lies.

The first wave swept in as a single breaker estimated at six metres from trough to crest, twice the height of the sea wall. It crashed over the parapet into the lines of parked cars, sweeping them up and washing them into the avenue in a tangled mass of crushed metal. The water poured on across the avenue and the sidewalk, swamping the ground floors of the cafes and buildings fronting the ocean. The wave's force had by now diminished, absorbed first by the sea wall and subsequently obstructed by the barrier of wreckage it had piled up in front of it. Fortunately, too, its length was hardly greater than that of a storm-generated wave. The suck back came quickly and the retreating water tore gaps in the sea wall, but the two subsequent waves that followed were puny by comparison.

In the ferry terminal to the south of the town, the long mole provided some protection. A jetfoil bound for Tenerife had departed just before the initial jolt and experienced only some momentary turbulence out in mid-ocean, but other vessels in the port had their moorings snapped and a twenty-five-metre schooner was carried up bodily onto the dock and left stranded. Many smaller craft were broken apart as a result of being repeatedly dashed against piers and docks.

There were no more waves or tremors and the shaken citizens were left to pick up the pieces of their shattered seafront. Two hundred had been

275

injured but the death toll was remarkably low for such a disaster: only five people lost their lives, most trapped in their vehicles.

The world had just been given a foretaste of what was around the corner.

The first jolt was severe enough to be felt forty miles away on neighbouring Hierro and La Gomera and registered on seismographs around the Atlantic basin. In Washington, the instruments in the USGS Earthquake Information Center rapidly computed the epicentre, and experts, who were monitoring tremors from the island, alerted the White House Situation team. The quake measured 5.3 on the Richter scale and was followed by a second jolt of 4.1 magnitude. USGS was in contact with La Palma Volcano Observatory on the island, whose own measurements located the epicentres directly beneath the volcano at a depth of around ten kilometres.

Chapter 25

Goodwill, Maine. Saturday, eight a.m. Don Egan arrived for work at his offices on the Green to find Annie Pellew already at her desk.

'Morning, Annie, looks like another scorcher ahead.'

'Ninety-five, if you believe the forecast.'

'Great for the parade anyway.'

'Jack Pearl reckons we're building up to a storm later and he's not normally wrong.' Annie liked to look on the dark side of life.

'Someone to see you,' she said, her mouth pursed with disapproval.

'This early? Who is it?'

Annie sniffed. See for yourself, she implied. Don went through and found Natalie Maxwell running a comb through her hair. 'Don,' she greeted him, planting a kiss on his cheek.

'Hi, Nats,' he said warily. 'Haven't seen you to speak to since the party. Great evening. How you been keeping?'

She shrugged. 'Here and there. Mom and Dad are stressed. It's the Yacht Club regatta dinner tonight. I'm staying out of their way.'

Don wanted to ask where was Rick? but like everyone else he had heard the rumours so instead he said, 'So what brings you here?'

She looked down, her lip caught against her teeth. 'Don, I have a favour to ask.'

'Go ahead.'

'Those surfers you picked up last night.' She shot him a quick up-and-under glance. 'They are friends of mind.' She saw his expression harden. 'I don't know what it is they're accused of exactly, but I'm happy to go surety for them if you'll let them out.'

'Gee, Nats, I'd like to help.' Don rubbed his face. 'It's not that easy though. These friends of yours, they're facing some pretty serious charges.'

'Don, I know both these guys. They're here to surf and have a good time. The last thing they would want to do is harm anyone.'

'Nats, I really wish I could help, but it's not just in my hands.'

Her jaw tightened impatiently. 'Don, do I have to get Mr McGaffey involved?' Jock McGaffey was the Maxwells' lawyer. 'It'll come down to the same result in the end and just make a lot more work for all concerned.'

Annie Pellew appeared in the doorway. 'Mr McGaffey is out of town this weekend,' she informed Don poker-faced and returned to her desk.

Natalie had gone pale with anger. 'They didn't have anything to do with the fire!' she burst out.

'Nats, they were found on the scene with a load of gas.'

'The gasoline was fuel for the jet skis,' she interrupted. 'You've no right to hold them for that.'

'Godsakes, Natalie,' Don told her, 'there have been three fire outbreaks in the past twenty-four hours, all deliberately started. The tanker is due in harbour today carrying twenty thousand tons of LPG that could go up like a bomb and flatten the entire town if a spark got to it. Maybe these friends of yours are innocent, but I can't take the risk. So far as I'm concerned it's safer for everyone if they stay locked up through the weekend. Monday the tanker will have gone and a judge will let them go maybe.'

Numerous groups on the web carried details of the latest tremors. Special interest user groups were monitoring seismographs in the region and subscribers like Ray Burns were able to watch the needle traces in real time. There were cameras mounted to observe a number of the Cumbre Vieja vents, but none covering the harbour at Santa Cruz. Information relating to the tsunami therefore emerged only patchily.

Ray Burns subscribed to several web notice-boards hosted by the science groups on which updates of activity on La Palma were posted.

Returning from a foray into town to smarten up for the parade, he checked his computer and noticed flags up on his screen. It took him some minutes to reach the most dramatic posting:

Hey, all you folks on the East Coast! Check out the latest from the new DART buoy! Then go to www.santacruzdelapalma.sp to read about the flooding there. Time to head for the hills or what?

Ellsworthy, Maine. Midday. The private jet flared out and touched its wheels to the tarmac of the small airstrip. It had been leased for the trip at a discount from a West Coast media combine in return for exclusive access. K. Zamos was still negotiating the details as he came down the steps, a phone pressed to his ear. 'It's the big one, the biggest. Yeah, the King himself will feature for certain, definitely. He's setting the whole deal up, for Christ sakes,' he yelled into the handset.

With him he had brought a four-man camera team pulled off a film set and Carly, a hotshot writer with *Dude and Rude*, Zamos's personal fiefdom and currently also his personal assistant, plus a shitload of cash. All were red-eyed from the long flight, snappy and stressed. A lot was riding on this gig and not only money. Careers were at stake. Theirs. Pull this one off and they would be made for life. Blow it and they were through.

Zamos was going out on a limb for the King. Correction, he was going out on a limb for the Gimp, whose dream this had been. It was a house of cards founded on the obsession of a crippled wave rider with a busted knee and a wild theory. It was crazy, but fortunes had been wrung from dreams before. The whole surfing business was a gamble anyway.

It was Zamos's fervent belief, his prayer literally – he had been on his knees in the toilet during the flight – that the King had one more punch left in him, one more epic effort that would send him to his grave a legend for all time.

A red roadster left the apron and shot towards the aircraft. The top was down and the wind blew the driver's black hair out behind her in a shining sheet. Dark angel, the image flashed through K. Zamos's mind.

'So what's this?' red-headed Carly snarled under her breath. 'Where's the limo?'

The Jaguar squealed to a halt at the foot of the steps and the driver pushed back her sunglasses. 'K. Zamos, welcome to Maine. Natalie Maxwell, your personal transport. Step in.' She patted the leather passenger seat. 'There's a van for the rest of the crew. Sorry I can't fit you all in, guys.'

'We figured first to send you all to the Inn,' Natalie shouted as the car shot away across the tarmac. 'Then we thought, no, for you guys something special.'

'Whatever.' Zamos was dismissive. This was business after all. 'Where's the King?'

'Tied up. You'll be seeing him later.'

She took him the back way around town. They rattled over the bridge at Indian Point and she dropped a gear and stamped the throttle. The low-profile tyres scrabbled for grip in the dust as the power burst through and the red car tore howling up the narrow road.

The woods closed in, shading out the sun. A mile further on the entrance to a private road opened discreetly. Lodge gates flashed past as she took the corner in a shower of gravel without slackening speed. Pines gave way to ancient oaks and beeches; the air became cooler. The drive opened out into a shaded turning circle fronting a century-old mansion. She braked the car exactly in line with the portico.

'Don't bother with your bags. They'll be taken care of.'

Zamos took in the house, the gardens, the view and the private beach. He looked at the girl. 'I'll bet,' he grinned, 'you call this place a cottage.'

'Exactly right,' she agreed. 'All our other houses are much, much larger.'

The Gimp was frantic. He and the King were still in jail. Natalie had sent in a phone and she was working on getting them a lawyer, but it was the weekend and Don was playing hardball.

'See that Zamos stays away from town. If he talks to anybody and learns the King is locked up the deal is dead in the water!' the Gimp told her, his voice sharp with urgency, when she phoned to report.

'He's impatient. He wants to know why you haven't called him already.'

'I'll call him very soon. Now you know what you have to do next.'

Her hand shook as she ended the call and dialled the number he had given her. She was getting further into this than she had ever bargained for.

A voice answered, 'Aviation Rentals. How can I help you today?'

She took a deep breath. 'Hi, I need a helicopter . . .'

The Lobsterman. Two p.m. Down on the Neck, Jean-Alice gulped from a mug of coffee behind the counter. She had hired four extra staff for the weekend, two in the kitchen and two on the tables, and still they were being run off their feet. The big rush had started at eleven when the first tourists hit the Neck for the mid-morning snack or brunch depending on if they were early risers or not. By twelve the lunch crowd were forming a line outside. Since then there hadn't been a minute to draw breath that Jean-Alice could remember.

'So long as they picked up the guys that started it, that's all that matters,' she said to Rick.

Rick made no comment. Natalie had left a dozen messages on his voicemail that he was so far ignoring. Who had been picked up or why was Don's business and he was determined to stay out of it. 'I guess we won't know for definite till the forensic reports come through.'

'Meanwhile any news of those visitors missing in Maple Cove?' Jean-Alice asked.

'Nope.' Rick shook his head. 'We had the woman's brother in this morning, come to help look for his sister. He is all broken up. Seems like they were very close, twins almost. Don and I drove him out to the cove, showed him the car and the bikes. Then he wanted to meet with Abby. She was crying; she's convinced if only she had notified the cops earlier when the couple failed to show it might have made a difference. But like Don said to her she gets no-shows and failed bookings all the time. How was she supposed to know?'

'What's the brother going to do?'

'He says he'll stay till something turns up. Abby found a slot for him at the motel.' Rick heaved a sigh. 'Like you say, they're gone and they're not ever coming back.'

'I guess it means they were caught in the wash from some ship, the same one that swamped the boats in the harbour. The first day of their vacation too, poor people.'

Rick was devouring a steak sandwich at a stool at the end of the counter next the kitchen hatch. The locals end it was called. Jean-Alice tried to keep a place there for friends who worked around the Neck. The whole of downtown was crammed with visitors and there was a line of people waiting to eat outside every establishment in town today.

Jean-Alice left him to attend to the customers. Rick wiped his neck. He was short on sleep with a long day ahead still. The fire had been put out, but it had taken four appliances and much of the night. A communications mast had been lost but the power sheds had survived. Now all that was left was a smouldering scar in the forest and a badly spooked town.

Today's parade would go ahead, starting with a minute's silence for the missing couple from New York. Rick had already cleared it with Mr Schaffer. He was touched, he said. The search for his sister and her boyfriend was still continuing along the coast north and south and on the outer islands. Tomorrow a Coastguard underwater team would begin diving in the Gurge.

Meanwhile there were still no whales being sighted and *Pequod*'s sailing had been cancelled for the second day running. None of the fishermen had seen any sign even of a dolphin and Patsy was in despair even though Rick pointed out that Saturday of Founders' Week was a poor day for passengers.

'All the tourists will be staying ashore to enjoy the action here.'

'Darn the tourists! It's my whales I care about; something's scared them off their feeding grounds and I'm damned if I know what it is.'

285

The TV over the bar was showing sport highlights, but the noise in the place was so loud it was impossible to hear. The news bar at the bottom of the screen spoke of casualties in the Canary Islands. Somehow all that seemed old and stale now.

Jean-Alice returned. 'Another beer?' Without waiting for an answer she slid a bottle across and laid her arms on the counter facing him. 'Just between friends,' she said, dropping her voice to avoid being overheard, 'looks like there's some repair work needed on your engagement.'

Rick's jaw hardened. She saw and put a gentle hand on his. 'You and I go way back. Remember when you used to scuffle around in here on your butt as a toddler? So I can say what has to be said. Are you just going to hang about like a sick dog while she makes hay with surfers?'

He shrugged moodily. 'If that's who she wants it's her choice,' he muttered, looking away.

'And that's it? Doesn't sound like you to give up without a fight. You always used to be the other way. Or is there something going on with you and Sarah Hunter the way people say?'

She saw the coldness come down over his eyes like a shutter. There were parts of him that would always be out of reach to her. 'Okay,' she apologised, 'I'm sorry, none of my business.'

There was a long pause before he spoke. 'Sarah's taking her revenge for things that happened between us a long time ago. That's all back in the past and neither of us can change what's been and done. If Natalie chooses to take the stuff Sarah's spreading seriously that's up to her.'

Jean-Alice looked relieved. 'It's your life. Just thought I'd give it a shot.'

The noise level in the diner increased as she spoke. Whale Morrissey barged through the door. He saw Rick and surged over with a cheerful bellow. A man in a white sun hat who had been occupying the next-door stool pushed some money across the counter and vacated his seat hurriedly.

'Thanks, bud.' The Whale plumped his mountainous bulk down. 'Boy, it sure is a scorcher today!' he gasped. Sweat was pouring off his face in cataracts. 'Hi, Rick. Say, Jeannie, you got ten pounds of ice?'

'What do you want it in?'

'A bucket of beer!' His belly laugh boomed through the diner. 'No, just bring a glass of the stuff and tip it down here.' He held open his shirt. 'Cool me off!'

'Jump in the harbour would be better,' Jean-Alice shot back, pushing a foaming glass mug across the counter.

Whale gulped and wiped his hand across his mouth. 'Man, I needed that. Hottest day of the year, I reckon.'

'So is Don Egan going to charge those two surfers or what?' Jean-Alice remarked.

The Whale was studying the specials board. 'How's that?' he asked distractedly.

'I said is Don going to charge those surfers with fire-raising?' Jean-Alice repeated and the Whale rolled his great shoulders.

'Hey, we all know Don. He's an easy-going sort of a guy most of the time, but once he gets an idea in his head it stays in there.'

A grizzled old lobsterman sitting across the counter had picked up on their conversation. 'The surfers show up here and we have three fires in two days. You call that coincidence? Jail's the best place for those kind of people.'

Jean-Alice pushed back a stray strand of hair. 'Beats me why anyone would want to do something that dumb, start a fire in the forest.'

The old man bared yellowed teeth wolfishly. 'Who knows what their kind think? Trouble-makers is what they are. Lock 'em up and good riddance, I say.'

'Maybe they were planning to have a barbecue or something,' Rick suggested mildly.

The Whale snorted. 'Try telling that to Don. One of the guys picked up was the one with the limp. I seen him hanging around this town before. What's he want with this place? Can someone answer me that?'

Rick got up to go. 'Parade's coming up. So long, Jeannie. See you up at the start line, okay, Whale?'

'Sure, be right with you, Rick. Jeannie, gimme a roll with a big juicy piece of lobster meat inside, will ya? Hell, make that two rolls. Gotta keep my strength up today.'

288

'Coming up, Whale.' Jean-Alice yelled the order through the hatch. 'Rick.' She ducked out under the counter and followed him to the door. 'Listen,' she muttered, catching his arm, 'that stuff I was saying back there. Don't take it too hard. Hang in there, kiddo. Natalie's a fine young woman, just a little wild at times. I guess it's hard feeling tied down, I wouldn't know.'

Rick gave her hand a quick squeeze. 'Thanks for that. It's good to know there's someone who sticks up for her.'

'Dolt.' Jean-Alice hugged him back. 'It's you I'm sticking up for. I don't want to see you hurt.'

'Goodness, it's hot.' Jessica Gardiner, Lloyd's mother, fanned herself. 'I wish we were out on the river again instead of stuck downtown.'

'It's so close,' Julie her friend sighed. 'I'm sure there'll be a storm tonight. Everyone says the weather has to break soon.'

So far as the Indian Patch children were concerned, the biggest hit of the day was the troupe of stilt walkers specially brought down over the border from Quebec. Lloyd Gardiner had counted six differently costumed figures tottering over the crowds on Bay Road. There was a splendid witch, a drooling-fanged vampire, Uncle Sam with his striped pants, even a Princess Diana, and Lloyd's personal favourite, a male dressed all in black with a great sweep's hat.

The sweep fascinated Lloyd. The actor had a cunning trick of ducking out of sight behind trees or down side streets, hiding himself away, then suddenly popping out again somewhere completely unexpected. The fellow must know every inch of the town around the harbour. Even Goodwill locals were amazed by his cunning.

His narrow black trousers clung to his stilts and his tailcoat was theatrically threadbare so that he appeared gaunt as a scarecrow. His energy though was phenomenal; he pranced and whirled and stooped and sprang up again, plucking at people's hats or tapping their backs with his long cane. While the rest of the troupe swayed elegantly among the throng, graciously bowing when addressed, the sweep by contrast was impish and mischievous, calling to them in a mocking French accent. He took particular delight in teasing the surfers, tugging at their tangled hair with bony fingers, spinning away wildly before they could catch him.

He seemed especially amused by Lloyd. Whenever they met, which was often because the boy stalked him constantly, his manic laugh would ring out and a leering grimace twist his grease-painted mask. 'Aie, aiee, munchkin, where have you been?' Lloyd would pretend not to notice the swaying figure sliding up behind him, only to squeal with pretended alarm as the white-painted fingers closed on his shoulder.

The harbour was filling up with sailboats, all kinds from dinghies to twenty-five-metre schooners belonging to New York bankers. Pride of place went to *Elise 2*, Elliott Maxwell's $20 motor yacht now berthed at the Yacht Club dock. Elliott was club president and marshal of the regatta. His boat served as judges' vessel for the races. She was a handsome enough craft, but it was an absurd amount of money to pay for a boat, let alone the running costs. Natalie refused to go aboard any more; she said it gave her claustrophobia.

The parade was slated to kick off at four p.m., but events were pushing it behind schedule. One was the arrival of the gas tanker. As Rick was leaving the Neck he saw through the haze off Long Island the silhouette of a large vessel standing in towards the Sound.

He called Jack Pearl.

'Is that the gas tanker I can see? I thought the company cancelled on us when they heard about the fire last night.'

Jack made a weary expletive as if he had asked that same question. 'They did and now they've changed their minds. Don't ask me why. The ship will anchor in the Sound as arranged and, assuming no more bonfires, discharge of cargo will commence tomorrow morning.'

'Why not start tonight?'

'Because they want to be sure the place isn't going to catch alight again, they say.'

'Discharge will take, what, six hours?'

'Did the last time that I recall.'

'So if they start at eight they'll be through by two. Meaning they're aiming to sail on the afternoon tide, nicely screwing up the finals of the regatta.'

'I worked that out too.'

'Well, thanks a bundle for letting me know, Jack. Now I'd better tell Elliott Maxwell the good news.'

By custom the parade formed up in the supermarket parking lot by the bridge over Indian Creek. Many floats were recycled year after year, but an awful lot of work went in all the same, cleaning, patching and redesigning. This year's theme was history, appropriate since it was the town's tercentenary. Beth Robbins and Mrs Mather, who coached drama at the high school, had run up between them some pretty authentic-looking examples of seventeenth-century costumes.

Before the floats set off, Rick called for a minute's silence. Everyone taking part bowed their heads while Rick read out the name of Randall Baines and Kimberly Schaffer. A solemn moment.

By tradition the parade was headed by the band followed by the town's fire department, engines polished and gleaming. This year Rick and his cousins had elected to go for a float of their own featuring *Pequod* instead of joining in with the Bearskin Neck association of traders. Rick had borrowed a low-loader from Chance Greene and with Paul and Magnus made a mock-up of an old-time whaleboat pursuing a very lifelike Moby Dick. The scrapwood boat

had sails and sheets and looked properly professional and the whale was painted white with a
figure of Captain Ahab, complete with false leg,
clinging to its head.

The drivers climbed into their cabs and
started their engines. The band were poised,
sweating in their costumes, instruments at the
ready. The cheerleaders thrust their shoulders
back. The drum majorettes lifted their batons.
The parade marshal gave the signal, and with a
roll of drums and led by the flag, the parade
moved off.

Overhead a blue-and-yellow helicopter circled
in the sky, filming the scene. It wheeled and
dipped, the sun flashing on its canopy, before
skimming away out over the Sound.

Out at Maple Cove, Ray Burns was preparing a
comparison chart. Assuming that a tsunami
travelled at a constant speed of approximately
550 miles per hour as most authorities agreed,
and took five hours to cross the Atlantic, then a
wave generated by a tremor in the Canaries at
say eight a.m. local time would reach the coast of
Maine at one p.m. Canary time, which given a
five-hour time zone difference would be
eight a.m. Eastern Standard Time. So allowing
for adjustments of international time zones a
tsunami triggered in the Canaries would impact
in New England at precisely the same time of
day.

The calculation could be done both ways. If

an incident occurred in Goodwill Sound at say six-thirty p.m., then it should be possible to link it back to a seismic event on the other side of the ocean that took place at a similar time.

Using as his source the official incident recordings published by government monitoring sites, Ray constructed a list of every significant tremor and eruption posted during the current crisis. Take, for instance, the unexplained wavers or series of waves that had apparently struck the Sound on Thursday evening. Could they be linked back to a corresponding incident on La Palma recorded at a similar hour?

The answer was chilling. Seismic charts for the island showed a distinct peak in activity at around that time when fresh eruptions burst out.

But that surely was coincidence. It had to be.

Chapter 26

From the cabin of the helicopter the view was spectacular. The air was clear and every island and inlet in the Sound was revealed spread out below in perfect detail. Natalie could pick out her father's boat, a fat white blob over by the Yacht Club, and the crowds lining Bay Road for the parade. Rick would be down there with his float. She felt a pang of guilt at not being with him and Reb.

K. Zamos and the cameramen were happy as a bunch of schoolkids. This was what they had come to see. The helicopter was large and well equipped. It needed to be to take all these people. The cost was something she was blocking out. She had charged it to her dad's account. Her life seemed to have slipped a gear somehow, leaving her adrift.

Zamos was giving instructions to the pilot telling him to fly back down the Sound. 'I want to check out that bank at the entrance by the cliffs. What do you call it again?' he shouted to Natalie above the racket of the engine.

'The Reef. Here they call it the Reef. The bottom drops away sharply, like an underwater precipice.' The Gimp had emphasised this in his briefing over the phone. 'Make sure he gets a good look. Point out how the water changes colour, how that indicates the steep dropaway.'

But Zamos didn't need explanations. He had the chart and could read it. 'Man,' he was saying to Carly, 'check out those depth markings. The seabed falls away like a wall.'

'See the contour lines beyond? That's an underwater canyon running all the way out to the abyssal plain. It's incredible; as if someone took an axe to the continental shelf.'

In the row behind the cameramen were discussing angles and light values. 'Hey,' one said suddenly, 'where did that come from?'

They all looked. He was pointing to a swiftly moving line – a dark smudge against the smooth blue – speeding landwards from the Reef.

'Looks like the making of a heavy swell.'

They all watched.

'Growing stronger,' someone said.

'Six foot easy.'

'That's solid. Man, wish I was down there in the water right now with my blade.'

'Gary,' Zamos rapped, 'get a shot of this.'

'Camera is running.'

Natalie watched spellbound. As the helicopter

wheeled again, turning to give its passengers a better view, Curtain Bluff came into her field of vision through the starboard side windows. Inexorably the line of the swell bore down on the white cliffs. 'Impact!' one of the cameramen shouted exultantly as a burst of white spray blossomed silently at the rock face.

Natalie bit her tongue.

She checked her watch. Time to be heading back.

She shouted to the pilot, 'Okay, we're done. Take us back in.'

The cameraman heard her. 'Speak for yourself, lady. We're not wrapped up here yet.'

'I'm not sure we have fuel?' she looked at the pilot.

He glanced at the gauges. 'I can give you fifty minutes, an hour maybe.'

'Fine,' Zamos said.

Natalie thought rapidly. 'Set me down on the Neck, then. There's a pad by the marina.'

'I know it.'

'You're leaving us?' Zamos said, surprised.

'I have stuff to do. You guys carry on filming. The pilot will drop you off at the Point when you're done. I'll meet you there.'

Zamos's gaze narrowed. 'Bring the King with you this time.'

'I'll tell him that,' she promised.

'I'll spell it out. He doesn't show, the deal's off.'

* * *

Goodwill Sound. Elliott Maxwell never attended the Founders' Day parade, regarding it as a noisy irrelevance to the only important part of the weekend, which was the Yacht Club regatta. The only worthwhile event of the entire summer so far as he was concerned, to which everything else was subordinate.

He stood at ease on *Elise 2*'s stern deck under the awning in his best white linen trousers and a shirt of sea-island cotton. It was too hot for the blue blazer. Although the sun was not yet over the yardarm champagne was being served to his fellow committee members in silver goblets inherited from his grandfather and engraved with the Maxwell monogram. The pre-regatta drinks party hosted by the club president on board his vessel was a century-old tradition.

'Darling, *so* good of you both to come,' his wife's voice swooped and fell as she passed among the guests in the main saloon. 'And such a glorious *day*! So much cooler out on the water.' The French doors to the stern had been thrown open, allowing a large party to circulate. Dress code for the women was casual, interpreted as understated elegance with minimal jewellery. Elise herself had upstaged everybody in a floaty silk dress from Milan, but then she was the hostess and it was her boat. Elliott regarded her with satisfaction. His wife was beautiful and fascinating still and on the whole compliant where his wishes were concerned, unlike his daughter. He sighed. Where the devil was Natalie?

Mindy McNeil, Cole's mother, had just asked the same question. 'And Rick is such a nice young man too,' she added brightly. 'I do hope everything is okay.'

Elise's blue eyes narrowed. Mindy's sugary sweetness was not lost on her. The woman had obviously picked up on the gossip going round. Natalie's erratic behaviour was becoming increasingly difficult to explain.

Fortunately little Izzy Jenks, Rick's second cousin or whatever she was, chose this moment to appear with a tray of canapés.

'Natalie will be joining us shortly. At the moment she is ashore helping with the parade,' Elise was able to respond having taken a mouthful. 'She has a great many friends in town.'

From the helicopter the picture was confused. Another swell line was moving on up the Sound with breakers observable on the beaches of the outer islands, but at the same time its shape was becoming less distinct. The camera team was divided over what was happening. Gary pointed to white water along the northern shore between Curtain Bluff and Maple Cove. 'Like the right-hand edge of the swell is speeding up, moving ahead of the rest.'

'There are ships down there,' Zamos observed.

Natalie was peering over his shoulder. 'The big vessel out in midstream is a tanker carrying liquid gas for the power station.'

'And the smaller one to the left?'

'*Elise 2*, a private yacht.'

'Some yacht. Who's the owner?'

Natalie kept silent. Red-haired Carly shot her a shrewd look. 'Your daddy's, huh?'

Natalie shrugged. 'He enjoys his toys.'

Zamos chortled. 'Better get on the horn to him. Looks like they're in for stormy water down there.'

The pilot was squinting through the Perspex windshield. 'Here's the marina coming up.'

Natalie had her plans in motion. Thank God for cellphones. She keyed the number of Brandie, the girl from California whose partner Mel rode the big bike. 'Time to roll! Round up the gang!' she shouted into the handset as the helicopter circled over the harbour. 'Have them meet at the corner of Bay Road. Yeah, that's the place. Everyone you can find. The King's instructions! And bring chains!'

The parade was getting into its stride. The lead floats were almost level with the entrance to Bay Road and crowd turnout was great in spite of the baking heat. The band was playing with gusto, attracting enthusiastic applause. Beth Robbins had organised clowns to pass out candy along the route, which was making the kids happy. Fruit might have been better for their teeth, but heck, it was a parade for heaven's sake.

Rick drove carefully, keeping his speed to a crawl. The longer they could spin out the afternoon the better. People were saying this was a record turnout. A successful Founders' Day weekend set the tone for the rest of the season. For a town like Goodwill, dependent for much of its income on attracting visitors, that was vital.

His phone beeped with a message and he scanned it, keeping one hand on the wheel. No text, just a picture. The bright sun made it hard to figure what it was. That was the downside of these tiny phones with their two-inch screens. It was like squinting through a keyhole in bad light. Whatever it was would keep for later.

They rolled on at a snail's pace. Rick waved to people on the sidewalk, calling out to friends. A helicopter lifted off from the harbour and went skimming away up the Sound. Some friend of the Maxwells most probably dropping in for cocktails on the yacht. Up ahead, the stilt walkers hired to entertain the visitors bobbed jerkily above the heads of the crowd like oversized string puppets.

The downdraught from the helicopter whipping her hair round her face, Natalie Maxwell ran along the dock from the marina helipad onto Bearskin Neck. 'Brandie!' she shouted into her phone. 'Are you guys ready?'

'And waiting, kiddo. Where are you now?'

'On my way. Where's the parade?'

'I have the band in sight.'

'Then let the show commence.'

* * *

Downtown Sheena Dubois was out on the street with her camcorder taping interviews. Folks were having a good time. No one seemed much bothered about the tsunami risk. 'Lady, with three thousand miles of God's green ocean between us and that volcano or whatever it is, me, I sleep soundly.'

Sheena grabbed an iced tea from a stall at the bottom of the Green and headed off west in the direction of Indian Point Bridge to meet up with the parade. Pausing at the corner of the road, she shot some clips of the crowd by the old Ice Factory where a pair of stilt walkers made a pleasing tableau with a family of kids. It gave her a jolt to spot Tab Southwell, Doc's son, in the viewfinder. He was all on his own and had a lost look. Doc had told her the boy was upset, blaming himself for letting down the missing tourist couple. Sheena would have liked to go over and chat with him a moment, maybe cheer him up, but she felt awkward. What was the etiquette for introducing yourself to your lover's son?

You need to end this thing, girl, she told herself, not for the first time. It's bad for you, bad for the boy, bad for Donna. The only one enjoying himself is Doc.

On Bay Road the whistle and thump of the band was growing louder. Lloyd Gardiner looked up at the soot-blackened face of the stilt walker and laughed. The face grinned back. '*Pas beaucoup de*

302

temps maintenant! Not long to wait now, my *leetle* friend!' he cackled.

Lloyd's sister, Betsy, waved to the princess figure across the road. The families had secured a good position from which to watch the parade on the harbour side of Bay Road by the old Ice Factory. At their backs the fairground rides were temporarily deserted as the crowds crammed on the sidewalks to cheer the floats. Peering round the stilt walker's legs, Lloyd glimpsed the sun flashing on the band's instruments as the music drew closer. From behind came deep hooting horns – the ships in the harbour joining in the chorus. Everyone was cheering, clapping, waving hats, throwing streamers.

His mom had tight hold of both children by the hand. 'The sweep will look out for me!' Lloyd protested, but she hung on all the same. 'Those boats!' she yelled. 'Such a noise!'

'Here, son,' Dad said. 'Ride on my shoulders. You'll see better.' He swung the boy lightly up. Lloyd was thrilled. He could see the entire band now spread out in formation with the lead floats following. He was almost on a level with the sweep.

More spectators were crowding up to the corner, wanting to catch a glimpse of the approaching band. Lloyd could feel people pushing against them from behind. A couple of dudes in board shorts were trying to shoulder through to the front. His dad turned and said sharply, 'Hey, mind who you're shoving, feller, there are kids here.'

Goodwill Sound. On the bridge of the SS *Marie-Sainte*, a Quebec-registered bulk LPG tanker, Captain Roland Leclerc conferred with the pilot on the approach into Goodwill Sound. Leclerc was a French-Canadian with twelve years' service in the merchant marines of Canada and the US. This was his third year in command of the *Marie-Sainte* and by now he was almost as familiar with the channels as the pilot.

Almost but not quite. Al Smither, a Down Easterner from Portland, was ten years older than the Canadian with a lifetime's learning on this coast. He had piloted boats and ships in and out of harbour from Boston to Halifax in all weathers and there wasn't a channel or a bank, a reef or a current that he couldn't follow in his sleep. He had seen it all and then some, he liked to say.

'The yachts are crowding the channel,' Leclerc observed studying the vista before them. The bridge was 100 feet exactly above the water-line. It had to be high to see over the bulbous white tanks that squatted on the ship's mid-section, tanks holding enough liquefied gas to fuel the town for five years. Only a fraction of her cargo was destined for Goodwill, the rest would be offloaded at Portland. From this height there was an excellent view of the inner Sound currently jammed with yachts and pleasure craft. Leclerc's professional eye automatically registered several larger vessels among them, including the catamaran ferry from St John, Nova Scotia, the *Pequod* at her usual berth, and a big motor yacht off their port quarter that looked as if she was waiting for the tanker to pass before getting under way herself. Safety regulations required all vessels within a half-mile radius of the gas tanker to heave to until the latter was safely berthed. A Coastguard cutter proceeding ahead of the tanker was present to enforce compliance.

Al Smither shifted the gum he was chewing to the side of his mouth. 'Regatta,' he said simply. He was a man of few words. Some trips Leclerc had passed an entire day up here on the bridge without a single exchange between them of a non-professional nature.

Abruptly the pilot stiffened. 'Watch your course!' he snapped to the helmsman. The electronic position indicator on the screen directly before the pilot had slipped a fraction of a point to portside.

The helmsman touched the wheel delicately. The ship weighed 20,000 tons, small for a bulk tanker but huge in the confined waters of the Sound. All her control systems, speed, heading, power, were computer controlled. The men were only present to make tiny adjustments within parameters set by the software. And to take over in an emergency. Left to itself the ship's electronic brain was perfectly capable of bringing

305

the *Marie-Sainte* safely up the deep-water channel to its designated berth alongside the outer mole. Leclerc and the pilot were mere observers. If there had been a genuine need to adjust the course the computer would have foreseen it minutes ago and made the alteration. It might not even have bothered to inform the bridge. In a real sense, Leclerc thought sadly, mariners were becoming redundant. The next generation of vessels would sail without the trouble and expense of crews.

'*Capitaine*!' the helmsman's voice interrupted his thoughts. Leclerc glanced, not at him or at the view outside, but at the control screen, in itself a measure of his own reliance on electronics. A red warning indicator had appeared and beneath it a terse message: SPEED OVER GROUND 0.5 KT.

Leclerc's senses came instantly alert, digesting and analysing the meaning behind that bald statement. *Marie-Sainte*'s forward speed, currently limited to a crawling two knots, was falling away faster than the computerised engine management system could cope with. Instinctively his eye flicked to the power indicators. Both engines were at their minimum rev settings. No warning signals were being received from the slowly rotating screws under the hull. The rudders were still amidships as they were meant to be. The engines were not overheating; fuel was flowing normally; gears were working smoothly.

The likeliest cause was a strong current flowing outwards from the Sound, as might be met for instance when the tide was running out. The extra resistance would account for the slowing of the ship's forward progress. Except that this was high water, the current should be flowing into the Sound, not out.

A second later, while all these thoughts were still passing through his mind, another light flashed up, accompanied this time by an audible warning, a definite signal of unease on the part of the computer. A new message appeared on the screen: DEPTH 2.0 METRES.

Leclerc's attention sharpened instantly. The echo locator beneath the bow had registered a sudden rise in the seabed ahead. The ship was not about to run aground, not yet, but the preset margin of safety under the keel had been reached.

And as if this was not enough, the warning buzzer sounded again, a different note this time, and a third message joined the others on the screen: COURSE ERROR 3 DEGREES PORT. On the approach map the icon representing the vessel was edging off the designated track. A fourth message underneath the third added detail: RATE OF DRIFT 0.5 KT.

The GPS receivers that continually updated the ship's position to within a metre had detected that she was being offset sideways through the water, a movement known as drift. The strong counter-current coupled with slow forward momentum was causing the *Marie-Sainte* to lose steerageway, allowing her bow to fall off. So now a third complication had been introduced.

Captain Leclerc glanced towards the pilot. He was in an awkward position. Under maritime law and the laws of the United States of America in whose waters he was sailing, control of the ship's handling was vested in the pilot with his specialised knowledge and experience of these confined waters. In a wider sense, however, responsibility was still the captain's. If he, Leclerc, had good reason to feel that the ship was being mishandled and failed to act promptly to rectify it then he might find himself being charged with negligence. Further than that, for Leclerc to stand by and watch his beloved command being put at risk was more than he could bear.

Fortunately, however, he and Smither had worked together on this route for a number of years and the Canadian had formed a high opinion of the pilot's judgement. The position was serious and their options limited. The ship was losing speed, probably as a result of an unusual tidal flow in the channel. The obvious solution was to increase power, but the sudden loss of depth ruled this out on safety grounds.

To underline the urgency of the situation an alarm from a different quarter now broke in. The officer on watch in the starboard wing of the bridge called out suddenly, '*Capitaine*, look over there on the harbour, smoke!'

The parade column was temporarily stalled on lower Bay Road. Rick had a two-way radio in addition to his phone that was supposed to link him in with the other Selectmen and marshals. When he tried to contact Chance Greene up in the lead vehicle all he got was static.

He switched off his engine to let it cool and wiped his face. It was still hot as hell. The crowd was getting bored and starting to drift away down towards the harbour. He remembered the picture message on his phone and called it back up, hunching over the screen to shut out the glare. He swore softly, angrily. The image was perfectly plain now. An interior shot of what might have been a party. A big couch and on it Natalie sitting next to a surfer.

'Shit!' He flung the phone across the cab in a rage. It bounced off the far door and fell into the foot well.

'What's the matter?'

He looked up furiously. Reb was standing by the window. 'I came down to see what was stalling us,' she said. 'What happened, did you drop your phone?'

'Yes, dammit,' Rick said gritting his teeth. He wasn't about to confess to the snapshot message, not yet anyhow.

'Is it working okay?'

'I don't know. Screen stays dark. I must have broken it, damn.'

'It's on the business, isn't it? In that case we have insurance. You can order a replacement, maybe upgrade to a newer model at the same time.'

'A new model is about right,' he said savagely.

His sister frowned. 'Come again?'

'Jesus, I don't know what's going on any more.'

She looked at him worriedly. 'Natalie?'

He grimaced. 'Some anonymous caller with my best interests at heart, hah.' Briefly he told her about the photo.

Reb's breath hissed through her teeth. 'Sometimes this can be a very small town.'

'Yeah, well, right now there are a couple of guys I wouldn't miss.'

His radio crackled afresh at that moment. Chance Greene's voice came through sounding angry. Rick pressed the transmit button. 'I'm back in the float. What's the matter?'

There was another burst of static. Round about people in the crowd were moving up towards where the band should be, craning their heads to see what was going on. The music seemed to have stopped, Rick realised. He turned off the engine and opened the door of the cab. 'I'm going up to see what the problem is,' he said to Reb. 'Take over for me, will you?'

He jogged along the column. Several other drivers were doing likewise. When they reached

310

the head of the parade a mass of people were jammed together. 'Selectman, let me through please,' he called. He felt a hand on his shoulder, turned and saw Sheena with her camcorder.

'I'm right behind you,' she said.

'What's cooking, do you know?'

'It's a sit-down.'

'A what?'

'The surfers, they're blocking the road up ahead. You'll see.'

On Bay Road the band had finally come into view, followed by the lead fire appliance. Loud cheers broke from the waiting crowd, which increased as the first floats appeared round the bend. The fire volunteers rang their bells in appreciation and waved back to their supporters.

Lloyd Gardiner was cheering with the best of them when all of a sudden the two surfers crowding behind them shoved him and his dad roughly aside and sprinted out into the roadway. Others followed, guys and girls linking hands to form a line across the road in the path of the firemen. For a moment the crowd cheered, thinking it was all part of the entertainment. Then as more surfers emerged from the throng to take their places squatting on the ground in front of the lead truck, the cheers died away to be replaced by laughter.

'What's going on?' Lloyd tugged at his dad's ear.

'I'm not sure, son,' Ted Gardiner said. 'Looks

like some sort of a protest to me. I guess they'll sort things out in a minute or two. Just have to wait and see.'

His wife nudged him. 'What's it all in aid of, can you make out?'

'Search me, hon. They don't seem to have any banners or signs that I can see. Just democracy in action, kids,' he told the children.

The lead elements of the parade had descended into rowdy chaos. There were so many people milling about in front of the fire tender that it was hard to separate out protesters from spectators. Around twenty young kids were squatting in the road in a straggling line, chanting slogans. It was impossible to make out their message amid the noise of people shouting. A boy held a sign up to the crowd with FREE THE GOODWILL 2 scrawled in different-coloured marker pen; one or two others had brought along surfboards which they were using to fend off Don's officers. Meanwhile a girl in her teens had crawled in behind the front wheels of the fire appliance and two of Freddy's men were attempting to drag her out. It looked as though she had chained herself to an axle though. A fireman caught hold of her legs. She kicked out wildly and her shorts slid down, exposing her pale rump. The girl squealed, the crowd roared and the men retreated red-faced.

Rick felt the anger that had been rising inside him beginning to boil over. He rounded on the nearest bunch of surfers. 'Okay, you've had your fun,' he said dangerously. 'This is a hot day and we have a busy programme to get through. If you kids know what's good for you I suggest you haul your sorry asses out of here before tempers get frayed.'

'Yeah, and screw you too, Jack,' an older dude with sun-toughened hide the colour of mahogany and a greying ponytail spat in the dust. 'You let our buds out of jail, we unleash your pretty red pumpmobile, *capisce*?'

More surfers were strolling up to join the protest. Meanwhile the spectators were enjoying the diversion and waiting to see what would happen next. Chance Greene saw Rick and bullied his way over. 'Well, don't just stand there, man. Do something!' He was puce in the face with rage.

Rick stood his ground. 'This is a job for Don's people,' he snapped back. 'The law can deal with it.'

Flecks of spittle showed at the corners of the developer's mouth. 'Are you blind or what? You don't know who is behind this? Take a look around you, man!'

At that same moment someone with a loud-hailer started up a chant: 'What do we want?'

The protesters on the ground supplied the answer. 'We want the King!'

'What do we want?'

'The King! The King! Free the King!'

It was a rehearsed routine and the cheerleader with the megaphone was Natalie. She had scrambled onto the hood of the tender and was standing legs astride, head thrown back, hair wild, haranguing the spellbound tourists. 'We're sorry to spoil your parade, folks, but we need your help. Why? Because two friends of ours have been thrown in jail.'

A buzz of excitement ran through her listeners. This was drama. 'Why?' someone, a man, called out.

'You ask why?' Natalie shouted back, her eyes flashing. 'That's what we ask too. No charges laid, no legal access. A corrupt town council and a—'

She got no further. With a bellow of fury Chance Greene launched himself at the tender, pulling her down and tearing the megaphone from her hands. Three surfers seated nearby jumped on him and wrestled it back. Larry Hageman waded in to separate the fighting parties. Natalie was knocked flying against the tender and slid to the ground.

Rick felt as if his chest was about to burst with rage and frustration. Swearing out loud under his breath, he plunged into the melee, caught Natalie by the arm and yanked her to her feet. 'What the blazes do you think you're playing at?' he stormed, barely restraining his temper.

'Let go of me!' She shook him off.

'Dear,' Jessica Gardiner muttered to her husband, 'this is turning ugly. I think we should get the kids away.'

'Just a bit of roughhouse,' he laughed. 'The cops can handle it. Nobody's getting hurt.'

From the sidelines the confrontation seemed to have cooled. The cops contented themselves with keeping marchers and protesters apart. Lloyd Gardiner was growing bored. He looked around him and tugged at the sweep's coat-tails. 'I smell smoke,' he called up importantly.

'*Comment?*'

'I said I can smell smoke,' the boy repeated louder. 'You know, like from a fire, or a cigarette,' he added truthfully.

'*Tu demande une cigarette?*' the sweep cackled, throwing up his painted hands in mock horror. '*Quelle affreux! Mais non, mais non,* you are too young, my *leetle* friend!'

'No, stupid,' Lloyd told him crossly. 'Don't you speak English? I smell smoke!'

'Hey, hey.' His father squeezed his knee. 'That's not very polite. Say sorry to the gentleman.'

There was a crackling sound from somewhere nearby. Lloyd craned round to look. Being up on his dad's shoulders, he had a good view. A thin tendril of dark smoke puffed from a freshly broken window in the front of the big brick building behind them.

'There is smoke. I can see it now!' he cried excitedly.

'What's he saying, Daddy?' His sister tugged at her father's other hand.

'I'm not sure, honey. I don't see the smoke he's talking about.'

'I can smell something though, can't you?' the children's mother chipped in. 'Maybe it's someone cooking hotdogs.'

At that moment uproar broke out.

'It's the old Ice Factory!' a voice shouted. 'It's burning!' Other voices joined in with cries of alarm. The crowd surged this way and that, some moving back from the scene, others pressing forward for a better look. The protesters began unlocking their chains and scrambling hurriedly out of the way.

Jostled from every side, Lloyd clung on tightly to his father's shoulders. The smoke from the broken window thickened, spurting out in thick black greasy coils. More smoke was leaking from cracks and openings in the roof, drifting away in a cloud that grew denser as he watched.

And then the sirens sounded.

Chapter 27

Out on the yacht, Elise was saved from having to answer further questions about her daughter by a cry from the bridge on the deck above. There were answering hails from the men in the stern followed by sounds of running feet.

'What's all that?' a guest asked. 'Did I hear somebody calling fire?'

Mindy peered from a window. 'I can see smoke,' she called in some alarm. 'The wind is carrying it this way.'

'What the devil is going on over there? Can you make it out?' Outside in the stern Elliott Maxwell called up to a crewman on the bridge deck, who was filming the band with a camcorder.

'There's a building on fire, Mr Maxwell. See that smoke over to the left on the harbour?'

The guests crowded to the rail to look. There were more shouts from the bridge above and a throbbing ran through the boat as the main engine kicked in below decks. 'They've drawn up the gangway. Are we pulling out?' a startled woman asked Elise excitedly.

The engines throbbed suddenly. Elise felt the deck tilt beneath her. Glass tinkled and Mindy let out a nervous giggle. 'Oops!' She clutched at the back of a settee. 'Almost forgot my sea legs there.'

Someone on the bridge was volleying urgent orders. Elise recognised the captain's voice, but it was impossible to make out what he was saying above the din. Guests were abandoning their drinks and pushing past one another to get out from the saloon. Through a nearby porthole she saw the harbour front moving by as the bow swung out from the berth.

Aboard the bridge of the *Marie-Sainte* a computerised voice intoned, *'Proximity alert starboard! Four hundred metres!'*

The deep-water channel did not follow the centre line up the Sound, but held towards the northern shore at this point, bringing incoming vessels appreciably close past Two Bush Island. The *Marie-Sainte*'s drift was carrying her near to the rocky outcrop.

The officers in command on the bridge were now being assailed by numerous visual advisories as well as two distinct audible warnings. The ship was losing steerageway and being dragged towards rocks. Increasing speed and putting the wheel over was ruled out by the shoaling water.

Leclerc's mind raced trying to isolate the mechanism responsible for what was happening.

Even more worrying, if that were possible, was the outbreak of fire on the harbour front. The *Marie-Sainte* was nothing less than a floating bomb of highly volatile liquid propane gas. In consequence her firefighting capabilities were state of the art. At a touch of a button from the bridge, Leclerc could drench the entire vessel from end to end with high-pressure foam throwers and water sprays. Strict regulations prohibited the use of a naked flame on or anywhere near the vessel and the same applied to the isolated terminal berth during discharge. Any fire incident in the vicinity of the vessel provoked an immediate emergency shutdown of all vents and valves and full deployment of firefighting crews both on the ship and on land.

Leclerc's gaze swivelled in the direction of the officer's pointing arm. The smoke source appeared to be located on the southern side of the harbour front and the offshore breeze was carrying it towards them. There could be sparks in that smoke and it was imperative that avoiding action be implemented immediately. Leclerc's reaction was instinctive. His hand reached for the red fire alarm button on the instrument panel at his side and he pressed it once. The response was instantaneous: high-pitched bells erupted deafeningly in all parts of the ship. The yellow-suited fire parties already standing by for the docking manoeuvre sprang into action, fanning

319

out along the main deck. At the same time the alarm button triggered the spray circuits, enveloping the huge gas tanks in a curtain of fine water mist to cool the metal and dowse any drifting sparks.

Al Smither had still not spoken, but now he opened his mouth. Leclerc could guess at the order he would give and mentally readied himself. In spite of the seriousness of the position a part of Leclerc's mind was calculating the manner in which the American would frame that command in the most economical way. Sometimes it seemed to him as though the pilot's early life must have been spent in an orphanage run by Trappist monks where every word uttered had incurred a heavy fine. Undoubtedly Smither's upbringing had taught him to hoard each syllable, weighing its expenditure as carefully as another man might spend a banknote.

Before the American could give voice to his decision though, before Leclerc could satisfy his curiosity, there was a further interruption. The second officer claimed their attention again.

'Sir, vessel manoeuvring near the channel!' he called.

On Bay Road, bells were clanging. There were cheers from the crowd as the fire engine released by the protesters pulled away from the line of floats and screeched to a halt outside the burning building. Lloyd thrilled at the sight of the firemen in their helmets and yellow and black protective gear leaping down to uncurl hoses, clipping them to hydrants in the road.

'They're breaking down the doors! They're inside the building, pulling the hoses after them!' From his father's shoulders Lloyd kept up an excited commentary.

'I want to see too! I want to see too!' Betsy Gardiner was jumping up and down trying to get a better view.

'Darling, I just can't lift you any more, you're too heavy. Ted, don't you think we should move back a little out of the way?' Jessica Gardiner urged her husband, keeping her voice calm for fear of alarming the children.

'Gee, I don't see any danger if the kids want to watch,' her husband reassured her. He was enjoying the action as much as they were.

'What about the V-Bs, where have they gotten to?'

Stretching up, he scanned the crowd. 'Brook is right across the road from us. He has Paula with him and Julie. Hi, Jules.' He waved to her. 'Come over and join us!'

Julie was waving back. 'It's safer over here by the ocean,' she signalled laughing.

As one man, Leclerc and Smither swung to focus on the new threat. The motor yacht off the portside, which had been tied up alongside the club jetty a minute ago, was getting under way. She appeared to have dropped her mooring and a wake frothed under her stern as her screws began to bite.

Leclerc had no means of telling if she was a victim of whatever current or tidal flow was affecting his own vessel or was simply putting distance between herself and the fire and there was no time to find out. The yacht's bow was now approximately half a mile distant on a converging course and regulations required both vessels to make an immediate course change to widen the distance between them. This at a moment when the tanker's manoeuvring ability was severely compromised by other factors.

Simultaneously the pilot rapped out the first of his orders. Shifting the gum into his cheek, he opened his mouth and enunciated unhurriedly but clearly, 'All stop.'

Instantly, the executive officer, another French-Canadian, acting with a speed that could only mean he had foreseen the order, rammed the engine control indicator into its central position. The effect of this was not immediate. Unlike an automobile, the tanker possessed no brakes to halt her progress. All that had been done was to decouple the slowly rotating propeller shafts from the turbines. The blades continued to bite at the water and the *Marie-Sainte*'s progress was slowed fractionally, but not halted.

It was a decisive action, however, because it demonstrated how Smither intended to handle the multiple problems that had suddenly arisen.

By taking this action the pilot had increased the range of options open to him. He was slowing the vessel and thus buying himself time. He had also left the way open to engage reverse thrust if it became necessary to check forward momentum completely. He was dealing with the most compelling of the problems facing them: the risk of running aground in shoaling water. The trade-off though was a loss of control, of steerageway, to use the technical term. As expected, Smither now moved to address this problem.

He spoke again out the side of his mouth. 'Engage number one bow thrust half power.'

Leclerc permitted himself a silent nod of approval. This was precisely the action he would have taken himself. He did not say so aloud because it would only distract the other bridge personnel. In the present emergency it was essential that the chain of command remained distinct. Inset into the bows of the tanker on either side were enclosed sideways-thrusting props used for manoeuvring in confined spaces. A similar pair in the stern of the ship assisted the procedure. By means of adroit usage of the thrusters it was possible to turn the vessel around in tight berth approaches.

As if to confirm Leclerc's attitude Smither spoke again. 'Engage number three stern thruster half power.'

Again Leclerc found himself approving. Deprived of steerageway by reduced speed, the American had taken steps to reassert control over the vessel. The power of the starboard bow and stern thrusters would counteract the tug of the current that was threatening to swing them onto the rocks of Two Bush Island.

The navigation screen continued to flash its warning messages. The depth reading remained unchanged. That at least was a positive sign. Smither now moved to reinforce his position. 'Main engines half slow astern,' he ordered.

By this order, which would reverse the thrust of the still slowly revolving shafts of the main screws, the pilot was electing to slow the ship carefully. The fact that he already had his bow and stern thrusters in operation to counter the drag of the current meant that he could afford to disregard the potential for the ship to turn in towards Two Bush Island. He was like a rider confronted with a bolting horse, who grips with his knees and increases the pressure on the bit steadily, reasserting his authority calmly instead of snatching at the reins in a panic.

Leclerc studied the screen. The icon representing the ship's position had steadied, indicating that the bows were no longer swinging, but the rate of drift remained at half a knot. The current must be a strong one to push a 20,000-ton tanker about like a toy boat. He glanced out to his right at the island. The rocks looked very close. As yet though the thrusters were only running at half power.

Reaching down the bridge binoculars, Leclerc focused on the column of smoke rising over the harbour. Spray from the water foggers cooling the gas tanks obscured the view but he could make out figures massing in the road and the flashing lights of emergency vehicles. What in heaven's name was going on across there? Behind him the second officer was on the radio talking urgently on the Coastguard frequency, asking was it safe to proceed to berth?

He checked the screen again. The tanker was almost stationary in the water. Smither had reasserted control, using the side thrusters to counteract the pull of the outward current. The depth sounder had even edged up a little to a point where the warning message disappeared from the screen. For the first time since the start of the emergency Leclerc felt himself start to breathe a little easier.

Smither too was studying the screen and shaking his head slowly from side to side in the manner of a puzzled dog. Leclerc saw his gaze flick to the island off their starboard and back, then the pilot turned towards him. 'What was your draught at St John?' he asked brusquely.

Leclerc shrugged one shoulder, a typically French gesture. 'Seven and one half metres as normal.' His tone was curt. The pilot was implying that the tanker might have been overloaded, causing her to squat in the water and exceed her stated draught.

'The load was the same as always,' he said, meeting the American's eye squarely. 'No change. It has to be the tide.'

Smither held his gaze a moment, then nodded. 'The tide,' he agreed.

There was a cough from the executive officer. '*Oui?*' Leclerc half turned. The man jerked his head at the navigation screen. Leclerc focused his gaze and his eyes narrowed.

The readings were changing. The speed counter was ticking up, 0.5 of a knot, 0.6, 0.7. There could be no doubt: before their eyes the ship was gaining momentum. And another thing: the depth gauge had altered too. It now read 2.5, half a metre more water under the keel than there had been five minutes ago.

Captain and pilot exchanged glances. Leclerc was the first to speak. 'The current must have reversed itself.' It was the only possible explanation that presented itself.

And then, as if to remind them that the danger was not yet over, another voice interjected with the artificial nasal tone of the electronic synthesiser.

'*Collision alert portside! Eight hundred metres closing.*'

In the manual this category of warning was described as 'an imperative action message', meaning it would continue to flash and the alarm keep sounding until action was taken to remedy the situation.

Leclerc was already acting on the instinct instilled from long training. His left hand moved outward and up to the horn button, pressing it hard. Three blasts of compressed air forced through the metal vanes of the horn's brass throat and the Sound throbbed to the deep bass note. This was his response as master, an immediate warning action taken for the safety of his vessel.

The motor yacht now also sounded its horn, the blasts reverberating off the hills. There were figures visible moving urgently on her deck as if preparing to fend off a collision. It looked to Leclerc as though she too was in difficulties, as if the same current that was affecting the tanker had her in its grip. Her speed was still low and she seemed to be having difficulty maintaining steerageway. At a guess she would not be equipped with side thrusters to help her out of her present situation. The strong tidal flow was sucking both vessels inexorably closer to one another.

'*Switching to anti-collision mode!*'

On the *Marie-Sainte*'s bridge the navigation computer had gone into overdrive. Alarm bells were sounding all over the ship. Leclerc wondered how his engine crews were feeling as they heard the watertight doors being slammed shut, trapping them in a steel coffin while the fire bells remained clanging overhead.

'*Collision alert warning portside six hundred metres!*'

Leclerc felt a real shaft of fear twist his stomach. Unless one or other vessel succeeded in pulling off a radical course alteration, it was

inevitable that they would collide with potentially catastrophic consequences.

Elise 2's skipper was Nick Costakis, an ex-US
Coastguard lieutenant-commander with twelve
years' experience handling cutters and small
ships. Nick had a long familiarity with this coast.
Prior to the fire breaking out he had noticed a
disturbance in the water of the Sound, which he
had put down to the tanker approaching at too
high a speed. During his time in the service, Nick
had formed a low opinion of many commercial
skippers.

When the fire in the nearby Ice Factory was
drawn to his attention, his seaman's instinct was
to slip his moorings and get the hell out of the
area. He gave orders briskly and the crew
jumped to. Nick was an exacting skipper, who
expected commands to be obeyed promptly.
Sloppiness or lack of discipline were not
tolerated aboard his ship.

A vessel such as the Maxwell yacht, virtually
an ocean-going ship, was equipped and maintained to near-naval standards and the main
engines started electronically on command.
Contrary to what Leclerc on the *Marie-Sainte*
supposed, *Elise 2* possessed side thrusters fore
and aft. Nick used them now to edge the yacht
rapidly out from her berth. In less than five
minutes she was nosing her way out into the
main channel.

Nick focused his binoculars on the tanker. She

328

was making directly for them and appeared to be picking up speed. According to his radar she was making four knots, faster than he would have thought safe in these confined waters. He ordered a five-point course adjustment to bring the yacht round on a parallel course.

Elliott Maxwell came puffing up the companionway from the lower deck. 'What in blazes is going on?' he demanded, gaping at the dock now obscured by smoke.

'Fire outbreak,' Nick said over his shoulder, keeping his eyes on the tanker. 'Just taking us clear, Mr Maxwell.'

'Of course.' Elliott had a high opinion of his captain and deferred to him in all matters of seamanship. Through the smoke he could make out figures and vehicles moving. 'Looks like Fred Tarr's boys are dealing with it.'

Nick made a non-committal noise. The fire no longer bothered him; that was somebody else's problem. He was waiting for *Elise 2*'s bow to come round. 'Steer zero five zero, I said,' he repeated sharply to the helmsman.

The seaman cleared his throat. 'Not responding, sir.' He was a Newfoundlander, a steady, reliable man. He had the wheel hard over.

Elliott Maxwell swung around. 'What's wrong?'

'Must be the wash from the tanker holding us back,' Nick responded tightly. 'Increase revolutions two thousand,' he ordered.

'Revolutions two thousand, aye aye,' the first

officer repeated. There were two officers on board beside Nick. The yacht was almost as fully manned as the tanker. On the engine indicator panel the counter climbed to the new power setting.

'Steer zero six zero.'

'She's crabbing, sir. I can feel it.' The helmsman was sweating. The yacht was being carried sideways through the water and her bow remained obstinately pointed straight at the oncoming tanker.

'Is there a problem with the steering gear?' Elliott asked puzzled.

Nick Costakis turned his head to look briefly at him. 'The gear is fine and so are the engines. There is nothing wrong with the ship; the problem is the wash from the tanker which is pushing our bow round.'

'Engage portside bow thruster,' Nick ordered. 'Half power.'

There was a short wait. 'She's holding, but she's still not coming round,' the helmsman reported.

That was something, Elliott thought. The yacht was no longer crabbing sideways. The tanker was sounding its horn now, the blasts assaulting the ears deafeningly. Damned cheek, he thought. This was all their fault.

Nick read his thoughts. 'She is probably having the same trouble as us,' he observed. 'The pilot has approached too fast and his momentum is pushing him on.' He turned to his officer. 'Give me three-quarters power on the port bow.'

'Three-quarters on port, aye aye.'

Elliott watched the ship's prow anxiously. It seemed to him as if it was starting to swing. He fervently hoped so. He wanted to suggest to Nick that he use the opposite stern thruster to apply more pressure aft, but checked himself. Nick was the skipper and he knew what he was doing. There was the risk that if the current eased or reversed itself then they might lose control.

A ping from the computer station made him jump. The GPS display was indicating a rearwards drift. The ship was actually being carried backwards. Elliott felt a fresh twinge of alarm. At this rate they would fetch up on the rocks.

Nick ordered a further increase in engine power. The water close inshore was turbulent now, waves slapping against the mole. 'We have plenty of power in reserve,' he remarked.

'Yes, of course,' Elliott agreed with elaborate unconcern. The tanker was closing in rapidly, it seemed to him, and still sounding her horn angrily. Her huge storage tanks loomed against the sky.

'She may be experiencing similar problems, too. Having made her entry into the Sound at too high a speed she now has to either turn in towards us or risk running aground,' Nick remarked, his voice as cool as if discussing the weather. 'Mister Mate, maximum thrust on the port side.'

'Max thrust port,' the first officer repeated.

A minute passed and another. The tanker crept inexorably closer. Her foredeck and tanks were partially obscured in a foggy mist. 'She has her fire-suppressant sprays in action,' the first officer said.

Elliott stared over the bows. It seemed to him that at last they were swinging over. Yes, it was true. His heart lifted. The yacht was at last responding. She was edging round gradually but surely onto the new heading.

'Steady,' Nick ordered the helmsman. 'Hold her at that.'

'My God!' exclaimed the first officer suddenly, 'what in hell do they think they're doing?' He was staring in horror at the tanker.

Even as *Elise 2* turned her bows away, the *Marie-Sainte* was swinging over onto a fresh collision course as if pushed by an invisible hand

Nick turned to Elliott. 'Mr Maxwell,' he said formally, 'I am going to order collision stations. All passengers are to come up on deck at once and put on life vests. At once, please.'

Jack Pearl, the harbourmaster, was out on the end of the dock yelling into his hand radio. 'Dumb idiots!' he shouted to anyone who was listening. He had seen it all before; big ship skippers making their approach too fast. 'The tide race catches them and they have to go full astern, kick up a wash. There'll be boats swamped. Christ Almighty, some people never learn!'

332

The *Marie-Sainte* was closing on the mole rapidly. From the froth under her tail he could tell the pilot had thrown the screws into reverse, side thrusters too. Her bow slid round to port and she heeled over. Shit, Jack thought, she was slewing sideways like an iceberg she was so darn huge. And here came the wash. 'Jeez-us!' he yelled, turning to run for the ladder to the upper level as a crest higher than a man swept down on a line of small craft, popping their mooring lines like so many strands of dental floss.

Jean-Alice heard the sirens too and like the others figured the noise was all part of the general excitement. The Lobsterman had emptied out as everyone disappeared to watch the parade and she was shutting the doors behind her to nip up to the top of the Neck and do likewise, when a couple of figures came running back towards her from the seaward end of the dock. For a moment she thought they must be hurrying to catch the floats go past, then she saw the tanker looming behind and the swell of the wash headed straight for the dock and she stopped dead.

A burst of white spray shot up at the far end of the dock where *Pequod* rode at her moorings. The thud of the wave's impact reached her in the same second and the next moment water was streaming in sheets across the roadway.

My God, Jean-Alice thought, someone will have to pay for this. And then she thought, The parade! And she turned and ran, ran along the Neck up towards the junction with Bay Road.

Lloyd was worried for the sweep. For a minute he thought the stilt walker had vanished again, then he saw the stovepipe hat bobbing tall above the crowd on the other side of the road. How had he gotten over there? The sweep saw him and waved both hands excitedly. Lloyd waved back. 'Look,' he called down to Dad, 'the sweep likes the fire too.'

Ted Gardiner was looking. It struck him that the stilt walker's gestures and manner were increasingly bizarre, not to say frantic. He wouldn't be surprised if some kids found that kind of behaviour alarming.

'Mommy.' Betsy jerked her mother's hand. 'Mommy,' she said plaintively, 'my shoes are wet.'

The protesters had taken themselves off. Natalie ran through the smoke swirling from the burning building. She caught sight of Rick by the entrance and jerked to a halt, her mouth working wildly, her face deathly white. 'Rick,' she cried desperately, 'you've got to believe me, this wasn't part of the plan.'

He looked back at her and his eyes were dead as Greenland ice. He waved her away. 'Get the hell out of here.'

'Rick, oh God, I'm sorry, I know what this place means to you,' her voice was anguished, 'I know how it looks, but I swear to you the surfers had nothing to do with any fire.'

He stared her down unspeaking. She might have been a stranger. 'Rick,' she pleaded, 'don't look at me that way. You know me better than that.'

His voice was harsh, bleak as iron. 'I used to think I did. I guess I must have been thinking of someone else all that time.' He turned on his heel and vanished into the smoke.

'Rick!' Her cries pursued him despairingly. 'Rick, listen to me, please!'

On the bridge of the *Marie-Sainte* there was alarm bordering on panic. Both main engines were running full astern, but the tanker's forward momentum continued.

'We must put the wheel over! We have to!' Leclerc said to Smither. The American was looking round wildly. The tanker was being carried inexorably towards the harbour entrance. In another few minutes she would plough through the moored craft to slam into the dock with catastrophic consequences. The only alternative was a radical course change to port, cutting across the path of the motor yacht now rapidly closing with them.

Shouldering the helmsman aside, Smither took the wheel. His finger jabbed at the buttons on the control station, jumping the starboard bow thruster and its opposite number on the stern quarter to port to full power. With maximum thrust exerted from countering directions fore and aft, at this speed the ship would turn in her own length.

Everybody on the bridge tensed, watching the bows come round. 'During the turn we shall be exposed to the full force of the current,' Smither said. Leclerc nodded. The ship was edging broadside on to the current and the risk was that she would lose steerageway and drift out of control into the harbour mole.

Slowly, slowly the bow came round. Leclerc shifted his gaze to the yacht. The people there had realised what was happening. The water under her stern was frothing furiously as her screws raced to give every ounce of thrust to carry her out from under the looming prow of the tanker. He reached for the tannoy switch. 'Attention all ship! Collision stations! Collision stations!'

The bridge personnel were all outwardly calm, but signs of strain were evident in clenched fists and tightened jaws. Leclerc picked up the direct-line phone connecting to the engine room.

'Sommer.' A woman's voice, Anna Sommer, thirty-seven years old, married, two teenage children. Female officers were the exception still. Anna was a chief engineer and a good one, as such virtually unique in the profession. Leclerc could imagine the feelings of the engine room crew sealed below with no chance of escape.

'Sommer here!' Anna repeated impatiently.

'This is your captain,' Leclerc spoke rapidly

into the mouthpiece, 'we are experiencing manoeuvring difficulties in the Sound. There is a small fire on shore, but it is not a threat at present. I shall shortly call for full power ahead on both main engines.' He was letting them know they were not forgotten down there in the bowels of the ship.

'*Entendu, mon Capitaine*. Standing by for orders,' Anna responded. There was the briefest of pauses, then, 'You can count on us.'

'*Bien.*' He hung up. Anna he could count on certainly, but of the crew under her he was not so sure. They were inexperienced. It only required one to crack and decide to save his own skin. Panic was as contagious as fire. Anna would stay at her post, but could she handle the engines alone?

'Jess, have you got Betsy? Honey, come between your mom and me and hold on tight to us. Right, now keep together, everybody, and we'll head up towards the Green. Nothing to worry about, just wet feet that's all.'

Lloyd's heart was thumping, but with Dad he knew they would be safe. Dad was strong. He wouldn't let anything happen. Then he remembered the sweep. Where was he? Lloyd twisted round on Dad's shoulders to see behind. How would the stilt people manage with people pushing and shoving around them? Suppose the water got too deep for them? Who was going to help them?

'The sweep, Mom, we should wait for him!' he pleaded.

'He'll be fine. He doesn't need us with those long legs,' his mother gasped. She had taken his sister Betsy on her back and was struggling to keep up.

Betsy could feel her mother's laboured breathing and her fear communicated itself. Dad was right behind, using his strength and weight to shield his womenfolk from the mob pressing in around them. The speed and suddenness with which the afternoon had changed bewildered the little girl. It was better for Lloyd because he was up and could see in part what was happening.

No one ever found out who was the first to cry 'Tsunami!' but the effect was drastic. A mass of people, men, women, children and old people stampeded into flight, streaming back from the water. The only escape routes were the narrow lanes leading westwards up to the Green. In excess of three thousand spectators now funnelled into these, pushing and jostling, those in the lead being forced on, stumbling and tripping, by people behind, while those still trapped near the waterside threw themselves shrieking on the packed backs of those in front.

Jessica's head was filled with vivid TV images of the Indian Ocean disaster of four years earlier. At her back she was sure she could hear the roar of a giant wave sweeping up the Sound. Fear of a wall of water about to break on the harbour front drove her and all the other families in a headlong rush for high ground.

For Lloyd Gardiner there was one terrible memory. He looked back and saw the sweep behind them, borne along in the mob, lurching from side to side as he struggled to control his unwieldy stilts. Then all at once he seemed to stumble. Powerless to help, the boy watched the stick-like figure sway, arms flung out in a desperate attempt to recover his balance, then topple in a tangle of broken limbs.

'Mom!' Lloyd cried. 'He's down!'

The last image he had was of a black-sleeved, white-painted arm clawing at the empty air.

'Officer! Officer! What's happening out there? Someone answer!' The King pounded on the steel door of his cell.

'Shut the hell up down there!' Logan Clancy yelled back. He strode down the passage, yanked back the hatch on the King's door and glared through. 'What's the matter now?'

'What's going on out there? What's all the screaming?' The Gimp was shouting too.

'Waves in the harbour. None of your goddam business.'

'Waves! How big? Tsunami?'

'Yeah, giants like you never seen!' Logan taunted them. 'Whole town flooded. You guys scared? You should be, ha, ha!'

'Screw you, buster! Let us outta here!'

'The hell I will. You scumbags can stay here

and drown like rats. See if I care.' Logan banged the hatch shut.

On the bridge of the tanker all eyes were on the yacht. The bows of the two vessels were barely two hundred metres apart. Alarms were sounding: proximity alerts, fire alerts and now the depth sounder was flashing urgently.

'Sir!' The first officer grabbed at Leclerc's arm, pointing. The indicator was showing barely two metres under the keel again. Smither had already seen it. The ship was broadside on to the current and it was overpowering the thrusters, dragging them down onto the footings of the mole. 'A few more minutes only,' the American said tersely, 'and her head will come round.'

The minute the ship's bow started to turn into the current then the odds would start to rebalance in the *Marie-Sainte*'s favour again. Instead of presenting the full length of her hull to the force of the current, the tanker would be knifing cleanly through with her prow as she was designed to do. Instead of relying on the feeble impulse of her manoeuvring thrusters she would be able to deploy the massive power of her twin main screws to drive them out of trouble.

Until that point was reached, however, all they could do was wait and pray.

The helicopter swooped low over the town, skimming the steeple of the church on the Green for the camera crew to snatch pictures of the fire.

Carly scrambled from side to side trying to make out what was happening in the harbour. That yacht was awful close to the tanker. She could see people crowding the upper deck. They must be terrified.

K. Zamos was excited too.

'Hey, you guys,' he yelled at the team, 'quit horsing around! You're supposed to be checking out ocean waves not house fires.'

Carly's phone buzzed in her pocket. She hunted it out and flipped the top open, but the call had dropped out. The number was unfamiliar. She was dialling back when the call repeated. 'Hi!' she shouted, cupping the handset to her ear.

'K? . . . that K?' The voice was ragged against the background noise. Ragged, but unmistakable.

'Oh, my God!' she whooped, 'it's the King! Hey, this is Carly.'

'Carly? . . . are you?'

'Carly Testarosa from Oahu, remember?' The others were crowding round. 'I'm in the chopper with K and the guys. We're out over the Sound.'

'How's . . . that?' The connection was fading in and out.

'Gimme that.' Zamos snatched the phone. 'King, this is K. Where in hell are you?'

'. . . bad stuff . . . cops . . .'

It was impossible to make out the words through the static and the clamour of the helicopter. Zamos had his free hand clamped against his other ear to keep out the noise. 'You're breaking up. Where are you?' he yelled frantically.

But the connection was lost.

The *Marie-Sainte*'s bow was less than two hundred yards from the centreline of the yacht, which was straining to pull ahead out of the tanker's path. With the ship rigged for emergency collision stations the entire accommodation block aft was now locked down with gas-tight seals on all doors and hatches, giving an impression of detached silence from the scene of impending disaster beyond the armoured windows. Officers and crew were wearing life vests with respirators slung around their necks. They had exercised the scenario a dozen times; this time it was for real.

From the bridge where Leclerc stood, *Elise 2* was now almost totally obscured by his own vessel's massive superstructure. He could only imagine the terror of the people on board as they saw the leviathan bearing down on them. The tanker's engines were still running astern endeavouring to hold them back, but her forward momentum was still three knots plus, a hundred metres a minute. When they collided the tanker would strike the smaller boat with the impact of a 20,000-ton axe blade swiping in slow motion through its hull.

Leclerc was bracing himself for the shock, trying to estimate the probable damage to his own vessel. The enormous gas tanks were heavily protected to withstand any collision. Even so he pictured an escaping gas cloud carried landward by the onshore breeze, enveloping the harbour. In the right concentration and with one building already alight, there would be a high possibility of explosive ignition resulting in a catastrophic conflagration ripping through the town.

The depth sounder switched from intermittent beeps to a continuous howl. Leclerc glanced at it out the corner of his eye. The gauge was registering one metre only. The current was still carrying them inshore. In any other conditions he would have been panicking, but all his concentration was taken up with the imminence of a collision.

He switched on the tannoy speaker and inflated his chest to issue a final brace warning when a quiver ran through the hull and a flash of pure terror ran through him. The yacht was completely hidden now. Had they hit? Surely there would have been more of a jolt, even allowing for the disparity in size? The depth gauge was still emitting its shrill wail and there was something odd about the ship's motion suddenly, an unnatural lack of vibration, a rigidity almost. He and Smither turned to one another, realization dawning in the same instant.

The pilot pulled himself together. 'Aground,' he said with his habitual economy with words. His shoulders sagged.

Leclerc was the first to recover. With the ship

aground command passed back from the pilot to his own hands. He straightened up. 'Stop engines,' he ordered.

A strange quiet settled over the tanker. The depth sounder was actually reading zero; the first time Leclerc had even seen that. From the wide windows of the bridge the nose of the yacht could be seen sliding past their bow to safety. At least that danger was now eliminated. Leclerc switched his attention to the burning building on the harbour front. Smoke was still pouring out, but there were appliances at the scene.

'All sections report damage,' he now ordered. The immediate need was to ascertain how badly the ship was hurt.

'Pressures normal in all tanks,' the first officer reported. That was one relief at least; if a tank had ruptured the gauges would instantly detect the drop in pressure and sound an urgent alarm.

The bridge phone rang. It was Anna Sommer. 'Engines stopped. No damage to propulsion systems. Main screws run free; rudders respond normally. No unusual vibration detected in shafts. All subsystems functioning normal.'

So the ship's power plant was intact. That much was good.

Smithers was on the radio reporting to the harbour authorities. No, there was no danger of a gas leak. All tanks were secure. Yes, they would need tugs in all probability, but first of all divers would have to go down to check the hull for damage.

The first officer shook his head. 'High water on a spring tide,' he said glumly. 'We could be stuck here a month.'

Chapter 28

Mid-Atlantic Ridge. Ten p.m. The USS *Tarp* was steaming westwards at economical cruising speed. Dr Mary Sennett had eaten and watched a movie that she had seen already on the trip out. That was one trouble with long voyages, never enough DVDs.

She went up to the communications centre to book a sat phone call home. Everyone aboard was permitted a certain number, but one of the satellites was down temporarily and restrictions had resulted. She ran into Wanless coming down. He was looking worried.

'Everything okay?' His wife, she knew, was expecting a baby, but the birth was not due for another month.

He shook his head morosely. 'Nothing to lose sleep over. Woods Hole have been on. One of the buoys is acting up. They can't work out if it's the telemetry or a malfunction of the gauge.'

'Even money on a communications glitch, I'd say. Which buoy are we talking about?'

'Zero-eight.'

Mary suppressed a momentary sinking feeling. Zero-eight was the code number of the final buoy in the series. The one that had been deployed only yesterday. 'It tested out perfectly. We ran the checks together.'

'I know, that's what I told them. The darn thing was performing perfectly up until that last big jolt. Since then the data stream has been erratic apparently.'

'What does erratic mean in this case?'

Wanless sighed. They were standing outside by a companionway and the wind was ruffling his sparse hair. He smoothed it down ineffectually. 'According to Woods Hole the pressure gauge is overcompensating.'

'Meaning it is set too high at the base?'

He nodded. 'And so giving misleadingly high readings compared with others in the network. I checked the data and there are a couple of spikes.'

'Big ones?' Mary looked at him sharply.

Wanless rocked his head in a yes–no manner. 'High, but not worryingly so. I told them it was more likely to be telemetry corruption of the data stream.'

'And did they buy that?'

'Kind of. They are running test transmissions now. I guess they'll let us know if they have any success.'

Mary went on her way with a worried frown. Out over the stern the night sky was black and starless.

Mid-Atlantic, USS *Thresher*. The executive officer knocked at the door of Captain Krauss's cabin. 'Sir, situation report as requested: the coolant pump is unchanged. There has been no detectable deterioration since this morning. The chief is confident it will get us home to Virginia. Our speed and endurance remain unaffected.'

'Except for our noise level,' the captain pointed out. 'The Russian seems to have moved west into deeper water as we anticipated. We're picking up intermittent bursts of active sonar from him which suggests he's lost us and is searching.'

'I agree, sir, and in light of that I have been looking at the chart. Seismic disturbance from that volcano seems to be picking up again, at least one big jolt in the past four to five hours.'

The skipper nodded. 'Yes, I heard about that. We're due to pass close in to the island. This might be an opportune moment to reconsider our projected course.'

'I'm glad you suggested that, sir.' The executive officer sounded relieved.

'We'll go up to the op centre and take a closer look at the chart.'

In the submarine's operations room a navigating officer projected a 3-D image of the ocean bed around La Palma on a forty-inch flat panel display for them. 'On our current projected track zero nine hundred hours tomorrow should put us exactly here, sir' – he pressed a key to illuminate an icon – 'twenty-one miles off the southern tip of the island.'

The captain studied the chart while the other officers waited on his decision. 'Volcanic activity is concentrated along the central spine of the island, correct?'

'Yes sir,' the executive officer confirmed. 'There seem to be four to five main vents spread out from north to south with a subsidiary one down on the west coast here by Puerto Naos.' He indicated the place.

The captain frowned. 'Suggestion time, gentlemen. Let's have your tactical assessments. You first, Leo.'

'Yes, sir,' the executive officer answered. 'My concern is possible turbulence resulting from seismic activity on the island. Not so much the physical threat as the degradation of our sensory capacity due to background noise. The Russki could make use of that to mask a radical course change. He could then drift off up the ridge and lie in wait for us as we emerge. With the racket our pump is making he'll have no trouble tracking us.'

'Sound thinking.' The captain nodded. 'Anyone else?'

The navigating officer spoke up. 'We could take the La Palma to El Hierro channel, passing to the east of La Palma.'

The captain shook his head. 'That would cost us time and still leave us having to cross the ridge to the north of our present position, which is exactly what the Russian boat will be expecting us to do.' He stared at the chart, tapping his fingers together. 'If it weren't for our pump I might agree with you, as it is our options are narrowed. We will maintain our present course and heading till zero nine hundred hours tomorrow. We will then be well inside the zone of turbulence with our own noise masked. I have in mind to loiter in the area for a few hours. If the Russian has been pretending to have lost us it may force him to show his hand. If not, we will move out westwards at creep speed hoping to pick him up on our passive sonar as we approach the edge of the turbulence zone before he can hear us against the background of noise from the volcano.'

He looked round the room. 'Everybody clear on what we intend to do?'

'Yes, sir,' came the response.

'Maintain present course and speed.'

Charco Verde, La Palma, Canary Islands. Ten p.m. In the deserted fishing village, shadows moved. The ruddy glow from the lava flow spilling from the crack that had opened in the mountainside north of the village bathed the handful of low buildings in a sinister half-light. Ash coated the roofs of houses and lay in drifts along the narrow streets. Smoke eddied downwind bringing a metallic sulphurous stench. Somewhere an abandoned dog lifted its muzzle to the shrouded moon and howled.

In the beginning it had spewed out fast and fluid, a torrent of white-hot rock covering almost half a mile in the first four hours. Now it continued more sluggishly like a slow-motion avalanche, smothering everything in its path.

From the lower slopes the flow had streamed through the cultivated ground till it reached the orchards behind the village. For two days the villagers had gathered to watch its progress. Families with property in its path clutched one another, weeping and beseeching God to turn it aside. In vain. The smoking tide of lava, its crust covered with grey slag where it had cooled in contact with the air, with gaping cracks exposing the blazing core within, continued on its course undeflected. Walls and buildings crumpled before its weight. Houses blazed briefly or were brushed aside ruined. Alleyways were cut across by a terrifying wall of moving rock.

And all the while it was headed unswervingly for the harbour.

Under the portico of Carlos's hotel, a torch beam flickered guiltily. Hours earlier the Guardia Civil had evacuated the remaining inhabitants, bundling them with their meagre possessions onto a convoy of vehicles and sending them over the mountains. Few had resisted; the inexorable advance of the lava flow, creeping through the fields, burning everything in its path, terrified everybody. Now only Carlos remained.

The ash clung to his shoes as he picked his way along the deserted street. The rumble of the advancing lava filled the darkness, the hiss of steam mixed with a constant grinding and crushing that boomed and rattled among the empty houses like an approaching storm. As he grew closer the noise intensified, fumes stung his eyes, catching in his throat. He rounded a bend and recoiled suddenly, throwing up his hands against a blast of heat. Twenty feet ahead the front of a house to his right burst apart, collapsing outward into the street in an avalanche of rubble. Through clouds of choking stone dust he dimly made out the red crackle of flames and a steaming avalanche of burning rock. Stones and rubble crashed about him. Right in front a river of semi-molten rock two storeys high had gouged a path clean through the houses.

The lava flow must have speeded up, crossing the alleyway behind and burning the building from the rear. The narrow street was half blocked by debris embedded with glowing lumps of lava. He would have to hurry to make it past before the flow closed off the street altogether. Two houses on, another alley to the right would take him down to the harbour. Defiantly, he started to pick his way across the rubble. He had gone a few steps when a loose beam twisted underfoot. He fell awkwardly, landing on a heap of burning stones. He sprang up again, yelping with the pain. The lava stream was moving far faster suddenly. With a rattle of stones part of the crust split apart, exposing a white-hot interior. He gasped again as the heat smote him. With terrifying speed a slab of fluidised rock oozed out behind him, swallowing the road where he had a moment before been standing, cutting off the way back.

Panic gripped him. His fingers clawed at the smothering rubble, tearing fingernails, leaving bloody stains on the smoking stones. He could smell his own hair burning, feel the skin of his face and hands blistering like cooked meat. A shuttered wall loomed up, blocking his path; terror lent strength. Hunching into a ball, he hurled himself shoulder first at the darkened window, felt glass shatter and the wooden staves burst under his weight. He dived through the gap, thudding onto a solid floor with a bone-jarring crash. His head smacked the flagstones and his senses spun. Drunkenly he fought himself to his feet, saw a patch of light, reeled towards it, clutching blindly in the dark for support, stumbling over obstacles, and emerged gasping in a rear yard.

The lane beyond was smoke choked between high walls. No way of telling where he was. He glanced left, saw a dusky glow of flame, turned the other way and fled. Moments later he was collapsing in the safety of the square.

* * *

In the hotel bar, Carlos poured himself a stiff tot of *cocal*, the dark Canary rum, and tossed it back in a single gulp, steeling himself for what had to be done. Footsteps crunched on the gravel in the forecourt and a thickset figure with bowed shoulders approached the circle of light around the doorway. 'Juan?' he called softly.

'*Sí, compadre*. I am here.'

'Are the others with you?'

'All but Olivero. His house is locked and there was no answer to my knocking. Tomas says he saw the car being loaded earlier.' The man's shoulders shrugged eloquently. 'His wife's family live in Santa Cruz.'

Carlos made a brief hissing sound of contempt. With tremors still shaking the ground and thunderous detonations echoing from the volcano summit, it was remarkable more hadn't voted with their feet. Juan owned the local garage, the other two with him were fishermen. The livelihoods of all four were bound up in the village, its harbour and beach.

'His cousin's daughter was on the mountain yesterday when the geologist was killed.' They were still discussing the absent Olivero.

'The one who works at the observatory? Who went to Madrid to study?' The island was small enough that everything was known.

'*Sí*, the same. She was here last week with her boyfriend, *un Americano*.'

Carlos listened, frowning. 'Did that fool Olivero tell the girl what we planned?' he interrupted. The others exchanged glances and shrugged. Who could say?

'The wind is freshening,' said the oldest of the group, a dark-skinned fisherman with a wall-eye named Pedro de Vera. 'We had best hurry.' All of them were nervous, anxious to get the business over.

'Follow me.' Carlos led the way round to the shack at the back of the hotel where the building supplies were stored. 'One box between two of you. Use the handles and don't drop them.' There was no need for the warning; the men handled the wooden crates as if they were made of glass.

The job was almost done and they were bringing out the last when it started again, a faint vibration underfoot as if the earth's skin had shivered suddenly in a chill breeze, the throb of an unseen pulse beating, the mountain's heart quivering under stress.

Chapter 29

Goodwill. Seven p.m. Rick picked his way through the burned-out shell of the main factory floor. Freddy's boys had dowsed the flames, helped by the wash from the tanker that had flooded the road outside to a depth of eight inches before receding. A few dying wisps of smoke still wound up through the gap overhead where a part of the roof had collapsed. Across from the charred stairs, the sperm-whale jawbone loomed blackened and scorched, symbolic somehow of his family's story.

Rebecca rubbed at the soot with a handkerchief. It came away black. She sighed. 'Thank the Lord Mom and Dad weren't around to witness this,' she said.

Rick put an arm around her shoulders. 'The place is Chance's anyway. I guess now he'll go ahead and pull it down.'

His sister dabbed at her eyes. 'It makes me so sad. I know it's just an ugly old brick shed, but it was ours for so long now it feels like a piece of me is gone too.'

He hugged her tight. 'We are here and we'll survive. This is our town. Nothing will ever drive us out.'

'First Mom, then Dad and now this. It's hard, Rick, and it's worse when you are a woman. I don't even have the name any more.'

'Maybe so,' he comforted her, 'but Mike's a good man and your boys are Larsens through and through.'

She brightened a little. 'That's true, isn't it? Little tykes, you know I told them to stay on the float with Patsy while I went to check the store was okay? Well naturally the moment I was out of sight they jumped down and ran right in here while the place was still ablaze. Freddy Tarr had to collar the pair of them and throw them out by their scruffs.'

The Chandlery had suffered some minor leakage, nothing significant. The same went for the Lobsterman. All the premises on the Neck had good storm protection. They had to. Several boats in the marina had capsized and a number of others had been swamped or thrown ashore. It might have been much worse. The real damage was to the town's reputation as a safe family vacation spot.

'Natalie got some of her paintings out, I hear,' Reb said.

'So it seems,' he acknowledged.

'I always liked that one she did of Dad.'

'Me too. It was a good likeness.'

Reb shot him a glance. '*Pequod* okay?' she asked.

Rick scowled. 'She had a big scrape along the starboard from midsection to within ten feet of the prow. Paint all scratched off down to bare metal. The wash from the tanker broke the tail painter on *Sequoia* and swung her through a hundred and eighty degrees of arc till the bow mooring parted and she took off like a torpedo. She hit the pier first, then *Pequod*, ended up on Chance Greene's new breakwater.'

'Is the hull holed?'

'No, the fenders took the impact. It's a paint job, that's all.'

'Lucky for you, then. Mike says *Sequoia* is on the rocks.' *Sequoia* was a former Canadian naval cutter now in private hands that had put into the Sound with engine trouble a fortnight ago. 'According to Mike she was thrown right up onto the boulders. If her back isn't broken already, they'll do it pulling her clear.'

'Pity, she was a handsome boat.'

'She was the only total loss. Plenty of other boats got tossed around. The outer harbour had the worst of it. Whale Morrissey lost some gear. He's suing.'

Fire and flood: was Goodwill jinxed?

Many families were pulling out ahead of tomorrow's regatta. On West Street and Bay

Road queues of vehicles were headed north for the Causeway to the mainland.

'I've tried telling them,' Beth Robbins said to her sister-in-law dispiritedly.

'I know, but they don't listen.'

'But it's just the boats in the harbour, nothing to do with any tsunami wave!' Beth was almost in tears with frustration. 'That darn ship, it's way too big for the Sound. We should never have gone over to gas.'

'It was the environmentalists trying to close down the hydroelectric dam on account of the fish. We should have stood our ground.'

'Well, at least it's just us now.' Beth wiped her eyes. 'No more dumb tourists to bother about.'

'The surfers are still here,' Abby reminded her.

Chance Greene had no doubts about who was to blame for the parade disaster. 'Of course it was the surfers!' He hammered the table. 'That fire was no accident. Anyone who says it was is a damn fool! We locked up a couple of their guys and this was their way of striking back at us. Pull them all in, I say. Lock the bastards up!'

'We don't have the space,' Don pointed out.

'Run them out of town then!' Chance was beyond reasoning. 'Ten thousand dollars I put up for that parade. Wasted because of a bunch of layabouts who right now are laughing at us.'

'A lot of us had cash sunk in the celebrations, Chance,' Rick reminded him. 'Time and effort too. Beth and Abby worked all winter sewing costumes for the parade.'

Jack Pearl chimed in, 'Personally I'm more concerned by the fact that there is a disabled tanker carrying twenty thousand tons of liquid petroleum gas aground in the harbour while this town appears to have a firebug on the loose.'

An emergency meeting of Selectmen and officials had been convened at city hall on the Green.

'We still have the two suspects in custody from last night,' Don said after a pause. 'But I'll be honest with you, unless forensic comes up with something I'm not going to be able to hold them beyond the weekend.'

'Then find a reason!' Chance barked. 'Good God, man, the town's on the edge of panic. What effect do you imagine it will have letting out the chief suspects?'

'Why exactly did your boys stop these two in particular?' Rick asked Don.

Don flicked his eyes sideways in the manner that indicated he was uneasy. 'Between ourselves we had a tip-off. Two people acting suspiciously in an SUV.'

'This was before the fire or after?'

'Half an hour before the alarm sounded. It's there in the log.'

'And this caller was who?'

Don's unease deepened. 'Annie answered the phone. She didn't actually speak to the person that called in the sighting. It was someone else relaying information from a third party.'

'I'm lost,' Rick said. 'Who did Annie speak to?'

Don had turned red in the face. 'The caller chose not to give a name,' he mumbled.

'You're telling us this was an anonymous caller?'

Don waved his hands as he tried to explain what had happened. 'I was on my way out. Annie picks up the phone. It's a woman. She says some person has contacted her claiming to have seen a couple acting suspiciously in the woods up behind the power station. No names, only that an SUV was involved.'

Rick felt exasperation wash over him. 'Two men in an SUV?'

'A couple were the words used. Sex wasn't specified.'

'So the caller could have been referring to a man and a woman?' Rick said.

'Or two women, come to that,' Jack Pearl chuckled.

Don shrugged.

Rick persisted. 'And the two fellows you stopped, they were in a pick-up, I heard?'

'Yeah, well . . .' Don rubbed his chin. In the harsh lighting his face looked worn and tired. 'It was one of those Sport Trac jobs, so you could call it either way.'

Rick knew the type, described as a crossbreed truck/SUV, essentially it was a crew-cab Ranger pick-up with a five-seat cabin mated to a short cargo bed that would take a trail bike or at a pinch a jet ski.

It was easy to blame the surfers for all the evils that had beset the town. Rick had a hunch the truth would prove to be a lot less simple.

Marie-Sainte, Goodwill Sound. Leclerc was bone weary. The Coastguard had finally left. Officers had spent two hours aboard and had departed with the ship's logs together with back-up copies from the computer systems. Charges were almost certain to follow, they had indicated. Leclerc would be informed of the specifics in due course. Al Smither had gone ashore with the officers to face further questioning of his conduct. Leclerc felt sorry for him. Meanwhile the primary consideration was the safety of the locality.

Preliminary examinations so far indicated no leakage from either the main tanks or any associated pipe work. No escape of gas had taken place or seemed likely to in the near future. The vessel was hard aground and the hull plates damaged over an area fifty feet back from the bows on the starboard side. Some leakage of water into the bilges had been detected and the pumps were holding it. Structurally at least one frame was probably strained. The big worry was that as the tide ebbed the ship's own weight would crush her keel deeper into the mud, causing further damage.

It was imperative that the ship be lightened as

quickly as was practical in order to reduce the strain on her hull. That meant emptying her tanks, either using additional piping to connect up to the discharge valves on the dock or, if that were impossible, by bringing in a relief tanker and transferring the contents of the tanks across. Leclerc had made these points as forcefully as he could to the Coastguard officers, but he was conscious that they, not he, would now make the decisions.

Another anxiety was for his crew. As he had foreseen, a number of the younger personnel were suffering from shock as a result of their narrow escape. He had judged it best for their morale to send them ashore for the night. A bus had been hired to ferry a dozen or more to hotels in Ellsworthy. All but one of the officers remained behind, but if an emergency arose it was now conceivable they might find themselves short-handed.

'They're saying downtown it was the wash from the boats, definitely not a tsunami,' Brook Van Buren said. 'There's nothing on the TV either.'

'That's just what they said in Thailand and look what happened, three hundred thousand dead!' his wife Julie countered.

'I know, but it's been what, two hours and the ocean hasn't moved. It looks like this time the experts are right.'

At the Indian Patch cottage the Gardiner and Van Buren families were still arguing.

'I don't care if it was a false alarm. I am not staying here with the children another hour,' Jessica stated flatly, looking her husband anxiously in the eye. 'I won't be able to sleep for worry in this place. Remember those pictures of the hotel in Phuket? The waves breaking four, five storeys high? They never found the bodies of the people inside.'

Julie Van Buren backed her up. 'Paula is simply terrified. "Please," she keeps begging me, "can't we go somewhere far away from the ocean?"'

'Lloyd is worried for that stilt walker, the sweep,' Jessica added. 'I tell him nobody was really hurt, but I wish there was a way to find out.'

'You could call the police department,' Julie said. 'I guess they would have a list.'

'There's no reason why we have to stay.' Her husband looked at Ted Gardiner. 'If you girls are determined we can leave tonight just as soon as everyone is packed up.'

'That's true,' Ted agreed. 'The tents and sleeping bags are loaded. It's still light, there's plenty of time. We can take off, drive inland till we find a place to camp.'

'Camping?' Jessica said doubtfully. The two women exchanged worried glances. Thunder rumbled in the distance. 'Sounds like a storm coming.'

'Okay, so an inn or hotel.'

'On a weekend in June? We'll be lucky.'

'They're saying on the TV you have to drive at least five miles inland to be completely secure,' Julie put in.

Brook put an arm round her. 'Then we'll make it ten miles and be extra certain,' he said laughing.

Jessica shuddered. 'Twenty miles won't be enough for me. Right now I'd like to put a mountain range between us and the ocean.'

'Don't fret, honey,' her husband soothed. 'Okay then, that's agreed. We pack up the cottage and head out.'

Jessica jumped up. 'Come on, kids,' she called, 'let's start getting your stuff together. Lloyd, collect up your PlayStation bits and pieces. Hurry now or they'll be left behind.'

While his sister and Paula ran around helping, Lloyd slipped out onto the porch and ran softly across the warm grass down to the water's edge to say goodbye to the river. The sky was dark overhead and an occasional spot of rain threatened a downpour to come. Cautiously he stepped out onto the pontoon. The wooden decking was wet, which puzzled him because there had not been enough rain as yet. The grass and rushes along both banks had the flattened, crushed look the way they had that time before when he had been down here and seen the river come up suddenly. He guessed that wake from the boats the parents were all talking about must have caused it.

'Lloyd! Where are you?'

His mother was calling. With a shake of his head, Lloyd ran back up to the cottage. He was going to miss this river with its mysterious tides.

Elliott Maxwell was bringing his yacht back to his private mooring below Indian Point. Natalie joined K. Zamos and the team to watch from the terrace. Her manner was subdued.

Zamos was in no mood for delay. 'You said you'd bring the King with you. Where is he?' he demanded.

She shrugged. 'I'm not his keeper.'

Redhead Carly said, 'He tried to call me, but we lost the signal.'

'So?'

Carly bared her teeth. 'So what's with the mystery? K told you, bring the King with you or no deal.'

Natalie's patience snapped. 'You want to know where he is? Okay, I'll tell, but you're not going to like it. He's in jail, that's where.'

'In jail?' Incredulity spread across Zamos's expression. 'In jail did you say?'

'They locked them up on a charge of arson, him and the Gimp.'

'Arson?'

Natalie scowled at him. She was done with crawling to this creep. 'Are you deaf or what? Arson, I said, like lighting fires. Forest fires in this case.'

K. Zamos wasn't used to being talked to like

this by young women or young men for that matter. He eyed her with a mix of surprise and respect. 'Did they do it?' he asked tightly.

'Of course they didn't, but the locals here—'

Carly interrupted. 'Localism, we've met with that before.'

'Shut up,' Zamos told her.

'It's a fit-up. The cops are doing tests on a container they found, checking for fingerprints. It'll clear them both, but till then . . .' Natalie shrugged. 'It's a jealousy thing.' Her shoulders sagged. 'He said not to tell you. I guess he reckons you'll pull out of the deal.'

There was silence. Zamos turned to Carly. 'You know,' he said softly, 'I think I like. In fact definitely I like.'

Carly nodded. Her eyes were shining. 'As a storyline it sure has drama. The jailed hero . . . will he get out in time? . . . Can the girl free him.

Zamos smiled. He had the picture now: the flawed hero on a trumped-up charge, a beautiful heiress, a surfing legend, a giant wave. It was an explosive mix and more, it was the stuff of fables. His gaze panned away up the Sound, picturing a hundred-foot wave breaking over the islands, the King poised on its crest. He felt a warm glow light in his heart. *Doomed Youth*, they would call the film. Box office magic, he could feel it now.

'Find him a lawyer,' he said happily. 'This story just gets better.'

* * *

367

Logan Clancy was on duty at the Green again. All the schedules were screwed up. His wife was furious. 'Think of the overtime I'll put in for,' he had told her.

'That skinflint Don Egan never pays out and you know it,' she stormed back. 'He makes out you came in voluntarily for the good of the community.'

'That's not Don's fault, it's the Selectmen with their budget. Don can't pay out money he doesn't have.'

Anyway so here he was, the only person in the building right now. Both cars were out on patrol in case the firebug struck again. Don was over at the council office. Even Annie had taken a rare leave of absence. Which left only the two surfers in the cells. Well, they could rot as far as Logan was concerned. He had told them so earlier and when they kept up their yelling Don had come back and removed their phone privileges as punishment. Any more trouble and the TV would follow. So now they were quiet. They had been fed, a half-pounder apiece sent in from Burger King. All Logan had to do between now and the end of his shift was turn off the lights at ten.

He settled down in the squad room with a second chair pulled up to rest his legs and the volume on the radio receiver turned low so he could follow the film on TV. The Red Sox were playing on one of the other channels, but watching a match alone was dull. Outside on the

Green, traffic was light for a Saturday. Half the town had pulled out already.

It wasn't till he went through to relieve himself that he heard the whistling. The men's room was situated to the rear of the cellblock with a high-set slit window opening onto the vehicle pound. Logan had his fly unzipped and was doing his business when this noise started up. At first he figured it for a bird or some kind of animal maybe, except there was more than one that he could make out and now and again he fancied he caught a murmur of voices.

When he was through, he zipped himself up and listened some more. The whistling was still there. It came and went, one side then another. Short and long notes at varying pitch very like a pair of birds calling to one another in the bush. Only now Logan was certain there was somebody out there.

Logan liked to work out regularly. Gripping the window ledge with both hands, he pulled himself up till he could peer through the opening. Outside, the fence around the pound ran back to the wall of the block a few feet away. Leaning against the top rail were three kids who could only have been surfers. It was one of them who was making the whistling; Logan could see his cheeks puffing out. The fellow stopped for breath and cocked his head to listen. A moment later there came an answering burst of notes from the direction of the cells.

'Hey, what the hell do you guys think you're doing?' Logan Clancy called out sternly.

The whistling stopped abruptly. The guys on the rail jerked round, startled to see Logan's angry face glaring at them through the slit window. The whistler, a kid with a buzz cut and a steel bolt in one eyebrow, squared his shoulders. 'Any law against whistling?' he answered sullenly.

'Don't get smart with me, punk,' Logan snapped. 'This is police property. Clear out.'

The boy scowled. 'We're not on police property this side of the rail. You can't touch us.'

'The hell I can't,' Logan growled. 'Communicating with prisoners without permission is an offence against the penal code. You stay round here one minute longer and I'll lock you up with your pals. You can whistle to each other all you want then.'

One of the others stepped forward. He was older and wore his hair long, tied back behind. He held up his hands palms outward in a gesture of peace. 'No one wants to make trouble, officer. We were just going anyway. Come on, Phil, we're done here.'

The buzz-cut youth stared back at Logan with undisguised hate. 'Screw you, mister, and screw your town!' He raised a clenched fist against the sky. 'Cumbre Vieja! Your day will come!' he shouted.

From the cells next door a voice roared out in answer, 'Cumbre Vieja! Cumbre Vieja!'

The echoes seemed to ring on and on.

Logan Clancy stormed round into the cellblock. His boots slammed on the concrete as he stalked to the end cell and pounded on the door. 'Shut the fuck up, you hear me in there!'

There was a chorus of mocking laughter from inside. 'Cumbre Vieja, asshole!'

Logan reached up for the power switch and pulled it down, plunging the block into darkness. 'You want to sing? Fine, sing in the dark, shitheads!'

Overhead thunder pealed. The weather had broken.

Mid-Atlantic Ridge, USS *Tarp*. Midnight. The news Mary Sennett had been dreading came through after two hours. Derek Wanless called the team together. In a brisk unemotional voice he informed them what they all knew from rumour or had guessed anyway. The tests on buoy zero-eight commanded by the telemetry experts at Woods Hole had failed to rectify the problem with the pressure gauge.

'There is nothing for it but to go back and send the submersible down to make a visual inspection. I've spoken to the captain and he is ordering a course change. If we make best possible speed through the night we should be over the deployment zone around ten a.m. local time tomorrow. Please arrange your schedules accordingly. That's all, goodnight.'

Mary went out for some fresh air. Suddenly home, which had been only two weeks away, felt like it was on another planet.

She felt the ship heel as the wheel was put over. They were coming round onto the reciprocal heading.

The fire mountain was dragging them back.

Chapter 30

Goodwill, Seafarers Motel. It was Beth Robbins who had the idea of putting Frank Schaffer in touch with Martin Seymour, the dowser.

'He can find things for people. Shelley Winter out at Hemlock Hill lost her ring and he ran a search and told her where to look and she did and he was right on the button.'

She was speaking to Don Egan. Don had dropped Frank off at the motel and Abby was showing him the room.

Don looked uncertain. He didn't know a whole lot about dowsing, he said.

'Listen, it can't hurt to try. And it will give the poor man something to do at least,' Beth urged. 'I feel so wretched for him not knowing what's happened to his sister.'

Don heaved a sigh. 'I guess there wouldn't be any harm running it past Seymour. If he feels he might be able to help then you could pass the message on.'

'I'll call Martin now.'

'Yeah, well just so long as it is understood this is a private thing between Frank and him. I don't want the department involved, that clear?'

'You got it. Thanks, Don. I have a feeling this could work somehow.'

'Mr Seymour? Hi, Frank Schaffer. It's good of you to see me.'

'Glad to meet you, Frank. My friends call me Martin. Come in out of the wet.'

The house had once been a small farm. Downstairs there was now one big living space, wood-floored with old beams. The furnishings were well used and there were books stacked on the floor. Seymour gestured apologetically. 'Sorry about the mess. I'm a bachelor.'

Frank Schaffer was younger than he had sounded on the phone, no more than thirty. He wore tan slacks and a polo shirt. He might have been almost any other tourist on Bay Road except that he had lost his sister and it showed.

'We're a close family. Kim and I were just ten months apart. When we were kids we did everything together. This thing is just devastating for Mom and me. Randy's family too.'

Martin dropped ice into tall glasses and topped them up with chilled coffee. 'Sugar?'

'Not for me.'

'If you don't mind getting wet again we'll take it out back.'

Outside, a grass field gave onto a yard with a

hip-roofed wooden barn and a loft over that Martin used for work. There was a big architect's table in the centre with skylights overhead that was spread with maps. Scents of summer hay lingered under the pitched roof.

'This is a large scale general map of the town,' he explained, 'two inches to the mile. They go larger but I find this size seems to serve best.'

Suspended from a beam over the table on a fine cord was a lead weight the size and shape of a green fir cone. He swung it gently. 'This is a plumb line. From the Latin: *plumbus* meaning *lead*. Masons have been using similar devices for thousands of years to drop a perpendicular. The great aqueducts of the Roman Empire, the cathedrals and castles of medieval Europe, all owe their existence to a simple weight and ball of string.'

Frank Schaffer took a gulp of coffee and nodded silently to show he was following.

'The technique I use is called "remote dowsing",' Martin went on. 'For instance here we have a plan of the Maxwell estate out at Indian Point. Elliott Maxwell is interested to learn if there was a Native Indian settlement on the property at one time. To begin a search I position the portion of the plan I wish to scry under the plumb and taking hold of the line gently like so' – he demonstrated using finger and thumb – 'take the tension off and wait to see if any vibration presents itself.'

Frank watched fascinated, saying nothing.

Releasing the line, Martin passed a hand palm down over the plan. 'Where I think I have detected a disturbance of the ground I make a mark in pencil. You can see here for yourself.'

Frank leaned forward over the table. Martin switched on the overhead lights and he saw lines of delicate pencil crosses tracing sweeping patterns on the surface of the paper.

'These are Indian settlements?'

Seymour shook his head. 'We think not. It's puzzling, but from excavations it seems more likely the lines indicate tide ledges from an era when ocean levels were higher than they are now.'

'Could this technique help locate my sister and her partner, do you think?'

'It's possible certainly. I have had some success in the past in finding items people have lost or mislaid.'

'Yes, Beth, Mrs Robbins told me. You found a ring for a friend of hers.'

'Of course, in this case it is a person rather than an object that we are looking for.' Seymour pulled the big map of the Sound towards him as he spoke and leaned over it thoughtfully.

'I guess the cove would be the place to start?' Schaffer said after a minute.

'Yes, yes indeed.' Martin straightened up. 'I was just picturing the place in my mind.'

'Beth said to bring along a picture of Kim and Randy.' Frank passed over a photo. 'This was taken earlier in the year when they came down to Poughkeepsie for the weekend. And this is her French scarf that she likes to wear. Her lucky scarf, we called it.'

Martin Seymour received both items solemnly. He adjusted the chart under the plumb line and with his hand smoothed it out on the table. 'I am going to ask you to concentrate on your sister and her partner for me. They cycled down to the cove, is that correct? Good, then try to imagine you are with them. Picture yourself a little behind, following as they ride down the path from the road.' He looked at the younger man. 'This will be hard for you, but it is important to try to establish a link between us and them.'

'I understand. I'll do my best.'

'Then we'll begin.' Martin stretched out his right hand to the plumb line and the lead weight quivered on its cord.

Eight-thirty p.m. Lightning crackles overhead while rain hammers down and this town simmers with anger and fright. In her tiny office Sheena Dubois rattled at her laptop. *Three hours ago a catastrophic accident was avoided only by a miracle. Shipping in the Sound was thrown into confusion when smoke was seen coming from that well-known town landmark, the old Ice Factory. Meanwhile a bulk gas carrier, the* Marie-Sainte *from St John, turning in the confined waters of the Sound narrowly scraped a collision with another vessel fleeing the flames. Officers aboard the* Marie-Sainte *blame unusually strong currents, but harbourmaster Jack Pearl says the tide state was normal for the time of year. A number of craft in the outer harbour were swamped by the tanker's wash and spectators watching the annual Founders' Day parade were forced to wade through foot-deep water along Bay Road. An inquiry is promised.*

The alarm was raised by Tab Southwell of Maple Cove, who was among the crowd watching the parade from the harbour side of Bay Road. Tab says he smelt smoke and thought he ought to take a look. His prompt action in calling for assistance prevented a major conflagration. The blaze was extinguished by volunteers from the Goodwill Fire Department, who together with vehicles were participating in the parade. Fire Chief Fredrick Tarr declared, 'It was fortunate we happened to be on the spot. There was some rubbish caught alight in the main hall and the fire spread fast with all the timber in there.' Tarr cited 'a cigarette or match' as the most likely cause, adding, 'This time of year we all need to be vigilant.'

Sheena's phone warbled. She glanced at the screen and sucked her teeth. Doc Southwell's number. Last night she had promised herself she would break this off. Maybe now was the time. She pressed the answer button.

'Hi.'

'Hey, can we meet?'

'Have you forgotten where you dumped me last night?'

'I'm real sorry. There were good reasons for

both of us, huh? Anyways I've got something for you.'

'What?' Sheena said in spite of herself.

'It's a present, a surprise. Meet me in the lane out back in half an hour.' The line went dead.

Martin Seymour was painstaking in his approach. 'Do you have a cellphone on you?' he asked Frank Schaffer. 'If so, please would you mind turning it off. I find the electromagnetic radiation degrades my own sensory perception. For that reason I never use one. In fact I don't even keep a TV or a radio about the house.'

Frank switched off his phone and placed it on a shelf over by the door.

They sat at the table. Martin had the plumb line between the finger and thumb of his right hand and held it still attached at one end to the roof beam so that the weight was suspended over the chart. 'This method ensures that the plumb weight never at any time comes in contact with the chart or the table,' he explained. 'The idea is that as far as possible it should remain isolated from all outside interference.

'Now,' he went on, 'I am going to ask you to place your sister's scarf that you brought along on the table between us if you will.'

Wordlessly Frank complied, laying the silk scarf neatly folded next to the chart.

'Perhaps if you were to shake it out a little that would be more natural seeming. Excellent, and if we both place our free hands on the scarf like so, now if you are comfortable we can commence.'

The chart of the Sound was arranged with Maple Cove directly beneath the hanging plumb weight. Martin held the line lightly, his elbow supported on the table. 'I simply ease the tension off a fraction,' he explained, 'just enough so that I can detect any vibration however faint.' He turned his spectacled eyes on the other man. 'Now this is the hard part, you must endeavour to clear your mind completely, concentrating solely on the scarf. Try to visualise your sister wearing it as you recall her. When you succeed in picturing her in your mind, hold that image. Cling to it, stay with it, don't let yourself be dragged away. If you find your attention wandering, snap it back; always the scarf and your sister together. Above all, don't attempt to search.' Martin emphasised the word. 'It's a great temptation to try to steer one's thoughts. You must resist. If your sister is out there and trying to contact us for help, it is vital your mind remains receptive. Otherwise it is as if you are talking across someone. You block out the message with your own sound.'

They sat in silence. Martin had the plumb suspended directly over the parking lot on the edge of the cove. 'This would be where your sister and her partner stepped off into the void, so far as our perception extends,' he said gently.

Several minutes passed. Martin's touch on the line did not waver. The plumb hung like a frozen bead of water suspended in space. The lamp had been turned down low and the rain drumming on the roof had a soporific effect on Frank. He remembered Martin's instructions and tried to bring up an image of Kim in his mind. He found it difficult.

After what seemed a long time Martin Seymour relaxed. He smiled at Frank. 'Nothing so far,' he admitted, 'which is quite normal. It usually takes quite a while before vibrations start to come through. I liken it to the process of tuning up an instrument. How are you feeling?'

'Okay, I guess. Quite tired. It's harder than it looks.'

'Yes, it is. Are you ready to continue?'

'Yes, I am.'

'Here,' Sheena said, 'you missed the excitement downtown this afternoon, didn't you? Take a look.' She snapped open the camcorder and passed it over.

They were in her car in the lane behind the cove with rain sluicing down the windows. Doc's present was a pretty gold and silver bangle. She was wearing it on her wrist.

Southwell peered at the screen. 'Hey, there's Tab!' he exclaimed.

'Where? I didn't see him.' Sheena took the camcorder back.

'Rewind a minute. A little further, stop. There he is, see? Coming out from the Ice Factory.'

'I must have gotten this mixed up. The fire comes after.'

'It was Tab. I saw him. Go back again. There, see? That's Tab okay.'

Sheena did not answer. Her mouth had gone dry and a knot of fear twisted in her stomach. Why hadn't she noticed this before? Had she skipped through or mentally blocked it out? Oh please, no, she prayed silently.

Doc was still speaking. 'Fred Tarr called me up earlier, reckoned the kid did well for a youngster. Is there any more? Run the clip on.'

With a sinking heart Sheena let the tape roll. Let me be wrong, she whispered silently to herself.

'This is insane! You're out of your mind! No one is going to believe this of my son.'

Sheena was relentless. 'Look, watch the tape again. Tab goes into the building. The time is in the bottom corner of the screen, five-twelve p.m. The alarm wasn't given till five-thirty. Tab goes in' – she ran the tape on – 'and here he is coming out again. The time now is five-twenty. Eight minutes he has been in there. What was he doing all that time?'

'Anything. He could be doing anything at all. Taking a piss probably.'

'Now he is looking round him, his manner is shifty.'

'He's thirteen, he's awkward; that's how kids his age act, for God's sake!'

'Watch some more. He moves away from the door. He hesitates, stops, looks behind him. His manner is definitely furtive, I would say. It's now five-twenty-six and look, there's a shot of the building, you can actually see smoke emerging from that upstairs window above the entrance. People in the crowd are growing restive. They know something's wrong, but they can't make out what it is. Probably they can smell smoke, but not see it yet.'

'Yeah, you say, you say,' Southwell muttered.

'I was there remember. Tab is still hesitating, then suddenly now he comes to a decision. He hurries back to the Ice Factory, see there, he's broken into a run. He pushes open the door and comes straight out again! "Fire!" he shouts.'

She stopped the tape. Southwell stared at the frozen image of his son on the screen shouting silently to them. 'It doesn't prove anything,' he whispered hollowly.

Sheena felt worn down suddenly.

'Arson is a copycat crime. Tab may not have started them all. I'm guessing, but I'd say somehow he found out about you and me. It upset him a lot; like you say, he's fond of Donna. She provides a degree of stability in his life when he is up here for the summer. The business with the missing couple may have tipped him over the edge. What I do know is that he was at last night's fire because I saw him there. That's typical of the pattern too; arsonists like to watch the results of their handiwork.'

Southwell had a stunned expression as if the

bottom had just dropped out of his life. His chest heaved. He seemed to be struggling to find words. 'We can work this out,' he said thickly. 'We can work it out together. I'll speak to the boy.'

'You have to do more than that,' Sheena said. 'Tab needs professional help. You're a doctor, you must see that.'

'Look, no one has been hurt by any of this. A few acres of woodland burned out, but that regenerates. The Ice Factory was a wreck; the building has been derelict twenty years. Chance Greene was going to pull it down anyway.'

'We can't just do nothing; he could be out there now with a can of gas for all we know!'

Southwell was still shaking his head. 'I don't get it, we were so goddam careful. How did Tab find out about us?'

'This rain is terrible. We're never going to find a place to stop the night,' Jessica groaned.

'We'll have to keep on till we find somewhere with vacancies,' her husband said wearily.

They had been driving for an hour and it was evident that his wife's predictions had been correct. Every place they passed seemed to have a No Vacancies sign hung out. Finally, following a twisting road signposted River Recreation Center they crossed a bridge and there was an illuminated board.

Ted braked. 'Here's a place.'

'White Water Rafting – Accommodation –

Camping,' Jessica read out. 'It says they have vacancies. Worth a try, I guess.'

'Looks a rundown kind of place,' Julie muttered as they ducked through the rain to the porch.

'I don't care if it's Tony Perkins on the set of *Psycho*,' Jessica told her. 'I'm not going another step.'

But the proprietor was welcoming and helpful. 'Two family units for the night? Yes, we can manage that for you. Pull round to the side and you can park right outside.'

'How far are we from the ocean here?' Jessica asked suddenly.

'Nearest beach would be Goodwill. That's about twenty miles by road.'

'And as the crow flies?'

The man shrugged. 'Hard to say exactly, ten, twelve maybe. The road twists a fair bit.'

The families exchanged glances. Lloyd was meanwhile studying the posters on the wall. 'Can we go rafting tomorrow?' he asked eagerly.

'Sure you can,' the man told him. 'Be outside here nine-thirty a.m. We aim to have you on the water by ten-thirty. They open the sluices in the dam a mile upriver at ten-forty-five.'

'We're on the river here?' Jessica sounded surprised. She squinted out the rain-sluiced windows of the reception area.

'Hard to tell in this weather, isn't it?' The owner grinned. 'The channel runs a hundred yards down the slope there. You can just make out the trees along the bank.'

'Can we go, Mom? Dad? Please say yes?' the children pleaded.

The adults conferred. 'I'm not sure. What level of rough is the ride exactly?' Julie enquired.

'Don't you worry yourselves, ladies. The sections are graded according to difficulty class two to five. Class two is suitable for children seven and older.'

'I'm seven next week!' Lloyd said anxiously. 'Is that okay?'

'Well, you look at least eight to me,' the guy told him. 'Seriously, folks, I take young kids on that stretch all the time with no problems. It's an exciting ride and we have full safety aids. There's a fully qualified and experienced guide in every boat. The kids will have a ball and it's a good way to get them accustomed to the river. Price is one hundred dollars a head for adults, fifty for each child.'

Ted made a quick calculation. 'We'll do it,' he said after a nod from Brook. 'Nine-thirty, right?'

'Here at reception. Bring swim suits and something like a fleece to keep the wind out. Avoid cotton, it dries slowly and leaves you cold. Synthetics are better. We have wetsuits to rent. This time of year I'd recommend one. Also have a towel and change of clothes for afterwards.'

'We got that. Meantime, where can we find something to eat? We're famished.'

'Dining room and bar through that door. Chef goes off at nine. Till then he does a mean steak.'

As they headed back to the cars to drive to the rooms, Jessica had one last question. 'What's the name of this river?'

'You didn't see the sign as you came over the bridge? It's called Dead River.'

Chapter 31

La Palma, Canaries. The helicopter fly-over was scheduled for five a.m. Later might have been better; the geologists wanted maximum light to check the crest, but the authorities were rattled. The latest quake had left fourteen dead on La Palma, eight of them from a single family whose apartment block collapsed, crushing four floors into a basement tomb. On the advice of the observatory the authorities issued a level four volcano alert: major eruption anticipated within twenty-four hours. Islanders were cramming onto every available boat and plane. Control in the capital was breaking down and answers were needed fast. So the aircraft was commanded for five, later changed to six for better weather.

Organisation fell down from the outset. The geologists, Felipe, Concha and Malcolm Mackenzie, plus a Portuguese added to the list at the last minute, assembled as before at the observatory landing pad. The helicopter, a

Spanish air force Bell Augusta operating out of Tenerife – since the latest quake aircraft were no longer based on La Palma overnight – had first to ferry a government official between two other islands in the group. It was then directed to the civilian airport down on the coast by the capital. By the time these problems were resolved and the aircraft took off on its mission with the scientists aboard, a further three hours had been lost.

The winds were coming from the south-east so that the caldera and observatory were socked in under a layer of ash that kicked up in a red dust-cloud as the helicopter lifted off again. The co-pilot yelled something back to Felipe as they wheeled away eastwards towards the capital. Malc tried to follow, but in the noise of the cabin the Spanish was too quick. 'What's he saying?' he shouted to Felipe.

Felipe translated, 'Visibility is very bad all across the island. We have to circle out over La Gomera and Hierro and approach from the south. It will take sixty minutes and cut into our fuel.'

'He's bullshitting us. Ask him how long can he give us over the ridge?'

Felipe nodded. There was a shouted exchange between him and the two pilots. Felipe turned back. 'The pilot says everything depends on the dust. If it is bad we can spend only a short time, enough for one pass only. This is because filters become blocked and the engines overheat, which would be bad for everyone aboard.'

Malc looked out at the swirling ochre-coloured clouds that clung to the mountains and wondered how these guys could fly at all.

The air was clearer once they were over the water however and became progressively better as they reached the precipitous cliffs of La Gomera and turned onto the new heading. After twenty minutes the immense bay of tiny El Hierro appeared below, glinting in the sunrise.

'Not much ash there,' Malc observed to Concha.

'No, they have been lucky. The wind favours them.'

'Let's hope the other elements do as well,' he replied. Her brow furrowed. 'I mean the ocean. If we lose Cumbre Vieja the folk down there won't have a lot of time to reach high ground.'

She looked at him and her mouth quivered. 'So you think it will happen? A day ago you called me stupid for thinking that.'

He shook his head. 'That was twenty-four hours ago; a lot has happened since then. Anyway I chewed you out for saying we could lose the American East Coast. I still think that possibility is remote.'

The co-pilot was saying something. 'We are lining up for the run in,' Felipe relayed. 'The pilot has to be very careful because the dust from the vents makes the helicopter radar blind.'

The poor bastards are shitting themselves,

390

Malc thought. Back at the base they've seen the TV; they reckon the volcano could blow at any moment. They're terrified of being burned alive. The pilot will give us one pass at medium altitude before announcing an abort and turning back, so we had better make sure every minute we have counts. In the next seat Felipe had obviously drawn the same conclusion and was readying his cameras.

They flew northwards. Ahead an immense dark cloud, towering up to 10,000 feet, hung above La Palma like a rusty shroud. Below, the ocean was shadowed, stained with muddied streaks from ash falls, and as they passed over the small town of Fuencaliente on the extreme southern tip the formerly neat white houses were blackened and deserted. A mile outside the settlement, the yawning chasm of the smoking cone boiled and fumed, occasionally spitting up showers of fiery sparks.

The helicopter banked round to let them take shots, but this was one of the lesser vents and they soon flew on, hugging the line of the western shore.

Malc tapped Felipe on the shoulder. 'He's taking us too far out. We need to be over the central ridge.'

The pilot shouted something back in reply. Felipe responded forcefully. A sharp debate took place.

'I told them they have to take us closer in,' Felipe translated for his colleagues. 'They are not happy. They say it is too dangerous. I have explained the purpose of the trip, that the data we have to collect is vital. If we cannot get close enough to obtain what we need, then the flight will be wasted and they will have to return, when it will be even more risky. So they will take us in, but as I say they are not happy.'

Still grumbling, the pilot banked away to starboard. Malc saw a fishing boat pass underneath, beating up north in the direction of Puerto Naos. Their shadow skimmed the dusty ocean below. They had dropped to around 3,000 feet. A black sand beach flicked by and the ground started to rise. Ahead he could see cliffs. Out the left side windows a smoke plume rose from the water's edge. He glanced at his map. They must be near El Charco. Trees below, shrouded in dust, grey as corpses.

Felipe was calling off map references to the co-pilot, who punched the coordinates angrily into his computer. Neither officer made any attempt to hide his disgust. Only the prospect of being ordered back a second time was driving them on.

The helicopter tilted and began to circle. They had reached the first set-down point and were looking for a landing place. Somewhere beneath in the dust and smoke should be what they had come to see: the southern end of the 1949 fracture line.

'*Jesu!*' The Portuguese behind Felipe crossed himself. Towering cliffs loomed ahead. The helicopter lifted a little. The dust clouds parted, revealing a lurid glimpse of a kilometre-high fountain of burning lava spouting like some hellish nightmare from the crater of Hoyo Negro.

Out on the ground it was worse.

The pilot set them down on the ridge at the first gap in the smoke that came up. When the scientists protested that they needed to be further in he yelled at them, 'Get out! Get what you came for. Every minute we wait here for you our lives are in danger!' There was nothing for it but to make their way on foot.

The dense ash falls near the vents and constant outpourings of smoke made the gloom so intense that at times the landing party had to grope their way. At Felipe's urging they improvised masks against dust and grit. The fumes worried him too. Methane gas was a known hazard of the ridge. There should be respirators, but somehow they had been left behind. 'Anyone who feels faint must stop at once,' he emphasised, 'and return to the aircraft. Work in pairs and watch one another.'

Malcolm took the girl. This sector of the fault was dramatic. During the eruption here in 1949 the ground had subsided vertically four metres along the crest of the ridge with a simultaneous sideslip of half a metre over a three-kilometre distance. The question was this, did this fracture extend far down inside the mountain or was it a surface crack? To use the technical terms, were they looking at a deep level discontinuity or a shallow geomorphological feature? Did it result perhaps from gravitational settling caused by the collapse of magma chambers supplying the numerous vents or were they poised on top of a line of cleavage that could shear like a plate of glass at the next big tremor?

'If it is a deep level rupture,' Felipe had theorised on the flight in, 'then we need to locate evidence of further shearing with movement in both vertical and lateral planes.'

In simple words they were looking for signs that the mountain was breaking apart.

'And if we find these indications? Then what?' Concha had wanted to know.

No one had had an answer to that one. Their job was to find proof, one way or the other. After that it was down to the politicians what to do.

Sweating in their flame-proof suits, wheezing and coughing in the foetid air, they set to work. The landscape had the devastation of a battlefield. Great mounds of blasted cinder and gravel, the slopes pockmarked by small lumps of tephra interspersed with craters formed where rocks had fallen like bursting shells. The Hoyo cone was barely two kilometres off. When the wind veered in their direction the fumes and noise from the screeching vents were unbearable and shrapnel showers of gravel swept the hillside. Any minute Malc expected to hear the helicopter's engines spooling up to take off as the pilots decided to pull the plug and abandon their passengers to their madness.

Between the four of them, they covered the best part of half a kilometre following the fault line, wading knee-deep through drifts of ash, scrambling past veins of razor-sharp lava. Everywhere along the crest the ridge bore traces of shallow cracking and folding. That was to be expected after the constant shallow tremors of the past weeks, but hard as he searched Malc found none of the gaping crevasses, the precursors to a major flank collapse that he dreaded.

He called to Concha. She shook her head too. 'I think we go back to the plane now, yes?'

'So long as we're out here let's do the job properly.'

He worked his way along another hundred metres. The girl followed reluctantly. 'There is nothing, we should go back, I think. The pilots are anxious.'

Malc gave up. She was probably right. 'Okay, let's head off.'

Relieved, they retraced their steps. Felipe and the Portuguese met them by the helicopter.

'We found nothing. You?'

'Likewise.'

'*Madre de Dios*, a mercy!'

The crew were agitated, jumpy. 'Hurry! Hurry!' they shouted through the door. 'Leave now!'

As they lifted off Felipe got on the radio to the observatory reporting the good news. 'Still as before, some crumbling and cracking, but no major slippage that any of us could detect. *Si*, Mackenzie agrees. We are on our way to the northern sector now.'

'For the last time!' the co-pilot added under his breath and muttered a quick prayer.

Malc clung to his seat as another air pocket jolted the Bell Augusta. They were skimming the crest of the Ruta de los Volcanes a scant 700 feet above the tallest of the smoking cones. So far they had counted five major vents all spewing ash and glowing pyroclast fragments. The sky overhead churned with red dust and smoke.

'Look, down there! See, there is a place!' Felipe shouted above the din of engines and rotor. Peering through the dust-streaked poly-carbonate window, the geologists could make out the scar in the side of the ridge, a vertical wall of rock that straggled the rutted remains of former lava flow.

The situation was deteriorating by the minute. Repeated detonations from the Hoyo Negro cone were shaking the helicopter, pebbles and lava stones pinging off the fuselage. The Portuguese was tugging at Malc's sleeve, also pointing downwards. Malc gave a thumbs-up sign to show he understood. Felipe was talking urgently to the pilot, who was shouting back at them, shaking his head in furious refusal. Malc caught, *No*! and *Prohibido*!

'Fifteen minutes! Tell the yellow bastard we need just fifteen minutes on the ground!'

he shouted to Felipe. He was struggling against the lurching of the chopper to focus his binoculars.

'What can you see?' the Portuguese was clamouring.

'Nothing, there's so much dust and crap I can't make out any detail!' Malc yelled back. 'Dammit, Felipe, the guy has got to set us down! That's what he flew us out here for, for Christsakes!'

Felipe was holding up his hands. '*Cinco! Cinco! Capitán,*' he pleaded. 'Five minutes, okay?'

The captain threw up a hand in disgust. Swearing under his breath, he scanned the ground and spat something at his co-pilot, jabbing a thumb downward. The nose dropped sickeningly as the machine spun on its tail, righted itself somehow, flared out and settled with a thump in a whirlwind of blown grit.

Malc and the others grabbed their gear and flung open the side door. The captain twisted round, his face under the helmet contorted. 'Five, okay! *Cinco* minutes! Then we go, you stay!' he raged. 'You stay here in the fucking *malpais* and die!'

Bending double, shielding his face against the stinging rotor blast, Malc ran towards the rocks, pushing Concha ahead of him. The four of them crouched on the ground, waiting for the blades to slow. Then Malc slapped Felipe on the shoulder and they set off in single file along the fracture line. Once again they were looking for tearing of the ground, recent fissures, signs of movement pointing to flank failure.

And praying they wouldn't find any.

But this time Malcolm wasn't so sure.

He had taken a dozen steps, when the girl at his side let out a cry and fell forward in the ash. He caught her by the arm, hauling her back up. 'Are you hurt?'

She coughed on dust and shook her head. Felipe was close behind. 'We must hurry,' he gasped, voice muffled by a handkerchief tied over his mouth. 'You and Concha go that way.' He pointed.

'No.' Malc jerked his head in the direction of the Hoyo crater. 'I want to try that way. I thought maybe I saw some ground disturbance among the rock falls as we flew in.'

Felipe stared at him. 'Okay, as you like. I will take the other side with Lopez. Do not go far. If the eruption gets worse, the pilots will not wait for either of you.'

'Is this where you saw the fresh faulting?' Concha screamed.

'I think so,' Malc yelled back. The shriek of steam from fumaroles on the ridge made talking next to impossible.

'I see nothing.' Her black hair escaping from under her yellow helmet whipped her cheeks.

'We'll try further along.'

'*Qué?*'

He took her by the arm and showed her.

'Down there, doesn't that look like fresh quake damage?' he shouted in her ear.

She peered down the slope, frowning. 'Maybe yes, but not deep.'

'We have to check. You wait here.'

'No, I come with you. I am not afraid.'

Together they slithered down a bank of gravel to a patch of broken ground.

'Not deep,' Concha said squatting in the dust. They were partially sheltered from the noise and wind. 'Just tremors, I think.'

Malc moved about, his gaze searching. She was right, he decided. The ground was cracked open in places, but it could just be the result of general tremors connected with the swelling of the Hoyo crater. And yet he was uneasy. Partly it was the extent of the fissures, the way they snaked through the ground and interconnected. He had the sense of something huge just around the corner. He checked his watch. They had been ten minutes already. As he opened his mouth to speak a deafening blast from the volcano blotted out the words. A glaring red cone pulsed vividly against the boiling smoke clouds. Sparks and globules of liquid lava splashed around them.

'Run!'

This time it was the girl who grabbed his arm. Ducking against the deadly rain, they pulled each other back up the slope. Dust-caked figures emerged from the smoke. Felipe reached out to help him up to firm ground. 'We came to find you. Hurry, the aircraft is about to leave.'

'Wait. I saw some cracking back there. I think we should check it out.'

'How bad? I saw nothing. Did anyone else?'

The other two shook their heads. Concha looked at him. 'It was tremor damage, nothing.'

'I disagree,' Malc argued back heatedly. 'We can't be sure without checking.'

Felipe was adamant. 'This is stupid. I cannot risk losing more lives. I am ordering everyone off the mountain.'

'We haven't examined anything like enough of this sector to be confident.'

'Are you mad? Do you want to get us all killed?'

Malc faced him. 'It's what we came here to find out,' he countered. 'If we don't survey the area properly we have no way of telling if the flank is stable. I'll do it on my own. The rest of you can go back.'

'We have the GPS,' Felipe said angrily. 'I am in charge here. The judgement is mine.'

Before Malc could argue further there was a whistling sound and everyone ducked. A glowing lava bomb the size and weight of a cement sack plummeted out of the smoke, hit the slope half a dozen metres away with an impact that made the ground shake and bounced off downhill. Smoking fragments showered the party.

'No more argument!' Felipe shouted. 'Back to the aircraft!'

Slipping and stumbling, they ran through the smoke. Well before the helicopter came in sight they could hear the rotors winding up. Christ, Malc thought, the bastards are going to bug out on us. And it would be his fault if they were stuck out here. Sand and grit stung their faces. Crouching, they staggered towards the noise. They could hear the pilots screaming at them to hurry. They reached the hatch and pushed one another through. Malc was last. As he hauled himself in the pilot was already lifting off. Gasping for breath, he collapsed in a seat next to Concha. Above the engine sounds he could hear Felipe calling in to the observatory. 'Everything checks out. No significant slippage on the fault line. Yes, we are off the mountain and coming in now. Over.'

They were the Spaniard's last words.

A lurid red glare enveloped the nose. There was a shattering crash and the starboard side of the helicopter opposite where Malc was sitting dissolved in a welter of splintered glass and metal shards. The cabin lurched violently and fell like a stone, canting over and flinging Malc from his seat. Freezing air blasted through the gap, driving a storm of wreckage into the interior. Malc grabbed out to stop himself being thrown out the gaping hole, but the aircraft was spinning violently, round and round, engines screaming at breaking point, bodies, rucksacks, pieces of equipment being hurled about inside.

Dimly Malc was aware of the cliff face racing

past outside the windows. The helicopter must have spun wildly, hurling itself off the mountain, and was plunging down the slope.

Moments later there came a second jarring impact, much, much worse than before, that slammed him up against what might have been the roof, he had no way of telling. An appalling noise of smashing and tearing metal and a series of violent jolts battered him half senseless. Dimly, he was aware of cries from the others. The cabin was thick with smoke and dust. They seemed to be sliding, falling, bouncing on rocks. All he could think about was the terror of fire.

Then suddenly the violent motion ceased. He felt wind on his face, somehow discerned a gap in front of him and on instinct rolled himself into a ball and threw himself through. He hit the ground with a thump that knocked the remaining air from his lungs, gasped, choked on a mouthful of dirt and pulled himself somehow to his feet.

The Bell Augusta lay crumpled like a broken insect, crushed between huge rocks on the ridge. Shattered metal everywhere. Smoke, steam curling. God, fire! Then through the hole torn in the side he saw the girl Concha slumped in her seat. He reached in and pulled clumsily at her. She moaned, half conscious, but resisted. Damn, she was still belted in. It took precious moments fiddling with the catch. He got an arm under her and dragged her out. The smell of smoke was strong now. Fear of fire was all consuming. He heaved her onto his shoulder and stumbled away, heart pounding, legs pumping, driven by adrenaline, the girl's body a dead weight dragging. A red glare splashed the rocks; he felt the thud of the fuel igniting and the heat at his back and knew the others were dead.

How far he carried her he had no idea. When his legs gave out he sank to his knees. The girl's eyes were open, staring. 'Are you hurt?' he asked her. She said nothing, but gazed around, her pupils dark with shock.

'Can you hear me? Are you hurt,' he repeated.

She moistened her caked lips. 'There,' she croaked. She lifted her hand from his shoulder and gestured at the ground. But by then, Malc had seen too.

'Jesus!' he whispered horrified.

They had found what they had come for. The evidence was there in front of them. Right where they had stopped, exhausted, the ground was riven with newly opened fractures spreading out from those of sixty years ago.

And that was not all. There was worse; along the line of the old fault a band of virgin rock showed fresh splitting, exposed where the ground had dropped away seawards.

The mountain was tearing itself apart.

The mountain was tearing itself apart and they were the only two who knew. The only two and with no way of warning the world. Felipe's last words had been catastrophically ill-judged. He had paid for it with his life.

Chapter 32

Goodwill, Bearskin Neck. Rick woke at five to five, moments before his alarm shrilled. The night had been humid after the rain, but this morning the wind had shifted round to the east and the greyness was damp and cool, heavy with sea salt. He kicked the sheets off and slid out onto the wooden floor in his bare feet. He was alone in his apartment above the store; Natalie had not passed a night here since the engagement.

In the slowly lifting darkness he slipped outside and started the pick-up. It was a three-minute drive to the Green. At the police department, Ted Hopper, one of the two night-duty officers, was behind the desk. 'Your day starts and mine ends,' he grunted. Ted was six months off retirement. He made the same remark every Sunday. Unhooking the key to the secure garage, he walked Rick through to the rear of the building.

'Don't you ever get tired of this job?' he said as they entered the garage where the vehicles were kept.

Rick shrugged. 'It pays the rent. I don't mind the early starts. Not in summer anyway.' They had this conversation over and over.

The dark-blue security wagon was parked up where he had left it yesterday over against the far wall. Waiting by the passenger side, shotgun in hand, was a lean, pale-faced man. Evan Kelso was the bank guard employed to handle the money. 'Morning, Evan,' Rick greeted him. Kelso nodded mutely. He almost never spoke. Perhaps it was nerves.

Before he climbed aboard Rick walked around and checked the tyres. The last thing he wanted on one of these trips was a flat. He slipped on the Kevlar vest and helmet, buckled on the gunbelt with the pistol that the firm supplied and climbed up into the driver's seat. At his signal Hopper pressed the switch to raise the garage door. 'All set?' Rick asked Kelso and received a nod in reply. He turned the ignition key. The clock on the dash said five-twenty-nine. Dead on time.

First stop was the bank on Main Street. Rick turned in behind Crocus Lane to where there was a steel gate opening onto a purpose-built bay and waited with the engine running for Kelso to collect the empty cashboxes that would be filled in Bangor and brought back to feed the tills and dispensers in Goodwill.

Bangor was 100 miles up Route One. At this hour with the roads clear Rick could reckon on completing the round trip in four hours flat. The bank allowed an extra hour for delays, which were seldom. If you could handle the early starts the money was good. He and Kelso made the same run every Sunday. Including bonuses, Rick's share worked out at thirty-five bucks an hour actual driving time. Kelso took home slightly less, but then all he had to do was look at the view and handle the bags at the stops. To Rick's way of thinking Kelso had the worse end of the deal; if anyone was going to stop a bullet it was him. Not that they had ever met trouble once in the four years Rick had been driving. And $175 a week went a long way in Goodwill.

They rumbled through the just-stirring town. There was a mist hanging over the Causeway. Lights burned in the hospital, but there were no signs of activity. Rick made a right onto the highway and started to bring the speed up. The engine was old and with the weight of armour she carried acceleration was slow. Beside his belt pistol, Rick had an M-16 clipped beside the door where he could reach it quickly in an emergency. The truck was supposed to be proof against small arms.

The road was deserted except for the occasional farmer in a pick-up and once a huge logging truck hammering southwards to a pulp mill. Outside Jonesboro they passed a couple of

RVs parked down near a creek, drapes drawn. Tourists exploring the backwoods.

The truck rolled on through patches of mist. There was no radio. Rick went through in his mind a list of things to be done today. If Natalie's father remained determined for the regatta to go ahead and enough tourists could be enticed back to watch, then the weekend might not be a total disaster after all. Chance Greene was going to speak to the local media first thing this morning about putting announcements out.

In the other seat Kelso chewed gum and thought about whatever, if thinking was what he did. All at once though he amazed Rick by speaking. 'So what you going to do now?' he enquired in his flat nasal drawl.

Rick started in surprise. 'What?' he said.

'I said, what you going to do now?' Kelso repeated unhurriedly,

He must have heard about the engagement, Rick realised. It was a reasonable enough question in the circumstances. A newly married man didn't jump out of bed at five every morning just for fun.

'I haven't given it much thought yet.' That much was true at least. 'I guess we haven't made any plans yet.'

Kelso made no response. Having got the one question off his chest he relapsed into his customary silence.

* * *

Charco Verde, La Palma, Ten-thirty a.m. local time. The last tremor had rattled the little town for a full three minutes. The ground had heaved and pulsed as if trying to throw off the weight of the buildings pressing on it. Not once but three times the ocean had run out, then swept back in, destroying boats already wrecked in earlier quakes. The waves had crashed into the sea wall, twisting railings, wrenching up paving stones.

The floor of Carlos's patio that was already buried in a foot of sand and dust had been heaved up from below, the tiles splintered and cracked as if some huge beast was breaking through from below. The ash clouds had cast a pall of gloom over the island and the temperature was in the sixties. Sweaters were the order of the day.

But still Carlos clung on. The vent beyond the rocks grew in size and power with each hour that passed, spewing ash and clots of hissing lava that coursed down the cone, armouring its flanks in a stony carapace. The sand on the beach was hot underfoot and wisps of steam could be seen rising in places. 'We cannot wait! We have to act now or it will destroy us,' he declared to the others. They nodded; none of them had any choice. Without the town they were nothing.

A dozen steel drums had been scavenged from a factory in the centre of the island; the explosives had been packed inside and the drums sealed up again. Carlos's cousin, who managed the quarry at Taburiente, had attended to the fuses.

It took two men apiece to manhandle each loaded drum out from the shed and heave it up onto the trailer that had been backed up outside. The trailer belonged to wall-eyed Pedro de Vera's daughter's husband; the tractor had been loaned by someone else. It had a hydraulic forklift to hoist the drums up onto the ridge. 'We pack the drums tight together against the side of the cone facing the ocean,' Carlos told them. 'The blast will smash a hole through the crust, split the rock apart and let in the sea.'

'Snuff the bitch out,' Pedro muttered darkly, in agreement.

Loading the trailer took longer than anyone thought. The drums weighed sixty kilos each and they were terrified of an accident, even though Carlos's cousin had said the *plástico* was hard to set off without a detonator. By the time the convoy started along the beach the tide was starting to turn.

Ahead of them the vent's cone sputtered and smoked like a devil's candle.

Ruta de los Volcanes. High on the smoking ridge Malc sat in the dirt, cradling his head in his hands. 'This is my fault. If I hadn't wasted time arguing with Felipe back there the helicopter would have gotten clear.'

The girl regarded him sternly. 'No, you were

right and we, the rest, were wrong. We should have looked harder and found the new faulting. What was it that you said? We were geologists, that was our task. Then we would not have been in the aircraft when the tephra bomb hit the rotor. Now the others are dead and we are alive. We have to find a way off the mountain to warn the observatory what is going to happen before more people die.'

Malc spat out a mouthful of dust and heaved himself to his feet. The girl was right, guilt and grief were unimportant. What counted now was to get word back. All the phones and radios had perished in the crash. They had to find a house and quickly.

'When they realise the helicopter is missing they will send out another to find us,' Concha said hopefully.

'Don't count on it. They were short of aircraft and with this amount of smoke and dust in the air we'll be hard to spot. Which is the quickest way to civilisation?'

'The nearest settlements are down on the coast. There may be phones still working in Puerto Naos or Charco Verde, but I doubt it. Otherwise our best hope is probably to continue along the Ruta towards Pilar.'

'If we come off the ridge and find the phones on the coast are down, then climbing back out again will take us till nightfall. I vote to follow the ridge.'

Driven by unimaginable pressure from below,

magma was forcing its way up swollen pipes, bursting through the overlying rock burden to outlets on the surface. If that process continued unabated, then all the ground between of the ridge crest where they stood and the shore five kilometres away to the west would slide catastrophically into the ocean, making everyone's worst nightmare come true.

They were entering the final phase in the eruption. The best they could hope for now was time, time to evacuate the population from this end of the island, time to warn populations around the Atlantic basin to be prepared to head for high ground.

Charco Verde. 'What if a spark hits the *plástico*?' wall-eyed Pedro de Vera asked nervously.

The tractor had reached the end of the beach. Tying handkerchiefs across their faces as a protection against acid fumes, the men climbed up onto the rocky outcrop screening the cove. The vent lay below them, a smoking pit disfiguring the little bay like a bleeding ulcer with the blackened cone rising in its centre. Steam and smoke hissed from the orifice in stinking gusts. As they watched, a gob of liquid red lava squeezed out over the cone's lip and slopped down the side.

Carlos wiped grit from his eye. 'This stuff is stable. They use it all the time in the quarry. If you set it alight it will burn not explode. For that you need a detonator, fool!'

The fisherman hunched his shoulders, hands in pockets. 'This is crazy. We have no business here.'

Carlos rounded on him, his eyes like flints. 'Would you rather take a job as a waiter on Lanzarote? Stop whining and be a man!'

His words put backbone into them. Under Carlos's direction they unhitched the tractor and used its hydraulic bucket to hoist an explosive-filled drum onto the outcrop. From there it was manhandled across to the far edge and lowered into the outer pit on ropes. 'Like a wine cask into a cellar,' as one of them put it.

'Less talking,' Carlos snapped. 'Fetch up the next.' In another hour the tide would be turning.

Atlantic Ocean. Eleven-thirty a.m. The PA system aboard the USS *Tarp* announced that a radar fix had been obtained on the transmitter aerial for the malfunctioning buoy in the DART network. Mary Sennett had passed a sleepless night and this morning the mountain seemed to loom huger than ever. An enormous black stain on the horizon, an anvil-shaped plume spreading out into the stratosphere, its vast shadow covering the ocean like a pall.

'Mount Doom,' someone quipped.

Mary didn't find it funny. The frequency and strength of tremors were increasing. You didn't need to be a geologist to realise that a climax of some sort was building. She just prayed they could locate the buoy and make the repairs

412

before the whole island went up, taking them with it.

Derek Wanless gave his team another pep talk. 'I won't pretend there isn't a degree of risk to our return. The people back home are relying on the DART network to provide timely warning of tsunami-type events. It's our job not to let them down. Preliminary evaluation of the test signals suggests that the problem stems from processor malfunction rather than a data transmission error. Retrieval will therefore be necessary. The captain has given orders to start preparing the submersible so that we can start deployment as soon as the ship is alongside the buoy. The quicker we get the job done the sooner we are out of here.'

Mary remained glum. She was doing the calculations in her head. Five hours minimum for the submersible to descend to the ocean floor, recover the pressure pack and return to the surface. Add time required to swap whatever component had failed, say two to four hours including testing. Another five hours to redeploy the pack and retrieve the submersible. Twelve hours minimum assuming testing of the unit could be completed while the submersible was making the second ascent. Navy regulations forbade night-time use of the submersible except in an emergency, meaning the redeployment phase would have to wait until tomorrow. At best, presuming the weather held, no cables snapped and all systems tested out satisfactorily, it would be a full twenty-four hours before they could up anchor.

Looking out over the rail, Mary half wished the mountain would explode, giving them an excuse to haul ass out.

As they steamed on they saw familiar sights, mats of floating pumice, poisoned fish floating belly-up. Ash drifted down out of the sky, coating the ship in a ghostly grey. The sun had been ringed with fire as it rose, now as midday loomed it had retreated into an ominous twilight.

'I feel as though we are entering the underworld,' she confessed to Derek.

He shrugged. 'Maybe we're the lucky ones. Think of those geologists out on the volcano even now.'

Mary shuddered.

USS *Thresher*. Noon. The trim control tanks hissed as water was pumped out and the huge vessel rose smoothly towards the surface. 'Periscope depth, sir,' the executive officer reported. 'Radar mast up. Negative air activity. Distance to land fifteen point eight miles. Sonar reports negative on the Russian still. One surface contact at zero-four-zero estimated small fishing craft distance two thousand five hundred yards inshore probably headed for Puerto Naos. The plot also shows the survey vessel USS *Tarp* approximately thirty miles to the north-west. *Tarp* is engaged in ocean buoy deployment.'

'Very good. Up 'scope.'

414

'Up periscope, yes, sir.' The glistening steel column slid swiftly up from the floor of the operations room. The captain took the handles, stooping to the eyepiece as it came level. The image was being simultaneously projected onto a computer screen for the benefit of the other officers, but like many commanders Krauss preferred the direct view.

'Sky is heavily overcast,' he muttered, scanning round. 'You'd think this was nightfall instead of the middle of the day. Heck of a lot of dirt on the water, ash and pumice mostly. You were right about the fishing boat, light blue, no wheelhouse, three men aboard probably hand lining.' He cranked up the magnification, bringing the scene into sharp relief.

'Looks like they've moved this far out to get from under the ash plume,' the executive officer suggested.

On the screen a moustachioed fisherman's teeth flashed as he hauled in a catch.

'He's happy,' someone commented.

'Wouldn't you be if you were him?'

The captain swung the lens round and whistled softly. 'Boy, lots of smoke out there, huge plumes of sparks. Those clouds must be twenty thousand feet—'

'Picking up strong seismic activity inshore!' a sonar operator sang out suddenly. 'Feels like another big tremor.'

'Can't make out what's happening from this distance. Plenty of red stuff jumping from the central area. Let's have some photographs for the log.'

For several minutes the sub crept along snapping pictures of the burning island.

'Looks like four separate cones all smoking,' the executive officer observed to his captain. 'Maybe it's true what they're saying about the island could break up.'

Krauss shook his head. He wasn't going to speculate.

'Captain, check out the boat, sir!' a junior officer, detailed to keep the fishing vessel under surveillance on the auxiliary periscope, interrupted suddenly. 'One of the Spaniards is in the water!'

'How did he get there?'

'Must have overbalanced.'

'In this sea?'

'Hey, those others don't look so good. The guy with the moustache just fell over in the stern sheets.'

'Shit, she's going down!'

Krauss swung the scope back round. 'I've lost her. Where'd she go?'

There was a moment's silence. Then the executive officer said, 'I think she just sank.'

The young officer, who had been watching, had a stunned expression. 'I don't get it, one moment she was there, the next she just went straight down like, like somebody pulled a string.'

The men in the command centre stared at the

screens. The sea was empty. The fishing boat with its three occupants, which had been plainly visible in the powerful periscope lens, had vanished completely.

Krauss was the first to recover. 'Check for other vessels in vicinity!'

'Negative on radar, sir.'

'Sonar is confused by seismic clutter, sir, but nothing close.'

'You certain of that? What about the Russian?'

'One hundred per cent, sir. We have their signature on file. If the Russian was within twenty miles we'd nail him even in this.'

Krauss was still scanning the surface, half hoping to see the fishing boat reappear somehow. 'Anyone pick up a mayday?'

'Negative, sir. There's some chatter, but all inland or around the other islands.'

'Wind speed?' He didn't know why he asked. The ocean was perfectly normal.

'Ten to twelve knots, sir, westerly. Sea state is normal.'

Whatever had sunk the boat, it had not been the weather.

'Sonar picking up hull crunching sounds, sir.'

No one spoke. The executive officer and the captain exchanged glances. 'That was quick, poor bastards.' The executive officer licked his lips. 'She must have gone down like a stone.'

'Yes, but why?' Krauss said.

'A whale caught someone's line, dragged them under?'

417

'No way,' the chief sonar operator cut in. 'If there was a whale we'd have picked it up.'

'Anyway the line would have broken first, surely?' another officer said.

'Yeah, but a boat doesn't just sink for no reason.'

'They were acting strange before that.'

'More noises, sir!' the sonar operator snapped.

Krauss stepped over to where the man was seated at his console. 'Engine?' he rapped.

'No, sir, sounds more like gas bubbles rising to the surface.'

'Probably escaping from the crushed hull,' the executive officer said.

Everyone waited tensely. 'Still picking up the sounds?' Krauss asked.

The operator shook his head. 'It's hard to make out; there's so much background stuff from the island.'

'I don't buy it,' the executive officer said. 'It's been what, a minute, a minute and a half? How does a small fishing boat reach crush depth that fast?'

Krauss's face was stony. 'Give me the last known position of the boat.'

'Fifteen hundred yards at zero-three-zero, sir,' the navigating officer came back promptly.

Whatever it was, the submarine was moving closer.

'Sir, seawater temperature is rising!' a technician monitoring the gauges called out.

Everyone snapped round. 'By how much?' Krauss asked him.

'Up two degrees to sixty-six. We must be passing through a thermocline.'

The executive officer was looking puzzled. 'A warm patch? Fuel released from the boat?' he hazarded.

'Sixty-eight degrees!' the technician called.

'Steam release from an undersea vent, more likely,' said the nav officer.

Then everything went crazy.

All at once the submarine lurched and began to drop violently. The periscope screens went blank. Alarms shrilled.

Charco Verde, La Palma. The placing of the explosives proceeded without a hitch. Carlos had thought the operation through fully. Each barrel was hoisted up and lowered into the pit on the far side of the rocks. While the last barrels were being brought up, Carlos scrambled down into the pit, braving showers of sparks and the occasional lava blob to hook up the fuses.

Each barrel had been fitted with electric blasting caps or detonators and wired up with a lead line running out through a predrilled hole in the lid. All lids were then sealed with waterproof sealant. The main charges were C-4 plastic explosive. C-4 consists of 90 per cent by weight RDX or cyclonite mixed with binders, plasticiser and petroleum oil. In appearance it is an off-white solid with the feel of soft clay. It is the ideal

419

explosive material: powerful and extremely stable.

All that remained was for Carlos to wire up each barrel to a capacitor box supplied by his cousin from the quarry. It was essential, the cousin had explained, that the wires for the detonators be twisted together to prevent stray radio signals from causing premature detonation. If the wires were not twisted or shortened, one lead could act as an antenna with the other forming a ground. Then the signal might induce sufficient current to heat up the filament inside the detonator and set off a charge.

Carlos's cousin had used exploding bridgewire-type detonators. A small-diameter wire took the place of a filament. A capacitor supplied a 300-volt current which discharged through the detonator causing the bridgewire to explode, initiating the secondary explosive.

The capacitor box was a sophisticated device that would pass the detonating current from the firing unit to each detonator simultaneously or in sequence depending on how it was set. For today's operation this one was set to fire the charges together in a single blast.

The final barrel was lowered into place on top of the others. Carlos located the tail of wire protruding from its cap, wiped it clean, twisted the bare wire ends together, inserted them into a junction box and tightened the plastic-coated screw. Then, as his cousin had instructed, he took a minute to check all twelve connections, making sure each one was tight. The fumes from the vent, a mix of hydrochloric acid and sulphur dioxide, were very thick down in the pit. His head was spinning and he had to fight constant nausea. Finally he unwound the end of the firing cable reel, fitted it into the junction box and twisted the screw tight on the socket.

'Here,' he gasped to Pedro standing on the rocks, 'take this. You'll have to help me up. I'm all done in.'

With Pedro's help he scrambled back onto the outcrop and together they paid out the cable and passed the reel down to the men on the trailer. Away from the fumes of the pit, Carlos felt his strength returning. 'Okay,' he told the driver, 'take us back across the beach to the wall. And drive slowly or you'll snap the cable.'

The wall was a section of breakwater 200 metres off erected by the town some years back, part of an abandoned attempt to extend the seafront promenade. They stopped the tractor on the far side and everyone got off to cluster round Carlos as he fumbled to connect up the capacitor box for firing the charge.

'Are you sure we have enough *plástico*?' Pedro de Vera asked.

'Twelve barrels, sixty kilos each, that makes more than seven hundred of explosive,' Carlos told him. 'My cousin said it is enough to blow a hole in the island and sink it!' He laughed shortly.

He checked the wiring and connections and

charged up the capacitors. A pair of lights glowed a dangerous red. Carlos set his finger on the firing switch. 'All ready?' he said. 'Get down behind the wall then, fool!' he added to Juan, the youngest of the bunch.

'I want to see the blast though,' the young man protested.

'You'll hear it and that will be enough,' one of the others quipped and the others chuckled. Now that the job was almost behind them they were quite cheerful.

'Ready?' Carlos repeated and this time every-one crouched.

'Wait,' Pedro de Vera said suddenly.

'Now what?' Carlos demanded irritably.

'Who is to set off the charge?'

Carlos blinked at him. 'Are you saying you should be the one?' he said furiously.

Pedro responded with dignity, 'Everyone helped equally. I say we should have a vote.' There were murmurs of assent from the others.

Carlos scowled at them. 'Who paid for the *plástico* and the barrels, eh? Answer me that! Who set the fuses? I saw none of you down in the stinking pit with the sparks flying.'

There was no argument. Everyone looked away. 'Of course you should do it,' Pedro de Vera said hastily.

Carlos snorted. He spat into the sand and rubbed his hands. '*Atención*!' he shouted.

* * *

Ruta de los Volcanes. One p.m. Still limping, Malcolm Mackenzie staggered along the ridge beside Concha. The Spanish girl had taken charge. She knew the island, but even she was finding it hard to navigate in this changed landscape. Hundreds of acres of forest on the slopes had been burned out, paths and cuttings buried under drifting sand and ash. Both geologists were coated in powdery red dust. It choked their throats and stung their eyes. From time to time gusts of smoke from one of the vents on the ridge enveloped them in an acrid cloud, leaving them gasping for breath and staggering like a pair of drunks.

It was dark under the ash plume and chilly. For easier walking they had stripped down to shorts and T-shirts, dumping their fireproof coveralls beside the track. Their water bottles had been lost in the aircraft and Malcolm's thirst was overpowering.

Somewhere up ahead in a defile between two hills lay the camping area at Pilar. From there a narrow road wound steeply down to the cross-island highway and the tunnel under the ridge to the capital Santa Cruz. With luck they would be able to phone from Pilar or at least find a vehicle to give them a ride into the city.

Tremors still quivered underfoot, but perhaps because they were moving away from the immediate eruption zone their intensity seemed to be easing. Yet vast quantities of smoke and ash were still pumping into the atmosphere behind them, obscuring the sun, leaving them groping in an ominous twilight among charred trees and poisonous rocks.

They had been walking an hour when Concha paused at a path leading away down to their left. 'I think that leads down to Puerto Naos and Charco Verde,' she said, shaking the dust from her hair and pointing. Trickles of sweat glistened on her ochre-dusted throat. 'If we followed it we might be able to link up with a road that would take us to El Paso.'

'That's taking us away from the highway though and anyway I thought all the towns west of the ridge were being evacuated.'

Concha shrugged. 'We might run into an army patrol. They would take us back with them. By now they may be out searching for us.'

Privately, Malc thought that unlikely. Even if the helicopter's disappearance had been noticed, with so much on their plates it would take several hours for the authorities to muster resources to mount a search.

'The walking will be easier downhill,' Concha reasoned wearily. Her face was drawn. Exhaustion and strain were taking their toll.

'I can manage,' he told her grimly. 'We should meet the road in another mile and then the going will be easy.'

'The military will have radios. They will be in contact with Santa Cruz. If we meet up with them we can pass a warning on quickly.' She hesitated, then went on, 'Besides, I have family down on the coast.'

'On the coast, where?'

'The town we went to, Charco Verde.'

Malc remembered. 'Where the fresh vent appeared, the one on the ocean.'

'*Sí*, that is the one. I do not know if the vent is still there any more. When I spoke to my uncles they were planning to blow it open and let the sea in to snuff it out.'

Malc shook his head. Her words took a few moments to sink in. 'What did you say?'

She repeated, 'My uncle and his friends, the men in the village are afraid the new vent will ruin their beach and drive the tourists away. So they have collected explosives to blow open the cone and—'

He stared at her in horror. 'They told you this when we were there? And you did nothing?'

She scowled. 'It was not a big thing, just a small vent of no significance, but it will ruin the lives of the people in the village.'

'My God,' Malc croaked. 'Fire and water! Phreatic reactions! Do they mean nothing to you?'

Concha stared at him sullenly. 'I understand these things. There will be steam explosions, yes, but the men will be a safe distance when they detonate the charge. No one is going to get hurt.'

Malc groaned. Did kids like her learn nothing these days? 'They could trigger a fuel–coolant interaction, an FCI!' he stormed at her.

425

She looked blank. 'An FCI? What is this?'

'It's the key to what happened at Krakatoa!'

Fuel–coolant interactions, FCIs, Malc explained to Concha, were a hazard first encountered in the steel-refining industry where it was discovered that water coming into contact with superhot fuel, in this case molten steel, could sometimes flash explosively into vapour, flinging out hot droplets of fuel and generating further explosions in a chain reaction. Later a similar phenomenon was observed in nuclear power stations where liquid sodium was being used as a coolant and molten uranium oxide the fuel that triggered the reaction.

'I do not see the connection,' Concha objected. 'Lava streams often reach the ocean and there is no explosion. Steam, yes, but no explosion, no FCI.'

'That is because, except on rare occasions, extremely rare luckily for us, lava entering the ocean doesn't mix, instead there is a clear boundary between the two liquids. Water at the boundary edge is heated into vapour and boils away, but this is a comparatively gentle process. There is no violent mixing of the type to generate explosive power.'

As the girl listened in dismay he told her about the Heimaey experiment in Iceland. 'Back in 1973 in Iceland there was a small town with a similar problem to Charco Verde. A lava flow was pouring into the harbour from a nearby vent, threatening to choke it off. Engineers had the

426

bright idea of blowing a breach in the side of the lava stream to crack open the crust and divert the flow out into the open ocean. Luckily at the last minute scientists did some calculations and tumbled to the potential risk.

'They realised that detonating just ten kilograms of explosive could trigger a chain reaction resulting in a blast equivalent to four million tons of TNT.'

Concha leaned against a boulder, a hand on her chest. 'And Krakatoa,' she croaked.

Malc ran his tongue across his cracked lips. His throat was sore from dust and fumes. Talking was painful. 'Krakatoa was always a mystery. How did a comparatively small volcano detonate with such incredible violence? Well, now we know. Krakatoa was an island. One of the earlier blasts must have shattered the cone, cracking open a breach in the side and allowing the sea to pour into the white-hot heart of the caldera. It set off a terrific explosion, but worse was to come. That blast opened the way down into the subterranean magma chamber, an immense lake of molten rock underlying the volcano and whose heat was driving the entire system. Imagine the energy that must have been released as the sea swept in! The explosion was cataclysmic! The entire planet rang with the shock wave.'

'Malc, I swear I knew nothing of this.'

'Your uncle and his friends, how much *plástico* did you say they have?'

She stared at him in horror. 'Carlos said more than seven hundred kilos.'

'Christ Almighty, they could smash the entire island apart!'

Chapter 33

Charco Verde, La Palma. One p.m. Carlos finally pressed the switch on the capacitor box to complete the firing circuit. The system worked flawlessly. The current flashed down the lead cable in a high-voltage burst of energy discharging simultaneously to twelve separate aluminium-cased high output detonator tubes embedded in blocks of C-4 plastic explosive in the barrels packed against the vent's cone. In the same microsecond twelve gold bridge wires vaporised in an intense burst of flame, setting off 80 milligrams of PETN initiating explosive.

The PETN in turn caused the detonation of the secondary detonation charge consisting of a full gram of RDX. Immediately on ignition the RDX began to burn with incredible speed, generating enormous volumes of superheated gas. This blazing jet of gas sliced through the surrounding blocks of C-4 plastic explosive of the main charge.

Seven hundred and twenty kilograms of 90-per-cent-pure RDX detonated against the cone wall of the Charco Verde vent with a stunning blast. Five hundred metres away, Carlos and his little group sheltering behind the wall were hurled backwards off their feet into the sand. Carlos felt a wave of superheated air tear over him accompanied by a blinding storm of sand, grit, rock particles and ash. When he came to he was half buried in debris and completely deafened. His eyes were swollen so that he could see only blurred shapes. He dragged himself up and staggered dazedly past the groaning bodies of his companions. Moving as if in a fog, he stumbled to the wall to peer over towards where the cone had been.

At first all he could make out was a white fog. His ears were still singing or so it seemed till he realised that what he was hearing was actually the violent screech of steam blasting from what remained of the vent. Clouds of white vapour dazzling against the ash-filled sky were boiling upward at an incredible rate. From where he stood he could feel the ground shuddering under the fantastic pressure building up below.

The sand cracked open, shooting out jets of black ash and peppering the beach with hot stones. Torrents of scalding sparks and pumice rained down from overhead, accompanied by blasts of stinging sand.

The ocean rose and fell, its surface grey with ash and pumice. Rollers swept the shoreline.

Patches of water churned and boiled, frothing with steam. Mud geysers bubbled and spat mats of dirty yellow scum accompanied by a gagging sulphurous stench. The tide ran out and back restlessly as if recoiling each time from the scalding shore.

For a moment the noise seemed to slacken, but then followed a series of tremendous cracks echoing across the beach. Gouts of fire from the vent spouted up hundreds of feet into the air, falling back as deadly rain. Peals of ominous thunder rolled seemingly under the earth. The sand heaved and quaked. There came a salvo of deep coughing sounds like the discharge of heavy guns. With more spouts of fire a number of red-hot boulders were shot out from the vent, whizzing up to an immense height, trailing bright tails of smoke before toppling over to plunge back into the ocean in clouds of steam.

Was this what was meant to happen? Were these the death throes of the vent? Carlos had no way of telling. What was done was done. They had acted as men, risked their lives to save their town. Now all that was left was to save themselves.

Tearing himself from the shelter of the wall, Carlos ran back to the others. '*Vamos!*' he screamed, shaking the dazed men. 'Onto the tractor! We have to clear out of here now!'

Like sleepwalkers they obeyed, helping one another onto the trailer. Carlos took the wheel, brushing aside glass from the shattered windshield. He turned the key in the ignition and prayed the engine would start.

As he did so there came a sound like the end of the world. Carlos's last and final impression was of the beach turning to fire.

USS *Thresher*. 'Sir, gaining depth, four hundred feet per minute!' a watch officer barked.

'Shit!' The colour drained from the executive officer's face. The *Thresher* was dropping down an elevator shaft.

Krauss's eye snapped to the gauges. They still had 6,000 feet beneath the keel, 4,000 to reach crush depth, the point at which, according to the people at the Groton Electric Boat Company who had built the sub, their hull would cave in under two tons to the square inch of pressure.

'Hard a port,' he rapped to the helmsman. 'Engines two thousand. Planes to half rise. Blow main ballast.'

The *Thresher* was in the grip of some vortex or current that was pulling her under. She needed power to break out. At the same time Krauss needed to avoid too violent an ascent or they might porpoise to the surface.

'Still going down!' the executive officer called. 'Four hundred a minute.'

'Seawater hitting seventy degrees!' the technician watching the outside temperature gauge reported.

This was screwy; the ship was diving deeper, but the water was growing hotter.

432

'Depth eight hundred!'

Krauss turned to look at the executive officer. His face was a mask of strain. 'Methane!' he said tersely.

Methane gas. A fissure opening in the under-sea bed was venting a lethal cocktail of fumes into the ocean. Methane, a colourless, odourless gas that formed an explosive mixture with air and asphyxiated victims who inhaled it. Like the fisherman on the boat who had fallen overboard. And there was another known peril from methane at sea. A sudden venting of large volumes of methane gas could drastically lower the density of the water so that it would no longer support the weight of a ship or a boat. For a vessel to enter a zone of methane-rich water would be like trying to float on air; it would sink uncontrollably, literally like a lead weight plummeting to the bottom.

Just as the *Thresher* was doing now.

'One thousand feet!'

At the same moment a giant hammer slammed into the submarine.

As the sound of fresh blasts echoed among the hills, Malc and Concha stared at one another in horror. '*Madre de Dios*, they have done it, the fools!' The girl's voice shook. 'They have fired the charge.'

The detonations swelled in intensity and volume. Billows of steam and smoke soared up from the direction of the coast, boiling into the

433

sky. Flashes of crimson light bathed the overcast atmosphere. Flaming lava bombs scorched the clouds, arcing over the scene leaving trails of twisting smoke.

Malc grabbed her arm. 'Inland,' he said fiercely. 'We must get off the mountain!'

He led off at a stumbling jog along the path heading for the camping ground. The wind was blowing from the west, carrying with it a thickening cover of ash. Very soon a steady drizzle of warm pumice was falling about them and the light had faded to a sickly yellow, making it hard to pick their way. Malc was working out calculations in his head. They were near the northern end of Cumbre Vieja and some four miles from the coast. The weakest sector of the mountain slope, the area most vulnerable to breaking up, lay in their rear. Yes, but that counted for nothing in the event of a truly major blast. Seven hundred kilos of RDX might in theory trigger a multi-megaton explosion.

He tried to visualise the shattering of the cone in the midst of the little bay, the sea pouring into the vent. There would be steam of course, that was only to be expected, and explosions caused by vapour pockets. That had to be what they were hearing now. But as Concha had pointed out, volcanoes frequently erupted into the ocean without triggering a cataclysmic reaction.

Unless of course one included Krakatoa. Malc winced to himself. Even that was only a theory, one explanation among several. But water was a

434

key element surely? Krakatoa was an island. The cracking of the chamber roof would almost certainly have resulted in an inrush from the sea into the white-hot furnace of exposed magma. And the resulting explosion had blown more than six cubic miles of island twenty-five miles up into the atmosphere.

Jesus, Malc thought as he uttered a silent prayer for them both. Jesus, what hope would there be then for any of them on the island?

USS *Tarp*. Two p.m. The *Tarp*'s skipper had given orders for the submersible to be swayed out and lowered into the water.

The ship wallowed on the swell alongside the transmitter buoy, maintaining position with her auxiliary screws. Thanks to her GPS and computer-controlled engines she could hold an exact position over any point on the ocean bed for as long as was needed to complete her mission.

Mary Sennett had gone below to check the video links were functioning normally. The *Tarp* at that moment was exactly fifty-one miles north-west of Charco Verde. The clap of Carlos's initial 720-kilogram charge detonating was heard distinctly by those on deck, but not below. There was no doubt at all, however, as to the subsequent eruption. The sound of the explosion and the shock wave reached the ship simultaneously. Mary saw the image on her screen shudder at the same instant the thunder rolled

435

outside. For a split second the thought flashed through her mind that the ship had hit a mine. Afterwards she could never understand why she should have had such a mad idea. Snatching down a life vest from an overhead locker, she tore on deck to find everybody staring open-mouthed at the mountainous column of burning smoke belching up on the horizon.

The moment of stunned amazement was replaced by urgent activity. The captain rapped out orders, sharply recalling his crew to their duties. The submersible was swung back in. Hatches and watertight doors were latched down and loose gear secured. Soon like Mary everyone was pulling on life vests and checking their boat stations. The ship turned her bows towards the island and they all waited.

Mary saw Derek Wanless slip away below and followed him down to the lab. She found him seated at the communication console activating the satellite uplink. 'You're running an emergency data dump, aren't you?' she said. 'I'll help.'

'Just a precaution,' he said tersely. 'No point in letting all our hard work go to waste.'

Mary took another seat and her fingers rattled at the keys, preparing files for uploading, selecting the most vital first. 'Just as well we performed a full back-up last night,' she said.

Wanless did not reply. Each was privately calculating the likelihood of their greatest fear: if the volcano's flank had slipped then a monster wave could be racing down on them even as they sat here. Mary glanced at her watch: 2.08 p.m. Four, maybe five minutes since the sound of the blast reached them. How fast would the wave travel? This was a factor she and Wanless often debated. Some authorities reckoned up to 500 miles an hour; others put the figure at much less. Suppose one halved the maximum possible and took 240 mph as a working speed. That posited a wave travelling outward at four miles a minute. Such a wave would take exactly thirteen minutes to reach the *Tarp*. Putting the ship about and cramming on full power with the engines would make almost no difference. *Tarp*'s maximum speed in open water was less than thirty knots. The best she could hope for would be to delay the inevitable by two minutes.

The next question was, how big a wave should they anticipate? This was more difficult. Estimates of the size of wave that might be generated by a flank collapse of Cumbre Vieja varied hugely from a wild 500 metres to as low as one tenth of that. Taking the lowest figure for argument's sake, a 50-metre, 160-foot wave racing outward at 240 miles per hour. No, that did not bear thinking about.

Yes, but short-length waves diminished rapidly in height as they travelled further from their source, dissipating their energy over an expanding area of ocean. This fall-off was most pronounced in the initial stages. A tsunami might be expected to shed up to half its height in the first fifty miles travelled. So a seventy-foot wave, then, might be anticipated to appear on the horizon in the next four to five minutes.

The PA loudspeaker crackled, startling them. 'Attention, this is the captain speaking. We can expect to experience large waves over the next few minutes. Make sure your life vests are buckled on. Do not, repeat do not go on deck unless directly instructed by a ship's officer. This threat status may persist for several hours. You will be informed when it is safe to stand down. Until so informed all personnel will remain on high alert and wearing life vests is mandatory at all times. Good luck.'

They waited, counting the minutes. Rumblings from the island persisted, but much diminished in volume. The eruption appeared to be declining. A seventy-foot wave, Mary thought, picturing a monster wall of water. But the *Tarp* was a navy ship, she was built to take heavy seas, she reminded herself.

The PA clicked again. 'Captain again. We have a wave moving towards us. Looks to be around ten metres. We'll meet it bows on. Hang on, people.'

Mary and Wanless exchanged nervous smiles. Ten metres, thirty-five feet. It could be worse, but maybe this was only the beginning.

'Here we go,' said the captain a minute later. The sea state grew more turbulent. They felt the deck tilt and lift sharply. Mary dug her nails into the palms of her hands and tried not to look out the porthole. She could sense the engines running up to full power, but the *Tarp* held steady heading for the crest. The slide down the back slope was easy by comparison. The ship levelled out, wallowing in the trough.

Several more minutes passed. 'Another coming,' the captain's voice informed them calmly. 'This one is bigger. Nothing we can't handle though.' Down in the lab, Mary clung on tight to the arms of her seat.

The second wave felt a lot larger to Mary or maybe it was just that the face was steeper. Water crashed across the decks as the *Tarp* struggled sluggishly up and through the crest. The plunge down into the trough seemed endless. She was finding the pitching of the boat uncomfortable.

The captain spoke again. 'Thought you might all like to know that according to our calculations here on the bridge that last wave was more like fourteen metres which makes a personal best for this ship.' Mary could hear laughter in the background and grinned. Some of the guys on board were absurdly young. 'Also,' the captain continued, 'our navigator has personally measured the smoke plume of the volcano behind all this mess and it tops out at fifteen miles high. One of those facts to use when impressing the folks back home.'

Santa Cruz de la Palma, the island's capital. The city was slowly recovering from the shock of the previous afternoon's tsunami. The fresh eruption brought a renewed outbreak of panic. The pressure wave caused a two-centimetre bounce in the barometers at the volcano observatory, but physical damage was mainly broken windows and cracked masonry. A section of cliff face overhanging the LP-1 highway running south to the airport collapsed, blocking both lanes of the road.

At the first sound of the blast many residents rushed out into the streets, then ran back again, remembering the waves that had inundated the seafront. Although it was only a little past two in the afternoon a chilly twilight gripped the city, made worse by widespread power outages. Vehicles crawled along, their headlight beams obscured by thickly falling ash and pumice. Many side roads were blocked by rubble and there were numerous petty accidents.

The town swarmed with refugees from the countryside. The Madrid government had stepped up evacuations. Three jetfoil ferries from Tenerife and Fuerteventura had been pressed into extra service. At a pinch they could carry fifteen hundred passengers apiece. Others were said to have been leased from Spain and Italy. They would not be available for several more days. Now it was looking as though they would be too late.

Every flight off the island was booked solid. But the constant need to sweep the runway clear of ash and the reluctance of pilots to risk clogging their air filters limited departures. Even before the tsunami a third of the population had fled. Ten thousand more had joined them over the past twenty-four hours alone, many pushing their way on board the ships with no more than the clothes they stood up in.

More than twenty thousand remained. They were mainly the elderly, the poor, the sick and those who cared for them. In any tragedy the same cast of characters. Those left behind could only wait and pray. Every church was filled. Priests fainted with exhaustion after conducting services around the clock. God is here. God will protect us. The pious burned candles, unbelievers cursed. Tales of theft and looting abounded. Immigrants were to blame as always. Anyone with African features risked being stoned in the street. As if they hadn't enough problems just staying alive. They skulked in the shadows of abandoned buildings like ghosts, uttering their own prayers.

But it would take more than prayers, more than candles, more than promises of ships that never came.

Chapter 34

Washington. Eight a.m. News of increased activity on La Palma had been flashed around the world. Professor Jean Ballister was on CBS.

'Information is still sketchy,' she informed the nation, 'but one thing is evident, the situation has taken on a new dimension—'

The anchorwoman interrupted. 'We have just had a flash from the Defense Department. The USS *Tarp* reports encountering two extreme sea waves fifty miles north-west of La Palma. Estimated TC amplitudes . . .' She paused. 'I'm not sure what that means.'

'TC, trough to crest,' the professor put her right. 'It's the standard measurement for wave height. Amplitude refers to the difference between the two.'

'Oh, okay. Then, estimated TC heights thirty-five and forty-five feet. Velocity between two and three hundred knots.'

'Yes, these are splash waves rather than

tsunami. Imagine you throw a rock into a pond; you get a high initial splash that disappears almost at once. You also get a series of ripples that fan out to the banks. The splash wave is dramatic, short-lived and decays rapidly. These are what the ship experienced.'

'So no threat to us here?'

'From these particular waves? Probably not; they might make a few surfers happy down in Florida. It's what may follow that concerns me—'

The anchorwoman interrupted. 'Professor, from the information coming in it looks like things on La Palma are pretty bad. Ash falls in Santa Cruz, detonations shaking the capital. The government is appealing for aid in getting people off the island. We have some footage here from Spanish TV channels.'

The screen cut away to show that what had once been the beach town of Charco Verde was now completely hidden by a monstrous smoke column seething with steam and ash rising tens of thousands of metres into the air.

'What do you think, Professor? Let us have your frank opinion.'

Jean Ballister pursed her lips tightly. 'The eruption has ratcheted up at least two if not three levels in the past few hours. That's a huge magnification. The potential is extremely alarming. The question we scientists must now be asking ourselves, is what factors can trigger a VEI scale four or five level eruption?'

'And what would your response be, Professor?' her host demanded eagerly.

'The only explanation for such a rapid escalation in violence that I can think of is that seawater has somehow penetrated into the magma chamber.'

'What does that mean in layman's terms?'

On the screen Jean Ballister's face was grim. 'It means,' she leaned in towards the camera, 'it means that we may just be looking at Krakatoa Two.'

USS *Thresher*. 'Sir!' a helmsman's urgent cry cut through the clamour in the attack centre. 'Port rudder failing to respond!'

Seven hundred feet below the surface of the ocean, the USS *Thresher* finally pulled out from the methane vortex that was sucking her downwards. There was water on the attack centre floor and the emergency lighting had cut in. As the vessel stabilised to an even keel once more Captain Krauss ordered engines stop and called for damage reports from all sections.

'Sir,' the chief engineer officer reported, 'the number two coolant pump is screaming worse than ever. My boys are working on it now. Till then power output on the reactor is down to fifty per cent.'

'Damn it, just when we can do with the extra.'

'Yes, sir, I'm sorry. Pulling out of that dive threw one helluva load on the reserve systems. The gauges were in the red zone.'

'Hot as hell in here, Sam. Can you fix that?'

'No problem, sir. One of the main air-con fans has slipped its drive belt. You'll be breathing fresh air in a few minutes.'

'What about the rudder?'

'Helmsman says we have to strip down the hydraulic linkage. Should take around an hour. With luck we can fix the problem without surfacing. Otherwise it could mean sending out a diver.'

'I don't want to order that unless we absolutely have no choice. Not in these waters with a methane release threat.'

'No, sir, I understand that. We'll do our best.'

'Can we do anything to stop this leak in the roof?'

'Most likely a ruptured seal in the periscope from diving in the extended position. I'll have someone take a look.'

Dismissing the chief, Krauss returned to studying the chart. They were still less than twenty-six miles from the island with a seized rudder and barely half power available on the reactor.

There was a discreet cough at his side. The executive officer had joined him. 'I think you should know, sir, just before we stopped engines the helmsman on the starboard rudder also experienced rudder seizure. He thinks it has cleared, but we can't be certain till we get under way again.'

Krauss felt an icy hand clutch his heart. With

445

one rudder out the *Thresher* was controllable, just. Running the port screw at slow reverse would probably counter the turning effect, enabling them to hold a course. With two rudders locked they would be helpless, trapped in an orbital pattern that tied them to the danger zone.

Another rumble from the island sent a fresh bout of tremors through the boat. Cumbre Vieja was not finished with them yet.

CBS, Washington. Professor Jean Ballister was speaking again. 'The profile of a Krakatoa or a super-Krakatoa-type eruption follows a distinct pattern. Towards the final stage ash and pumice discharge escalates dramatically with explosions increasing in frequency and violence. The ash cloud reaches to a height of fifteen miles plus with explosions coming more or less continuously. Krakatoa's end came when a single catastrophic blast collapsed the caldera. This was followed by two more similar-sized detonations culminating in a final paroxysmal detonation that ripped the island apart, destroying it utterly. The first explosion occurred at five-thirty a.m. local time and the fourth and last at ten-o-two a.m. Ten cubic kilometres of rock was hurled into the atmosphere over a period of four and a half hours.'

'So what you're telling us,' the interviewer said, swallowing, 'is that the worst is yet to come?'

'It is.'

'And are we talking killer tsunami here?'

'If the eruption develops into a super-Krakatoa, shattering the island apart, then, yes, it will pose a serious risk to the eastern seaboard.'

'And in your opinion this is now the probable outcome?'

Ballister shook her head. 'I'm a volcanologist, not an oceanographer. But,' she added, and everyone's attention sharpened, 'there is a sure way we shall know if and when it does happen.'

'And what is that?'

Ballister indicated the map. 'We spoke earlier about the USS *Tarp*, the survey ship that is attempting to repair a DART buoy. Her last given position puts her approximately fifty miles off the coast of La Palma.'

'So if the wave is large enough to threaten us here she would be able to transmit a warning?' the interviewer said.

Ballister was still looking at the map. 'If Cumbre Vieja blows apart and its west flank falls into the ocean, the splash wave will reach half a mile high. The *Tarp* won't stand a chance.'

The anchorwoman fixed worried eyes on her. 'So what you're saying is, if the *Tarp* goes down and we lose radio contact with her it will be a sign that . . .' Her voice faltered.

Professor Ballister supplied the answer. 'That something wicked this way comes? Yes, it will.'

Chapter 35

Goodwill. Eight-thirty a.m. Rick's sister Rebecca woke early to open the store. Sundays in summer were busy days with boat owners in the marina working on their vessels. She unlatched the shutters and propped the doors open front and rear to air the place and expel any lingering dampness from the flooding yesterday.

Cousin Paul drove past in his truck bound for the dock to check on *Pequod*. From out beyond the harbour came the offbeat clank of the dragline dredger working to deepen the channel so as to enable that damned tanker to be towed off somehow. A low mist obscured the islands in the Sound and the gulls were crying.

There was no TV in the store. Reb felt, and her brother agreed with her, that there was always plenty of work that needed doing around the place. She did have a radio though for the weather bulletins. She switched it on.

'. . . *indications of a major eruption in progress on*

*the island of La Palma in the Canaries group.
Federal government experts are describing the threat
as "Krakatoa Two"* . . .'

'Oh, my God.' She put a hand to her throat. Her first thought was for her family. Mike was still asleep in bed and the boys, where were they?

She ran to the shelves behind the counter and started pulling down boxes of high-value electrical components. Then she carried armfuls out to the car and dumped them in the trunk. This was crazy; it would take all day to strip the place on her own. She dialled home. 'Mike! Mike, wake up!' she yelled down the phone. 'Get the boys dressed and haul ass down here!'

And where was Rick when he was needed?

Frank Schaffer woke up in the spare bedroom at the farm. Light was slanting in through the attic widow and when he threw back the shutter there was an apple tree outside almost within reach. He showered in a whitewashed bathroom with a wood-plank floor. Last night they had worked together with the plumb line for two hours before Martin called a halt.

'We are on the verge of a breakthrough all the time, I can feel it,' he said wearily. 'There's something blocking us and I can't figure out what it is.'

'Is it something I'm doing wrong?'

'No, no definitely not. We're probably trying too hard. The power won't be forced. You have to let it flow through at its own pace. I can

449

definitely feel a presence out there and it wants to communicate I know, but the message isn't getting through for the moment.'

He looked apologetically at his guest. 'I'm sorry, this is agonising for you. I feel I'm letting you down. Maybe we will do better in the morning.'

It was still raining when they went back over to the house. They sat for a while over a bottle of wine. Frank talked about his sister and the family while Martin found steaks in the freezer and they ate them in the kitchen. When Martin offered a room for the night Frank was glad to accept.

'Good morning,' Martin greeted him on his appearance in the kitchen. 'I hope you slept well up in the little attic. The last occupant to stay in that room was the farmer's widowed mother, who lived to be ninety-three. There's coffee brewing and if you say the word I'll rustle up a couple of eggs.'

They breakfasted on the porch. The air was damp and fresh with a misty overcast. 'Looks like being a cooler day,' Martin observed, pouring himself more juice. He never touched coffee before a session, he explained.

'Kim, my sister, is just the same,' Frank said. 'She says caffeine is a drug.'

'When you're done,' Martin said, 'we'll go across to the barn.'

The chart and the plumb line were just as they had been left last night. Before they took their seats, Martin recited the Lord's Prayer. 'I do this first thing each morning,' he explained. 'It's my way of cleansing the room of negative influences and channelling energy towards the light.'

Sheena Dubois also woke early for a Sunday. She had passed a restless night. Doc had been upset when they parted, understandably. He was also angry. He would do anything not to get Tab into trouble with the police. 'Leave it to me; I'll straighten him out,' he promised. 'I won't let him out of my sight.'

'Are you crazy? You're worked off your feet as it is. What are you going to do, ask Donna for help?'

He shut his eyes. 'Jesus,' he whispered. 'If she finds out I'm finished.' He sat with his head in his hands. 'Maybe if I send him back to his mom.'

'Suppose he does the same thing there? You have to think this thing through, for God's sake.'

'I know, I know,' he groaned.

'The cops have evidence. Freddy Tarr's men found a container up in the woods, a bottle or something that had held gasoline. Don Egan sent it off to be fingerprinted.'

Doc scowled at her. 'They can't prove anything. So what if his prints were on some bottle? He was up there watching the fire. So were you. So were two dozen other people. Anyone could have handled the thing.'

He needed time, he begged her, to work things out. That was what men always asked for.

Today she woke to the news from La Palma on every channel. The TV footage was alarming. Professor Ballister had captured the headlines with her 'Krakatoa 2' remark. Was America really under threat? Africa was thousands of miles away, but memories of the Indian Ocean quake were fresh in people's minds. Down in Florida many residents on the Keys were quitting their homes for the safety of the mainland. The authorities meanwhile were appealing for calm. Warning systems were in place, no tsunami had been detected. But some experts remained sceptical. 'This is typical government reaction,' one scientist was quoted as saying. 'Ignore all warnings and rely instead on a multi-million-dollar detection system that will provide exact data on the wave after it has struck.'

The man had a point, Sheena reflected. She checked her to-do list and called the jail. She asked to speak to Don. Annie Pellew was sniffy, but finally put her through.

'Don, morning. How you keeping?'

'I'm busy right now, Sheena. What do you want?'

'You still holding the King?'

'How was that name again?'

'Don't play games, Don. There isn't time. You know who I mean, the King of the Mountain. The surfers' leader of choice.'

'What's it to you if we are?' Don was sulky.

'Local news story. Maybe national, who knows? Could be big.'

'I can think of bigger stories.'

'Like the tsunami?' She heard Don suck in his breath. 'The experts are calling this Krakatoa Two now.'

'Yeah? Well, you don't want to go believing every dumb thing you get on TV. You sound like those idiots down in the cells.'

'They reckon the big one is just round the corner, huh?'

'Ask them that, why don't you?'

'Just what I want, an interview.'

Don snorted. 'Don't make me laugh!'

She tried another tack. 'How are the forensics coming along? Any joy on the finger-prints?'

'I won't ask where you got that from.'

Sheena laughed lightly. 'And I wouldn't tell you if you did. So, Ellsworthy didn't find a match then?'

'Who are you trying to kid? This is Sunday. The lab doesn't work over the holiday.'

'Is it true Miss Maxwell hired a lawyer?'

'They don't work Sundays either. Least not any that I know of.'

'Money talks, Don. She'll find one. And twenty bucks says it's not a match.'

'Why don't you get lost, Sheena?'

'Without the prints what do you have? Motive?'

There was a snarl down the line. Sheena chuckled. 'No motive either then, and they have an alibi for the Ice Factory fire. Even you can't pin that one on them. Let them go, Don, before a judge orders you to.'

The sound of an expletive crackled over the wire and the phone went dead. Sheena smiled grimly. She had owed the surfers that much. Even for Tab's sake she wasn't about to see someone railroaded for arson. Don's attitude surprised her though. He wasn't usually so intransigent. Maybe he was pissed off with the King for going behind Rick's back with Natalie.

Speaking of which, why wasn't Rick answering his phone?

Goodwill. Nine a.m. The sky was still overcast when Rick eased the security truck into its parking slot in the police department garage and switched off the engine. He climbed down and stretched his back. He and Kelso stowed their weapons in the back compartment and Rick locked the truck and handed the keys to Kelso to drop off at the desk. 'So long.'

Kelso nodded as he always did and moved off without speaking. Sundays he went to church and then worked his garden. He had the straightest hedge in town.

Rick was crossing over to his pick-up when he saw the red Jaguar swing around the Green and halt in front of the building. Natalie was out and through the doors without a glance. Evidently she was in a mighty hurry.

It had been Rick's intention to check on the store, and then give Chance Greene and the other Selectmen a call. Now suddenly he didn't want to see or speak to anyone. Starting up the truck he drove off down to the harbour. Mike's pick-up was parked outside the store. It looked like he and Reb were loading up a shipment. Why they should be doing that on a Sunday he couldn't imagine and right now he didn't care. Chance Greene's big Porsche SUV that cost as much as a house went streaking along Bay Road, horn blaring. The tanker was still stuck fast on the mud outside the mole with Jack Pearl's boat alongside and a Coastguard launch as well. There were any number of people about fussing with boats or hurrying along the dock, but that was pretty much standard before regatta day and he paid them no attention. *Chimay*, his dad's boat, was still berthed where he had left it. He threw off the lines and jumped down into her. The tide was running out strongly and the engine started first turn, the screw biting the water throatily. Moments later he was heading her out through the harbour mouth towards Greenstone Island.

His phone was in his pocket, but he left it switched off. He needed time alone to think.

Meanwhile the King was growing frantic. He paced like a caged animal, two strides to the door, turn and two strides back to the barred window. Back and forth, back and forth. It drove the Gimp crazy.

'Take a break,' he said from the bunk where

455

he sat resting his knee. 'You're only making it harder on yourself.'

Frustration and rage twisted knots in the King's belly. The phone Natalie had sent in was out of juice and power to the cell had been cut off overnight in reprisal for whistling and pounding on the door. Further occurrences would be punished with a trip to the isolation cell.

He halted by the window. It faced the parking lot. Opposite was the fence where from time to time some of the guys stole down to whistle messages before the cops chased them away. The fence was clear at present. Soon the sun would be burning off the mist and the waves would be sweet and here he was, the King of the Mountain, locked up like a dog!

The glass was protected by a grill that unlocked with a key to open the window. Bars on the outside. The only way out was through a steel door that was locked and bolted from the passage. The King felt smothered. The air was stale, his throat dry.

Footsteps rang on the cement stairs leading down to the cellblock. Logan Clancy's face appeared in the hatch. 'Chief Egan says to turn the power back on, so you guys got TV again. Any trouble and it goes back off for the rest of the day.'

He snapped a switch and the overhead light clicked on. 'Shit to that!' the Gimp yelled. 'Where's our lawyer?'

* * *

456

Pastor McCabe let himself into his church on the Green. The door was unlocked. This was Goodwill, a God-fearing town still. These past days though the words came uneasily. Last winter he had conducted funeral rites over a coffin filled with stones. The people here had their own customs; the man had been a lobsterman, a member of his flock. Respect was due to the family. Friday had seen another death and two more missing. Rumours abounded, of catastrophe and God's punishment.

'Hey,' the Gimp said, 'check this out.'

His attention was fixed on the TV. Shots of tossing ocean backed by towering ash plumes and spouts of fire filled the screen. The Gimp turned up the volume and the commentator's voice-over picked up. '. . . *evacuating towards higher ground. The sudden extreme hike in activity has caught authorities by surprise . . . geologists say swarming seismic tremors may signal even more violent explosions to come . . . talk of Krakatoa Two type eruption possibly within the next twelve hours . . .*'

'Shit!' the Gimp breathed. 'Oh shit! Oh shit! Oh shit!'

The plumb line was behaving strangely. There was no other word to describe it. Last night the cord had hung lifeless; this morning it seemed to have taken on a life of its own. Almost from the moment Martin Seymour took it up the weight began to quiver and swing as if possessed. Before long the chart underneath was covered in pencilled crosses.

'I can't figure this out; it's making no sense. Yesterday we had no response, now it's as if there's a whole torrent of influences breaking through. Trouble is now there is almost too much.'

'Is there anything specific relating to Kim?'

Martin shook his head distractedly. 'Nothing, yet I can sense the air vibrating all around us. It is so strong I can almost feel it pulsing against my skin.'

Frank looked around him in dismay. Maybe it was only the draught from the window, but it seemed to him that he too could feel the air throbbing in his ears. Were those ripples in his water glass? Surely that was impossible.

Rebecca ran round to the Lobsterman to hunt out Jean-Alice. Whale Morrissey and a bunch of other locals from the harbour were inside watching CNN and arguing. Jean-Alice was behind the bar talking with Sarah Hunter.

'Hi,' Sarah greeted her. 'I was just coming round to see you.'

Reb's mouth tightened. 'If you're looking for Rick I can't help you.'

'Is that can't or won't?' Sarah's eyes flashed.

'Take it how you like.'

Jean-Alice intervened. 'Hey, girls, come on now, keep it friendly. Sarah just stopped round to say goodbye.'

'You're skipping town? After all you've put Rick through?'

Sarah held up a hand in surrender. 'Okay, so I fought for your brother. I loved him, always did. What would you have me do, roll over and let the Maxwell bitch walk away with the only guy that ever treated me halfway decently?'

Reb's stare grew less steely. 'I hadn't thought of it from your side. I guess maybe in your shoes I'd have done the same or more even.' She shrugged. 'So why are you pulling out?'

It was Sarah's turn to hunch her shoulders. 'What's to stay for?'

'I don't know, Rick's not the only single guy in town,' Jean-Alice said. She glanced at Reb. 'Latte for you? On the house.'

'Thanks.' Reb climbed on a stool. 'The way things seem to be between those two, who knows how they'll end up?'

'You mean that surfer guy Natalie's been seeing?' Jean-Alice shook her head. 'Just engagement nerves. Lots of girls get jumpy when they feel the knot drawing tight.'

'Not just girls,' Reb countered. 'I remember one time Mike and I had a row before we were married. He took off for a week. I figured he'd jumped a ship and I'd never see him again.'

'Natalie's got to be crazy if she picks a dumb surfer over Rick Larsen,' Sarah said. 'As for Rick . . .' She sighed and shook her head sadly.

'He's been in here, her surfer,' Jean-Alice said meditatively. 'Big fellow, he even makes me feel

459

fragile. And driven. Kind of guy talks in mythic terms, "the unridden realm", "the brotherhood of danger", "coming home on your shield", like a character in a comic book sometimes. Don't get me wrong. There is a kind of legendary quality to him. Men like him are born to ride giants and slay dragons. I can see how a girl's head could be turned.'

In the cell behind the Green, the man they were discussing raised his fists heavenward and beat a thunderous roll on the metal door. Up at her desk in front, Annie Pellew, watching the same TV pictures, pursed her lips and glanced across at Logan Clancy. Logan shrugged. Let the jerks hammer. They could rot down there for all he cared.

The King swung to face the window. He squeezed his fists and uncurled them slowly, flexing his fingers powerfully. He filled his chest, tensing the muscles till his back rippled and the joints cracked. He took a step forward and thrust his fingers through the steel mesh of the grill protecting the window. The Gimp watched awestruck as he took a hold and heaved backward.

'Christsakes,' he shouted, 'you go busting up the cell and the cops will—'

He didn't finish. The cell had been constructed to resist attack, but right now the King had the strength of a berserker. With a rending sound the upper edge of the mesh ripped out of

460

the surrounding metal frame. The King flexed
his grip again and braced himself for another
mighty heave. The veins in his arms bulged and
tightened. Slowly giving way under the immense
strain, the grill tore loose all down one side. With
a yell of triumph, the King took a fresh hold
lower down and lunging backwards, used his
weight to wrench the rest away.

The Gimp stared slack-jawed at the opening.
'Jesus!' he whispered.

Pastor McCabe faced his congregation from the
front of the church. The hall was full, he noted.
In time of threat people were reminded of God's
power. He looked in their eyes and felt their
concern, their fears for homes, for family, for
each other. Somehow he must find words to
bring courage and endurance.

'We pray,' he began quietly and every head
bowed. 'We pray to Almighty God for strength
to carry us through whatever trials he may lay
before us . . .'

Across at the farm, Martin Seymour snatched his
hand back from the cord as if he had
encountered an electric shock.

'What is it? Did you feel something?' Frank
questioned him eagerly.

Martin turned towards him. There was
puzzlement in his eyes and something else, fear.

He took a moment to speak. 'I'm not sure
what it was. Never before have I experienced a

461

tremor so strong, as if the whole earth rang like a bell.'

The two men stared at the plumb. The lead weight was quivering still. It seemed to have taken on an eerie life of its own, swinging in jerky parabolas across the chart of the Sound as if possessed.

'It's like . . .' Frank tried to speak, struggling to find the words. 'It's like something terrible passing over.'

Martin's face was ashen.

Out in the Sound a damp mist hung over the water and clung to the whaler's cabin windows. There was no wind to speak of, but a brisk chop made the boat roll. Rick held his course by compass bearing, keeping a watch out for other craft. Not that he expected to meet many. Few workboats would be out on a Sunday and this fog would put off the marina types.

He passed Two Bush Island and thought about the couple still missing. A clump of bluebottle jellyfish floated past, ragged survivors of a once great armada. No whales though still, not even a dolphin and few birds. The boat's motion was easing off, a sign that he was coming under the lee of Greenstone Island. He checked the radar and there it was showing up dead ahead around two miles off.

Ten minutes later he was inside the arms of Greenstone Bay.

The crude jetty he had built had barely

survived the rigours of last winter. It needed attention, but there had been no time that he could see, looking back, to spare for its repair. Rick brought *Chimay* alongside, backed the engine, then threw her into idle. He made fast then cut the engine and stepped ashore.

The silence was total. The fog deepened the stillness, damping the wave rhythm, absorbing and deadening the thud along the shoreline. The house lay up an overgrown path, but today instinctively his feet turned away. The house was symbolic of too many unanswered questions for the moment. He paced along the silver beach, soothed as always by the cleanness and purity of the sand. A stone uncovered by the retreating tide caught his attention. He stooped, picked it up and rubbed it clean. Even on a dull morning the translucent marble glowed as if lit from within. A Goodwill greenstone as fine as any he had ever held.

An omen, no, a talisman. He slipped it in his pocket for safekeeping. And then he paused. Could that have been thunder? Surely not? And yet it seemed to him that a faint rumble had troubled the bay for an instant. He strained to listen. Yes, surely there it was again, a throbbing, infinitely remote yet deep, almost below the threshold of human hearing, an ominous thudding that seemed to come out of nowhere and roll through the ground underfoot.

* * *

'In God we Trust, that is the American way. The same creed that first brought our ancestors to this shore, that sustained them through the hardships of their new existence, that gave them strength to rebuild after the Great Storm. The creed that supports us now and in years to come through danger and difficulty . . .'

There was a sound of running feet outside in the porch. The west door was flung open and the figure of Whale Morrissey burst in upon the congregation. The pastor broke off in mid-sentence as heads turned in the pews to gape at the intruder. The Whale staggered to a halt in the middle of the aisle. He was purple with exertion, sweat pouring down his face and his eyes were wild.

'It's gone!' he gasped incoherently. 'The island' – he shook his head to clear it – 'the volcano just blew up. Krakatoa! Krakatoa!' He repeated it as if the word were the clarion call to rouse his audience from their stupefied amazement. 'Krakatoa!' he bellowed, inflating his chest till the rafters rang. 'KRAKATOA TWO!'

Chapter 36

Cumbre Vieja, La Palma. Malc and Concha staggered in single file along a narrow path that clung to the steep side of a hill. They were passing through a nightmare landscape of burned-out forest, torched by blazing lava bombs. Those few trees that remained stood shrouded in dust like ghostly sentinels of the dead. On and on they stumbled in frantic haste. Their position now was desperate. Ever since the first huge explosion the tremors and detonations bursting from the new vent had continued without let-up and the ground underfoot shivered and bucked at every other step.

As they rounded a huge boulder a brilliant flash, a hundred times more vivid than anything that had gone before, etched the rocks with blinding intensity. In the same moment they were slammed against the ground as the shock wave burst though the valley like an invisible fist, bending and snapping tree trunks, scattering

465

boulders and triggering off avalanches of scree and stones.

Malc grabbed out instinctively as they both fell and by sheer luck caught a hold on a deep-rooted clump of juniper that withstood his weight. Stones and rocks rattled down from the upper slopes, but he clung on, keeping his head down. A whirlwind of suffocating dust followed in the wake of the blast, filling mouth and nose and ears and sealing his eyes. The violence of the concussion had smacked the air from his lungs and he just lay there gasping and choking as the dirt filled his throat. For a while it seemed it was a question of whether he let go and fell to the bottom or passed out from lack of oxygen and was buried alive.

Repeated detonations shuddered around him. An immense thundering, interspersed with deep chuggings, as if the vent was clearing its throat, filled the valley. Over to the west he could dimly make out a roaring column of flaming ash shooting skywards. Vast billows of smoke, white and black, shot through with crimson fire filled the sky, expanding at a colossal rate. Spurts of blazing lava flashed and darted among the boiling vapour. On and on the smoke poured out, choking off the light. Concussions like a great door slamming shook the hills. The ground heaved and juddered. Heat beat down from the burning clouds accompanied by storms of searing ash and gravel.

For what seemed an age, Malc braced himself,

waiting for the final detonation; the one that he guessed would mark the moment when the roof of the main magma chamber fell in on a hundred million tons of liquid magma. At long last though the thunder of the explosions appeared to have subsided and the avalanches of stones and dust lessened. Spitting the dirt from his mouth, Malc dragged himself to his knees and scrambled back on the path.

He looked around for what had become of Concha. The girl had been a few paces ahead when the blast hit. Now she was nowhere to be seen. 'Concha!' he yelled. He had to bellow even to hear himself. Smoke was still belching from the new vent at a prodigious rate. He had to strain to see even a few yards. 'Concha!' The dirt in his lungs, the swirling dust, turned his voice into a feeble croak against the echoing thunder from the mountain. 'Concha!' he called again despairingly.

This time there was a faint answering cry from below. Peering down the slope, he made out a face staring back from a heap of rust-blackened clinker. She had slid down thirty feet of scree to fetch up against a precariously wedged boulder. 'Hang on!' he told her.

Like most volcanologists Malc was an experienced rock climber. He moved out to the side so as not to bring more scree down on her and, choosing a place where there were trees and bushes to provide hand holds, slid down till they were level. Then it was simply a matter of

467

crawling sideways across the slope to where she lay. 'My foot is stuck,' she told him as he reached her.

'Is it broken?'

'I don't think so, but each time I try to reach round and free it the rock tilts and I'm frightened if it goes it will take me with it.'

The boulder was wedged across the girl's leg and wobbled at the slightest movement on her part. Clearly it could fall away at any minute. The girl's face was bloodied from her slide down the mountain and her shirt was in rags. Otherwise she seemed unhurt. Taking off his belt, Malc fastened it around her wrist. Holding tight to the other end, he wrapped an arm around a young pine. 'Okay, I've got you now. See if you can free the foot.'

'It's not coming,' she gasped.

'Keep trying. I've still got you.'

She wrenched at the leg and the rock tilted ominously. Concha let out a cry of pain. Malc could see that the rock had slipped and was still lodged across her leg. The position was now worse.

'See if you can undo the boot.'

Concha struggled for a couple of minutes, then lay back defeated. 'It's no use. I can't reach round to get at the foot now.'

'Okay, I'm going to let go of the belt for a minute and try to get in closer. Maybe I can work you out from underneath.'

As the words left his mouth a fresh paroxysm

of detonations rolled deafeningly among the hills. The girl's chest heaved and she bit her lip. 'You don't have to stay here,' she gasped.

Malc twisted his head round to look over his shoulder. He froze. Fountains of lava were bursting out all along the mountain ridges. Through the smoke the fierce red glow of multiple lava streams could be seen spewing out from a dozen separate vents.

Cumbre Vieja was on fire! The detonations on the coast had fractured the underlying magma chambers. Short of a miracle it was only a matter of hours before the straining fractures of the southern ridge burst open all along their length.

Across the globe, twenty thousand recording devices leapt into urgent action charting the jolts as they radiated through the earth. Computer systems seized the data, processing and analysing. Within minutes they had the epicentre pinpointed and a profile of the event. That in turn triggered automatic alerts and a blizzard of e-mails to phones, mailboxes and Internet noticeboards: BREAKING NEWS! CUMBRE VIEJA, LA PALMA, CANARIES GROUP. MAJOR NEW ERUPTION ESTIMATE VEI 6!

Even as Malc struggled to free the girl, half the outside world was watching images of the blast on their screens in real time.

USS *Tarp*. The smoke clouds were unlike anything Mary Sennett had ever experienced, even in photographs or in the movies. The sky

469

overhead was almost pitch dark and this was still only mid-afternoon. The ship was sealed and battened down, every window and porthole smothered under a blanket of sticky ash. The rain of stones and pumice was so thick that personnel could only venture outside in hard hats with protective clothing including facemasks against the swirling dust. Already the fallout was a foot or more deep on the decks and cabin roofs.

The ocean surface was unrecognisable. In place of the blue Atlantic they were steaming through a sea of ochre-coloured mud and thick rafts of floating pumice. Early on in the eruption the ship had been caught by salvoes of lava bombs, huge lumps of semi-molten rock that screamed down out of the smoke like exploding shells. One of these had hit the upper bridge, seriously injuring an officer, badly burning others and starting a blaze. The ship was now being conned from the operations centre on the lower deck.

Half blind and wallowing under the weight of stone and dirt clogging her decks, the *Tarp* battled a succession of monstrous waves that reared up out of the darkness to the east like black cliffs. Twice already it had seemed to Mary and her colleagues that the ship was done for. Again and again the PA alarm bells pealed as the captain warned of worse to come.

Lightning blazed savagely overhead. Vivid sheets that flashed and glared against the overcast without respite. The communications gear and most other instruments were down, circuits burned out by the constant violent electro-magnetic discharges. As the alarm bells pealed yet again and iron-stained water hammered at the ports, the ship rolled drunkenly in the trough of another wave. Mary looked out and screamed.

Beneath the blackness of the swirling clouds the ship shone from end to end with a ghostly luminescence. The tip of every antenna and radar dish, masthead and railing glowed with a flickering corona of fiery jets that pulsed with eerie radiance.

A hand caught her shoulder. Derek Wanless had seen it too. 'Corposants!' he shouted above the storm. 'St Elmo's fire! The old-time sailors called it a sign of God's protection.'

West coast, Morocco. 4.14 p.m. local time. The ominous stain on the horizon to the south-west had darkened and spread as the afternoon wore on. By three p.m. the rumbling from the mountain sixty miles off was like the thud of distant artillery and the jolts of heavier shocks could be plainly felt through the ground. Shards of floating pumice were washing up along the shore and each retreating wave left behind a thin rim of rust-coloured dust. The Watchkeeper was their leader. He made everyone pack up their gear and stow it in the big Land Rover ready for departure. Afterwards though the younger guys broke out their boards and patrolled the break line two hundred metres out till he called them in.

'We're the sentinels here,' he reminded them mildly from the roof of the stable where he had set up the camcorder under a makeshift shelter. 'It's not our turn to play heroes.'

'Man, that sucks,' a dreadlocked Australian protested. 'No one owns a wave. We can all be giant-killers too if we want.'

The Watchkeeper made no answer. He had the camera hooked up to the sat phone via a PDA. All it needed now was to hit the button and the PDA would dial the number and start feeding live images via satellite to an Internet site stateside.

Dreadlocks was defiant still. 'A hundred foot, I could handle that.'

'Who said a hundred?' the Watchkeeper called down.

'You did, man. You said the King was hoping for a hundred-footer.'

'That's across the pond. Three thousand miles away. This close in' – the Watchkeeper shrugged – 'you'd be looking at three hundred.'

'Three hundred feet!'

The Watchkeeper eyed him pityingly. 'That's metres, dude.'

In the silence that followed each member of the group tried to picture the effect of a thousand-foot monster breaking across the beach at sixty knots.

472

'You said we'd get a warning?' a girl with a thick tan asked anxiously.

'What d'you call that?' The Watchkeeper gestured out to sea. Another lurid flash had splashed the towering cloud peaks with crimson fire as the terrible volcanic furnace below the horizon blasted yet more explosive energy into the atmosphere.

Five minutes later the shock wave hit and everything changed. The kids were still debating whether to stay or go when the ground heaved and bucked as if someone had detonated a mine. Mud walls cracked, sand-dunes shuddered and slid in clouds of choking dust. Violent thudding sounds battered the eardrums in rapid succession, drowning out the screams of the girls, followed by a prolonged roaring that rolled over the beach like an avalanche. The surfers clung to one another as aftershocks continued to hammer the sand. Fissures snaked across the ground and a palm tree swayed and toppled. On the beach the ocean frothed and churned.

The Watchkeeper was first to recover. 'Out!' he shouted to the others. 'Get in the truck! Hurry!'

'Out boards! They're still down on the beach.'

'Forget your boards, there's no time. If the wave comes you'll have no chance. Get in the truck and drive like hell inland. Don't stop and don't look back. Just keep your foot down!'

They needed no urging. Flinging the last of their stuff in the back, they piled into the truck.

473

Only Dreadlocks hung back. 'What about you? Aren't you coming with us?' he called as the Watchkeeper sprang for the ladder to the roof.

'I'll take the bike. There's things I have to do first. Go now! Go!'

Chapter 37

Dead River, Maine. The morning session of white-water rafting had been cancelled, but the afternoon run was scheduled to go ahead as promised. Lloyd Gardiner was thrilled.

'No, no way,' the innkeeper assured both sets of parents. 'There is positively no risk at all up here. We are more than fifteen miles from the shore, maybe twenty miles even. The line from the government is that in the event of a tsunami being detected, which by the way hasn't happened yet' – he paused and took a drink of water from a plastic cup – 'if there is a tsunami sighted,' he corrected himself, 'then residents of the "at risk zones",' he made inverted comma signs with his fingers – 'have to move back three to five miles from the coast. So far as we've been told,' he continued, 'this only applies at the moment to the people down in Florida. The state of Maine is not designated as part of the danger zone. Nowhere in New England is included in the danger zone according to what they are showing on the TV.'

The families had been holding a worried conference. 'I don't know what to think.' Jessica's grip tightened on her husband's hand. 'Half of me longs to be back home, but this is the children's vacation and I don't want to ruin it.'

'Right where we are standing now, ma'am,' the proprietor told her, 'is more than two hundred feet above sea level. The way they are talking now these waves aren't going to hit more than thirty feet tops and that's down in Florida. Wildest guess I heard was a hundred feet. Imagine, if the coast was right across the room that wave would still top out a hundred feet below you.'

The women laughed nervously. Lloyd's dad looked impressed.

'Seriously, folks, I can say in all honesty you haven't an iceberg's chance in hell of seeing hide nor hair of a tsunami out here.'

'Hey, mister,' Lloyd said. 'How come then they cancelled the rafting?'

Everybody laughed at the break in tension. 'They didn't cancel the rafting, son,' the man told him earnestly. 'It's like this: in order to have a real fast flow in the river we wait for the electric company that owns the dam upstream to open their sluices and release the excess from the lake. Now what I'm trying to tell you is that on account of all the uncertainty connected with the tsunami scare the company held off. They just didn't feel it was appropriate to have a whole lot of extra flow at the mouth of the river. As of this moment, what they are saying now is the afternoon release will go ahead as scheduled at four-thirty.'

'Can they hold the water back that long?' Brook asked.

'Sure, no problem, this is summer.'

'Lot of rain last night,' Lloyd's father quipped.

'Which is good. Means there'll be plenty of water coming down for you good people when you go out on the river. Now how about it? You made up your minds yet?'

'I guess so.' Jessica grinned at her husband. 'Haven't we, children?'

'Oh, Mom, please, please, please!'

The man grinned. 'All right now! Three p.m. assemble here. We'll kit you out with wetsuits for those that want them plus life vests and helmets for everyone. Then we bus you up to the launching area, aim to have you on the water by four, leaving time for instruction from your guide, familiarisation with the equipment. You ride the river down for approximately ten miles till you reach the bend just here by the hotel. Your guide will put you ashore right there at the landing stage. Anything you chose to leave on the bus will be waiting for you when you return. There will be hot showers and changing rooms at your disposal and the restaurant will be serving food, because believe me you will have worked

477

up some appetites. This will be the ride of your lives, yessir!'

Goodwill. Midday. Captain Leclerc was fighting officialdom. 'I demand the return of my crew!' he shouted down the phone at Con Wolfowitz in the Coastguard office. 'You have no right to detain them. They have seamen's visas and their papers are in order.'

The windows in Con Wolfowitz's office faced the Sound. As they talked he could look out to where the tanker lay like a beached whale outside the mole. The TV was showing footage of a devastated townscape somewhere in North Africa, shattered streets choked with wreckage, upended vehicles buried in a sea of mud and sand.

'Sir,' Con explained patiently yet again. 'Members of your crew quit the ship last night voluntarily of their own accord. They were then permitted to land on humanitarian grounds because your ship was deemed unsafe due to stranding and risk of explosion. Once ashore they became the responsibility of the US Immigration Service.'

'Yes, yes, I understand that, but the fire is out, tugs have been ordered and I want my crew back.'

'Sir, before we can allow that to happen there will have to be an inspection to declare the vessel safe again.'

'But she is safe. The hull has not been holed;

478

no tank has been breached; the machinery is functioning. You inspected her yourself last night,' Leclerc pleaded.

Con became blunt. 'Captain, your vessel is carrying a highly dangerous cargo; she is currently stranded on the mud in a crowded harbour unable to move under her own power and to cap it all we have a tsunami scare. I don't blame your crew for not wanting to return on board. Frankly I'd feel the same way in their shoes.'

'If you refuse to help me, then I will speak to the Immigration Service; I will demand they return the men, forcibly if necessary.'

'Immigration will not do that until our safety experts have declared the vessel safe, which is not going to happen until the salvage company sends a tug to tow you off the mud. Once we can get you back afloat, the inspectors can go aboard and conduct a proper check. As soon as that is signed off, then your crew will be returned aboard and we can all get on with our lives.'

There was no response from the other end. 'Captain, did you hear me?' Wolfowitz said.

'Yes, Commander, I hear you,' Leclerc said tersely. 'And if a tsunami does appear on the horizon in the meantime, what am I supposed to do without a crew? Answer me that, Commander.'

But Con Wolfowitz, looking out at the huge white tanks and their 20,000 tons of liquid gas, could think of no adequate reply.

* * *

Natalie was powering up the coast road in the Jaguar when she heard the siren. She looked in the rear-view mirror and saw a police cruiser showing its lights angrily. Now what? she thought, pulling over.

'Yes, officer, what is it? Oh hi, Logan, was I speeding? I'm sorry.'

'Hi, Miss Maxwell. No, it's nothing like that.' Logan looked embarrassed. 'Would you mind popping the trunk a moment, please?'

'Why sure if it makes you happy. All I have are groceries.'

She flipped the latch and the lid rose. Clancy rummaged inside a moment. 'That's fine, ma'am, thank you. I have to ask you to follow me back to the station though.'

'What now?'

'Yes, ma'am, right away. Chief Egan's orders.'

'Why? What does Don want from me?'

'I couldn't say, ma'am. Just following orders.'

'Am I under arrest for something?'

'Not unless you refuse to cooperate, ma'am. Then I was told to detain you.'

'On what charge, for heaven's sake?'

Logan reddened. 'Aiding an escaped felon, ma'am.'

'An escaped felon! You thought I had a felon in my trunk? Oh my God.' Realisation dawned. 'He broke out? What have you done with him?'

'Can't tell you that, Miss Maxwell, but it's best if you come back right away.'

* * *

Goodwill PD was chaotic. The front entrance was crowded with people wanting advice and assistance so Logan took her in through the back. Don had greeted her grimly with none of his usual affection. 'Just what was in those packages you handed over to the prisoners this morning?' he demanded brusquely when Annie Pellew showed her into his office.

'Nothing, a phone, spare batteries, some magazines he asked for,' she shrugged. 'Why, is there some law?'

'Has either of them tried to contact you since then?'

Her jaw lifted. 'I don't think I have to answer that.'

'You do if you don't want to be pulled in for aiding the escape of a felon.'

'He's not a felon and you've no evidence against him!'

They glared at one another. Don sighed. 'I don't understand any of this. We two used to be good friends. Now here I am threatening to lock you up. Everything's gone crazy today.'

'I'm sorry, Don. I know this is hard and you have your job to do. After I brought in those things I told you about I left and I haven't heard anything from him since, or any of his buddies. The first I knew something was wrong was when Logan pulled me over.'

She went with him back to the cellblock. Don threw open the door. 'There, see what your friends did.'

Natalie gasped. The cell was a shambles. The wire grill had been torn loose from over the window. The glass frame itself was buckled and smashed and, most incredible of all, one of the steel bars set into the recess had been wrenched from the concrete, leaving a gaping hole.

'Boy!' she said, stunned.

'I know, looks like we had a bear in here,' Don spat. He turned to Natalie. 'This is no joke. The mood your friend is in, if he's stopped he might do anything. Somebody could get themselves killed. If he's stopped and resists arrest my boys would have no choice but to use their weapons. So if he does contact you, for his own safety I suggest you urge him to give himself up.'

At that moment Natalie felt her cellular vibrate in her pocket. She felt a moment of panic in case Don might have heard. 'May I go now?' she said.

Back in the front office there were still more people wanting help. Don looked exhausted. 'I guess we'll get through this somehow,' he said. 'You don't happen to know where Rick's gotten himself to, do you?'

She shook her head. 'I haven't spoken to him today. As a rule he does the cash run first thing Sunday morning. Nothing's happened to him, has it?'

'No, not so far as I know. He brought the van back as usual, only then he seems to have taken off, nobody knows where, and he doesn't pick up his phone.'

'Well, I'm sorry I can't help you then.'

The moment she was back in the car she dug out her phone. But she was wrong; the message wasn't from the King. *Morocco 1623 local. Heavy detonations from east. Strong tremors followed by major suck out. Ride the mountain, Wave Slayer!*

Don Egan had too many other things on his mind to bother with runaway prisoners. With every TV channel and Internet portal pumping out footage of the super-Krakatoa blast on that damned island and huge waves swamping coast-lines from Portugal and Spain to the tourist beaches of southern Morocco, panic was spreading faster than a bush fire in August. After consulting with State, Don had ordered the beaches closed until further notice. Meanwhile every phone and cellular was ringing and the station was under siege by persons wanting advice or help leaving town.

'We can't tell you what the situation is, we don't know any more than you guys!' Don repeated again and again to distressed residents.

'Have you gotten through to State Emergency yet?' he shouted repeatedly to Annie.

'I told you I'm trying, only the lines are busy. All you get is a message saying there will be an official announcement shortly.'

'Well keep on trying. We have to get guidance on how to handle this thing. Everybody is going crazy out here.'

To distraught citizens he could only give the

same response: 'Go back home. Watch the TV and wait for directions. If an evacuation is ordered instructions will be broadcast by vehicles with loudhailers. We'll make sure no one is left behind.'

Don personally dialled the Emergency Center at Bangor. 'According to what we are getting from Washington the risk zone doesn't extend north of Jacksonville,' he was told. 'It's strictly a Florida and the Gulf States emergency.'

'Does that mean I can open the beaches again?'

'That would be a judgement call for you on the spot. We can't advise at this point in time.'

A half-hour later, though, talking to the Coastguard he was told the risk zone now extended north as far as Cape Cod.

'What's so special about Cape Cod? Or is it that they reckon not enough people live north of Boston to bother rescuing?' he demanded furiously.

'Search me,' came the answer. 'We just pass on what we're told. I guess though they have to draw a line somewhere.'

'That's it?' Don raged. 'Some bureaucrat down in Washington draws a line on a map and says disregard every place north? Is that supposed to make us feel secure?'

'Look,' the officer explained patiently, 'nothing has changed. Evacuation orders have so far only been issued for Florida and the Gulf coast. North of Jacksonville certain areas may be at special risk due to topography. Inlets, bays, places where the continental shelf is particularly narrow.'

'Jesus,' Don told him, 'all those factors apply to us!'

'Yeah, yeah, but don't forget distance counts too. You guys up on the border are way down off the bottom of the scale dangerwise. Confidentially, the Canadian authorities aren't issuing warnings to any of their citizens.'

Chance Greene was worried too. He was in his offices on Bay Road, trying to file a claim for fire damage on the old Ice Factory. If he could get the claim in ahead of the mass of flood claims that were bound to result from the present emergency he stood a better chance of a pay-out. Unfortunately it seemed other people had had the same idea. 'What do you mean you're not taking any more claims today? You are supposed to be running a twenty-four-seven hotline!'

'Yes, sir, but due to the current national emergency situation—'

'What emergency? There's been no emergency declared that I heard.'

'That's not our understanding, sir. We've been told that the president is about to go on air to declare a national emergency.'

'Shit!' Chance rocked his head back and forth. 'Does that go for Canada as well?'

'I couldn't tell you that, sir. You'd have to ask them.'

Chance slammed the phone down and called a friend in Montreal, another developer.

'Chance, my old friend, where are you calling from?'

'My office in Goodwill. Where did you think?'

'You are not concerned for the tsunami down there?'

'Yeah, well, word is the only ones in any danger are the people living down in Florida or the Gulf.'

'I wish I shared your confidence, my friend, but that is not what we are being told by our experts.'

'No?' Chance felt his heart sink.

'I am watching the TV as we speak. The compulsory evacuation of St John and Halifax; the Bay of Fundy closed to all shipping except for rescue craft; all inhabitants of the Maritime Provinces to move back ten kilometres inland. Even in Quebec there is anxiety.'

'In Quebec? But Quebec is built on a cliff, for God's sake!'

'Ah, for the docks, you understand.'

'I seem to recall you had land down there,' Chance said with satisfaction.

'Alas no longer. Some weeks ago when all this problem with the volcano first erupted I had a good offer and I thought, why not? So I wish you well, my friend. If there is anything I can do . . . ?'

Chance rang off in a fury. He turned up the volume on the office screen. A news announcer was speaking, but it was the rolling news bar underneath that transfixed the developer: TSUNAMI WARNING: FLORIDA WARNED WAVES COULD REACH THIRTY FEET. WHITE HOUSE CONFIRMS ENTIRE EAST COAST MAY BE AT RISK. RESIDENTS OF COASTAL AREAS ADVISED TO EVACUATE FIVE MILES FROM OCEAN.

Bearskin Neck. The only people welcoming the turn of events were the surfers. They packed into Jean-Alice's cheering and chanting. Shots of massive waves battering beaches on the far side of the ocean were being beamed to cellphones and the kids crowded round whooping and cheering.

'You kids better finish up now,' Jean warned them crisply. 'This place is closing down for the duration.'

'Bummer, man, we have to be out on the water soon. Gotta keep our strength up,' they protested.

'You guys are selfish, you know that? There are people in this town could lose everything, houses, jobs even. You ever figure that?'

They stared at her blankly. Youngsters who had never known what it meant to be tied down, to have responsibility.

A boy in board shorts shook back a tangle of salt-blonde hair, his eyes were puzzled. 'We don't make the waves, we're just here to surf them. We're not doing any harm.'

'Yeah,' his buddies backed him up. 'You guys stay off the beaches you'll be okay. Leave us alone to have our fun.'

Stung to sudden anger, Jean-Alice rounded on them. 'Is that all this means to you, a bit of fun?' She snatched one of the phones out of a girl's hand. 'Just look at these breakers, why don't you? They are hundreds of feet high. Whole cities are being trashed out there, homes destroyed, thousands dying as we speak, and you talk about having fun!'

Feet shuffled and faces fell as her words struck home. 'Jeez,' someone said, 'we know that stuff, but it's not like there's a whole lot we can do to stop it or anything.'

'The ocean has the power, lady. It can't be tamed. You have to ride with the flow.'

One more platitude, Jean-Alice told herself silently, gritting her teeth, and so help me I will belt someone hard.

She was aware of a growing noise outside on the dock, a chorus of acclamation that was soon audible inside the diner. 'The King! The King!' The ones in front moved aside as the Gimp came shouldering through. Jean-Alice's eyes widened as she saw who was with him. 'So they finally let you bums out, huh?' she said tightly.

The King made no answer. His eyes were bright. Elation at his escape had instilled in him a messianic conviction in his mission and his fervour was communicating itself to his followers. More surfers followed him in, packing the place out. He raised his arms and an expectant silence fell as they waited on his words.

'Guys, our time is near. A break is running like

no break any person on this planet ever saw or most likely will ever see again. You are the witnesses; summoned to see history in the making. You will be the storytellers; your voices will pass the legend down to generations of surfers yet to come. "I was there that day!" you will tell them. "I saw the great wave. I saw the King of the Mountain slay the giant!"

He looked around him and his gaze locked on Jean-Alice standing hands on hips looking at him tight-lipped. 'Ma'am, I heard you ask what motivates us. Well, let me tell you, we are committed to testing ourselves to our personal limits. Each time we paddle out every one of us has a personal inspiration and his or her own particular challenge. We will not settle for failure or second best, no matter what the cost to ourselves. We seek out life's challenges wherever they may be found. Maybe that seems selfish to you, but to us it's a calling to something beyond ourselves, a higher purpose.'

He turned back to face his supporters. 'Friends, before we set out I want to thank you all for being here today, for your support and encouragement. I know we will all remember this day. And I'd like to share with you a poem that has given me strength in dark times and may do the same for you when you have need of it.

'I have a rendezvous with Death
At some disputed barricade,
When spring comes back with rustling shade

489

And apple blossom fill the air –
I have a rendezvous with Death.

'But I've a rendezvous with Death
At midnight in some flaming town;
When spring trips north again this year,
And I to my pledged word am true,
I shall not fail that rendezvous.'

Behind him in the mob, Jean-Alice glimpsed
Natalie Maxwell.

Greenstone Island. Rick walked back along the
beach and up the path that led to the house. The
path that he had worn with his own feet carrying,
dragging or wheeling building materials. The
house was not large, just five rooms with a
kitchen and bathroom out the rear, laid out in
the shape of an L. He had always envisaged it as
somewhere to spend the summer, a place to
escape to. In wintertime it was too bleak for
serious habitation. He pictured himself spending
time out here with his family, showing his kids
how to fish, handle a boat, collect gulls' eggs.

Natalie liked to join in the fantasy too. She
was sick of great houses, she claimed, and longed
for the simple life. Or thought she did.

Late last fall he had finally gotten the main
roof shingled, which had been a huge step
forward. With shutters on the windows and
doors front and back it meant the house was
weathertight. So far this summer he had ferried

over a stack of wood that he had been hoarding and later if he could get some time off he planned to board out the rest of the top floor.

The key would be under the stone where he always left it. He was stooping for it when he checked himself suddenly.

The doorstep was a massive old millstone that he had found out back. Two years ago, he had spent most of a weekend out here humping it round into position while Natalie kept him going with cans of beer cooled in the ocean. Afterwards they had scoured it clean with a wire brush, uncovering the mason's initials carved in the rim.

Now the weathered stone surface was disfigured by a recent stain that looked to Rick's eye like dried blood. A seal's perhaps or a bird's, there were no sheep left on the island now.

Rising, he tried the door. It opened, creaking on its hinges, sending a shaft of light into the narrow hallway beyond.

It was empty, but the door to the left-hand room was ajar. Rick moved towards it. He heard a noise, something between a cry and a groan. Jesus, he thought. Gently, so as not to startle whatever was inside, he pushed the door open. The room inside was one which Natalie had partly furnished with unwanted items from her parents' place at Indian Point. There was a big old couch that had formerly stood on the porch there and a Persian rug that her dog had chewed a piece out of. Lying on the couch was a young woman with a dead white face. Her eyes were closed and she was covered by the rug, which had been thrown over her to form a crude blanket. Slumped at her side, clearly in the last stage of exhaustion, was a man in shorts clutching a cup.

'Kim,' the man groaned oblivious of Rick's entry. 'Kim, please, you must drink something.'

The woman stirred a hand fractionally, whether to bring the cup closer or to push it away was unclear.

At that moment the man caught sight of Rick in the doorway. The blood drained from his face. He set the cup down on the floor and made an effort to rise, but sank back gasping.

'Who are you?' he croaked.

Rick ran up the hill behind the house to the summit where he knew he could get a signal for his phone. He dialled the emergency number. 'Put me through to the Coastguard,' he told the operator.

According to what the man Randall had been able to tell him, Kim had torn her leg badly on the rocks in the Gurge. He had managed to keep her afloat on some driftwood and dawn found them washed up in Greenstone Bay. 'Somehow I got her ashore and there was the house. I imagined that all our trouble would be over, but then we found the island was deserted and there was no food. By this time, Kim was delirious. I tried to build a fire to summon help, but it kept going out and then last night it rained and Kim was getting weaker. I had just about given up when you walked through the door.'

Rick couldn't imagine how anyone could have survived that long in the water. It had been a hot night though which would have helped and according to Randall they had floated into a warm current that eventually brought them into the bay.

Rick had wanted to ask him about Maple Cove and the swell that had washed them into the Gurge, but it wasn't the moment.

'Helicopter is on its way.' The operator spoke. 'Should be with you in ten to fifteen minutes. Confirm location of incident is Greenstone Island, Goodwill Sound. Two casualties for emergency evacuation.'

'Right on the button, lady. You want I shoot off a flare when I hear the aircraft?'

'That won't be necessary, sir. Please remain with the casualties until the paramedics reach the scene.'

As Rick ran back down the hill it seemed to him he could detect a distant thunder in the air as if a great storm were rolling in behind the mist.

Goodwill. Frank Schaffer was adamant. 'I'm not concerned about risk. The plumb is plainly telling us to go look in the bay. You said that yourself. I'm going down there to see for myself. Stay here if you prefer. You don't have to come along. I appreciate all you've done and I can take it from here.'

'Frank, all I'm saying is we should inform the

authorities first,' Martin Seymour tried to reason with him. 'How is it going to help your sister, or your mother come to that, if you go and get yourself into trouble?'

For a mild man Frank Schaffer was utterly determined. 'I hear what you say, but I'm going down to the cove right now. I've listened to the police and the Coastguard and I'm sure they've tried their best, but they haven't found Kim. You're the only one who's helped. I trust you and I trust the pendulum. Its message is clear. I'm going down to the cove to find Kim. So are you coming with me or not?'

Chapter 38

Cumbre Vieja. Prone among the ash and dust of the hillside, Malc Mackenzie jabbed doggedly once more at the rock crevice with a Gerber hand tool that he carried hooked on a belt loop. Despite being forged of tempered Swiss steel, hardened and honed to a four-inch point, the spike was making little impression on the basalt surface of the huge boulder trapping Concha by the foot. The girl whimpered and struggled, twisting and straining frantically to free herself. Sometimes she let out a cry of pain, at others she screamed at him to get out and leave her to die.

The tempo of the eruption was increasing. Detonations were coming in series now like an artillery duel, deafening bangs that set the ground shaking, accompanied by salvoes of lava bombs shrieking out of the murk like lethal rockets interspersed with shrapnel storms of burning pumice. Worst of all were the clouds of noxious gas that swept down the valley from freshly opened vents along the ridge to the south, leaving them choking and gasping for breath, eyes streaming, lungs straining for air. It could only be a matter of time, Malc knew, before they were caught by a *nuée ardente*, a pyroclastic flow of incandescent ash and pumice mixed with superheated volcanic gas sweeping along the valley, incinerating everything in its path.

Fear made him redouble his attack. Wiping the dust and sweat from his face again, he worked the tip of the spike into a crack and levered with all the force he could bring to bear. The steel slipped suddenly. 'Aiee!' the girl cried sharply.

'Sorry,' he gasped.

'No, it's good. I think maybe . . .' the girl told him, straining at her foot.

Malc blinked and looked again and saw that a piece of rock had cracked off. 'Here, let me see if I can get this out of the way.' Scrabbling with his fingers, he succeeded in pulling out a lump. With a cry of relief Concha twisted free.

At that moment all hell broke loose. Another shattering blast shook the hills. Shock waves snaked through the earth like ripples on the ocean. The slope shivered and fractured, kicking up clouds of suffocating dust. The boulder that had been pinning Concha lurched suddenly and crashed over right where she had been lying. With a gathering rumble it slithered downwards, tearing the ground from under the two. Caught in the avalanche, Concha tumbled down the slope. At the last moment, Malc managed to throw out an arm and grab her back and stop her from pitching headlong into the smoking chasm below. For several moments the two clung like broken insects to the wreckage of the hillside while stones and rubble rattled over them. Then as the paroxysm subsided, slowly, painfully, they clawed their way back up to a patch of level ground.

Even here, though, safety was only an illusion. The two geologists gazed about them in dismay. Everywhere they looked cracks and crevices gaped across the ground. Raw earth showed where vertical fractures had dropped the ridge face by three and four metres. With every fresh blast those same fissures would deepen and spread.

'*Madre de Dios*!' the girl choked. 'The whole ridge here is breaking up.'

Malc took her arm, hustling her away. 'We have to get off this section, and fast before it takes us with it.'

Concha wept. 'My poor La Palma, poor *isla bonita*.'

Chapter 39

Goodwill, Maine. One p.m. The King was back where he liked to be, in control. Already his attention was moving forward. He hunched over the TV in the back of K. Zamos's blacked-out Suburban drinking in data. 'Where's this, Morocco? Shit, feature those breaks! What's been happening? Did anyone speak to the Watchers?'

'There's a message from someone called the Watchkeeper.' Natalie read it over. 'He sounds brave.'

'Yeah, one of the best. I hope he makes it. He's put himself in danger to make this work. I'm not going to let him down. We stand and fall together, the Watchkeeper and I.'

The Gimp took over. 'Morocco is down. There's been no word since. Our government is predicting wave heights on the East Coast in excess of a hundred feet!'

The King breathed deeply.

'Any word on the Azores yet?'

The Gimp was checking on the computer. 'Looks like the waves are breaking on the outer reefs. Reports of a seventy-footer, but the boys were closed out, couldn't find an entry point.'

There were gasps from the listeners. Seventy feet was a world record.

'And?' The King could tell he was holding something back.

The Gimp shrugged in his cold way. Life and death were all the same to him. 'Hodson and Delray wiped out.'

'Both down?'

The Gimp said nothing.

'Shit, man, they were good buddies. I'll miss them.'

'I told you the Azores weren't the spot.'

'Seventy foot, huh?'

'Ours will be bigger, I promise.'

'You'd better be right.'

'On my grave.'

One-fifteen p.m. The red medevac helicopter from Ellsworthy clattered overhead heading out over the Sound and word spread rapidly. The missing couple from Maple Cove had been found. It was incredible but true. They had washed up somehow in Greenstone Bay where Rick Larsen had found them, half starved, battered and suffering from exposure, but alive. The helicopter was bringing them in now.

'Jeez, Rick,' Don Egan exploded when Rick radioed in to say he was on his way back in

Chimay, 'you picked a fine time to go AWOL. We really needed you back here.'

'Yeah, I heard from the paramedics. Didn't realise things were that bad. What's the latest?'

'Depends which agency you talk to. Looks like there have been one or more major blasts, but the big one may still be to come.'

'So we're waiting for the other shoe to drop?'

'That's my reading.'

Maple Cove. Doc Southwell called home. 'Donna, where's Tab? He's not answering his phone and I've great news for him. Rick Larsen just phoned in and guess what?'

'Oh, my God, that's wonderful!' Donna cried when he told her. 'Tab will be so relieved.'

'Yeah, but listen, that's not all. I just had his mom on the phone.'

'Diane? What does she want? Tab's not due back for another two weeks.'

'It's this damn tsunami scare. She doesn't like him being so close to the ocean.'

'Why she's forever going on about how they're only half a mile from the shore where she lives. Tab was saying so only the other day.'

'I know, I know. Anyway she's threatening to drive up here and grab him back. I wanted to warn him in case she shows up suddenly.'

'That's just dumb! It's six hundred miles for heavensakes. She couldn't get here before midnight. I mean we're going to be okay here, aren't we?'

'Sure, sure, the house is safe. We're way too high up the hill. All the same it's better if you and Tab pack a bag each and meet me out here at the hospital. Listen, honey, go get Tab for me.'

'He was watching the newscasts on TV in here with me just a minute ago. It looks really bad in some of these places; it's beginning to scare me.'

'Those places are all a long way off, thousands of miles. Now call Tab, okay.'

'I think he went up to his room. Hang on, I'll call him. Tab! Tab!' he heard her shouting. 'It's your dad on the phone! Tab! Tab!' she called again. Then the sound of her footsteps clattered down the wooden stairs and she snatched up the phone again. 'He must be out back. I'm just checking the yard. Tab! Tab! Oh God, I can't see him anywhere.'

An awful premonition seized Southwell. 'Jesus, Donna, I told you not to let him out of your sight!'

'I know, I know! He was with me just a minute ago. He must have slipped out when you called me!' she wailed. 'I don't understand it. He always tells me when he's going somewhere.'

'I'm coming right over.'

'You want I should call the cops?'

'No, no! I don't want them involved again. It only upsets Tab and besides, they have enough on their hands.'

'What should we do then? I'll take the car and try down in the cove. That's his favourite place.

And there's no phone coverage. That must be where he is. I'll get the car.'

'No, Donna, for God's sake! Don't go down there, it's unsafe!' he cried frantically.

But she was gone.

At Goodwill PD Annie Pellew was trying to locate Frank Schaffer. 'His phone is turned off,' she told Don. 'Should I leave a message?'

'He was staying out at the Seafarers, wasn't he? Try there first.'

Annie dialled the number and got Beth Robbins. 'You know I was going to call you, Annie, only things have been so crazy this morning,' Beth said. 'Half our guests are checking out thanks to what they see on the darn TV. We're having to make refunds; what else can we do?'

The two women discussed the situation for a minute before Annie put the phone down. 'Beth Robbins says Mr Schaffer didn't sleep in his bed last night,' she reported to Don. 'She says he went out to see Martin Seymour that does dowsing for objects. I called his house and no answer there either.'

'You could try the hospital,' Don suggested. 'Maybe the brother had the news from someone else and is on his way over.'

Annie looked down her long nose. 'I already did that. The sister is conscious and asking for her brother. What do we tell them?'

'Tell them we're still trying to locate the guy.

And send a car over to Maple Cove; that's the only other place he might have gone that I can think of.'

Annie glanced at the status board. 'All our vehicles are committed.'

Maple Cove. Mack and Brandie had argued all night. In the morning Mack announced his decision. He would make the break. He was tired of second place behind guys like Coughlin, young chargers without his experience. He was through with taking orders. He rode out to Ellsworthy on the bike where he rented a 1200cc, 165h.p. direct-drive Yamaha PWC that the agent swore could hit forty knots with two bodies up. The machine came with a trailer and another fifty bucks bought him the use of a rattling GMC Safari minivan, a vehicle that Mack personally despised but that would serve to lug the Yamaha as far as the ocean.

Brandie would drive for him. She was strong and she was fearless on the water. 'But who's going to shoot film?' she wanted to know. There were a couple of groms he might recruit, Mack said. Young guys, but he had seen footage of them in action and they were standouts both. They had a machine that they shared. He had floated the idea with them and they were interested.

'Can we trust them? Suppose they split to the Gimp? He'll tell the King and then what?'

Mack felt they had to take the chance. 'This is

a once-in-a-lifetime. We don't seize it we're done, screwed for ever. There's no retake.'

'It seems, I don't know, kind of disloyal somehow.'

'Brandie, no one owns this wave. It has to be ridden and I aim to be one to do that.'

'All the same.'

'Just call it me straight, are you in or not?'

She shrugged. 'If this is what you want.'

The rented minivan with the trailer behind sped along the cliff road, stereo blasting hip-hop in a thumping mix that rattled the woods. The track down to the beach was barred off. Mack halted to let the girl lift the poles for him to pass. Van and trailer rattled down the slope in a cloud of dust. He pulled into the parking lot and killed the engine and the music died. Brandie followed on foot unhurried. She inhaled the air. 'Mm, smells sweet. You sure this is the place?'

'You better believe it.' Mack was already climbing down.

'So do we wait for these guys to show or what?'

'Beach closed by Police Order . . .' He was reading from a notice fixed to a pole. 'Five-knot speed limit. No water-skiing eight a.m. through five p.m. No PWCs . . . Man, this town sucks. Scott said they'd meet up with us out on the Bank. Guess they figure to make their own way there. Let's offload the gear and run the jet down to the water.'

The inside of the van was a jumble of surfing gear and personal effects. The girl slid open the side door to reach out a stretchy pink rashy. Straightening up, she pulled her T-shirt casually over her head with both arms and chucked it in the back.

'Man, it's glass out there.'

The girl stared across the wide strip of sand running down to the smooth cove, the small island out in the bay. Everywhere was quiet. Not a leaf stirred in the woods. Only the ticking of the engine block cooling broke the stillness.

Brandie tossed her hair. 'It's flat,' she said disappointedly. 'And so darn quiet. Can't imagine anything ever happening there. Maybe we should have stuck around with the rest of the guys.'

Mack gazed to the south-east up the Sound, his expression brooding. 'Figure the shape of this bay, the way it angles to the ocean. Notice how those offshore islands narrow the channel down. The incoming tide gets squeezed, then *kaboom!*' He clenched a fist. 'Nowhere to go but up.' His voice hardened. 'Yes, this might just be the spot.'

His eyes went back to the ocean again. 'The swells are building across the ocean even as we speak,' he said to the girl, talking half under his breath. 'The King wants this one for himself. He's been stalking it for weeks now. The Gimp has watchers out on the coast of Africa, on Bermuda even, passing him condition reports. K. Zamos has flown in from the coast and you know what that signifies.'

'I don't feel good about going behind his back though.'

'Hell, he doesn't own the wave. It belongs to all comers. I've had taking orders. It's a question of respect.'

'Well, in *that* case,' the girl mocked him. 'Heck, let's get this show on the road. We haven't been in the ocean all day.'

Mack climbed back into the van, swung around and reversed the trailer down across the beach. Together they hauled the Yamaha free from the trailer into the water. When they were satisfied Mack ran the van and empty trailer back up onto the road and parked under the trees. Returning, he repositioned the poles across the track.

'There's another notice.' The girl pointed when he rejoined her. 'Something about currents by the island. Say, do you think this is where those two dudes went missing the day we blew in?'

The man glanced briefly, incuriously, and chewed his lip. 'More likely just a story cooked up by locals to scare us off.'

Down in the water they fitted the rope onto the transom ring and hooked on the board for the trip out. Both were wearing full wetsuits. The surface was getting choppier, they noticed. Mack took that as an omen. 'Head out past that island,' he ordered. 'The sets look gnarlier there and we'll be out of sight from the Sound for longer.'

506

The girl climbed on and started up. The engine fired first kick, settling into a throaty roar. Plenty of power. Mack ran a final check of the equipment and settled himself on the pillion seat. 'Okay,' he shouted in her ear, 'let her rip!'

Mike Caine, Rick's brother-in-law, jogged back along the Neck to the Chandlery. The tanker *Marie-Sainte* was still aground outside the mole and the dredger had ceased work. The waterfront was a scene of frenzied activity with bigger boats putting out for open water, while at the same time many of the boat owners were hauling their craft out and onto trailers. The Neck was choked with vehicles fighting to get out with loads or in to pick up. Mike found Reb and the boys in the store, packing cartons.

'The boat is gassed up full,' he told his wife. 'I'm going to take her out now. Con Wolfowitz reckons ten miles out for security, I want to allow a couple of hours to be safe.'

'Can we come along, Dad?' the boys demanded eagerly.

'No, you two stay here and look after your mom. She needs you.'

Rebecca's face was drawn. She hugged her husband tight. 'I wish you wouldn't go,' she whispered. 'It's dangerous out there.'

'Look,' he said, 'we went through this last night. After this store the boat is our biggest single asset. Even a small tsunami, if there is such a thing, will smash up anything it catches in

507

harbour. Out on the ocean there's nothing to fear. We can ride out any wave.'

'We have insurance though. So what if the boat is lost? We buy a fresh one.'

'We went through that too. Payout could take months and we'd miss the lobster season. It would cripple us just when we need the money most. Let me do what I have to. You clear out with the boys to Ellsworthy and stop over with Uncle Stu and Aunt Julia till the emergency is over.'

'Okay,' she agreed wearily.

'Promise me you won't leave it too late? Don't hang on here and get trapped.'

'I promise. But it's you I'm worried for.'

'I'll be fine. *Pequod* will be with me.'

'Is she seaworthy? Patsy was in here and said there was trouble with a rudder.'

'Magnus and Paul are fixing that now. As soon as she's ready we'll head out. We'll sound the horn before we go.'

'We'll listen out.'

'And mind you get the boys out of here in good time. I don't want to save the boat and lose my family.'

Reb watched him go with a cold hand on her heart.

Curtain Bluff. Sheena was on her way out to Ray Burns's place again when her phone trilled. She glanced at the screen, Doc's number. She jabbed the button. 'What is it?'

508

'It's Tab. He's taken his bike and gone off. We're searching for him everywhere.'

She spun the car. 'I'm coming!'

Goodwill. Half a mile away, the boy they were all concerned for cruised down the hill into Bay Road, weaving in and out among the vehicles leaving town. At the turn to the Neck he braked to let vehicles past. A throbbing sound was approaching, and glancing left he saw three big bikes cruising up from the direction of the bridge, heading a long procession of trucks and SUVs.

The bikers rolled majestically closer. Their machines bore surfing insignia, Tab saw, and the riders' hair streamed behind them. At the junction of Main and the Neck their leader halted, holding up his right hand palm forwards, and behind him the rest of the convoy stood still. Taking up the flag he carried, he thrust it high in the air and his voice rang out above the traffic sounds. 'To the glorious dead!' he cried. 'To our comrades in Morocco, in Spain and on the Azores! May we meet again in Valhalla!'

'Valhalla!' the cry came back from fifty throats. 'Valhalla!'

Rick headed *Chimay* back down the Sound at a rapid clip. The sun was dissipating the mist, but visibility was still hazy. The water was dotted with departing craft seeking the security of open water, mostly larger vessels and working boats, whose owners didn't want to risk them being

509

swamped. There was a lot of radio traffic. Rick listened in to some of the exchanges.

From habit he kept to the northern shore. There were figures on the sand in Maple Cove. He put the binoculars on them, but couldn't make out the faces. The water was growing choppy. There was white surf around the rocks of Two Bush Island. The current must be flowing fast through the Gurge.

The tanks and superstructure of the *Marie-Sainte* were just coming into view, looming ominously over the mole of the harbour. If a big wave did reach as far as the Sound the tanker could pose a major hazard. No wonder a lot of boat owners wanted to get the hell out.

His cellular beeped. The boat had come within range of the mast on the end of the dock. The caller was old Phil Rebold, manager of the Main Street bank. There were generally two kinds of bank managers who came to Goodwill: young ambitious types who stayed a short while before moving on and older ones looking forward to a quiet retirement. Mr Rebold was one of the latter.

'Rick.' He had a deep unhurried way of speaking. 'I should like for you to come back into the bank if you will, please.'

'I'm out on the Sound. Why, is there a problem?' Rick asked.

'Not a problem exactly, just something that has to be done right away. You can probably guess what it is.'

'No disrespect, Mr Rebold, but I've a lot on my mind right now. If you could just say what it is you want.'

The bank manager coughed. 'The delivery you made this morning; it has to be returned right away.'

Rick couldn't believe what he was hearing. 'You're saying you want us to run the cash back?'

'I would rather not discuss such matters over an open line, but yes,' Rebold said. 'It is not my decision,' he added, 'head office called.'

'Let me get this straight,' Rick said. 'Bangor are telling you that it will be unsafe to leave that much cash in the vault in town?'

'I suppose it does amount to that,' Rebold agreed calmly. 'You have to understand that the bank has an obligation to take the greatest possible care of depositors' funds.'

Why was it, Rick wondered, that whenever you were borrowing it was the bank's money, but if there was a question of risk the money belonged to the depositors?

'That's not showing a great deal of faith in our chances here, would you say, Mr Rebold?'

'I'm sure I couldn't answer that,' Rebold replied stiffly. 'The point is the money has to be returned directly. I've spoken to Kelso. If you'll just bring the van around as normal, he'll have the sacks bagged up and waiting.'

Rick felt a rising anger. 'There's no "has to" about this,' he said.

Mr Rebold's voice deepened. 'I would remind you that you are under contract,' he said tersely.

'A contract that provides for me to drive a van for you once a week and I've performed for this week.'

The phone crackled as the signal started to break up. After a moment the manager's voice became audible. He spoke evidently choosing his words with care. 'Rick, this bank has always treated you and your family with respect, with trust I might say. We have supported you; we have been here when you needed us. In return we expect a degree of loyalty. Do I make myself clear?'

A chill came over Rick. This was what happened when you owed the bank: they owned you. His voice hardened.

'Mr Rebold, I am a Selectman; my loyalty to the town comes first. I'm sorry but you'll have to find someone else to drive the money back, either that or trust your own vaults.'

Rick cut the connection and dialled the Chandlery to let Reb know he was coming in, but the number was busy. He was trying her cellular when something made him pause.

Something was wrong, badly wrong. It had to do with the boat.

Chimay was moving backwards.

Chapter 40

Cumbre Vieja, La Palma. Titanic explosions shook the hills. The mountain was tearing itself apart.

With a desperate spurt Malc and Concha had reached El Pilar at the head of the trail at last. Ahead of them, half buried under mounds of pumice, the remains of a metalled road ran down through the hills to join the new highway at El Paso on the plain. Ash and gravel were falling so thickly now they had to cover their faces in order to breathe. Malc was exhausted but he staggered on, the girl clutching at him for support. The road ran downhill clinging to the hillsides through sharp corners and steep-sided valleys. There was constant danger from avalanches as well as from lava bombs and falling rock. Often they had to force a path through thigh-deep drifts of hot ash, scramble over landslips or jump crevasses torn by tremors. In some places the roadway had fallen away completely and they had to clamber round the gap like mountaineers hugging the rock face.

Dizzy from exhaustion, from the heat and fumes, half blind and deafened by blasts, bruised and bleeding from the never-ending hail of stones and gravel that plummeted out of the sky, they stumbled on through a darkness relieved only by spouts of fire.

Explosions were now coming from the new vent so fast one upon another that it was no longer possible to distinguish individual blasts. Their numbed ears registered only a continuous wall of noise. Lava bombs began falling again, not singly as before but in salvoes and sticks. Some buried themselves where they fell, others bouncing off rocks careered and slithered down the hillside, setting off more landslides. A third kind, hotter than the rest that blazed with a white heat, burst on impact in showers of searing shrapnel.

Shortly after this the noise shifted to a series of immensely powerful grunts or gasps as if the volcano was struggling to clear its throat. Each sound was accompanied by spouts of blazing lava that shot thousands of feet into the air. The eruption was now clearly approaching its climax. In desperation Malc pulled the girl in under an overhang to escape the storm of burning droplets that swept the valley. At one end a fallen boulder partly obstructed the opening, forming a kind of cave. They crawled in together as far as they could go, crouching under the low roof.

'Get down!' he yelled. 'And cover your ears! This is the big one coming! When it does, open your mouth and scream as loud as you can to equalise the pressure.'

Concha nodded her head to show she understood. Her dark eyes were huge, rimmed with dust. Suddenly pulling Malc close, she flung her arms around his neck, kissing him with all her strength. In the midst of death and destruction an affirmation of hope.

The third and final detonation was the most terrible of all. Brilliant red and yellow flashes burst from the cone, drenching the land in fearful light. With a scream like ten thousand jet engines roaring at full power, a flaming column of superheated gas and pumice shot more than forty kilometres to the edge of the ionosphere. A fraction of a second later came the pressure wave that stripped the hillsides bare for a radius of five miles from the epicentre. A blizzard of splinters and razor-sharp rock shards hurtled outward, shredding everything in its path without mercy. Man-sized boulders slammed into the hillsides like giant cannonballs, shattering on impact. Buildings that were still standing were reduced instantly to rubble and dust. A reinforced concrete lighthouse a mile from the cone had steel doors and window shutters blown out and the top three storeys snapped off like a broken tooth.

The sound of the explosion was clearly heard on Bermuda almost 3,000 miles to the west as a rumble of gunfire. On La Palma its effects were annihilating. Malc and Concha were partly shielded by being down in a valley with hills between them and the blast site. Even so the effects at that range were similar to being caught up in a high-speed car smash. The pressure punched the air from their lungs, crushing their chests and cracking ribs like breadsticks. Malc's head was kicked back against the roof of their crude shelter, fracturing his skull and knocking him unconscious. When he came to he was half suffocated, buried under a wall of debris and bleeding from ears and eyes and nose. Concha pulled him clear, but he couldn't understand a word she said. The blast had burst both his eardrums and done the same to her.

But worse was to come.

The earth cracked open and the mountain slid. The impact of the blast ripped into Cumbre Vieja's entrails like an exploding shell, shattering and destroying. As a vast cloud of smoke and fiery debris vomited out over the ocean, the shock wave punched through the island, ripping and fracturing. Magma pipes all along the volcano ridge erupted into fury as the chambers below were torn apart, releasing the pent-up pressure of a thousand years. The surging lava flows burst through subterranean lakes of trapped water, flashing them into instant steam with the explosive force of nuclear bombs. Fault lines snapped like gaping jaws, the fractures rippling along the ridge, cleaving the basalt cliffs.

The ground quivered and heaved. Rocks shot out of the shaking earth, buildings tottered, highway tunnels collapsed, roads buckled. Deafened and bleeding, Malc and Concha clung to one another praying. On and on went the destruction, a constant thunder of noise that swelled and grew like an avalanche that overwhelmed the brain.

With cracks like shellbursts, cleavage lines split their way through the dark heart of the volcano. As fracture met fracture, widened and spread, the speed of the collapse increased exponentially, ripping its way through twenty kilometres from the ancient caldera of Taburiente in the north of the island down to the twin cones at Fuencaliente at the southern tip.

And the mountain slid again. With a cacophony of sound, of crackings and splinterings of rock, of explosive fracturing and phreatomagmatic eruptions, the western flank of Cumbre Vieja broke free from the main mountain, fracturing along the summit line as if split by a cosmic axe stroke. All the westward side began to move, the land surface subsiding toward the ocean with a slow but terrible collapse that gathered momentum as it went, shaking and rumbling with an awesome power that levelled the ruined buildings, crumbled roads to dust and devoured trees, people, power lines, animals and vehicles, plunging them into the water in an almighty crashing avalanche of burning rock in a geological cataclysm the like of which had not been experienced on the planet in at least a hundred thousand years.

As the pace of collapse accelerated great blocks of material split off, tumbling into the water, plunging down to the seabed. Behind them they left a vertical cliff like an exposed wound two kilometres high, whose surface glowed red hot from the terrific friction generated by the sliding rock masses grinding past one another. Half a trillion tons of rock was on the move, thundering six kilometres down to the ocean bottom.

And the ocean returned. Hidden by an enormous pall of dust and smoke, with a thunderous roll like an artillery barrage, the water crashed back into the vast gap ripped out of the volcano's side, surging half a kilometre up against the newly cut cliffs. Steam erupted in boiling clouds as water came in contact with the searing rock face. Cliffs shattered as if torn asunder by explosive charges. On and on the chaos of destruction thundered. Minutes later the reflected wave was roaring back outward into the ocean still two hundred metres from trough to crest. The event the world had been dreading had finally happened: the La Palma tsunami was spawned.

USS *Thresher*. It took fifteen minutes for the exposed flank mass of Cumbre Vieja to reach the abyssal plain four miles down and fifty miles out. On the submarine the pressure wave from the big blast made the 20,000-ton vessel vibrate like a bell. Captain Krauss felt the tremors running up from the deck through the soles of his shoes into his legs as he braced himself against the periscope stack. They seemed to go on and on. The rumblings and thuddings reminded him of attack practices with simulated depth charges and undersea mines.

Since the last blast an hour ago the *Thresher* had been at full alert condition while they crept away westward, hoping to put as much distance as possible between themselves and the next blast. By Krauss's reckoning they had made around twenty-five sea miles. It made him feel a lot more comfortable. Even a volcano in its death throes, he felt, would scarcely be capable of lobbing sizeable rocks fifty miles.

As it happened fifty miles was exactly the distance that the Cumbre Vieja landslip ran out.

The first Krauss knew of this was when abruptly the *Thresher* juddered afresh. 'Turbulence!' he shouted automatically. At that same moment something struck the sail with a heavy clang and he thought, Shit, now what? This was going to be different.

Just how different he was about to learn.

The rumbles and shaking broke out afresh. The vessel was tossed and buffeted by unseen currents like a toy in a washtub. Light fittings popped and warning bells shrilled as rocks and debris cascaded about the hull. 'Collision stations!' he had time to shout before something huge slammed into the stern section. More alarms sounded. There were cries over the intercom. Krauss thanked his stars that he had ordered heightened alert with watertight doors sealed and hatches dogged down. He prayed there was no damage to the running gear.

More rumblings and crashes echoed through the boat. A red emergency phone blinked on a control panel. Krauss grabbed it. 'Captain.'

'Sir, this is the chief. The main propeller is cavitating badly. It must have just taken a knock.'

Cavitation was a vibration set up by air pockets forming around the propeller blades.

'Can you keep her running for the next few minutes till we get away from whatever this is?'

'Sir, we'll do our best, but we need to reduce power two thirds to avoid straining the shaft.'

'Understood.'

Outwardly calm, Krauss swore to himself silently. At one third remaining power the submarine could manage barely ten knots, hardly more than creep speed.

'Sir,' the executive officer was calling his attention to the inertial navigation plotter. 'Looks like we're in the grip of a major current here.'

Krauss looked and gaped in disbelief. According to the plotter the vessel's actual speed over the ground was an astonishing forty-eight knots. 'That's unbelievable,' he gasped, stunned. With the engines powered down there was no known current with that kind of power. The submarine was literally being sped through the water like a missile.

The executive officer shook his head. 'Whatever is happening back there must be helluva big,' he said weakly.

The *Thresher* shuddered afresh as more detonations thudded around them. 'Hold her steady!' Krauss rapped. 'Maintain current course and depth.'

'I'm trying, sir!' the senior helmsman gasped. 'She's being thrown around all over though.'

'Do your best, son,' Krauss told him. He reached for the PA button and pressed to speak. 'This the captain—'

It was as far as he got. There was a terrific crash on the starboard side and the vessel was plunged into darkness again. The deck tilted sharply. There were cries from forward as men were hurled against machinery. Choking fumes filled the attack centre. 'Masks!' Krauss had just time to shout. With a sickening sensation the submarine plunged towards the ocean floor.

USS *Tarp*. 'Here, put this on, Mary.' Derek Wanless bundled a thick orange immersion suit into her hands. 'Skipper's orders. We're all doing the same.'

Mary bit down on her lip to keep back the choking fear that churned in her stomach. If the suits were being issued there was a real possibility of the ship going down. Kicking off her shoes, she rifled through her shoulder pack for a few precious items to slip in her pockets.

'Take some chocolate, you may need it,' Wanless advised. 'And hurry.'

Mary stepped into the bulky suit and pulled up the zips. It felt horribly bulky and clumsy. I'll never be able to move in this thing, she thought. Much less swim. Derek showed her how to tighten the seals at cuffs and neck.

'I did a survival course on these things, but I guess I didn't pay enough attention,' she told him with an attempt at humour.

'Don't worry about it. If the worst happens and we have to go overboard this thing will keep you afloat for a week.'

Her knees were shaking though as she followed him out the door and up the stairs to main deck level.

'Hurry along there!' a sailor shouted to them. 'Everyone into the main saloon. Sit down on the floor and link arms!'

Dry-mouthed with fear now, Mary took her place, squatting down between Derek and Felix. All the academic staff were present, some strained, others determinedly cheerful. From time to time instructions from the captain came over the loudspeaker. Lightning flickered and blazed. Peals of thunder hammered overhead. Outside it was now almost too dark to see. Only in the west did any light linger in the sky. To the east an immense darkness pulsed with streaks of fire. *Götterdämmerung*, Mary thought, the Twilight of the Gods.

The loudspeaker crackled again. The captain's voice, calm and collected: 'Here we go again, people. A big one this time. Hang on and we'll do our best. God bless us all and bless America.'

'Amen,' everyone chorused. Arms tightened as they felt the bow start to rise.

Mary stole a glance at the window and froze. Ahead of them reared a wall of water, mountain-high, lightning-crowned, vast, omnipotent and deadly. Its cresting summit seemed to scrape the darkened sky. Up and up the *Tarp* climbed, steeper and steeper. They could feel the engines labouring. The ship rolled wildly, burying her bow. Foaming water burst over the decks, hammered against the portholes. There came a falling sensation . . .

And then hell burst in on them.

Chapter 41

Goodwill Sound. Rick's instinct was to ram *Chimay*'s throttle open. Even shaking under full power though, the workboat barely held her own against the current. This was crazy. The tide should have turned by now and be running the other way. The vessels up ahead in the Sound still seemed oblivious to what was happening. They were cramming on full speed in their haste to reach open water. The current would only seem like a bonus to them. But Rick's heart went cold at the thought of what must follow. He glanced over his shoulder half expecting to see a glistening wall of water bearing down on him from astern, but there was nothing. The monster must be building out there in the haze. Riding down on the unsuspecting town, silent and unseen.

There was only one course to take and he took it. Putting the wheel over slowly, he brought *Chimay* carefully about till she was facing out from the Sound ready to tackle the threat head on when it came. The speed of the current made the manoeuvre difficult; *Chimay* rolled as she came broadside on and a roller smacked into the side, drenching Rick from head to foot. He held her steady though, straightening her up on her new course. The ocean foamed past slapping at the stern and the boat bobbed along jerkily with the tide stream pulling her.

A handsome forty-foot Bermuda sloop, newly built for an English banker by Hinckley, was overhauling him to starboard. A couple on board gave him a cheery wave from the cockpit; they looked to be enjoying themselves. Rick wondered whether to try warning them over the radio; hell, though, they would find out soon enough what was in store, and it was the people back in town who were most in danger. He picked up the radio mike and gave the call sign for Goodwill harbourmaster. 'Jack, this *Chimay*, do you copy?'

The response was immediate. 'Rick, I was wondering where you had gotten to.'

'Jack, I'm out in the Sound experiencing a strong outflow current. Can you see any sign of suck back where you are in harbour?'

'Suck back? What are you talking about?'

'Take a look off the end of the goddam dock, for Christ's sake!'

Leaving the radio on, while he waited, Rick dug out his phone and speed-dialled Reb's number. Dammit, the line was still busy. He punched in the number for Jean-Alice's and swore again as he got her voicemail. 'Jeannie, pick up will you? This is urgent!' No response.

He was listening out for the radio with his other ear. Other mariners were starting to register the current. Anxiety was spreading around the Sound.

Rick hesitated a moment, then dialled the first number on his speed-dial list. 'C'mon, come on,' he muttered.

The phone clicked, but there was no sound. 'Nats?' he shouted. 'Nats, can you hear me? Where are you?'

But the connection had gone. Either that or she had rung off.

That was the point that Rick knew he had to turn back.

Maple Cove. 'What's that?' Brandie shouted. Ahead of them across the mouth of the narrow channel that separated the island from the shore a broad line of leaping spray had blossomed into existence. Through boiling surf they could make out jagged teeth of rocks guarding the entrance.

'Just keep going! Keep going!' Mack yelled into her ear from behind.

'Hang on then!' She twisted the throttle and the Yamaha surged forward in instant response. Spray flew past blindingly as they sped howling up the channel, a broad arrow of foam streaming in their wake. Brandie felt the adrenaline squirting through her bloodstream at the sheer exhilaration. She loved jets, the crazy speed, the pin-sharp steering. And this baby was quick! One hundred and sixty plus horses and every one of them raring to race. Even with two up they were hitting thirty-five easy.

'Stoked, girl!' Mack was urging her on. 'Give it the gun!'

The waves were getting more solid. The jet was bounced from crest to crest, crashing through the seas with bone-jarring thumps. As the channel narrowed, so the current speeded up and the sea state grew rougher and more confused. Bursts of spray exploded around them, breakers leapt out of nowhere, slamming into them, leaving them breathless. The lightweight Yamaha slewed under their impacts. Brandie struggled to hold the stern steady. The seas grew steeper with plunging breakers crashing on the rocks, flinging up clouds of spray. The water was ice cold; it lashed at her numbed fingers like glass.

'It's pulling us faster!' she screamed at Mack. The current was tearing at the machine as the waters of the cove forced their way outward through the tight gap. Squinting through her goggles against a blizzard of spray she glimpsed a dark pit yawning right ahead and hooked a sharp left. They clawed up the face of a gnarly six-footer, pitched over the top and instantly found themselves floundering in a wild slalom of ferocious cross-currents.

'I don't know what to do!' Her voice was stretched by panic as they rolled and pitched dizzily.

'Hold straight. Cut through this shit!' he yelled back.

Another trough opened right in front of them. The nose pitched down, almost tossing them off, and the stern fishtailed as they slewed across the slope, clawing for grip. A black spine of sharp rock loomed off Brandie's right elbow and she leaned frantically over to pull them round out the way, feeling Mack hanging on behind. Surf crashed over them as the Yamaha buried its nose deep. She twisted the throttle savagely, felt the jet pump bite, and the machine ploughed on gamely.

Somehow they struggled out from under. The current was carrying them back towards the right again in a dizzying arc. Terrified of hitting the rocks, Brandie fought with all her strength and weight, but felt the nose tilt over. They were turning back on themselves. The nose came round again, they were spinning. Jesus, she thought, we're in a whirly!

Pain shot up her right leg. Something hard banged the bottom of the hull. Shit, if they hit the rocks now they were dead. The Yamaha bucked and bounced. They were picking up momentum, spinning faster and faster. Round, round and down . . .

Goodwill. The King had readied his crew for action. Horns blaring, they raced through town down to the dock, led by K. Zamos in the Suburban with red-headed Carly at the wheel and the helicopter camera team in the back, the Gimp's jet towing behind. The rest of the convoy followed: the back-up rider Sharkbite Coughlin and his driver with their own jet ski, then four more teams of PWCs with camera agents to cover the close-up action from the water.

Only one team was missing. 'What's happened to Mack and his girl? Why aren't they here?' the King demanded.

The Gimp shook his head. 'They haven't shown. I don't know why. I called Mack's phone, but he doesn't answer.'

'Not like him to chicken out.'

'I'm thinking he's maybe playing his own hand.'

The King's mouth was grim. 'Just him and Brandie? No camera team?'

'He probably figures to use ours if he can race ahead and drop in on us.'

'If he tries we drive him under, right?' The King's expression was bleak. This was war.

The Gimp got the message.

The convoy screeched to a halt alongside *Pequod*'s berth. Patsy Easton was at the head of the gangway as the teams piled out and swarmed aboard. 'What's this? Who are you guys? We're not taking passengers.'

Red-headed Carly pushed past onto the deck. 'Where's Paul Olsen?'

'He's busy right now. Don't bring all that kit aboard. What's all this about? This is a private ship. You've no right to push your way on board.'

'Yeah, you think so? Read, girlie, and weep.' Carly waved a bunch of papers under Patsy's nose. 'This is a charter agreement signed by your boss putting this boat and crew at our disposal any time in the next ten days. We're exercising the option as of this minute and we have cash for the balance. Default on the contract and we sue and you lose the boat. Understand what I'm saying? So go find Paul and tell him his clients are coming aboard and to get this tub under way.'

Patsy stared at the woman in disbelief. 'A charter? Now? Are you out of your skull? Haven't you seen the TV? There's a tsunami coming through any minute. It's dangerous out there.'

Carly's upper lip curled. 'Why do you think we're here, huh? You take us for whale watchers or what? Now go find Paul and have him send someone to get that crane working. Some heavy-duty machinery alongside needs swaying up on deck and like you say, there's not a whole lot of time.'

Patsy gaped at her for a second in sheer bewilderment. Surfers and photographers lugging gear were pushing past onto the deck. The dockside swarmed with husky bodies unhitching trailers, manhandling jet skis and rescue sledges into position for hoisting. The huge surfer leader was down among them giving orders. Natalie Maxwell was with him, talking urgently into a phone. A young man lugging film equipment up the gangway pushed a camera in Patsy's face. 'Smile.' He grinned irritatingly. Patsy elbowed him aside and ran down the companionway to the engine compartment to find Paul.

The world was going mad.

Up in town, Tab Southwell bumped over the cobbled lane running down to the new marina. Chance Greene had wanted to rip the cobbles out, make it smoother for his customers' vehicles, but the council had refused him. A steady stream of boats on trailers towed behind heavy-duty SUVs and trucks were pulling up the ramp to the entrance. Hammers were ringing along the Neck as owners boarded up their premises. The air was muggy and though the mist of the morning had lifted the ocean was still hazy. It was hard to figure what might be out there. Tab half hoped it was true that a wave was coming to sweep the whole rotten town away.

The matches were snug in the pocket of his pants along with a throwaway gas lighter. Down in a boatyard there was always plenty of trash for burning and paint and stuff, varnish, oil rags that would catch alight easily. It would make something else for his dad's scabby girlfriend to write about in her stupid paper.

Inside the marina gates people were hurrying up and down the walkways between the berthed boats, humping loads of equipment ashore.

Those unable to haul out their boats were determined to strip them of every movable fitting. Tab saw sails, radar receivers, depth sounders, seats and cushions, crockery, even a fridge being barrowed along the swaying pontoons. No one took any notice of him as he wandered around. 'No, no, I'm managing just fine,' one white-haired old guy thanked him when Tab offered help with an aluminium mast. 'Look after yourself, son.'

Dads were yelling at their families to hurry along and arguing over how big a wave was coming, whether it would break over the mole and how much damage it would do. 'The first wave will hit Maine at three o'clock,' a sun-burned man was telling anyone who would listen. 'That's official.' Tab checked his watch. Another hour then.

He wandered around some more and even climbed down aboard one boat that looked to have been abandoned. No one bothered him, they were all too busy. Tab toyed with the idea of setting fire to a yacht, picturing the blazing craft drifting among the other vessels spouting flame and smoke, spreading panic and confusion. That would teach them all a lesson. Or maybe he should try somewhere on shore like a paint store.

Tab fingered the matches in his pocket.

Sheena sped down the hill into town in her car. Donna was searching the cove and the last thing

Sheena wanted was a confrontation with Doc's wife. If Tab had gone back there well and good, his parents could pick him up and take him home. If he was in town looking for another building to burn then he had to be found and stopped. That much she owed Doc.

She circled the Green, but there seemed few people about. Most that she did see were loading vehicles or boarding up storefronts. She was reminded of small towns in Florida getting ready for a hurricane. Could this be as bad? It was hard to imagine peaceful Goodwill getting trashed. There was activity outside the police department building. Maybe someone there had seen Tab.

She half wondered whether to try the Ice Factory and made the circuit back down to Bay Road again. A stream of vehicles was pulling up from the marina; weekend sailors moving their boats out of harm's way, and on impulse she made a left onto the Neck. If any place was at risk this was it. An air of ominous calm lay over the dock. The Lobsterman was shut, which was a sure sign of bad things to come. Sheena stopped the car and climbed out for a look around. The doors of the Chandlery were open and inside Reb and her sons were stripping shelves. Further down the Sail Loft sported a CLOSED sign and next door the windows of the Candy Shack were boarded up.

Pequod was still berthed at the end of the dock though and that surprised her because most of the larger vessels had taken off. Vehicles were massed alongside and people were running up and down the gangway ferrying equipment and shouting to one another. Sheena could see a crane hoisting what looked like a jet ski up onto the stern deck. A young woman in a striped top was giving orders from the bridge deck. That would be Patsy Easton. In the background, out beyond the mole, the looming bulk of the gas tanker brooded over the scene. Sheena fished out her camera-phone and snapped off a couple of shots.

Jean-Alice appeared, walking briskly up towards the head of the dock.

'Have you seen Tab anywhere?' Sheena asked.

'Tab? Tab Southwell? No, I haven't seen him since yesterday I think. Why, who wants him?'

Sheena flushed. 'He's gone missing. They can't find him anywhere. Donna is down searching the cove. His dad called me,' she added lamely.

'Sorry, can't help. Do they think he's on the water?'

'I'm not sure. I just came down to look. You staying?' she added.

Jean-Alice shrugged. 'Everything I own is wrapped up in the diner. Besides, this town has stood for two hundred and fifty years, I reckon it's good for a few more yet. If I see the kid what do I tell him?'

'Hang on to him and call his dad. Donna's worried for him.'

'Will do. Take care of yourself now.'

'Wait. What's happening with *Pequod*?'

'Didn't you know? They're hoping to surf this tsunami that's coming through. If it does. They've chartered *Pequod* to take them out off the Bank.'

Sheena sprinted to *Pequod*'s gangway and leapt aboard. Up on the bridge deck, she pleaded her cause with Patsy. She had forgotten about Tab. Anyway he was Doc's problem, Doc and Donna's. 'Do this for me, Patsy, please, please. I really need this break. It's the perfect story and it'll be huge, huge. Just take me along with you. I won't get in anyone's way.'

'Jeez, I don't know, Sheena. Paul's pissed off enough with all these surf guys showing up.' Patsy wavered. 'Well, I suppose we could stretch to one more. Keep your head down till we're safe out of the Sound, okay? Anyone asks, you're one of the crew.'

'You won't see me. Listen, I just need to fetch my big camera. I'll be right back. Don't go without me.'

Frank Schaffer and Martin Seymour drove over to Maple Cove in Frank's rental car and parked under the trees near the van with the trailer. They read the notice on the barrier. 'So long as we're not intending to swim I guess it's okay to go down,' Martin said.

'I need to check once more just in case,' Frank

said. 'For Kim's sake. I sort of feel I owe it to Mom too.'

The gravel of the track crunched underfoot as they descended. 'The cops said they cycled down, Kim and Randall. The boy saw them and the bikes were found later. Over there by the parking lot, I think,' Frank told the older man.

In the parking lot there were more warning notices. 'Looks serious,' Frank said. 'I guess these signs weren't up when Kim came by.'

At the edge of the sand they halted. 'Someone was down here recently.' Martin pointed to the tyre tracks. 'Seems like they launched a boat.'

They moved on along the beach. 'Here are some more tracks,' Martin said, 'different ones.'

'Narrow feet, probably a woman.' Frank's voice trembled. 'You don't think . . .?' He gazed at Martin, a wild hope breaking out on his face.

'That's the Gurge,' Martin said quietly. The entrance to the channel had an ominous quality, the water lapping darkly at its rock pinnacles. It was hard to imagine anyone being foolhardy enough to venture out there.

'Who's that?' he said suddenly, shading his eyes to look. Away off in the distance at the far end of the beach opposite the island a small figure with a bright scarf was waving wildly at them.

Frank was breathing hard. 'The pendulum was right. Something is going on down here!' he cried. He broke into a run along the beach.

The tide was sucking back out before their

eyes, exposing wide stretches of sand. The entrance to the Gurge was quite close now. Panting after Frank, Martin could see broad pools around the rocks separated by patches of mud.

Reluctantly Martin followed as Frank splashed out across the still wet bed of the cove towards the woman who had been waving at them. Crabs and other small creatures scuttled away into crevices and pools at their approach. The sand quaked under his weight, sucking at his shoes. 'Frank, I'm not sure this is a good idea. We are way out from the shore. If the tide comes back in fast we could be cut off.'

Bearskin Neck. 'Ten minutes!' Patsy shouted after Sheena as she ran back to the *Pequod*'s gangway. 'Ten minutes, no longer. If you're not back too bad; we sail without you.'

'I'll be ready, I promise.' Sheena raced down the gangway.

Down in the marina, Tab moved out onto one of the further pontoons. The tide looked to be running out. He could see the bottom of the harbour quite clearly and crabs crawling about under the timber piers. It struck him as unusual and he recalled with alarm what he had seen on the TV about tsunamis and suck back. 'Hi,' he said to a woman he recognised hurrying past with a cool box, 'take a look at what's happening with the ocean.'

The woman checked herself in mid-stride. She wore calf-length slacks and there was a smudge of dirt on her blouse. 'Were you talking to me?' She shaded her eyes to look at him. 'Tab, hi, is something wrong? Are you here with your dad?'

'It's the ocean; it's getting shallower. It's kind of weird, don't you think?'

The woman shook her head. 'I'm sorry, I don't have time to chat. You know you really shouldn't be hanging around down here. It isn't that safe just now.' And she bustled off.

Tab tried another person and again received a brush-off. By now the water was running out so far that the larger boats on the outer pontoon were grounding their keels and starting to list. And still nobody seemed to have noticed anything wrong.

Sheena Dubois tore back along the dock to the marina's side entrance. Thank you, God! she shrieked to herself. This was it, the break she had been waiting and praying for all these years. The King of the Mountain was going to ride a tsunami and she, Sheena Dubois, would be there to capture the moment on camera.

To reach his new marina Chance Greene had built a walkway giving boat owners direct access down to the pontoons from the Neck with its stores and eateries. It was also a useful short cut through to the other end of Bay Road. Some whim of building regulations had caused gates to be fitted each end but they were seldom locked.

Sheena pushed the first gate open and ran onto the bridge, hearing the gate clang behind her, and darted down the fenced-in walkway towards the marina. Her apartment was only a step from the main road entrance on the far side.

She reached the second gate and pushed the bar. The gate stayed shut. It was locked. The last person through must have tripped the catch. Damn, now of all times. Impatiently she rattled the grill, trying to attract the attention of people on the pontoons. No one even glanced in her direction. They were all too busy with their stupid boats. Sheena swore; she was wasting valuable time. Giving up, she ran back along the footbridge towards the Neck. She reached the gate she had come in by and pushed to open it. It stayed shut. She pushed harder, but it didn't budge. The catch had locked shut behind her.

She was trapped.

The dredger had ceased working. On the bridge of the tanker, Captain Leclerc strode to the edge and focused his binoculars. 'Contact the harbourmaster,' he snapped to the third officer. 'Ask him why work on clearing the channel has halted.'

'*Oui, mon capitaine.*'

The answer came back promptly. 'They say it is the tide, sir. The dredger no longer has depth to manoeuvre.'

Leclerc made no response. Frustration was burning him up. Almost twenty hours since the ship had gone aground and what had been done to get her off? Nothing, nothing at all. A tug had been promised, but there was no sign of it and not even a suggestion now of when it might be expected. Leclerc had raged and pleaded, pointing out that with every rise and fall of the tide that passed the *Marie-Sainte* became more firmly wedged, but his protests fell on deaf ears. And now the dredger had given up. She was actually sending her crew ashore. Leclerc could see them going over the side into a boat.

His own crew was ashore too. There was no work for them to do of course, but it irritated Leclerc. Now that the fire risk was extinguished there was no danger to anyone. The chief engineer had made a thorough inspection below decks and aside from some minor straining the hull was intact.

Leclerc had tried to speak with the Coastguard. They at least were anxious to see the tanker moved. At present though they were completely taken up with this tsunami scare. And that was a fresh anxiety. Every sea captain's urge when faced with a threat was to put to sea. If a tsunami were to strike in the next few hours and catch the *Marie-Sainte* helpless . . .

'*Capitaine!*'

He was startled out of his reverie by a sudden cry from the young third officer, who was pointing over the side.

'*Capitaine*, look! The tide, it runs out! All the way!'

540

Leclerc ran back to the side of the bridge and stared over. The boy was right. The ocean was retreating, draining out from the harbour. Before their eyes, rocks and sandbars that only a few minutes before had been underwater were emerging into the light. Already the mud at the base of the mole was exposed; a pair of lobster boats moored alongside had grounded, leaning on their sides against the stonework, bottoms exposed.

And the *Marie-Sainte* was being affected too. Leclerc could feel the tanker tilting as the support of the water at the stern sucked away. Mother of God, if this went on much further she could break her back. The hull would crack open, splitting the tanks; there would be a gas escape, an explosion, and utter devastation.

Other vessels had seen what was happening. Sirens were going off, a general alert sounding. People were running along the harbour back towards the town, waving their arms and shouting.

A cold horror seized Leclerc's heart. There could only be one explanation for the ocean running out in this manner. The same phenomenon was observable on any beach as a breaker moved in. The advancing wave climbed over the water in front causing a suction effect. Often the pull was strong enough to drag swimmers off their feet.

But a suck-back effect on this scale was something unheard off. It would have to be a truly enormous wave to drain all the water from the Sound like this. A wave like no other. A great sea wave. A tsunami!

Over at the marina, Tab Southwell had finally located someone to take him seriously. A middle-aged couple stopped to listen. The woman frowned at him, but she did look at the water. 'Wow, that is shallow,' she said to the man with her. 'The boy is right, it does look kind of strange.'

'And it's still running out,' Tab told them. 'See that boat,' he pointed to a thirty-foot lobster cruiser leaning over on its side. 'She's resting on the mud.'

The woman chewed her lip. She glanced worriedly at her companion. 'Is it my imagination or is that water draining away as we watch?' she said.

The man gripped her wrist and started to back away up the pontoon. 'Hey!' he shouted to people further up on the dock. 'Get out of here! The ocean is running out fast. It's a suck back! A tsunami is coming!'

Tab took up the cry. 'A tsunami! A tsunami!' And suddenly with one accord everyone on the marina started to run.

Maple Cove. 'Two people in the water. They're being swept out into the Sound!' the woman gasped as Frank reached her. 'Call the Coastguard! Hurry!'

'Two people?' Frank's heart leapt. 'Where? Where are they? I don't see them.'

'Out there, beyond the island.' Donna pressed her hands against the pit of her stomach to ease the pain of breathing. 'The current took them. I saw their heads in the water.' She sucked in another lungful of air. 'Have you seen a boy? Thirteen, fair hair?'

'A boy?' Frank was bewildered.

'My stepson, we think he came down here.' Donna struggled to get the words out. 'Please, please get help, those guys in the water . . .'

Frank gripped her arm to steady her. 'Lady, do you have a phone?'

'No use,' she gasped, 'no signal, the cliffs . . .'

Frank took charge. 'Martin, I saw an emergency post on the beach back by the parking lot. See if there's a landline connection there to call for help. If not run back up to the top and go to the nearest house. Tell the Coastguard two people are in the water in trouble. Hurry!'

Martin Seymour blinked at him, nodded and turned away, breaking into a stumbling run. Frank turned back to the woman. 'The water has run out. If I cross to the island could I reach them from the far side?'

Donna swallowed and shook her head. 'Don't know, maybe,' she told him.

'I'm going to give it a shot. You stay here.'

'No, I'm coming too. The boy, my stepson, he may be out there.'

* * *

543

Up on *Pequod*'s bridge, Patsy Easton felt the ship lurch and reacted faster than most. One glance over the side told her all she needed to know. A scientist by training, she recognised what was happening and had made the connection. The tide was running out, draining water from the harbour as if someone had pulled a plug. That meant a suck back and a heck of a wave on the way. One half of her thought, Oh my God, that serves those idiot surfers right! The other half, the scientist, experienced an adrenaline rush. Either way Patsy didn't hesitate a moment. Whirling on her toes, she ran for the cabin, knocking a photographer out of the way, and yanked the horn cord hard and held it down.

Down on the Neck, Reb and her sons froze in their tracks as the blast of ships' horns split the air for the second time in two days. 'Gee, Mom, is that another fire?' Leif asked hopefully.

'Yeah, can we go watch?' his older brother pleaded. 'Just for a minute, please.'

Reb waved them savagely to silence. The blaring sounds repeated again and again. Other ships were joining in with a crescendo of frantic alarm. Mike Junior made a face. 'Sounds kinda serious.'

'Man, it's the wave!' his younger brother Leif yelped excitedly. 'Let's go see!'

'Boys, jump in the truck,' their mother barked.

'What about all this junk?' Mike Junior indicated the stacked cartons. 'You want us to load it up?'

'Do as I say and don't argue!' Reb snapped. 'Outside, into the truck. Move, the pair of you.'

There was shouting outside and a noise of running feet. A vehicle went speeding past the windows. Rebecca's phone trilled urgently. She snatched it up as she ran.

'Yes?'

'Get out!' Mike's voice, hoarse with urgency. 'Get out!'

'Where are you, Mike? We have to stay together!' she cried frantically.

'Just get out! Take the boys and run! Run now! Run!'

Chapter 42

Rick spun the wheel over and for the second time *Chimay* dug her blunt snout gamely into the current. A fresh deluge of water crashed against the windows of the small cabin, but she was used to toughing it out. Her bows lifted again, she shrugged off the weight of the heaving breakers. Her stern slewed a moment as she turned broadside on, but Rick steadied her as a man might steady a startled horse and she butted her bow bravely into the teeth of the tide stream again. Two Bush Island was still off to starboard so she had a bit less than a mile to make before the wave caught her.

The current was slackening though. He watched the land crawl past. He must be making two or three knots which was better than before. Straining to see through the streaming windshield he thought for a moment he could make out figures on the island. He put the Nikons on them and whistled. Two people, one of them a woman from the bright scarf. They must have crossed over from the beach while the tide was running out. People were insane. Didn't they realise the risks? There was no way he could get in close enough to help them even if he wanted to.

He threw a glance over his shoulder, half expecting to see a wall of water powering down on him from astern. Was it his imagination or was there already a shadow thickening the haze out on the horizon? Big waves on this coast were spawned off Goodwill Bank where the continental shelf took the plunge down to the abyssal plain. But the mouth of the Sound was offset from the Bank so that entering waves were deflected northwards around Greenstone Island onto the cliffs at Curtain Bluff. That twist of physical geography made Goodwill a sanctuary, a safe haven for shipping.

But there was one flaw in the design, a crucial weakness in the shield system protecting the Sound. Certain storm systems tracking up from the south-south-east, from the direction of Africa, had a tendency to generate waves that approached Goodwill Sound full on. Such storms were rare, but deadly. It was just such a storm that in 1812 had descended on the coast, driving the ocean before it up the Sound and overwhelming the town. As a consequence the town fathers had sanctioned the construction of the high mole running out from the southern edge of the Sound as a bulwark defending town and harbour.

For two hundred years the mole had defended Goodwill. Now it was about to be put to its severest test yet. And *Chimay* had to reach it first.

He risked another glance astern. And there it was, a band of darker blue topped by a silver rail where the sun caught the crest. A mile in his rear? No, less than that, half a mile at most and closing fast. Twenty knots? Fifty even? Impossible to tell. All he could do was cram on all possible speed and pray.

Pray he could make the mole in time.

Out the corner of her eye Brandie glimpsed a black spike of rock shelf flash by like a shark's fin. The muscles in her shoulders and arms ached from clutching the machine's handles and when her breath choked on gulps of water it scared her in a way she hadn't known before. The force of the current pulling them out was growing stronger and the Yamaha lurched, picking up speed. It was almost tearing them from their seats.

Just when Brandie thought she could hold on no longer, the drag slackened, leaving the jet ski bobbing on the surface like a lump of debris spat out of a mill race. Open water surrounded them. They were through the channel and out in the Sound.

Easing the throttle back, she let the jet idle. 'God,' she coughed, 'that was heavy.'

'You did great.' Mack patted her shoulders.

'Some ride, hey?' he chuckled, spitting over the side. 'Now for the big one.'

Maple Cove. Donna and Frank splashed across the shallows to Two Bush Island. The distance was further than it looked. Also the water was deep in places and they had to detour through thickets of exposed seaweed. By the time they made the island both were soaked.

'I don't see anybody,' Frank panted. 'But if they're being swept out we should find them around the far side.' Without waiting for an answer he set off clambering towards the north end of the island. Donna followed, picking her way over the weed-covered rocks, arms spread for balance, struggling to keep up. If only they could find Tab safe.

After about two hundred yards Frank found his way blocked by a sheer drop. The water was deeper here, slapping against the rocks. 'No go,' he reported, returning to join Donna. 'We have to climb back, try another route.'

She halted for breath. 'Is Tab out there?' she gasped.

'No, but it's hard to see from here. We need to search further over. Come on.'

Back on the shore, Martin Seymour staggered along the beach to the Coastguard emergency phone in the parking area. He had to pause a moment to catch his breath before making the call. There was a lengthy wait before the operator came on. 'Coastguard, please state your position.'

'Maple Cove, Goodwill Sound.'

'Your name and address please, sir.'

Martin complied.

'And the nature of the emergency?'

'Two people, maybe three, in the water. They're in trouble.'

'Are they in a vessel?'

'I don't think so. No, they're in the water.'

'Max three persons, okay. Do you have visual contact with them?'

'I'm sorry, what was that again?'

'These people in the water, can you see them from where you are?'

'Uh no, I think they've been swept round the far side of the island into the Sound.'

'Two Bush Island, that right?'

'Yes, yes.'

'Okay, sir. Now please listen carefully. We are experiencing a great many calls at this moment. We may not be able to respond to all requests for help right away. Also there is currently an urgent tsunami warning in effect for all parts of the coast. We are advising everybody to get back at least a mile from the shore.'

'But these people, they're in trouble.'

'Yes, sir. We will try to get assistance to you as rapidly as possible. In the meantime I repeat our advice is for you and anyone with you to get back at least a mile from the ocean without delay.'

Shaking, Martin Seymour hung up the phone.

550

He looked around for Frank and the woman, but they had disappeared over to the island. Before he could think of what to do next a vehicle came barrelling down the slope from the road above and slewed to a halt in a cloud of dust. Martin recognised the doctor. 'Hey!' Southwell shouted to him. 'Hey, have you seen my wife?'

'Looking for a boy? She went out to the island to find him.'

'My wife went out to the island!' The doctor stared incredulously at Martin. 'What, in a boat?'

'No, they went over on foot. The tide is out,' Martin told him. 'She thought she saw people in the water. The guy I was with went too. His sister is missing and her boyfriend. I just phoned the Coastguard,' he explained.

Southwell wasn't listening any more. He was staring at the cove where the receding waters had uncovered wide stretches of sand and weed. He turned an ashen face on Martin. 'The tide?' he cried almost hysterically. 'You idiots, don't you know what that is? It's not the tide; it's a suck back. It means a tsunami is approaching!'

For several minutes Mack and Brandie drifted in the Sound, recovering their strength while the jet burbled and spluttered gently beneath them. The exhilaration of those moments back in the channel was still with them. Mack was busy retightening the lashings of his board and other equipment.

'Hey, check that out!' he said suddenly with excitement. 'Awesome!'

Brandie straightened up to look. Her heart skipped a beat. From side to side of the Sound stretched a smoothly curving wave. It was twenty feet high.

Two Bush Island. Donna was gazing out across the Sound. 'Lots of boats on the water. Maybe one of them has seen something.'

Frank shaded his eyes to look. 'Is that a Coastguard launch, the one heading this way?'

'Where? Oh, I see. Yes, yes, I think so. Try to attract their attention!' Donna cried.

Frank took off his cap and waved it over his head. 'They've seen us, I think. They're circling. They can't get close though.'

The launch swung in parallel with the island and slowed. A figure on deck seemed to be trying to signal to them. Then a megaphone blared. 'Get back from the beach! High waves are coming. Get back from the beach immediately!'

Frank and Donna looked at one another. 'Oh my God!' Donna screamed. 'What are we going to do?'

Frank grabbed her wrist. 'Climb!' he told her. 'Climb as high as we can get!'

'We have to get them off!' Southwell cried. He was scrambling back into his car. 'If we hurry . . .'

Martin was staring at the surface of the cove. 'We're too late,' he croaked. A look of slow horror came over his features. 'We're too late. Look!'

Out beyond the island, the Sound was foaming back into the Gurge in a huge breaker.

'Turn into it!' Mack yelled in Brandie's ear. 'Meet the sucker head on.'

Brandie blipped the throttle and the Yamaha leapt forward. The wave was less than two hundred yards off now, sweeping inexorably down on them. Its face was glassy smooth, the slope not yet quite steep enough to break. It was swelling though as the Sound narrowed and the drag along the seabed increased, underwater turbulence shortening the wavelength and pushing up the height. Already she could make out the first streaks of foam appearing at the flank nearest them, signs that the crest was growing unstable as the water shoaled.

'You wanna try this one?' she yelled over her shoulder.

'Nah, way too small. We can do better. Save our ammunition,' he shouted back. 'We have bigger fish to spear.'

'My wife and son! I have to find them!' Southwell cried, shoving Martin away.

'Don't be a fool! You can't reach them in time!' Already behind them the ocean was streaming back into the bay, filling the channel between them and the island. Bursts of spray leaped up as the wave crashed among the rocks opposite. The island shoreline disappeared behind a curtain of thundering water.

Southwell slumped against the seat, waxen-faced with defeat. 'Come on!' Martin urged. 'We can't stay down here. We have to get up onto the road. Move over!'

Edging the shocked man over into the passenger seat, Martin climbed behind the wheel, slammed the door and threw the car into reverse. The Landcruiser shot backward and he stamped on the brakes just in time to stop from smashing through the rail over onto the beach. Grit spurted under the tyres as they surged forward up the gradient. Martin took one look back in the rear mirror and shuddered as a wall of water crashed over the patch of level ground, erasing the tracks the wheels had made only moments before.

Out on the water, Brandie screwed the throttle round to max, pumping fuel to the engine and sending the Yamaha scrambling up the face of the onrushing wave in a swooping curve. Gaining the summit, she leaned right and they skated along the back of the crest for fifty yards before curling down the rear slope, the slipstream tearing past at thirty knots.

Mack punched the air, stoked with excitement. 'Yeah, baby! Way to go!'

'Hang on!' Frank cried. 'Hold tight to me!' Crouching among the crags and grasses as close to the middle of Two Bush Island as they could get in the time, they linked arms, bracing themselves for the wave's onslaught. Already they could see the foam leaping among the rocks below. A roar like thunder filled Frank's ears. 'Hold!' he screamed.

There came a burst of spray. It grew stronger and fiercer, tearing and battering at them, crushing them against the rocks like insects. Frank tried to snatch one last gasp to fill his lungs for what was to come, but there was no air left, only rushing water that rolled on and on . . .

Goodwill Sound. The wave caught up with *Chimay* half a mile short of the harbour mole. Rick felt the stern of the boat start to lift. He glanced back. The wave was just starting to break, lines of foam streaking the face. The height he guessed was about equivalent to *Chimay*'s length overall. So long as she held steady and didn't fall away or broach, she should be able to ride it out.

The slope of the deck increased till it felt as if the bow was hanging almost vertical. She was on the wave now, being borne along with its momentum. There was a temptation to put the wheel over and attempt to plane down to one side, but that would be to risk sliding off and being buried under the weight of the breaker. Rick eased off the speed slightly. *Chimay* was lifting now, the body of the wave overtaking her.

under the keel. She shuddered as a ragged section of crest crashed over the stern, slamming Rick against the wheel. The boat sagged, wallowing under the weight of water filling the cockpit, while he fought to hold her steady, praying the hatch cover was latched tight and the engine wouldn't die on him.

It was an ugly moment. The sea was surging alongside and *Chimay* was riding low in the water, losing steerage. He got the pump going and in another half-minute the crest was past and the boat was levelling out on the back slope. Rick throttled back on the speed and set to work with the hand baler to help the pump out. The wave had carried the boat in quite a way. The mole was hidden now by the crest, but the white tanks of the *Marie-Sainte* were still visible, giving a fair idea of scale. Rick caught a moment's glimpse of his brother-in-law's boat wallowing between them, then came the *whump* as the wave struck the mole full on and the air was filled with sheets of foam.

Over on the *Marie-Sainte* Leclerc was one of the few actually able to see down on the wave as it rolled in. The alarm bells were ringing throughout the ship for collision stations and those few who had chosen to remain at their posts were braced for the impact. The tanker was positioned slantwise on to the wave's attack with the result that the stern would take the impact first.

'Perhaps the wave may lift the ship and free

us,' he heard the first officer say hopefully on his right.

The chief engineer snorted, 'More likely to twist the hull and break her back.'

'Enough,' Leclerc snarled. There was no torture like that suffered by a master whose ship was in danger and unable to manoeuvre. Even if the ship did by some miracle remain seaworthy after this they would never persuade the crew to return.

'*Alors*, here it comes,' muttered the chief.

For a ship the size of the *Marie-Sainte* a twenty- to thirty-foot storm wave is no big deal. Her designers had waves four times that in mind when she was ordered. But this was no ordinary wave, it was a tsunami. And the single significant factor about a tsunami is its wavelength. The punch a wave packs, its energy, is computed by a simple formula that multiplies wavelength by the square of wave height. Take a thirty-foot storm wave with a wavelength of three hundred feet and compare it with a tsunami of similar height and a sixty-mile wavelength. The tsunami's energy quotient is one thousand times greater than the regular storm wave's.

Incredible as it seemed, Leclerc felt the ship jump under the impact, like a heavyweight boxer taking a solid blow to the chin. Twenty thousand deadweight tons of steel and cargo was actually shifted bodily sideways a distance of more than thirty feet, deadweight being the operative term here since the *Marie-Sainte* was at the time firmly grounded on the mud of the harbour.

The wave surged up twice its own height against the port side of the ship, the side that took the impact, ripping off the side rails and sucking a steel door on the main deck level out of its frame and bursting several windows. Water surged inside the accommodation block, washing out a saloon and recreation room and pouring down a shaft into the galley below. On the exposed main deck, pipes and valves serving the fuel and water pumping system were wrenched from their fixtures and twisted out of shape. Four lifecraft were torn off their davits. Only the main gas tanks remained unscathed.

The floating bomb was still intact. So far.

Behind the mole on *Pequod*, Patsy Easton and Paul were frantically throwing out fenders and loosening mooring ropes, all the while yelling at the surfers to don life vests and stay away from the rails, when Patsy heard the thump of the wave's impact and twisted in time to catch exploding plumes of water bursting over the wall of the mole, high enough to blot out for a moment the hull and superstructure of the tanker beyond. The wave crashed over and down among the boats still trapped inside the harbour. Shit, here it comes, she thought, grabbing the bridge rail and hanging on tight as the surging ocean tore on over the wall across the inner harbour, rolling over boats, moorings, rafts and dinghies, sweeping them all before it towards where *Pequod* lay.

She felt the deck tremble under her, rolling and shaking. There were thumps and scraping noises alongside from wreckage washing against the hull. The wave was spewing over the wall of the mole into the harbour. The dock was flooded and now water was streaming across the Neck and chasing people on foot up towards the town.

A sudden crash forward made her jump. A lobster boat had rammed them under the bows. Patsy ran down to the foredeck.

Without stopping to think, Jean-Alice sprinted back to the diner. With practised speed she unlatched the heavy wooden shutters and swung them together over the windows, dropping the bar across to hold them in place. Feverishly she fitted the key in the lock of the main door, let herself in, heard the *whoomp* of the surge hitting the mole outside and slammed the doors shut again behind her. The flood boards for the door were stacked ready to hand. Hefting them one at a time, she slotted them into the steel grooves either side of the frame and hammered in the wedges to make a seal.

She ran into the kitchen. This was her liveli-hood. The front room could survive a drenching, but even a few inches in back would wreck the fridges and ovens, the dishwashers. The big walk-in freezer room that had cost $20,000 to build and fit out might survive. Its door was like a vault, but everything else was critical.

The kitchen door was solid and fitted with a seal on it that would hold back a flood for a while. She checked the stand-by generator that would run the freezers and the water-activated pump installed to take care of any leakage. All the electrical switches and fuses were purposely sited as high as possible. In the storeroom there was some dry food from the last delivery stacked on the floor. Working frantically she piled every flat surface with cartons of perishables.

The side-door fire exit! In her haste she had forgotten to check that. She darted back into the diner, locking the kitchen behind her. Until recently the only other access had been a narrow passage beside the kitchen where the garbage went out, but three years ago at Freddy Tarr's request it had been upgraded to a fire exit. The new door she had installed was fireproof and burglar proof, not that there was ever much crime in Goodwill but the insurance company had regulations. Jean-Alice cracked the handle open a fraction to peer out.

A cascade of dirty water spurted through the gap, soaking her shoes. Swearing, she slammed it shut again. The alley outside was six inches deep. The weight of the water shocked her. It took strength to force the door back against the inrush. Praying the catch would hold, she went to fetch a pail and mop up the mess.

Usually this only happened in winter during a storm.

Her phone rang, startling her.

'Jeannie, where are you?' Her manager's voice, concerned.

'In the kitchen, boarding up. Where are you?'

'On the Green. Bay Road is swamped. I called to warn you.'

'About the flooding? Thanks, but I was on the dock.'

'Do we have water inside? How bad is the damage?'

'None to speak of. I got the doors shut up just in time. What's going on, Mitch, do you know? Is it the big one?'

There was no answer. 'Mitch? Mitch, can you hear me? Are you there?' she shouted, but the line was dead.

Like a caged bird, Sheena Dubois ran back and forth along the footbridge hammering at the gates as she tried to attract someone's attention. The wail of the horns and sirens had been joined by the cries of people in the marina running back from the pontoons. 'Help me!' she yelled. 'Help me, please!' But the noise and pandemonium drowned her pleas.

The footbridge spanned a rock breakwater with a ten-foot drop. If she tried to jump she would break a leg or worse. She rattled the gates again in desperation. 'Help!'

And then suddenly among the people streaming past a face looked back, a face she recognised.

'Tab!' she screamed at the top of her lungs. 'Tab!'

Tab never knew what made him turn back. Maybe he had heard Sheena calling his name and it had belatedly registered. Even then he didn't take in who it was pounding on the locked gates of the footbridge. As a matter of fact it was never clear why the gates should have been locked. Afterwards there were people who claimed they never were; it was just that the catches were stiff. The woman had been hysterical with fear, they said. If she had only calmed herself down, taken a deep breath and tried the handle properly it would have opened and she could have freed herself.

Tab acted bravely. With the wave bearing down on the harbour no one would have blamed him for putting his own safety first. He was only a boy after all. Instead he made a wild leap between the two sets of pontoons and ran back up to the gate. He saw that it was his dad's girlfriend trapped inside, but he didn't let that make any difference. Perhaps he realised all along she was as much a victim as he was. There was no key that he could see. He looked around frantically, found a boat hook, seized it and started to lever at the lock.

Tab was a husky boy, driven by urgency. He wedged the spike of the boat hook in under the latch and heaved with all his weight. The lock gave suddenly, snapping open, throwing him off his feet. With a cry of relief Sheena flung herself through the gap. Tab picked himself up and they tore up along the pontoon to the road. In the same instant the leading edge of the first tsunami reached the marina.

To shelter the new moorings, Chance Greene had planned a breakwater extending out from the far side of the Ice Factory. There was trouble however from environmental groups and work was incomplete when the wave struck.

This was the shallowest part of the bay and the wave had broken already when it reached the pontoons. With no defences worth the name the surge burst in upon the massed boats like an avalanche. Yachts, motor cruisers and pontoons were all swept up and pounded into splintered wood and fibreglass shards. The whole mass was carried on the wave up over the flooded water-front into Bay Road. A thirty-foot family cruiser was thrown bodily across the road into the Pier Street parking lot and every vehicle in the place wrecked from water and mud damage.

Sheena and Tab felt the pontoon buck and disintegrate under them as they leapt for the pier at the end. Seconds later that went too, shattered from below as the sea erupted underneath, scattering planks and cross-beams, catching Sheena in the instant of jumping and catapulting her onto dry land in a heap. She lost her footing and fell and would probably have stayed down, but Tab saved her life again, not once but twice that day, reaching out to jerk her to her feet and pull her on up the slope to the entrance.

They made it through and across the road, running up Pier Street with lungs bursting and the blood pounding in their ears, running as neither of them had ever run before or would run again, with the roar of the flood chasing them, tripping and stumbling, their feet slipping on the cobbles, until Sheena knew she could run no further. It was easier to die if that was what it took and she sank fainting to her knees.

Chapter 43

The Causeway. Ray Burns cycled down the hill from Curtain Bluff. Away to his right the Causeway branched off ruler straight, running across the glistening salt marsh that separated Goodwill from Ellsworthy. Something was wrong though. There should not be that much water in the marsh.

Ray braked and slowed as he reached the dip where the creek ran under the road. The ditches either side were brimming over and in another moment his wheels were hissing through a shallow stream. The flooding grew deeper; soon the bike wobbled, forcing him to dismount. Ray rolled up his trousers and began walking. The water was ankle deep. By the time he arrived at the crossroads it was up to his calves. He could feel the current flowing in strongly and felt alarmed.

A car came down from the direction of the Causeway. It was piled high inside with baggage and household items. There was an elderly couple inside. 'Causeway's blocked,' the man told Ray.

'How deep?' Ray asked him.

The man was wearing a jacket and tie. His wife had a hat on. They must have been to church earlier. 'Couldn't tell.' The man shrugged. 'Might have been a foot, might have been a yard out in the middle. Didn't want to risk getting stuck. Have to try the bridge over Indian Creek if the road there's still dry.'

Ray swallowed. 'How is it in town?' he asked.

'Bad,' the man told him succinctly.

Ray watched them drive on slowly through the flood. It looked passable still. He hitched his pants up further and set off, dreading what he would find.

And yet the town had been spared the worst so far. The mole had fulfilled its purpose as the town fathers had intended. Its stout construction resisted a major part of the tsunami, reflecting it back up the Sound. According to experts afterwards this had the double effect of reducing the volume of water entering the harbour area and at the same time disrupting the following wave train, cutting the damage that would otherwise have resulted.

Out in the Sound its effects were dramatic in a different way. In *Chimay*, Rick was still baling when a second wave, travelling in the opposite direction to the first, burst out of nowhere, catching him completely unawares, swamping the boat and very nearly driving her under. He estimated this wave, which almost knocked him over the side, at ten feet minimum. Others said more. It actually did more damage to the boat than its big brother, stoving in the cockpit windows, snapping the wheel in two and carrying away all the instruments including the fish finder and the radar and radio.

If the engine had given up on him he would have been finished, but somehow it kept turning. Rick staggered back to what remained of the wheel and found enough control left to meet the oncoming seas. The next few minutes were a nightmare of surging currents and breakers coming at him from every quarter, while the boat sagged under the water it had shipped. Gradually, though, conditions eased and he started to take an interest in his immediate surroundings. The Sound was awash with wreckage, dismasted boats and flotsam of every kind. He saw a man's head in the water and managed to get a line to him. It was his brother-in-law Mike Caine.

'I saw you not far away when all this started,' he said when he hauled him aboard. 'Looks from here like your boat's still afloat though.'

Mike vomited up a load of seawater and managed a rueful look. 'I thought I'd come through, till that last one hit,' he said. 'I went up in the air and came down again that hard I swear I touched bottom.'

'Give me a hand baling out this water,' Rick told him. 'Then we'll get a line on your boat and tow her back in.'

Downtown, Goodwill PD was chaos. Officers were struggling to cope with dozens of injuries and homeless. The Bay Road was a shambles with almost every property under two feet of water. Don was on the phone hanging on for State Emergency, when Logan Clancy barrelled excitedly into his office. 'What do you want?' he snapped. 'I thought I sent you down to clear Bay Road.'

'That's it, Chief, I just came to tell you there's a bunch of surfers down on the Neck and I think I saw one of our fugitives among them. If you'll let me have a couple of vehicles I can bring the bastards in for you.'

'Jesus wept!' Don exploded. 'Have you no sense of priorities? The town has just been hit by a tsunami with maybe more to come. People are being injured, maybe dead even. I sent you down to evacuate the harbour area. Now get back there!'

'But, Chief, these guys bust out of jail!' Clancy protested.

'Yeah, well, we'd have had to let 'em out anyway by now, wouldn't we?' Don said scathingly. 'The charges wouldn't have stuck. Now scram!'

Logan went out crestfallen and Don continued trying to raise State Emergency Control. 'I'm real sorry, Chief Egan,' the operator apologised, 'all the lines are busy still. You want to hold?'

'No,' Don said wearily. 'Thanks for trying anyway.' He put the receiver down. It looked like they were on their own for the present at least.

Annie Pellew came in. 'Causeway's flooded out,' she told him. 'Ellsworthy says high-wheel trucks can still get through, but for how much longer they don't know.'

'Let's have another look at that big map.'

They stared at the large-scale plan of the town for a minute in silence. 'If the Causeway is out I don't like the way the hospital is stuck out there down by the marsh,' Don said. 'I think we should speak to Doc Southwell about evacuating patients. Give him a call, will you?'

Annie was back inside a minute. Her lips were pursed. 'I spoke to the hospital, but he's not there. They said he took off just before the sirens sounded. Apparently his wife is missing.'

The harbour was a mess. The marina looked to have been trashed by a bomb. A boat had smashed into *Pequod*'s side and at least three other craft had sunk. Rick and Mike made the boats fast to a vacant berth and climbed up onto the Neck. The scene was one of devastation. Floodwater was draining back off the dock, leaving stretches of mud and wreckage behind. The weight of the surge had burst in the doors of the Chandlery and the sales floor was swamped.

Cartons of stock lay on the floor soaked and ruined. 'Reb and the boys got most of the shelves cleared,' Mike said. 'I helped her drive a couple of loads out.'

'Yes, but where are they?' Rick asked.

'I called her just before the tsunami hit. She and the kids must have taken off in the truck.'

Neither of them had a phone any longer. Mike had lost his when he fell in the water and Rick's was soaked along with the rest of him. They went next door, but the Lobsterman was shuttered and locked. They ran up to the head of the Neck. There was a police barrier on Bay Road. Phil Hogan was there holding a small crowd back. Rick made out a fire truck further up. 'What's happening?' he asked Phil.

Phil looked harassed. 'Flood washed out the front wall of a building, collapsed the floors above. There's people trapped. Fred Tarr's boys are trying to reach them. They've sent for a back-hoe.'

'Which number?' Mike wanted to know.

'Sixteen,' Phil answered out the corner of his mouth. 'The Bakehouse.'

'Shit, that's where Mitch lived over,' Mike muttered to Rick.

Jean-Alice came to join them. She was distraught. 'I can't reach Mitch. His phone cut out while we were speaking and now he doesn't answer.'

'Phil, okay if I go through?' Rick said.

'Sure, Rick.'

'Stay with Jeannie, Mike. I'm going up to take a look,' Rick told him.

He ducked under the tape and walked quickly up the road. His wet pants and shirt clung damply to him. The damage along this part of the street was heavy. Around half of the premises were businesses of one kind or another. Rick passed a restaurant, an art gallery and a bar, all of them gutted. The seas had ripped and surged through the ground floors, pulling out doors and windows. Years of effort had gone into making these places nice and all wiped out in a flash.

The Bakehouse was an old brick building dating back two hundred years, it was claimed. All that was left now was a gaping hole in the block and a pile of rubble in the roadway. The suction of the retreating water had pulled out the front wall, tumbling the unsupported upper floors and roof into the road. The fire crews were labouring with shovels to clear a way through. Fred Tarr was directing.

Rick tapped him on the shoulder. 'Fred, how bad is it?'

'Bad enough. There's a pick-up truck underneath all of this.'

'Anyone inside?'

'Won't know till we get under to take a look.'

'Any word on Mitch? Jean-Alice thinks he may have been upstairs.'

'We found him. He was in back when the wave came through. Cuts and scratches where a ceiling came down on him and shaken up, but no bones broke. Luck I guess. He's up in that tender if you want to see him.'

'Lend me your phone and I'll tell Jean-Alice the good news.'

The backhoe with its big front loader came rumbling up on its huge tyres. Rick watched as under Freddy's direction a heavy section of roof was lifted clear. Now the rear quarter of a blue pick-up was plain to see. 'That's a Ranger,' one of the crew said.

'No way, a Mazda,' Rick heard a buddy contradict him. The two models were almost identical. Both types were common. Mike Caine had a Ranger in the same blue, the double cab version so he could tote the boys along.

Fred Tarr was looking at him and for a moment stupidly he couldn't think why. Maybe it was a kind of defence mechanism that rejected the evidence of his eyes even when it was in front of him. Then all at once it struck home and he felt sick.

He had to call Mike and he didn't know how he was going to do that.

Maple Cove. The level of the ocean was slowly subsiding again. From the top of the cliffs Martin Seymour could see the beach parking lot starting to emerge from the water. The surface of the bay was still heaving menacingly with whitecaps, slapping at the base of the rocks, and Two Bush Island was ringed with surf.

Southwell had a pair of Japanese binoculars out and was training them on the island. 'Can you see anyone?' Martin asked after a minute.

'I'm not sure. The surf gets in the way. I think maybe . . .' Southwell fiddled with the focusing. 'Yes!' he cried, his voice high pitched with relief. 'I can definitely see something moving along the ridge.'

'Who is it? Is it your wife? Can you tell?'

'I can't make out. They're among the rocks. There they are again now, moving up towards the top of the ridge. Here, you look.' He passed the glasses across.

'Where were they? I don't see them.'

'Along the top crest, near the middle. There's a pale-coloured rock. They're next to it.'

'I think I see the rock. Yes, I can see someone, one person . . . and another! Two people, one could be Frank, but I can't be sure.'

'Here, let me drive now,' Southwell said peremptorily. They swapped seats and Southwell started up the engine.

'Where are we going?'

'Down to the beach of course.'

'But there's nothing we can do. We don't have a boat and even if we did it's too rough to get near. We have to wait for the Coastguard helicopter.'

'You spoke to them already, didn't you?'

'Do you have a phone? Call them again.'

But Doc's phone was ringing even as they spoke.

'Southwell. Who is this?'

'Doctor, this is Annie Pellew calling for Chief Egan. Sir, we need you to come down to Bay Road in town right away please. There's a family trapped in a truck. This is an emergency, sir. Please come as quickly as you can.'

Down on Bay Road, urgent efforts by the rescuers had cleared the remainder of the wreckage and rubble from around the pick-up. Firemen were using power cutters to remove the crushed roof of the cab. Mike was going frantic with anxiety.

'Looks like the boys may be okay,' Freddy said to him. 'The back seats seem to have stood up better, less weight maybe.'

'And Reb? How is she?'

'Unconscious. The paramedics are with her. They've got an air line in and a drip. They are giving painkillers so we can work better to free her.'

Mike groaned. Rick had him by the shoulder.

'My guys are getting set to lift Leif out. Do you want to be there?'

'Yes, yes, let me see them.'

'This way.'

An ambulance sounded its horn nearby. Rick shuddered. Reb was not the only injury today. He took a paramedic aside. 'The woman in there, she's my sister, how bad is she?'

The paramedic was a young guy. He looked upset too. In a small town a tragedy touched

574

everybody. 'The roof of the cab caved in and crushed her chest against the wheel. We have to be careful moving her. That's what's taking so long. We have her in a neckbrace and we're just waiting on the doctor to check her over.'

'Southwell? Where is he?'

'On his way I guess.'

Pequod. The King was going frantic. Was the ship damaged? he demanded to know.

'A boat rammed us under the bow. Does that sound like damage to you?' Patsy yelled back at him.

'So how long till you can move it? When do we cast off?'

'I don't know. Paul is taking a look now.'

The Gimp interposed. 'If it's a question of money to get the boat shifted . . .'

'For God's sake,' Patsy stormed at them, 'there's been a tsunami. People are injured, the waterfront is destroyed. No one is going anywhere right now!'

Angry and embittered the surfers turned away. 'Is there another boat? Or could we drop in by helicopter?'

The King shook his head. 'Not big enough. We need a boat.'

'There's the yacht, Natalie's dad's yacht.'

'Too slow, we need a multi-hull like this one with the speed and stability. It has to be this boat. There's no other available. Believe me.'

* * *

Sheena Dubois was surprised to find herself alive. The flood had dropped her soaked, filthy, scratched, bruised but intact on the cobbles of Pier Street. Tab was equally bedraggled, but he helped her to her feet a second time and Sheena thanked him for saving her life.

'Any time,' he said awkwardly, embarrassed.

Sheena remembered something. 'Your dad was worried for you, and your stepmom. You should maybe call them.'

Down on Bay Road, Southwell still hadn't arrived. The paramedics had cut both boys free. Mike Junior had cracked his head. He was conscious but the paramedics were sending him off to hospital to check for skull fractures. Leif was in shock. He clung to his dad.

Reb was still in the truck. Rick prayed for her. Jean-Alice held his arm. 'She's strong,' she whispered.

SS *Marie-Sainte*. Aboard the stranded vessel officers were carrying out an urgent survey to try to establish how much more damage she had sustained. The ship had been lifted at the stern and her bow moved sideways. The chief engineer was concerned for the integrity of the hull at the point of contact with the bottom. He was worried that frames amidships had been over-stressed with a risk of failure. He wanted a full inspection undertaken by experts before the tug arrived to move her. Leclerc cursed. Everything was conspiring against them. It could be weeks at this rate before the ship was floated off.

Then out of the blue came a fresh panic. The young second officer manning the bridge summoned Leclerc over the intercom. He sounded agitated. 'Sir, there has been a loss of pressure from number three tank,' he reported.

The words triggered an immediate alert status throughout the ship. Once again all doors and hatches were sealed, respirators donned and living spaces in the superstructure pressurised to prevent escaped gas seeping inwards. The main deck areas damaged by the waves, the dining areas and recreation rooms, were isolated and watertight doors latched shut to leave a gas-free zone. Fire pumps were engaged and sprays turned on to dowse the leaking tank.

Leclerc returned to the bridge at a run accompanied by the chief engineer. The gas safety officer had been in the toilet. He was suffering from nerves, worried if he would see his wife and family again. He joined them looking pale. Together they studied the gauges.

'Well?' Leclerc demanded. 'How much have we lost?'

'I can't be sure.' The gas officer's skin was clammy. This was only his second voyage. 'A few hundred litres so far.'

'A few hundred! Is it continuing?'

'I can't be certain yet. It could be a pipe leakage or a valve may have been damaged. It might just be settlement from a vapour lock. I need to establish if the integrity of the tank is compromised. It will take a few minutes.'

Leclerc swore again. 'Then get moving! And inform the Coastguard. Stress there has been no vapour release detected.'

'Yet,' the gas officer muttered under his breath.

Maple Cove. Doc's phone went again. 'Dad? Dad, it's me, Tab. I'm down by the Green.'

'Tab, you're okay?' Southwell's voice broke. 'We thought you were out on the island.'

'Which island? I don't understand.'

'It doesn't matter. Listen, stay where you are. Don't go near the water. There could be more waves.'

'Okay. We only just made it out from the marina, Sheena and me.'

'You're with Sheena?'

'Yuh, we met up. Long story. Listen, Dad, they need you down here. There's a lady hurt bad.'

Goodwill Sound. The Coastguard launch was scouring the Sound for survivors. It was a grim task. So far they had rescued four people found clinging to boats and recovered the body of a middle-aged woman. Who she was no one knew as yet. One of the survivors pulled from the water needed medical treatment and all were shaken. Was that it? they wanted to know. Was that the big one or is there worse to come? Lieutenant

578

Rose, the commander, couldn't give an answer. He was hoping someone would tell him.

'We'll run you back ashore and get you taken care of,' was his standard response.

Fresh orders came over the radio. The CPO brought the message slip to Rose on the bridge. *Two or more persons stranded on Two Bush Island in the Sound. Respond.*

'They'll be the ones we saw earlier,' the CPO commented. 'Idiots must have crossed the channel during the suck back. Now they're stuck.'

'We'll take a look,' Rose said.

'They're sending a launch,' Southwell said to Martin Seymour, shutting up his phone.

'Great. It shouldn't be long now.'

'I wish there was some way to let Donna know. Do you think they can see us?'

They had tried tying a cloth to the end of a pole and waving it from the cliff top.

'Hard to say. They don't have glasses.'

'I'm needed in town. There's a woman injured.'

Bay Road. Rick sneaked another look at Reb. His sister's eyes were closed, her skin waxen.

'The Causeway is cut,' one of the fire crew was saying.

'I heard that, but they're saying trucks can still make it. And there's still Indian Creek Bridge.'

'Yeah, for how long?'

Rick listened sick at heart. A medevac helicopter had been requested, but the system was swamped with casualties all needing help. Southwell drove a big SUV, surely he could make it through the flooding.

But another wave could hit any time.

On the *Marie-Sainte*, the nervous young gas safety officer, whose name was Charles, was crawling on his belly through a tangle of pipework running under the main bulk tanks searching for leaks. Water condensing from the fogging systems dripped constantly about him. Each tank held 5,000 tons of liquefied natural gas under high pressure. Charles was sweating inside a chemical protection suit and a bulky respirator that impeded his movements and restricted his vision. Somewhere among the complex of tanks, pipes and valves gas was oozing out through a pin-sized crack. If that crack should widen while Charles was underneath then he faced death from a variety of causes, all of them unpleasant. He could be asphyxiated, burned alive or blown apart by explosion. Alternatively he might be frozen solid by a blast of gas escaping at 190 kelvin or, finally, drowned if the ship sank. At the present moment none of these possibilities seemed remote.

Attached to his belt was a gas detector which he pushed in front of him as he crawled. An amber LED was blinking intermittently indicating the presence of gas in the air but at a low non-explosive concentration. Charles was passing the detector along a balancing circuit designed to equalise pressure between tanks during discharge. A few feet up ahead jutted a tap controlling the circuit. If the leak was coming from this sector Charles hoped that by shutting off the valve he could isolate the circuit and solve the problem. Then he could get out of here.

By the time he reached the valve he was exhausted. Pausing for breath, he checked the detector again. The light was blinking faster than before and the meter showed a rise in gas concentration, but not yet worrying. Grasping the tap handle, he hauled himself out from under the pipe. There was barely sufficient space for Charles to squeeze between it and the next in the row. Kneeling, he gripped the tap in both hands and twisted it round. It moved quite easily which was a relief after all the effort of getting here.

Charles shut the valve right down and sat back on his heels to wait. He had to give the remaining gas a few minutes to clear before checking the level again. Pressing the radio talk button on his respirator, he reported in to the bridge. It was like talking underwater. He had to shout to make himself understood. Apparently there was no change in the computer readings up there.

After a while he checked his watch and consulted the detector again. Still no change. The LED still blinked. He gave it another five minutes. The gas should have dispersed by now. Just to make sure, he screwed the tap down hard.

There was a sharp crack from the base of the valve and a high-pitched whistle as a jet of white vapour shot outwards. The detector let out a shrill squeal. Its display was now glowing an angry red. Moments later the hold erupted to the sound of bells as the main alarm system cut in.

Now they were faced with a full-blown gas leak.

Doc Southwell's Landcruiser came bumping along the rubble. Now that he was here he wasted no time. He crawled in beside Reb, ignoring the mess in the cab, and made an assessment.

'You call the helicopter?' he asked the paramedics, climbing out again.

'They're sending one as soon as they have an aircraft available.'

'I'll speak to them.'

They let him have the radio and listened while he told the dispatcher exactly what he needed and why. The helicopter was promised for ten minutes max.

'Okay,' Southwell told the paramedics. 'We'll start moving her now. Keep her neck steady in the brace and watch the airway.'

It took four of them with his assistance to lift her clear and onto the gurney. When she was fixed Southwell checked her again and then spoke briefly with Mike and Rick.

'She's stable for the moment. Right now I'm more worried about the fluid in her lungs than the head injuries. She has major chest trauma and she needs surgery in a specialist unit. I've arranged for the helicopter to take her direct to Portland. The surgeons at the trauma centre there will take care of her.'

'Thanks, Doc,' Mike told him. 'We appreciate your coming out. We heard about Donna. I guess you must be worried sick.'

At that moment came the sound they all dreaded. Sirens.

Fred Tarr snatched up his radio. He listened a moment. His face turned white. 'Gas!' he shouted to the others. 'Gas!'

Chapter 44

'Gas escape! Gas escape!' The alarms shrilled through the tanker. Up on the bridge, Leclerc and the men gaped at one another for an instant in dismay. Then training took over. The computerised safety shutdown program which overrode all others was racing through its checks.

'Point of leak?' Leclerc snapped.

'Sector two, inter-tank balance valve on the relief line.'

'Volume of escape?'

'Two thousand litres a minute increasing!'

'Increasing?'

'Yes.'

'Action taken?'

'Isolating valve section. Reversing flow to drain circuit into receiving tank. Opening valves to standby emergency relief tank to reduce pressure in tank two.'

'Where is Charles?' Leclerc demanded.

'Down in the valve hold.' The chief engineer

tapped a screen where a light blinked on a diagram map. 'There, underneath tank two. He had located the initial seepage and was attempting to rectify it.'

'Can you reach him?'

'We're trying.'

As he talked Leclerc was glancing out the window. The flag over the Coastguard building showed a stiff breeze from the east. Onshore. *Merde,* he thought. A westerly would have carried a gas cloud harmlessly out to sea. As it was . . .

'Clear the area!' Freddy Tarr yelled. 'Move out of here. Now!'

Down on Bay Road the wail of the sirens merged with the throb of rotors. The red medevac helicopter was circling overhead. Freddy was yelling into his radio, trying to reach the pilot to order him back.

'Cut that out!' Rick snatched the mike away from him. Fred rounded on him, scarlet with rage. 'Stay out of this! I'm in command here!'

'The hell you are!' Rick countered. 'I'm boss of this town. I say we get Reb away. It's her one chance.' Delay was literally a matter of life and death. Already they were eating into Reb's so-called 'golden hour' – the first sixty minutes after the injury were crucial to her survival. Without invasive medical action the mortality of a severely injured victim increased by a factor of three times in the first thirty minutes' delay and by a further three times in the second thirty minutes. If the helicopter did not land now, Rebecca faced an agonising three-hour journey on rutted roads. She might die without ever seeing the hospital.

'You heard the sirens, man! There's a gas escape! The whole town could go up! We can't take the risk.'

'That's my decision and I say bring the aircraft in,' Rick yelled back, pointing out over the harbour. 'The tanker is to the north of us. It'll take a while for any gas to drift this far across and the rotor wash will blow it in the opposite direction. We'll be safer while it's overhead.'

Pushing Fred away, Rick ran to the side of the road. The helicopter, a new McDonnell Douglas 902 in red and white livery, was low overhead now. Rick signalled the pilot on down. Everyone ducked as dust and debris flew around. The machine settled on the Ice Factory forecourt, scattering pools of water. Before the rotors stopped turning the paramedics were hurrying the gurney along the sidewalk, Rick and Mike running behind with Jean-Alice. Reb was lifted onto the pivoting stretcher and slid through the fifty-four-inch side door into the cabin. Doc Southwell thrust hastily scribbled notes into the hands of the air medic and the machine lifted off again.

SS *Marie-Sainte*. The first officer handed Leclerc a phone. 'The Coastguard, they demand to know what is happening.'

Leclerc scowled at him and took the receiver. 'Commander Wolfowitz? Capitaine Leclerc here. Yes, we have a problem. A small leak in a relieving pipe that has become larger. No, not in a tank. All our tanks are intact. What is that? *Monsieur*, we treat all leaks as serious, even the very smallest.'

As he spoke Leclerc's eye was on the operation control panel of the computer system. The main tanks were shown as bright blue squares. Blue indicating full of gas. As he watched the valve icon at the side of tank two flipped from closed to open and the feed circuit pipe to the standby emergency relief tank changed colour from black to green and started to pulse, indicating that gas was moving along the pipe in the direction shown. His heart rate began to ease.

'Commander, I am pleased to report that we appear to have traced the leakage and are taking active steps to reduce the escape of gas.'

'You're telling me the damn stuff is still spilling out?'

Leclerc continued to observe the screen. 'We are taking steps to transfer bulk gas away from the zone currently affected by damage.'

'Dammit, just give it to me straight: is there a fire risk to the town or harbour?'

'Of course there is risk. Wherever gas is present there is a degree of risk,' Leclerc said, playing for time. Ah, there it was! The flow rate at the leaking valve was starting to drop away at last. 'Commander, the escape of gas is diminishing. The flow in the pipe has been successfully shut down. Our measures have been successful. The fire risk as you put it is over.'

Leclerc replaced the receiver. He looked round at the two officers. 'Well, what are you staring at me for?' he said.

The chief engineer swallowed. 'It is Charles.' He jerked his chin at the far screen, the one monitoring the layout of the gas decks. 'Down there. He has stopped moving.'

Hannah Morrissey, shrew wife of Whale Morrissey, hurried back to her house on Culpepper Street. She moved quickly, her little black shoes a blur like a doll on wheels. The wail of the sirens pursued her as she let herself in the peeling front gate. The door had three separate keys, remarkable in Goodwill where locals seldom bothered to lock up. Hannah shut the door behind her, tripping the latch from habit so that anyone else wanting to come in would have to ring the bell, even her husband. Where cash was concerned Hannah had a simple rule: trust no one. It had worked well.

Pulling off her hat, she ran upstairs with surprising speed for her age. Hannah might look frail but she came of seafaring stock and had never had a day's illness in her life. Her grandfather had immigrated from the Baltic. He had been part-Finnish, able it was said to whistle up a wind when needed. Certainly the ships he was master of made phenomenally quick passages.

The house was small: two sparsely furnished rooms up and down with a kitchen and bathroom tacked on the rear. Everything inside, carpets, furnishings, even the kitchen, was old and shabby and worn out. The few pictures and cheap ornaments had been passed down through their families. Hannah never bought anything if she could help it. She had been brought up to scrimp. Thrift was engrained in the fibre of her soul. Hannah owned four houses in the town besides this one and she hoarded the rents jealously.

Unlocking the door to the spare bedroom that doubled as her den, Hannah knelt by the hearth. The fireplace was taken up by a large wood burner very firmly bricked in. Opening the grate revealed an iron strongbox, requiring another key. Hannah did not trust combination codes. Inside were a great many small packets that chinked together when she lifted them out. Methodically, Hannah emptied their contents out onto the threadbare carpet. Each packet held a gold $50 coin in mint condition. Laying them out in rows of ten, she added up the total. There were 386 coins with a nominal value of $19,300 and with gold at its current level a street price of double that.

Hannah didn't trust banks either.

Out in the Sound, the Coastguard launch sped eastwards heading for Two Bush Island. It didn't take long, not more than seven or eight minutes before the island was well in sight. Lieutenant Rose slowed the launch as he studied the out-crop through his high-power optics. He picked out the couple close to the skyline and put the launch into a circular pattern while he decided how to play this one. Two Bush was not an easy recovery situation on account of the rock formations protecting the shore. Most times if the weather was reasonable he would move into the channel and launch the Avon inflatable with a couple of men to bring the people off. If conditions were bad he avoided the channel and put the inflatable on the south side. Or else skipped the whole thing and told them to send a chopper.

Today conditions were borderline. From the bridge Rose could spot cross-currents tearing at the mouth of the channel and four-foot breakers beating up the rock ledges. A boat landing was not going to be easy. On the other hand the two people on the island would probably not survive a second larger tsunami. He could call the chopper, but the chances of one being available were slim.

He decided to chance the inflatable. 'Launch the Avon,' he ordered.

Normally the launch carried two Avons, twenty-five-foot inflatable craft also known as RIBs, for rigid inflatable boats, with rigid hulls and powerful outboard motors. They were tough agile little craft ideally suited for this kind of inshore job. Unfortunately today's conditions were abnormal, as everyone was about to find out.

In the aftermath of the first tsunami the Sound was badly churned up with currents surging against the shore and running everywhere. For a few minutes the surface would be abnormally calm and the next four- and five-foot breakers would erupt all over, colliding and bouncing against one another. A strong circular pattern seemed to be developing with incoming flows tearing along the southern shore, sweeping round the harbour before streaming back east again out past Curtain Bluff. Near the middle of the Sound cross-currents breaking off from the main flow reversed themselves without warning, causing patches of violent turbulence.

The Avon launched with a four-man crew under Chief Bosun Kirk Kirkorian, a thirty-one-year-old bear of a guy, a qualified diver, who tried out for the US Olympic team two years back. If anyone could pull these people off it would be Kirk. All four wore full neoprene wetsuits and life vests. Meanwhile Lieutenant Rose used the loudhailer to direct the couple on the island down to a relatively flat spot where the rocks looked slightly less jagged. As it turned out this was an illusion.

The Avon bounced over the water rapidly. The sea state was rough with fast currents coursing clockwise past the island. As the boat neared the shore, projecting spurs of rock with dragon's-teeth spikes made the approach hazardous. Rose watched the Avon twisting about trying to find a way in. Kirkorian was standing up to see better and at times he was completely hidden by crests. The waves were bursting against the rocks, sending up great blasts of spray, and the man and the woman were hanging back, afraid to come too close for fear of being swept away.

Finally Kirk made his decision and the Avon lunged forward, rolling between the breakers aiming for what he took to be a clear spot where the crew could beach the RIB long enough to pull the couple on board. Conditions in the water were deteriorating fast at that point. In the log report afterwards Lieutenant Rose described the scene as 'a full sea state running', meaning like being out in mid-ocean during a full gale. Waves were riding up almost perpendicular. The heights were now hitting six feet, but due to cross-currents the troughs opening up when waves pulled away from each other at the same moment could be as deep again, opening up pits in the water that could swallow the boat whole.

With the Avon pitching through fifteen- to twenty-foot arcs events moved very fast. Kirk was using the full power of the outboard to hold the boat back as they surged in towards the rocks, but he might as well have saved himself the trouble. The hull was thrown forward, lifting at the same instant. It tilted as it came down and the portside bow bladder spiked on a basalt needle that ripped a foot-long gash in the armoured rubber. That was something next to impossible. The Avon's buoyancy tubes were internally sealed and made from triple-layer Hypalon-coated fabric, the same material used in white-water rafts and other high-abrasion environments. It was immensely strong, wear resistant and waterproof and had almost never been known to tear in Rose's experience. Yet that was what happened now. The gash deflated the Avon's bow, water poured in, the stern lifted and a following breaker flipped the boat on its back without mercy, spilling all four crew into the pounding surf.

'Avon Two crash launch!'

The rest of the crew on deck had seen the accident and the second RIB was swaying out almost before Rose's order was given. It sped across to the island and Rose watched anxiously as it wallowed in the steep swell. He saw two men hauled aboard. They appeared none the worse for wear. The current was sweeping a third man down past the island towards the mouth of the Sound. Rose kept the glasses on his bobbing head. In a complex rescue it was easy to lose a person in the water if you took your eyes off them even for only a minute, but the rescue boat had him marked down; it wheeled and ran alongside, pulling his black-suited figure in over the bow.

That left one.

The rescue boat was circling off the island. Rose saw the helmsman standing up. He was shouting to the people on shore. Was he preparing to bring them off too? That would be inadvisable with the boat grossly overcrowded. Better to bring the survivors of the first boat back to the launch before embarking on a second attempt. Besides, there was still another man in the water to be picked up. He shifted his attention to the people on the island and stiffened. There were three figures now among the rocks. Two shivering civilians clinging to a tall figure in black. Rose turned up the magnification. Yes, he was right. Kirk Kirkorian had fetched up on the island. Rose was down one boat and his best crewman and he was still no nearer to completing the rescue.

Worse was to come. Reluctantly abandoning their comrade, the second Avon returned to the mother launch. One man had to be helped aboard, grunting with pain from a fractured leg.

'It's just not feasible by boat,' the non-com in charge of the second craft told Rose frankly. 'The rocks there are lethal and the seas are surging every which way. It's impossible to anticipate. You wait for a calm spot and it just doesn't come. Anyone coming onto the rocks at the surf line runs a risk of severe injury. McGee's leg is busted wide open. Better we call in the helicopter. Either that or wait for the shitty sea state to settle.'

'Impossible even with Kirkorian to bring them out?' Rose hazarded.

'We can try if you want, Skipper, but in my opinion someone's going to get hurt. Kirk is big enough that he could swim off by himself and make it, plus he's wearing a suit, but he says he'll stay with the other two.'

Which was Kirk all over, Rose thought. He reached for the radio to call in air support.

'We have to move that ship. We've been lucky up till now, but if another wave comes through, a bigger one, who knows what could happen.'

The body of the dead officer had been brought ashore from the tanker and taken up to the morgue, where Doc Southwell had made a preliminary finding of asphyxiation due to an ill-fitting mask. For the town it had been an escape, but a narrow one and nerves were frayed. Meantime an urgent meeting was being held in the Coastguard building looking out over the Sound with its wreckage. Con Wolfowitz was present, so were Don Egan, Chance Greene and Jack Pearl. Rick Larsen was doing the talking.

Con shook his head. 'Can't be done,' he said flatly. 'She's fast on the mud; the crew has been taken off and the tug ain't coming.'

'We have vessels in the harbour that can handle a tow. There's *Pequod* for a start.'

Jack Pearl interrupted. 'You're crazy, you know that? The *Marie-Sainte* is carrying twenty thousand tons of gas in those tanks. *Pequod* couldn't budge her.'

'Come on, Jack. It isn't the size of the towing vessel but the angle of the pull. You know that as well as I do. And the tanker's officers are still aboard. If we clear her out of the Sound into open water better for them and better still for the town.'

'Suppose you do manage to tow her off, we don't know how badly damaged she is. The ship may not even be seaworthy.'

'Better then she sinks out off the shelf than here in the Sound,' Rick said brutally.

'You're just a bunch of amateurs, you know that? You'll wind up making more trouble for everyone.'

'He may be right, Rick,' Chance Greene said heavily from the other end of the table. 'There's plenty of other things need our attention. Evacuating the hospital for one.' He glanced at Don.

Don nodded. 'Word from Washington is the biggest wave is still to come.'

'How big are they talking this time?' Jack asked gloomily.

Don sucked his lip. 'Hard to make out,' he mumbled, avoiding everyone's eyes. 'They give out different figures. Thirty feet, fifty feet.'

Con glared at him. 'A hundred is what I heard.'

Don turned pale. 'That's down in Florida though, surely?'

Rick wasn't giving up. 'Face the alternatives. What happens if a big wave catches the

596

tanker? Right now she is lying broadside on to the tide. A tsunami will roll the ship clean over, break her in half. Jesus, she could blow up right here in the Sound. We could lose the whole town.'

'Better than losing a bunch of lives,' Jack was heard to mutter.

'How's that again?' Rick's jaw tightened.

'I said better the ship blows up than people lose their lives. Houses can be rebuilt.'

'Get this, Jack,' Rick told him. 'I didn't take on this job to see this town die. My people go way back in Goodwill. We fought the French and the British and we're not being driven out by any goddam tsunami.'

He looked around at the others, his jaw tight still. 'This is something we have to do for Goodwill, for our families, for our children and for those who went before. We owe it to them. Now who's with me?'

Over on *Pequod* the King had come up with a compromise. 'We both want this ship out of here, right?' he said to Paul. 'Okay, let's work together. You give the orders, we provide the muscle. My guys have worked around boats all their lives so they know what they're doing. First up we can lend a hand clearing that lobster boat away and checking for hull damage.'

Paul scowled and looked at Patsy. She shrugged. 'If we stay in the harbour and a big wave hits we're screwed,' she said flatly. 'We only just rode out the last son of a bitch.'

'And that was just a taster,' the Gimp threw in, keeping up the pressure. 'Believe me, I know. The main event is just two hours away. Wringing our hands and sitting on our butts is not an option.' His eyes burned as he spoke. They could still pull this off. The prize was within their grasp.

Feet sounded on the gangway. Someone was coming aboard at a run. It was Rick. He grinned at Paul and Patsy. Then he saw the surfers and checked himself. 'What are they doing here?' he snapped.

The King spoke. 'This is our boat, she's under charter.'

'The hell it is. I never signed up to that deal.'

The Gimp stepped up to bat, flourishing the contract. 'Your partner here wasn't so choosy. He signed an option and we're exercising. The vessel is legally assigned to us for the next twelve hours.'

Rick looked from the Gimp to Paul. 'You two went behind my back? You had no right.'

'Like hell we didn't.' There was raw anger in Paul's reply. 'Magnus and I've as much money in this ship as you. The price was generous and with the whales gone we needed the cash. We still do. Doesn't look like we'll get many more tourists this season,' he added bitterly.

Rick swung back to face the surfers. 'Contract or not this vessel is being commandeered,' he said in a steely voice. 'It's needed for urgent recovery work. You people have five minutes to offload your gear.'

'Recovery work?' Paul looked doubtful. 'What's that mean?'

'We're going to move the tanker.' In a few short sentences Rick outlined the plan.

Paul's jaw dropped. 'You're crazy. That's twenty thousand tons deadweight.'

'The tide is coming in. It will help float her off.'

'It'll never work. *Pequod* doesn't have the power.'

'I'll prove you wrong.'

The Gimp butted in. 'The hell you will,' he rumbled. 'We have a legal right—'

Rick cut him short. 'If you and your friends don't haul ass off this ship right now,' he said harshly, 'I'll have Con Wolfowitz at the Coastguard declare your project MUV, a manifestly unsafe voyage, which gives him legal authority over the vessel with powers to force you off. That could put you back in jail. Take your choice.'

But Patsy had turned away. She was gazing over the side. 'Stop fighting, all of you,' she said with a sob of bitter despair. 'You've left it too late. We all have.'

Up in the Coastguard building, Con Wolfowitz was watching the tide gauge indicator in disbelief. The trace, which within the last half-hour had first sunk back to something approaching normal and had then begun displaying the beginnings of a steady rise following the end of slack water, was climbing up the scale near vertically.

'What the hell's wrong with this thing now?' he barked. In spite of what had gone before or perhaps because of it, his first instinct was to blame damage to the gauge or just as possibly a software glitch. Because this was counter to everything he understood about what was supposed to happen.

Even as he said it realisation was dawning on him that this time he was actually witnessing first-hand the opening moves of the next assault. And he yelled across at his office assistant to get on the horn to all ships and vessels in the area.

'It's starting over,' he said. 'And it's starting bad.'

Out on the Coastguard launch, Lieutenant Rose was also struggling to believe the evidence of his eyes. The same was true of his crew. The tide was running in. A ferocious current had them in its grip and was sweeping them westward past the island. And everywhere they looked the water was eating up the shoreline, climbing rocks and beaches with a speed and hunger that said: This is no tide!

Other people had noticed already. Channel 16, the emergency frequency, was screeching with tsunami warnings. The crew were all staring at him, waiting for orders as if he had been trained for this or something. All Rose could think was that a tsunami was headed this way, a wave that could devastate the entire coast and the launch lay right in its path.

And meanwhile over on the island were three people who were his responsibility and who didn't stand a cat in hell's chance.

Up on the cliff overlooking Maple Cove, Martin Seymour saw the ocean swarming back in again and placed the call he had been dreading having to make. He dialled the number Southwell had left him to tell the doctor the rescue had failed. His wife was still out there on the island. She was still out there and another wave was on the way.

He heard the gasp, then Southwell's hoarse whisper like a dead man talking. 'I'm coming over now.'

'There isn't time. There's nothing anyone can do.'

Martin lowered his head in prayer.

Chapter 45

The surge rolled on slowly, inexorably. This time it was different: less violent but deeper and heavier and in its way more frightening. On *Pequod*'s deck, Rick and Patsy and Paul and the surfers watched from the side as waves flooded into the harbour for the second time. Behind the mole the water level climbed relentlessly. Patsy timed the rate at three feet a minute. When it reached the level of the dock it swarmed over, but it kept on rising. Rick heard mooring eyes popping out of the decks of boats that had survived the first wave.

He and Paul ran to their own mooring ropes, slipping them off just before they jammed tight. Looking towards the stern, he saw the surfers following suit. Maybe they did know what they were doing. He could hear the lobster boat scraping against their side and hoped it wasn't doing more damage. Another boat was being forced under as her anchor held. The water climbed up over her gunwales, filled her up and sucked her down.

He rejoined Patsy at the side. 'Jeez, when's it going to stop?' she muttered. 'That's what, two feet over the dock? And that's on top of a low tide. Add the two and you get thirty, thirty-five feet.'

'The last one went over the top of the mole in a straight run.'

'Yeah, but that was more of a wave. Why is this one different? I don't understand.'

Rick was trying to work it out too. 'It looks to me,' he said slowly, 'as if this wave is coming in trough-first without breaking. Maybe that's a good sign,' he added hopefully.

'Doing some damage,' Patsy said. 'Listen to that.' From inland came the sounds of splintering wood and crashing glass. A loose dinghy went careening by on the current, passing right over the dock into the flooded marina.

Rick turned to look up the Sound. It was an amazing sight. The mole and the harbour walls had all vanished, swallowed up by the surge. From shore to shore of the Sound there stretched a single sheet of water. It occurred to him that they were seeing the Sound as it must have appeared before the first settlers arrived to tame it.

'It doesn't feel right,' Patsy said. 'I keep thinking something bad is round the corner.'

Rick said nothing. He was watching a bright gleam on the distant horizon.

Out off the Bank the ocean was a hostile place. Steep-sided swells reared their shoulders out of nowhere, jostling for space at the entrance to the Sound. The tide flow was strong; Brandie had to run the engine just to hold their place. 'We're burning fuel,' she warned.

'We have plenty. I gassed us up to the limit before we kicked off.'

A flurry of confused seas tossed the machine around. Brandie gunned the motor. 'I sense like maybe something is about to happen.'

As if the ocean had heard her, a shadow fell on them. Slewing around they saw a massive chest with multiple savage heads rearing up behind. In seconds Mack was in the water, tightening the straps on his board.

'Go for it!' Mack yelled to her. Crouching over the bars, Brandie raced the throttle, adrenaline pumping. Was this it? Was this the big one? Big enough, she thought.

The beast was still building as she moved in on the flank, racking her speed, feeling Mack moving out behind her, readying himself for the slingshot manoeuvre that would catapult him past her onto the crest. She felt the Yamaha's stern slide and corrected. This was not the moment.

Now! Spotting her entry point, she charged the jet forward up the back slope. She was committed. There was no going back from here on in. The Yamaha tore up the slope, reached the crest and swung hard over. Behind her, forty-five feet of HAS tow rope tightened as Mack leaned outward on the turn. In a flash he was hurtling past her onto the lip. The Yamaha skimmed the crest and shot away down the face. Glancing behind, Brandie saw the lip curling over, pursuing Mack as he chased along the face. He was in the tube! He was in the tube!

Out in the Sound, Lieutenant Rose had seen it too.

'Stand by! Stand by!' he announced over the boat's PA system as he brought the launch round to meet the crest head-on. He took one last look out the port window in the direction of the island. Kirk Kirkorian had made an excellent chief bosun. He would be missed as a seaman as well as a human being and friend. Rose felt a personal sense of failure at having let him down.

Studying the wave as it moved down on them, Rose estimated its crest as a minimum of twenty feet.

On the chart Two Bush Island was marked as topping out at forty-four feet above the high-water mark. The figure was subjective because an island that small was subject to natural erosion as well as a regular winter battering from ocean storms. It was probably safe to assume that a few feet had been shaved off since the last mapping.

Taking forty feet as a safe benchmark, Rose judged that the surge had levelled off at around ten feet over the high-tide mark. In the past he had personally observed storm-driven breakers crashing clean over the island so he could form a fair estimate of the chances of the three people crouching together on the rocks as near to the summit as they could get. They were not great. A twenty-foot tsunami could be expected to run up at least one and a half times its own height against a small obstacle such as Two Bush Island. Quite probably more. Which didn't leave Kirk and the couple with him much leeway. Realistically it didn't leave them any at all. Probably the best they could hope for was to be swept clear and somehow picked up from the Sound afterwards. And the chances of that were almost as slim. In the aftermath of the wave the Sound would be churned up with tossing breakers and whitecaps. A survivor might be swept back miles out to sea. Kirk with his physique protected by a wetsuit might make it, but the two with him wouldn't stand a chance. Either way it was more likely that all three would shortly be pounded to death on the rocks.

The wave swept on. It wasn't moving that fast and its crest had already started to topple. But breaking early was a good sign. The wave would have dumped some of its energy before it reached the island. The first faint glimmer of hope flickered in Rose's heart. He gripped the wheel and eased the throttle forward. 'Hold on, boys. Here she comes.'

* * *

Engine roaring, Brandie raced the Yamaha into the cauldron. Her sharp eyes scanned the churning bowl for a glimpse of Mack's head in the surf. Just when she had begun to think he was gone, he came flying out the end of the barrel like a cannonball, his red board still strapped to his feet. Elated, she scooped him up and they peeled away into calmer water.

'Good one?' she shouted, light-headed with relief.

'Ace, but not awesome. That was just a taster. We can do better. This is definitely the spot though. All we have to do now is wait.'

The wave was breaking this time. Rick and the others watched tautly as the tumbling crest rolled towards the harbour like a wide carpet of foam reaching out for them. The height had dropped away some, he told himself, and the speed. Against that, with the mole underwater there was nothing to check the momentum. It was close now, very close. Still diminishing but not fast enough. Ten, twelve feet max.

'Back from the rail! Brace yourselves!'

For a second time spray shot up, drenching him. The impact felt long, but heavy, like a slow-motion punch. It pressed *Pequod* back against the side of the dock and held her there. Rick thought he could hear her plating grinding against the stone piers. Dammit, that would do some damage. Pray to God there were no leaks. He shot a glance at the shore. The flood was hammering the Chandlery at ceiling height. Jesus! How much more could the town take?

He felt *Pequod*'s hull grating underneath him again. Paul had hung out additional fenders, but the ship was riding way too high for that. Patsy was staring at him, her mouth made ugly with dismay. 'Rick, *Pequod* is shallow draught. What if she's carried over the dock? She could break up!'

Out at the hospital an evacuation was complete. The National Guard depot at Ellsworthy had provided a high-wheel truck capable of handling the flooded Causeway. Three patients had transferred out. One woman was probably well enough to have gone home, but Southwell judged it better for her to be moved out of town. The other two, the Schaffer woman and her partner, were still bed cases.

The only patient left behind was the corpse of the young officer from the French tanker, poor devil.

Southwell raced his Landcruiser down to the crossroads. Shit, that water looked deep. The creek was swollen beyond recognition. Even the rails had gone, swept away, making it impossible to see where the road ran. Dammit, he had to get through. Donna's life was at stake! There was no other way. Selecting low ratio, he moved down to the water, aiming as straight as possible for the far side. The distance, he judged, was around a hundred yards.

He hadn't gone far when he was regretting his

decision. The water was deeper than he had guessed, or feared. Certainly up to the sills already. No leaks yet, that was something. Keep going slowly, that was the secret, people always said. A small bow wave radiated out ahead but the motor was running smoothly.

He was over the middle of the creek now, he judged. He could feel the current rocking the vehicle. Two tons of metal or whatever it was and the flow was making it sway like a boat. Just as well he hadn't tried to swim or anything foolish. The big anxiety was putting a wheel off the road into the ditch. One rail was sticking out still and for a moment he panicked, imagining he was the wrong side. Calm down, he told himself. You're doing fine.

Two thirds across. The urge to press down on the gas was overwhelming. Just charge ahead and pray. But that would be fatal. Except that the water seemed to be getting deeper, not shallower. And there through the bushes on his right was more water flooding towards him. There was water everywhere he looked. Something was wrong. Something was badly wrong! This shouldn't be happening!

Up in town, an evacuation had been ordered of all buildings west of the Green. Don Egan ran from house to house up Washington Street from Bay Road, banging on doors. He got few answers. Most people down this stretch were long gone. As he reached the end of the block a torrent of water came rushing at him from the lane on his right, drenching him to his waist. He lost a shoe and stumbled. In a second he was down, rolling along in the torrent, fighting for breath. A hand reached out to grab him, pulling him clear. He struggled to his feet and looked up to see who had saved him. It was Whale Morrissey.

'I might have guessed,' Don gasped. 'No one else has a grip like yours. I owe you one, Whale.'

Whale's face was mud-flecked and his eyes were wild. 'It's a judgement,' he shouted back.

'Whale, your house is here, isn't it?'

A gleam flared in the lobsterman's eyes. 'She's in there.'

'Who, your wife, Hannah? Are you saying she's inside the house?'

Whale nodded. The lane was deserted but for them, the water tugging at their knees. A cat crouched on a wall, yowling at the destruction.

'It ain't safe down here. The flood is backing up on the other side. If another wave comes through it could bring down these houses, wash out all this part of town.'

There came a rumbling of collapsing masonry nearby as he spoke. More water surged deeper around them. Don held on to a phone pole for support. The Whale with his huge bulk and strength didn't seem to notice. Grabbing his arm, Don waded along the lane to Hannah's small front garden. The tips of the fence palings were sticking out of water that was already up to the windows. 'In here, right?'

Whale Morrissey forced the door back. The flood was black and ominous inside. Don could see Hannah crouched on the stairs. She had a leather bag like an old school satchel slung around her shoulder. She clutched it to her chest and glared at them. 'You're not taking me away!' she screeched. She looked mad.

'Mrs Morrissey, come along. You can't stay here. We'll help you.'

Hannah's eyes blazed. 'I can't. I must stay. It's all in here!' she patted the satchel. There was triumph in her face as well as madness. 'All of it. You shan't take it away. No one takes it away!' Her voice rose to a shriek.

'Hannah, the house isn't safe any longer. You have to evacuate. I'm ordering you to leave right this minute! Whale, fetch her down from there. We'll carry her up to the Green.'

Don stood aside in the small hall to let Whale past. The big lobsterman reached out an arm to pluck his tiny wife off the stair like a farmer gathering up a hen. Cradling her against his chest, he plunged back out into the flood. Don followed thankfully.

Outside, the flood was up to their waists now. Hannah shrieked and kicked in her husband's grasp. As they struggled along the lane with her there came a muffled crash. Twenty yards ahead Don saw the lower front windows of a wooden house explode outward as torrents of water surged through. The front wall bulged, then came a roar and the entire house dissolved in a wave of splintered beams and roof tiles. Floodwater surged greedily through the gap. Don gasped. A whole house gone, swept away, only the brick chimney breast left standing like a lone sentinel.

The flood tore out the pathetic garden of the cottage, smashing down the fence and spilling over to swell the water in the lane. With nowhere to run Don and Whale found themselves chest-deep in an instant. Don dodged a heavy beam sliding along on the current. It passed him by and struck Whale a glancing blow. He stumbled, spilling Hannah into the water.

Whale uttered a cry. The torrent caught Hannah and washed her down a dozen yards into a fence, rolling her like flotsam. Her flailing arms caught at a gatepost and she clawed at it to save herself. Don and Whale plunged into the flood in pursuit. Hannah held on desperately, wrapping her scrawny arms around the post, the water rushing past, tugging at her. 'Hang on!' Don yelled. 'We'll get to you! Just hang on!'

Hannah clung on frantically, teeth bared in her bony, straining face. Whale was almost up to her now. He reached out towards her. 'Take my hand, Hannah! I'll pull you over.'

Then something happened. The shoulder strap on Hannah's satchel snapped. Hannah screamed, an awful tearing sound like a tortured animal. 'My treasure!' she shrieked. Ignoring her husband's outstretched hand, she threw herself into the water.

The flood closed over with a swirl of bubbles and she was gone. Hannah Morrissey was gone.

Out at the crossroads the flood was growing deeper by the moment as the surge forced its way up the creek. Southwell knew there was only one thing left. If he stayed where he was the water would climb over the engine block and he would be finished.

Gritting his teeth, he rammed his foot down on the gas pedal. The Landcruiser surged forward, a V-shaped bow wave arching out ahead of it. Relentlessly Southwell kept up the pressure. He could feel the motor straining against the weight of water holding it back. If the air intake choked now or damp entered the electrics he was finished. He felt the left front wheel bump against something. A log, a stone, the side parapet of the bridge? No way of telling. All he could do was to keep going and pray. Spray splashed against the windows. The sheet of water ahead seemed never-ending.

Then with a gasp he saw that the level was dropping. He was coming through. With water showering from its flanks the Toyota stormed off the bridge onto land, picking up speed. Ahead stretched the road, still under water but passable, passable.

Southwell's shoulders sagged with relief. Now to reach the cove.

'Get below!' Rick shouted to Paul. 'Run up the engines.' Paul gaped at him for a second then ducked down the companionway at a run. Rick seized the wheel. Come on, come on, he muttered to himself. What's keeping you? With an effort he remained calm. Engines didn't start at the press of a button, or rather they did but only as part of a sequence. Paul was moving as fast as he could, but there were circuits to open and fuel pumps to prime first.

With a rumble underfoot the diesels broke into life. The gauges on the panel in front of Rick trembled and started to climb with maddening slowness. Patsy was signalling to him urgently from the deck outside. Rick's mind was racing. *Pequod* had a bow thruster only. Would it be sufficient to counter the pressure of the ocean flooding against her length? It was just possible provided he could add some forward momentum.

But there still remained the lobster boat jammed against the starboard bow. How would that affect the handling? Could they slide out past it? Only one way to find out.

'Okay,' he shouted. 'We're under way.'

Patsy had guessed what he intended and was hanging over the starboard rail, the King with her. Rick set the speed for slow ahead. The screws began to bite and a screeching sound echoed up through the hull. For a moment Rick feared it was the prop-shaft, then he realised it must be the crushed workboat scraping along the side below the waterline. God alone knew what damage it was causing.

Patsy ran forward to the bow, took a look and returned. 'All clear ahead. There's a sail yacht drifting fifty feet off but she's small and you can nudge her out of the way.'

'What's the ocean doing?'

'Maybe easing off a point, hard to tell. No worse anyway.'

That was something. If they could just hold on till the surge ran out of steam and began to recede they would stand a chance.

The scraping sounds alongside were growing worse. Patsy ran to see. 'Looks like the boat is filling and rolling over, sliding down our starboard hull as it sinks.'

'Jesus, I hope she doesn't hole us underneath.'

'If she goes over onto her side that might help us to get clear.'

'Let's hope.'

The noises eased astern as *Pequod* slowly edged her way forward along the dock. The bow thruster seemed to be holding its own against the surge. If they could bring the speed up a little, forcing water past the rudder, then that would increase the resistance.

'If I can just hold her at this it'll be something,' he said to Patsy when she next appeared.

'The water level on the dock has definitely peaked. There's been no rise in the past fifteen minutes.'

615

At some point the flood would go into reverse, presenting them with a whole different set of problems.

Magnus emerged from below. 'There's water in the starboard bilge so there must be a leakage down there. Nothing serious though that I could see. I'd say we got off lightly.'

'For the moment.'

'Yeah.'

It was another twenty minutes by the bridge clock before the surge finally and definitely could be said to have turned. Slowly the mole emerged from the frothing water and then the dock. From *Pequod*'s deck they watched the water streaming back off the land, carrying with it a dismal cargo of wreckage. 'They say these tsunami do as much damage on the way out as they do bursting in,' Patsy observed.

Rick was silent. At least, he was thinking, there were no bodies yet.

Then came a yell from the surfers in the bow. 'Wow, man, look at that!'

Rick looked. Out beyond the mole, the tanker was moving again.

Out in the Sound Rose put the optics on the island. The faint hope that had warmed him minutes earlier faded out as he scanned the lifeless outcrop. Even at reduced height nothing could have survived out there. His best bet would be to run round into the cove and maybe recover the bodies. With a heavy heart he clicked the mike to give the order.

Then, had there been something? he wondered. On that last sweep he had half imagined a flicker of movement at one point, but when he had looked again there was nothing. Check once more.

He focused the glasses, forcing himself to search slowly, methodically. Suddenly his heart leapt. Something was moving out there still! To his amazement and disbelief Rose made out an arm waving. 'It's Kirk! It's Kirk!' he yelled wildly, forgetting his dignity as a skipper. There were whoops from the crew. Kirk had made it through. He was out there still. Against all the odds he had somehow hung on, clinging to the scrap of land while the waves swept over. Human endurance was incredible.

Rose reached for the loudhailer again. 'We will get you off,' he promised. 'We will get you off before the next wave comes. You have my word.'

It was just that he couldn't think how.

Chapter 46

'Goddamit,' Rick said. 'Now is our chance.'

'To do what?' Patsy said.

'To get the tanker out of here. Move her down the Sound before the next wave hits.'

'Is she fit to be moved? Her propulsion gear may be damaged.'

'She's not under control,' Paul said. 'She's drifting.'

'Let's find out. If not we can give her a tow. Freed from the mud, *Pequod* is capable of keeping her moving.'

Paul scowled again. 'You're out of your mind. What are you going to use for a cable? Nothing we have will reach, let alone hold her.'

He had a point. Rick bit down hard in frustration. In normal circumstances they might have turned up a cable somewhere in harbour, but not in this chaos. Not in the time. 'We could rig something up,' he said lamely.

'The *Marie-Sainte* will have a cable,' said a

voice behind them. The King had been listening to their conversation. He addressed Rick directly. 'Drop me and Gimp here over the side with a couple of the jets. The two of us will scoot over. We have tow hooks and lines; we can drag the cable back between us, no problem.'

'You'll be towing against the tide. *Pequod* will never manage it. We don't even have a tow hook.'

'You can make fast to the stern anchor winch,' the King countered. His voice was compelling. 'I've seen it done. And the tsunami is running out right now. The Sound will be in stasis for the next hour. If we get our act together we can take advantage of that.'

He fixed his gaze on Rick. 'We do this, we help you shift the tanker out of the Sound, and you honour our charter, okay? We do our part and you drop us off at the mouth of the Bank. Deal?'

Rick felt the fuse of his anger kindle. 'We can use our own boat to fetch the tow across. We don't need help. I told you once already to get yourselves ashore. That goes for the machines too.'

The surfer's jaw hardened. 'You aim to handle two ships between just the four of you? I don't think so.'

'I can get volunteers if I need them,' Rick snarled.

'Sure you can,' the King riposted with a glance along the deserted dock.

'Rick,' Patsy sighed. 'Please.'

The colour rushed into Rick's face. He knew he was being stubborn. He couldn't afford to turn down any help. He and Patsy and the Olsens could barely manage *Pequod* by themselves, let alone tow a crippled tanker twenty times their size. The surfer's offer was a godsend. And yet . . . into his mind swam the image on his phone . . .

Indian Creek Bridge. The National Guard had the road barred. A soldier stepped out, hand raised. Natalie pumped the Jaguar's brakes, sending the roadster into a slide.

'Road closed, lady. Bridge is unsafe.'

'But I live up there. Can't you let me through?'

'Floodwater has pulled out one of the piers. Could drop the span any time. You'll have to find another route round. Sorry.'

K. Zamos was at the airport in Ellsworthy. The helicopter was gassed up, ready to roll. The camera crew was aboard. Natalie was racing to join them, but the roads were blocked. She wasn't beaten though. She still had the car and she knew the back roads. She scorched around the town looking for a way across the creek. There wasn't one.

She pulled over by the bus depot and called up Zamos.

'Yup.' Red-headed Carly's voice; her rival in the no-holds-barred, free-for-all catfight that infected every female that strayed into the King's orbit.

Natalie swore silently. 'I'm stuck in town. The bridges are blocked. You'll have to lift me out.'

'Ha, ha. No can do, honeybunch. You're on your own.'

'I'm on the flight, bitch. The King's orders.'

'We'll call you.'

'You'll do better than that.'

'Says who?'

'I say so and it's my name on the charter. You want to play hardball, find another aircraft.'

She shut the phone up. Someone was standing by the car. Tall, fair hair – Sarah Hunter.

'I was going to hitch a ride, but I guess there's no point.'

'You're leaving town?'

Sarah shrugged her strong shoulders. Her mouth was sullen. 'Why should I stay? I've nothing to keep me here.'

'I thought you wanted Rick. You tried hard enough to get him off me.'

'And you don't deserve him. You're like a spoiled child, thinking only of yourself.'

'I'm loyal to my friends. And I admire what they're attempting, something dangerous, heroic, bigger than themselves.'

'The surfers, what do they care what happens to this town, to all of us?' They were both of them mad at each other now.

'They have a dream!' Natalie exclaimed passionately.

'Rick has a dream too, to save this town!'

Natalie's eyes blazed suddenly. 'Against a tsunami? He's mad; it's impossible.'

'Maybe, maybe not, but I know one thing. If Rick Larsen was my man and he was going to risk his life, I would be with him. I would be at his side.'

A helicopter swung over the town, circled, hovered and dipped to settle somewhere near the bus depot. A moment later it was off again, headed over the harbour. It circled low over the Neck. Rick could see figures waving from the open hatch. The surfers were waving back and he knew, he just knew Natalie was up there. Bitterness closed over his heart.

He gazed round the stricken harbour; at the ship he and the cousins and Patsy had spent so much effort on, at the drifting tanker. To hell with her, he thought. He had other responsibilities.

He turned to the big surfer. 'Get your machines in the water. We'll take your help.'

'And?' The King waited.

'We'll do our best to drop you off in a good spot.'

The King nodded. He didn't ask for guarantees or make conditions. He didn't need to. They were both men of their word.

'Tow my ship with that little boat of yours? Idiocy!' Leclerc did not trouble to hide his anger.

'Your ship is unmanned and drifting. You are without power. It's a danger to shipping, a danger to the town and a danger to anyone on board. Commander Wolfowitz here will back me up.'

'The main engines are functioning. The problem is with the gearing which was strained in the tsunami. This can be repaired. My chief engineer is working on it now.'

'Captain, we don't have time to effect repairs. Another wave, a bigger one is coming through in one hour.'

Rick had boarded the *Marie-Sainte* up a rope ladder. It had been a stiff climb with a chilly reception at the end. At first the French master had been pleased to see him. He and the handful of officers left had willingly cooperated in getting a line across to *Pequod*. The current was swinging the tanker in slow arcs, which the captain was endeavouring to counter using bow and stern thrusters.

Leclerc turned to Wolfowitz. 'Commander, I appeal to you. My vessel is being hijacked . . .'

Con Wolfowitz was having a long day and it didn't look like ending any time soon. He had brought two men out with him, both packing side arms. 'Captain, your ship is a hazard to life. I'm ordering it out of the Sound with immediate effect. If you fail to comply you will be placed under restraint and the ship taken over. I believe this to be in the best interests of all concerned. Any questions?'

There could be none. Leclerc made a gesture of despair. 'Do what you must, Commander. This is not my country,' he said bitterly. 'I only ask you to bear witness that none of what has occurred has been my fault.'

'Rick,' Con said. 'Are you confident you can manage this?'

'We'll do our best.'

'Get that tow rigged.'

The tide was definitely flowing out now. Already the tanker was becoming unmanageable. Paul brought *Pequod* in as close as he dared with the *Marie-Sainte*'s bow swinging through thirty degrees. A line was fixed to the tow and lowered over the bow to the water where two jet skis driven by the King and the Gimp waited to drag it over to *Pequod*. When they had it under the stern, the King killed his engine, gathered up some slack on the line, and with a sweep of his arm hurled the coil neatly and accurately to a buddy up above.

'Reel in steady,' he shouted up. 'That tow will be heavy and it's easy to snap. We don't want to have to start over.'

Foot by foot the line was wound in on *Pequod*'s anchor winch. Rick watched anxiously from the tanker's foredeck as the heavy towing cable began to creep out across the water. They had tied it onto the heaviest line available, but even so the strain was considerable and made worse by the current affecting the two vessels. One moment *Pequod* and the tanker would be moving apart, stretching the line to breaking point, the next the enormous bulk of the tanker would rush down on *Pequod*, threatening to ram her. Paul would scuttle to get clear and two minutes later both ships would be moving apart again.

Finally though it was done. A flag went up on *Pequod*'s stern signalling that the hawser was inboard and had been made fast to the anchor winch.

Con prepared to leave. 'You staying here?' he asked Rick.

'Yes, Paul needs someone he can trust this end.'

'You'll be on your own, you realise? The speed things are moving I can't guarantee to spare a helicopter to lift you off.'

'I'll take my chances. If we can reach the open sea we should be okay.'

At the last minute an inflatable pulled alongside *Pequod*. It was Sheena. She had persuaded Mitch from the Lobsterman to row her out. Soaked and filthy, she was clutching her camera. 'I told you I'd be back in time,' she laughed to Patsy. 'What's happening?'

'Small diversion,' Patsy told her grimly. 'We're towing a floating bomb out to sea.'

Slowly, carefully, Paul inched *Pequod* out through the harbour entrance. The tidal flow was moving fast, hurrying both vessels on. It was necessary to build up speed to maintain the tow at an even tension. The *Marie-Sainte* was vastly bigger by a factor of twenty. The slightest jerk on the tow would part it completely or even pluck the anchor winch clean out of *Pequod*'s stern like a rotten tooth. The King was right, it was only the outflow of the current that made this mad undertaking possible at all.

The convoy passed Maple Cove to port. A Coastguard launch was hovering off the island. Rick recalled Con saying something about an operation to rescue a party stranded there. A helicopter had been requested, but there was a wait. The thought of helicopters brought his sister back to mind and he wondered how she was doing.

Captain Leclerc was studying his screen and frowning. 'Our speed is climbing,' he observed. 'Either your ship is more powerful than I thought, Monsieur Rick, or the current is driving us faster.'

Rick joined him at the console. It was true. They were making almost twelve knots. An extraordinary pace in the circumstances. Leclerc strode to the window and raised his binoculars to the horizon.

'Nothing yet.' Lowering the glasses again, he turned back. 'But something is out there. Something big that is gathering its strength, flexing its muscles.' Leclerc glanced at the clock. 'Half an hour to go before your friend the surfer said we should see the next wave. I am beginning to think he was correct.'

Dead River, Maine. Three-thirty p.m. Fifteen miles inland, the Indian Patch families, the Gardiners and the Van Burens, were preparing for their rafting trip on the river. Everyone was kitted out; all the women, moms and their daughters, were sporting summer-weight wetsuits. 'More as a precaution against bruises than cold this time of year,' the store assistant renting the suits advised. Ted and Brook said they would be fine as they were with just their shorts and T-shirts.

'Hey, Dad,' Lloyd complained, running out from the changing room, 'do I have to wear this dorky pants suit?'

'Better than getting cold, son,' Ted Gardiner chuckled.

'But I look so stupid!'

The assistant suppressed a smile. 'We do have a neoprene vest he could try. A lot of the older boys go for those.'

Lloyd's dad winked at her. 'What do you think, son?'

'Sounds okay to me.'

Brook Van Buren joined them. 'Any news on the tsunami yet?'

'Don't!' his wife rounded on him. 'We agreed not to speak about any of that. This is the last day of our vacation and I won't have it spoiled. We're here to enjoy ourselves.'

Goodwill PD. The fax machine on Annie Pellew's desk clattered into life. Annie waited till the printer had stopped churning before ripping the sheet off the machine. She scanned it briefly, pursed her lips and took it in to Don. She handed it to him without comment.

Don was still in his wet clothes. There had been no time to change. Didn't look like there would be for a while either. He took the fax, glanced at it briefly and his jaw tightened. He read the message again, his lips moving soundlessly as he checked to make certain he had understood it right. He looked up at Annie. 'When did this come in?'

She looked at him severely. 'I brought it straight through.'

'I'm sorry,' Don said. 'Did you read it?' He passed a hand over his brow. His face had gone pale.

'I read it,' Annie told him. 'You'll be wanting to call Fred Tarr then?' she added as Don still sat stunned.

Don pulled himself together. 'Guess I'd better,' he mumbled. He shook his head. 'I never figured it would come to this. I thought we could hold out.'

Annie said nothing. Things happened, her manner implied, and the work still had to be done.

Don picked up the red phone on his desk, the one that communicated direct to the fire department next door. 'Freddy,' he said hoarsely, 'hold on to your hat. I've had a message just come in from State Emergency—'

Fred Tarr interrupted. 'I had one too. Guess it says the same thing. I was about to call you.' He let out a sigh. 'So what do you want me to do now?'

'Freddy, I guess we have to pull the plug. Evacuate.'

'Yeah, but where to? The bridges are all cut. There's no way off the island.'

The message on both their desks was from Washington. The estimated height of the next wave was put at 50 metres – 150 feet plus.

Dead River. The ride up to the dam took twenty minutes. There were four other couples. The bus rattled along rutted logging trails through thick forests. It was all wild and remote and beautiful. 'So peaceful,' Jessica sighed to Julie as they passed a deserted lake. 'I'd love to have a place up here for summers together with the kids.'

'The cottage at Goodwill was pretty neat.'

Jessica shuddered. 'I could never go back there. Not after what happened.'

They pulled into a clearing. 'Leave everything you don't need on the rafts on the bus, towels, shoes, dry clothing. Everything will be safe.'

A steep path through rocks and trees led down the side of the valley to the river's edge where a man with a huge beard waited to greet them. 'Hey, you folks, you're here to ride the rapids, right?'

'Right!' everyone chorused.

629

'We have two kinds of rides, wild and very wild! Which is it to be today?'

'Very wild!' the kids squealed with delight.

'I didn't quite catch that, let's have it again, one more time!'

'Really, really wild!' Lloyd screamed at the top of his lungs.

'That's great. Tell you what,' the man boomed, 'you guys see that dam?' He pointed upstream.

'Oh my gosh.' Jessica quailed at the sight of the enormous wall towering over the valley. From where they stood it looked at least a hundred feet high.

'Behind that dam lie fourteen miles of water and in about twenty minutes from now the engineers will open the sluices and let the whole darn lot out!' the man roared. 'See those rafts?' He pointed to the bulbous inflatables lining the bank. 'We're going to put you people on board and wash you clean down the river six and one half miles! Yessir, you guys are about to experience a ride you will never forget!'

Each raft had a trained guide. The Indian Patch families took one raft between them. Their guide was a young woman. Her name was Sandy. She was twenty-three years old and this was her third season on the river. She checked everyone's life vest and safety helmet, handed out paddles and set them to work. 'Like this,' she demonstrated, digging in vigorously. The adults joined in. It was fun and they soon had the raft whirling down the river. 'That's the way! Get that speed up!' Sandy yelled.

'What do you do the rest of the year, Sandy?' Ted called to her.

'Work my way through college. I'm studying for a degree in tourism at the University of Maine.'

'You enjoy the outdoors then?'

'You bet. I get to do this all summer and in winter it's skis and snowmobiling. I hate the cities.'

'Is it true?' Lloyd asked her. 'Is it true what the man said that they're gonna let the whole dam go today for us?'

Sandy laughed. 'That's Hank, he likes to kid around. Seriously though, you guys are fortunate. Usually they make two releases on the dam, but today on account of the tsunami scare they held back on the morning release so you're in for a double helping now. Should be exciting! Everybody is going to get very wet! Maybe even thrown out the raft if you're lucky!'

The rafts were picking up speed. 'Yup,' Sandy cried happily, 'they're opening up those sluices. Okay, we have the first of the rapids coming up. Notice how the gorge narrows here making the water move faster. Expect some turbulence here, people. Paddle hard! And whee! Here we go!'

The raft dipped and shuddered in the fast-moving current. Lloyd saw rock teeth flash past. He bounced on the wooden bench seat, clinging hard on to the safety line attached to the buoyancy tube. The front of the raft tipped, sending a great splash of broken water crashing inboard, drenching him. There were squeals of shock from everyone. 'Paddle!' Sandy commanded, digging deep. On they sped, picking up more speed. The bow of the raft pitched down again and they lurched over the rapids into a cauldron of boiling surf.

'Hang on, kids!' Lloyd's dad shouted. He and Brook were plying their paddles, pulling the blades through the water, driving the raft on between the rocks. Lloyd screamed with excitement, exhilarated by the speed and danger. The gorge walls were narrowing, hemming the river in. Great boulders fallen from above reared their shoulders in the tossing water as the raft dashed past.

After several minutes the hectic pace slackened and they emerged into a wider, calmer stretch where the banks were lower, lined by trees in place of lofty crags. 'Well how was that? Good fun, huh?' Sandy's fair hair was slicked back like a seal.

Betsy giggled, 'Lloyd nearly got bounced out the boat.'

'Did not!'

'Did too!'

'I almost went over the side,' Paula's mother admitted laughing. 'If Brook hadn't grabbed me by the seat of my pants I'd be back there in the rapids.'

'If you do go in the water just relax, let

yourselves be carried along. You all have life vests so you won't sink and the current will take you round the rocks. Just keep your mouth shut and breathe through your nose and we'll pick you up again at the next calm patch.'

The sun was out. It was warm on the river. Lloyd felt himself drying out already. The water was not really cold.

'This is a breathing space before we move on down to the main event,' Sandy warned them. She gazed about her curiously. 'River certainly is high today. The water is up around those trees and you don't usually see that except in the winter floods.'

'Must be all that rain we had last night,' Lloyd's dad suggested.

'Even so . . .' Sandy shook her head, puzzled.

SS *Marie-Sainte*, Goodwill Sound. A while ago Greenstone Island had passed by on the port side. Rick had strained for a glimpse of the house, but it was hard to tell the state of the little bay from this distance. The jetty would be gone, but the house itself was set well back. It had survived storms and high seas before.

The tanker was riding the waves, her motion smooth. It was all easy, too easy. They were almost on the Bank where open ocean waves were first encountered. Something in the water off the port bow caught his attention for a moment. He narrowed his eyes, but without binoculars it was too far away to make out.

Most probably a seal or a bird feeding on the Bank.

'Yes, I noticed it too,' Captain Leclerc murmured beside him. 'But it is only a rock, an outcrop of that last island, what is its name?'

'Greenstone Island, its name is— What did you say that was? A rock?'

'Yes, I am certain that is what it was. I could see clearly with the glasses. Why?'

Rick felt the colour draining from his face. With one quick stride he was at the control console. 'Depth gauge? Where the hell is the stupid depth gauge?'

But it was too late. Even as he searched the screens a buzzer sounded and a message flashed up: DEPTH 4.30 METRES. Rick watched in helpless dismay as the display changed, counting down towards four metres.

There were sounds of running feet in the passage and the chief engineer burst in. 'What is happening?' he demanded. 'My gauges are going crazy! They say there is no water under the keel.'

Leclerc looked stunned. 'I do not understand. The chart here shows thirty metres over the boundary with the reef.'

'Idiots!' Rick gestured out over the bows. 'Because it's another suck back of course!'

Leclerc frowned. 'But that means . . .'

'Yes,' Rick said savagely. 'It means the next tsunami is building out there on the horizon.'

The captain shook his head in disbelief. He was still staring at the gauges, hoping to read

634

some explanation there. 'But a suck out that strong, big enough to drain the whole Sound . . .' His voice sank to a hoarse whisper as the implication hit home. 'Mother of God!'

The French-Canadians stared at one another. 'What are we to do?' the first officer cried.

'The fire launches!' It was the chief engineer who supplied the answer. 'They can make forty knots. If we launch now we can reach the shore before the wave. Quickly!'

They ran in a bunch for the exit. The emergency launches were located aft at the rear of the accommodation block. Taking the stairs three and four at a time, they gained the main deck level and the chief stormed through the fire door leading aft. Abruptly Rick checked and started to run in the other direction, going forward. 'Where are you going?' Leclerc cried after him.

'To the anchor to cast off the tow. *Pequod* draws less than two metres; she can slide over the Bank with luck, but this tub will ground in the next couple of minutes! When that happens the jerk on the tow will rip *Pequod*'s stern out. They won't stand a chance.'

'There is no time for that! They must fend for themselves. We have to prepare the launch and get clear.'

'Give me two minutes. I'll join you at the launch.'

Leclerc stared after him in the narrow passage, his face pale, mouth taut, fighting down his panic. The other officers were already through the far doors and pounding down the next set of ladders, screaming back at them to follow. 'Two minutes then, not a second longer or God help you!' He turned and was gone.

Racing along the deserted ship, Rick charged through door after door till he pushed open the hatch giving access to the outside. A keen wind blew in his face and the deck lurched underfoot. As the water drained out from the Sound, the fierce current was making the ship pitch like a barge.

Before him loomed the giant white insulated tanks filled with the gas responsible for all this grief. A narrow steel catwalk threaded between them towards the distant prow of the ship. Without pausing to think what he was doing, Rick set off at a run through a forest of pipework, his feet ringing on the steel grating. Once he caught his toe and went flying, but he picked himself up and ran on.

Past the foremost tank there was a rail and a gate to a ladder leading to the lower level. Rick kicked the gate open and flung himself down the rungs. He was now on the foredeck. This was where the tow fed in. The heavy line ran in over rollers down to a winch under the bow. Rick had worked on big vessels before. To reach the winch and cast off the tow he would have to locate the hatch leading to the forepeak below.

The hatch was set into a recess reached by four steps. It stood open. Rick dropped down and peered about. Inside, lights illuminated a dank area smelling of oil and paint. Most of the central space was taken up with two enormous winch drums. This was where the anchor cables were wound in, feeding to the cable lockers below. *Pequod*'s tow had been made fast to the starboard drum, the eye of the cable hurriedly fed through a loop of chain, doubled over and spliced off. The alternative, using one of the mooring fixtures on the deck above, had been rejected as carrying a risk of chaffing on a forward pull. Rick had supported the decision.

To cast off the tow it was necessary to slacken off the tension. Rick put his hand on the hawser. Even under the light pull at present it was as rigid as a steel bar. Rick searched about him. The simplest method of dropping the tow was to do exactly what it said: throw off the latches securing the anchor cable and let it run out into the ocean under its own weight.

To locate the latches took him a minute of valuable time. As he had feared they were electronically controlled. Worse, the switches were labelled in French. Rick swore as he tried first one set, then another, all the time conscious that precious seconds were slipping away. Finally he was rewarded. With much grinding and squealing the winch drums commenced to revolve, unwinding under the pull of the cable. The pace quickened as the weight increased. The noise in the low-ceilinged space was deafening. Rick covered his ears and retreated to the back of the compartment. At last with a final cacophonous rattle the tail end of the cable shot out through the eye and silence fell.

Rick heaved a sigh of relief. Peering through the cable eye he could make out *Pequod* still moving away. At least now she might stand a chance of riding out the wave when it hit.

Not so the *Marie-Sainte*. Even as Rick straightened up there was a hideous grinding crunch below. A violent shudder ran through the length of the tanker, hurling him against the bulkhead. There was a deafening crash and the compartment rang like a drum. The ship ground on and on under the momentum of the current, pulverising the reef. For a minute it seemed to Rick they might actually make it over and slide across into the safety of deep water on the far side. Then the dreadful motion ceased and in its place fell a terrifying silence.

He picked himself up, his head ringing from the noise. The lights had failed, plunging the compartment into semi-darkness. He stumbled to the ladder and looked up. His bones turned to ice. There was no patch of daylight overhead. The hatch had closed; the impact of the stranding must have flipped it shut. He sprang up the ladder and pushed against the handle. It stayed fast. He set his shoulder to the steel and gave it his best shot. Not the faintest movement.

The hatch had jammed. Rick was trapped.

Chapter 47

Dead River. The rafts were picking up speed again. The river bent around a huge rock and then suddenly a nightmare opened in front of their eyes. Barely a hundred yards away a waterfall had appeared. Blocking the gorge from side to side was a foaming crest twice the height of a man.

Sandy was the first to react. 'Everyone down in the raft!' she yelled. 'Link arms! Hold the kids tight!'

'What the hell is that?' Brook cried.

'It's a river bore. The river's reversed itself. It must be the tsunami . . .!'

And in a flash both sets of parents understood. Down on the coast a tsunami had struck. The ocean was storming upriver from the estuary against the flow at the same time the sluices on the dam were opened releasing millions of cubic feet of water downstream. The two torrents had clashed here, generating a monstrous swell that was wiping out everything in its path!

Lloyd felt his father's arms wrapping round him, crushing him in a fierce grip. Mom had grabbed Betsy and Betsy's face was dead white the way it went when she was scared. All the parents were clutching the children, linking arms with one another the way Sandy had told them. The wave was very near now, looming over them like a rampart.

'Hold tight!' they heard Sandy yell as a rush of water burst over the raft.

That was the last coherent thought any of them had for what seemed like an eternity.

Lloyd clung on to his father and he felt the raft tilt up and up. It started to slip back and he felt Dad's arms tighten about him as if they would crush his chest. He thought, If this thing topples over we could all drown! He had a flashing glimpse of sky. Heard his mother screaming, or was it Mrs Van Buren? Water poured over the sides, swirling round their knees. The raft wallowed. 'We're going to sink!' Lloyd tried to shout, but the words got stuck somehow.

The raft levelled out. Lloyd had a brief, dizzying impression of looking down on the river from an immense height before the raft tilted again, plunging them sickeningly down. This time the screams were a thin howling that could only come from one of the girls. They were skidding down the back of the wave, faster, faster . . .

SS *Marie-Sainte*, Goodwill Sound. Rick pounded at the hatch door. He hammered and kicked and yelled his lungs out, knowing all the while it was pointless. The three French-Canadian officers would be down on the boat deck, swinging out the emergency escape boat. They probably hadn't missed him yet. And even if they did respond, could they free him in the time left?

He stepped back, forcing his brain to work coolly. There had to be another way out, most probably down through the cable lockers into one of the lower decks. His instinct was right. Some light was coming in from outside through the cable eyes on either side of the forepeak. It took him only moments to locate a second hatch in the deck between the two winch drums. He dropped down a steel ladder into darkness. He fumbled for a switch but the power was off here too. Slowly his eyes adjusted to the gloom. A cramped compartment with sloping sides. Steel bulkheads glistening with moisture. The sound of waves booming against the prow. He was right in the forepeak of the ship here. Huge drums for winding cable loomed and the floor was sticky with grease. There was another hatch opposite in the stern bulkhead. He seized the handle, turned, and it opened. Relief.

He was standing in a narrow passage. Two doors either side, locked, probably storerooms. A fifth door at the end facing him; that would be the one leading to a cross passage or a stairwell. He wrenched the handle. Locked!

Damn! He might have guessed. All these hatches would have been sealed and the latches slammed down when the ship went to emergency stations at the time of the first grounding. Afterwards she had been all but abandoned. There hadn't been the manpower since to open up these decks again. And why should anyone bother now?

His eye lit on a grill set into the bulkhead and hope surged again. An intercom. There would have to be some means provided for communication with the bridge or engine room. But there was no one on the bridge now. He stabbed the talk button and shouted, 'Hi, anybody there? I'm trapped down in the cable locker. Someone let me out? Please!'

No response. He tried again. 'Captain Leclerc! Chief Engineer! Can you hear me up there? This is Rick Larsen from *Pequod*! I need help!'

Silence. No way of telling if the circuit was live even. Most likely it tapped into a central monitoring room currently unmanned.

How long before the others realised he was in trouble? They might even decide he had abandoned them, found a raft and dropped over the side. Anything was possible. They would be concerned for their own safety now, not his. If he had gotten lost so much the worse. It was every man for himself.

A sudden noise aloft startled him. A crash of metal resounding through the forepeak. He ran back through the cable locker and flung himself up the ladder to the winch room. 'Hi, I'm in here!' he yelled, hammering on the door again. Nothing. His shoulders sagged in disappointment. It could have been anything, a door slamming in the wind, a scuttle banging.

There was still *Pequod* though. Paul and Magnus would not abandon him. Yes, but how would they reach him? he asked himself bitterly. And Con Wolfowitz's parting words came back. *I can't guarantee to spare a helicopter to lift you off.*

He retreated back into the winch room and crawled into the empty cable eye, straining for a glimpse of his own ship. The stranding had left *Marie-Sainte* canted over to one side, giving him a view out over the ocean. The sight out there was breath-taking. The ocean was still draining out from the Sound. The tanker had grounded on a pinnacle of dark rock periodically visible among swirling currents. Through sheer bad luck she must have struck the highest point of the Bank. A few metres to one side or the other and she might have scraped over.

He climbed over to the opposite side to find the situation reversed. All he could see was empty sky. He tried shouting, 'Anybody up there? Can you hear me?'

There was no response. Straining to listen though, his ears detected another sound, a shrill, two-tone siren pealing out across the main tank deck and repeated urgently through every quarter of the vessel.

Rick's heartbeat began to race again. He recognised that sound. Less than two hours ago he had heard it carried on the wind across the harbour to the waterfront where Reb lay trapped in the rubble of the collapsed shop front. It was the gas alarm!

Maple Cove. 'A helicopter is on its way. I spoke with the Coastguard,' Martin Seymour greeted Southwell as the Toyota slewed to a halt on the cliff top in a shower of stone chippings.

Southwell stared incredulously at the cove. 'My God, it's happening all over again!'

The ocean that had pursued them up the beach had vanished and the cove was turning back into dry land again. Southwell snatched the binoculars from Martin's hands. 'Where are they? Is Donna still okay?'

'In the rocks near the centre of the island, about halfway up. There's a Coastguard swimmer with them. They tried to get a boat in before the last wave but it didn't make it.'

'I can see them. I can see Donna.' Southwell was squinting through the glasses. 'It looks like they are coming down to the edge. Jesus!' He turned to Martin with a look of horror. 'I think they're going to try to make it across!'

Martin gaped in disbelief. 'Look how far it is. They'll never make it on foot in time! They'll be trapped when the next wave sweeps in. Maybe they are trying to make it easier for the helicopter to land and pick them up,' he added.

'If it does come.' Southwell was looking at his watch. 'How long ago did you speak to them?'

'I don't know, ten minutes, fifteen.'

'Then what's keeping them?'

For several more minutes the two men watched from the cliff, searching the sky for approaching aircraft. The launch meanwhile had moved further offshore. 'Look,' Martin said, 'they're off the island now.'

It was true. Plainly visible even without the glasses, three figures were picking their way slowly out onto the bottom of the dried-out channel.

'I can't leave it any longer. I've got to help them. Come on!' Southwell was climbing back in the car.

'You're going to drive out? That's crazy. The track is all washed out. Wait for the Coast-guard.'

'I'm not waiting any longer. I have to do something. I can't just sit here and watch my wife drown!'

Seymour was right. The lower part of the track down to the beach had been torn away. Waves had gouged out stones and scoured gullies. Near the bottom they came to a halt at a five-foot drop. 'I told you it was no good,' Martin said. He sounded frightened. This was all slipping out of control.

'We'll see.' Southwell slammed the Landcruiser into low ratio. Turning the wheel, he aimed the vehicle at the side of the track and pumped the throttle.

'For God's sake!' Martin cried as the front nose-dived over the edge. The truck plunged downward on a near-vertical slope and slithered off a ramp of piled sand. A huge hole loomed; Southwell wrestled the wheel round. The Toyota tipped and swayed as they crawled their way over boulders and scree, then lurched through a deep pool and somehow clambered up over the rim onto level ground again.

'Anything's possible,' Southwell said grimly.

Martin gulped. They still had to make it across. And back.

The sand along the beach was flat and firm at first. The Landcruiser raced out, heading for the island. 'It's not all dry,' Seymour warned. 'There's a deep section out in the middle. You have to bear away to the right and go round.'

'I know what I'm doing,' Southwell replied through tight lips. 'I live out here remember.'

The going became softer though. They were forced to detour round wide expanses of rock and stretches of deep water. 'We're heading too far east,' Seymour said. 'We need to try to work our way back round.'

'I'm trying, I'm trying, dammit,' Southwell cursed. 'It's not so damned easy. Where are they now? Can you see them? Stick your head out the roof.'

Seymour climbed shakily onto the seat and

leaned out the sunroof. 'I can see them,' he shouted down. 'They're still quite near the island, moving the opposite way to us, parallel to the shore.'

Still swearing, Southwell swung the vehicle around and tore back the way they had come. They crashed through a shallow lake and found themselves confronted with a long ledge of rock. 'To hell with it,' Southwell said. 'We'll fight our way across.'

'They've seen us!' Martin cried down. He waved his arms over his head and shouted. 'They're changing tack and are heading this way. I think we should wait for them to reach us.'

'Let me take a look.' Southwell stopped the car and opened the door, standing on the sill. 'I see them.' He waved madly. 'Donna! Donna! Over here!'

'They're coming,' Martin said excitedly. 'They're hurrying as fast as they can. Those rocks are slippery though. It's slowing them down.'

'If only there was some way we could get to them,' Southwell said, biting his lip.

'I'll go out and help them.' Seymour clambered down from the sunroof. 'You turn this thing around ready to take off.'

'No, wait. I'll go, you stay here!' Southwell shouted, but the older man was already out and stepping onto the rocks. Southwell watched him go and cursed.

He backed the vehicle round, positioning it

ready to roll the minute Donna and the others scrambled aboard. He climbed back up to see how they were doing. The party was in plain view now, but they were moving slowly. Dammit, Southwell swore, I should be out there.

For a couple more endless minutes he watched as the group picked their way closer. Finally he could stand it no longer. Jumping down, he scrambled onto the rocks and set off to meet them. He had only taken half a dozen steps when he grasped why progress was so difficult. God, it was slippery! The rocks were coated in some kind of thick weed that acted like grease. Swaying perilously, he fought his way on. 'Donna!' he called and saw her wave back. 'Donna, this way!'

When finally they collided, she fell into his arms. 'Oh God, I'm so sorry. Tab's not here. I couldn't find him!' she wept.

'It's okay,' he told her, holding her tight. 'Tab is safe. I've left him in town. All that matters now is to get you back ashore.'

'Folks, I hate to break up a reunion scene,' the big man in the black wetsuit interrupted. 'But the party ain't over yet. We need to get the hell out of here before some serious weather comes our way.'

The words were hardly out of his mouth when from the mouth of the Sound a clap of thunder split the air.

* * *

SS *Marie-Sainte*. The impact of the tanker's grounding on the Bank had almost capsized the escape launch. Two of the French-Canadian officers had been thrown over the side. In terror for their lives they floundered in the water screaming for help. Leclerc dragged them back on board. The chief engineer had the motor running. 'Push her off!' he called to his captain.

'Rick! We must wait for Rick,' Leclerc shouted back, holding on to the painter.

'What happened to him? He was with us.'

'He went forward to drop the tow!'

'He is mad! The wave is coming. We must leave now. Otherwise we all drown!'

'No, I promised him I would hold the launch.'

In the well of the boat, the first officer vomited up salt water. 'Fools,' he croaked. 'Listen! Don't you hear that? It's gas! We are all going to die!'

Rick forced himself to think logically. First rule out what doesn't work. Doors are locked or jammed. Ceilings, bulkheads solid steel. No help within earshot. Which left only the cable eyes where the anchor chain ran out. The gap was way too small though for his shoulders. Or was it? He crouched down and slid his head and arms out. God, but that was tight. He pulled back inside. Think this through a moment. Even if by some miracle he did succeed in squeezing through, what then? Dive into the ocean? A forty-foot drop down to a solid reef a foot below the surface. No, try the other way. The ceiling in the compartment was eight feet, eight and a half. All he had to do was stand on the lip of the eye, reach up, grab the edge of the deck and haul himself up.

No way. Think again.

Wait. There was a rail round the prow surely? A safety rail to prevent accidents. And a rail had stanchions. If he could only grab a hold of a stanchion, then he might pull himself up.

He thought it through, step by step. It could work. It had to work. First though he had to make it through the eye.

Rick stripped. Undershirt, pants went. Shoes too, he would need bare feet to grip with. Take the upward-listing side. The slight angle of heel would work in his favour. He knelt again, slid his arms through and hunching his shoulders into his chest began to snake his way through the hole. Shit, this was painful. Even worse than before. No way would his shoulders fit that hole.

He struggled back and sat panting on the steel floor. His shoulders were bleeding where the edges of the rivets had rubbed. Give up? No! Try again then, and keep trying till he had worn away enough flesh to scrape through.

The alarm was still pealing. He breathed in short gasps, terrified of the first whiff of gas. His attention roamed the compartment. Was there really no other way? Nothing that would help? The empty winch drums, grease-stained and scratched, loomed in the half dark. Grease!

Scraping some off with his fingernails, he smeared it across his shoulders. Boy, it stank. This had better work.

Over on *Pequod*, Patsy had taken over the wheel from Paul. She felt the sudden lurch as the tow went free and shouted to Paul, 'The tow has gone. The tow has gone.' At the same time she reduced power on the engines and prepared to go about.

Paul came running. 'How did it happen? I didn't feel anything.'

'I don't know. I just felt it go that's all.'

A surfer came forward from the stern. 'Tow's gone slack.'

'I know. Did you see what happened?'

The boy shook his head. 'Nothing to see. Just the cable went slack and the other boat is left behind.'

Patsy was already on the radio. '*Pequod* calling *Marie-Sainte*! *Pequod* calling *Marie-Sainte*! Come in please.'

There was no answer.

'Maybe they dropped the tow on purpose,' Paul suggested.

Patsy rounded on him. 'Why would they do that?'

He shrugged. 'Had enough maybe?'

'That's dumb!'

Paul exploded suddenly, 'Sure it's dumb. This whole thing is dumb. It's a really dumb idea to be out here towing a twenty-thousand-ton bomb

651

out to meet with a giant tsunami! And we must be crazy to be going along with it.'

Patsy stared at him shocked. She shook her head. 'We have to turn around.'

Before Paul could say anything a surfer hailed the bridge from atop the roof. 'Hey, you guys down there. Take a look ahead!'

Patsy looked. And looked again. All she saw was a gleam on the ocean, like it might be the sun on the water. And then she understood. And then she thought, Rick is dead and so are we.

The King snatched her glasses and swung up onto the roof, elbowing aside the gawpers. He focused the lens and narrowed his eyes. His pulse began to race the way it did back on Maui when an all-time westerly was heading up towards Peahi. This was it. The clock was running.

There was a grunt behind. The Gimp had joined him. The King passed over the Nikons. The cripple looked and a deep sigh of relief gathered in his heart. The Fire Mountain had delivered. Three thousand miles away a cataclysm had flung the wave to end all waves towards this single point in space and time. And he was here to greet it. His fist punched the air.

The King took the glasses back. 'What is that, ten feet, no more surely?'

'What you're seeing is the tip of the iceberg,' the Gimp told him softly.

Two feet behind Sheena Dubois heard them speak and flipped the microphone button on her camera to catch the conversation.

'The tip of the iceberg,' the Gimp repeated. 'Underneath there's a thousand feet depth of water in motion. It's moving down on us at a hundred knots. In fifteen minutes' time when it hits the reef it's still doing sixty and all that energy transforms into height. It jumps from ten feet to two hundred in the space of a quarter-mile. This is what we came for. The all-time greatest board ride is about to be born!'

'We stop to drop you here and we all die. It's madness. Our only chance is to run to meet the wave before it reaches its full height.'

Paul was speaking. *Pequod* was tearing out into open ocean as the approaching tsunami sucked the water out from the Sound. Overhead the helicopter hung like a giant insect waiting to feed.

'Hell,' the King said. 'We had an agreement. Just swing out the jet on the end of the crane and set the Gimp and me down in the water. Then you can take off.'

'Do it then.' Paul covered his ears. 'On your own heads be it. Just get the hell off this ship!'

Sheena filmed the drop. It took all of three minutes. *Pequod* was working up to full power, her hull throbbing under the beat of the engines. The red and green lead machine was lowered over the water with the Gimp up front and the King with his yellow board behind on a BZ rescue sled. The jet struck the surface with a mighty splash, digging deep and throwing up a burst of spray. The Gimp wasn't fazed; he smacked the hoist latches and the machine ploughed clear of the ship's wake.

The second jet was put in the water with the camera crew. All the guys were jumping to go, stoked on adrenaline and glory. Sheena thought of matadors and gladiators, tornado chasers. Too young to die; too fast to live.

'Go boys!' she yelled.

The riders made a last check of their gear: straps, goggles, quick release system, vests, leashes, personal radios. The Gimp gave the thumbs-up signal and twisted his throttle. The motors roared. Creaming the surface, the twin machines scorched away. The King's fist punched the air. Do or die!

And up in the stern, Patsy Easton gazed back at the helpless tanker marooned on the reef and wept for Rick Larsen.

'They're off!' red-headed Carly shouted from the helicopter's nose. She was up in the cockpit, leaning over the pilot's shoulder.

Natalie peered out of the main hatch, screwing her eyes up against the slipstream. There was *Pequod* like a white bird on the ocean. Half a mile in her rear lay the tanker, squatting hugely on the massive bank that had emerged from the ocean like some prehistoric Atlantis returning from the waves. She saw the jet skis zoom away from *Pequod*'s side. Brilliant, she thought, but a shaft of fear pierced her as her glance lifted to the wave building out on the horizon. It looked endless, endless and beautiful, a line of brilliance drawn on the surface of the ocean.

K. Zamos was firing orders at everyone, at the cameramen to track the King, at the pilot to go lower. 'Follow them! Follow them!' he urged. 'Don't lose sight of them whatever you do.'

But the pilot was listening to his headphones. Some message was coming in. 'It's the Coastguard. They're worried for the tanker down there. They want us to take a look.'

'Out of the question!' Zamos exploded. 'They have their own helicopters. Our mission is at a critical point. Men's lives depend on us. Keep with the skis!'

Natalie pushed past the camera crew and their mountain of equipment to the cockpit. 'What's this about the tanker?' she asked the pilot.

'Some guys trapped on board. They were bringing it out before the suck back. Now the thing is stuck on the Bank and they can't get off. Looks like one bad situation.'

Natalie felt her stomach knot inside her. 'How many guys?'

But the pilot wasn't sure. 'Maybe one guy only. I didn't get the full story. You want we take a look?'

She hesitated. Sarah Hunter's words returned to haunt her. . . . *I know one thing. If Rick Larsen was my man and he was going to risk his life, I would be with him. I would be at his side.*

And while she hesitated there was another shout from Carly. 'Hey, down there, look! A second crew in the water! We've got competition!'

The King's earpiece crackled. Another jet ski in the water! Another surfer!

Someone was trying to steal his thunder. The King's great fist balled. Someone was trying to drop in on his wave and that person was going to pay the price.

The Gimp had heard too. Mack, he thought. Professional jealousy, but this was worse; it was a breach of trust, of loyalty. There was a traitor out there.

Rick had gotten his shoulders out. That was the good news; the bad news was that his chest was now wedged. He could feel his ribs cracking under the pressure as he strained and pushed back with his hands. God, they were going to have to cut him out of here. He paused for breath and as he did he twisted his head to look for *Pequod*. And that was the moment he had his first sight of the tsunami.

A moment of sheer panic brought him a few minutes more of existence. With a frantic heave he wrenched his bruised ribcage clear of the cable eye. There was no more time for planning the way ahead. He had to trust to instinct for self-preservation. Drawing his legs up and through, he crouched on the lip of the eye, gripping the upper rim with one hand. A deep breath and he straightened up, flattening himself against the side of the vessel, right arm outstretched, the tips of his right hand fumbling for a hold that would save him from toppling back onto the reef. His fingers felt round and fastened on a slim pillar. A stanchion, a rail stanchion; strength coursed through him. This he could do now. He firmed his grip and swung his legs up, pulling himself in and round, at the same time grasping up with his other hand for a wire, a post, the rim of a scuttle, any kind of handhold would do. His fingers brushed a wire, snatched, missed, then closed on a projecting bolt. It wasn't much but it gave the purchase he needed for that vital moment. He got a leg up and round another post. A second heave and he was up and rolling under the wire onto the deck. The open air had never felt so good.

The gas warning siren was still blaring. He picked himself up and snatched a look back at the oncoming wave. Jesus, he thought, that's going to be a big one. And he cast around for some cover.

From 500 feet, Natalie watched the jets drawing white tails across the surface of the ocean. The King's was a faster machine and bigger but it was towing more equipment. And Mack was closer. If the wave ran straight, he was perfectly placed to catch it before it reached its full height.

K. Zamos was getting jumpy. 'What's our man doing? That Gimp guy, does he know where he is? What's he doing moving out to the edge? This other guy is set to scoop him if he doesn't watch out.'

'He's looking for the spot, the entry spot,' Carly shouted. 'He and the King have it all planned out.'

'Yeah, well there's only one winner. I hope he remembers that.'

The pilot was talking again: 'Coastguard is back on. Can we overfly the tanker? Official request.'

'No way!' Zamos came back instantly.

Natalie felt her heart squeeze tight like a fist inside her chest. Rick and the King, each in his own way a hero, both needing her. What was she to do? How could she make a choice?

'Man, the other guy's going for it!' a cameraman yelled excitedly. 'Watch his smoke!'

The blood pounded in Natalie's temples as she stared down. The wave was building fast now. It was rushing on, swelling like a mountain. She saw the jet ski racing towards the lower edge nearest her, clawing its way up. She saw the surfer swing out and round, catapulting himself forward towards the crest. He had dropped the tow. He was almost on the crest.

But the crest was building faster than the board could move, piling up behind, growing and towering over him. There were gasps from the crew as an arm of foaming crest curved over, gathering the surfer in. 'He's gone,' someone said quietly. 'The beast ate him.'

They watched on in silence. The jet had over-run and the back slope was moving too fast to swing back on. The driver tried to ride the crest, searching for an exit point, but the wave was pitiless. 'Another down,' muttered Carly. 'Where's the King? Where's our man?'

'He's there!' One of the cameramen pointed. 'Right in position.'

The King and the Gimp had seen Mack wipe out. The Gimp grinned wolfishly and shook the spray from his goggles. Serve the bastard right for trying to steal their wave. He had no regrets.

He gave the King the high sign and saw the surfer's arm go up in acknowledgement. Time to move in for the kill. The tsunami was rolling down on them, building from the southern end over by Indian Point where the water was shallowest. The topography of the Sound, the slight angle of the underwater reef, meant the wave would build later and rise higher by Curtain Bluff. It left an entry point for a fast machine to catch the wave's rising shoulder and ride with it to the crest; a fast machine and daring riders.

The Gimp gunned the throttle, building up to full power. He could feel the King's weight behind. They had chosen a specially built board with a patented extended wing fin designed to lift ɪne underside fractionally above the water's surface, allowing the board to skim like a hydrofoil with minimal drag. Tests had shown speed increases of as much as 10 per cent. The extra speed would boost the jet's power in the crucial final seconds of the run-in, when every ounce of power was vital to catapult the surfboard onward and upward to the crest.

The wave loomed up like a mountain, blocking out the sun. The Gimp crouched over the handles, coaxing every last revolution out of the engine. They were climbing, climbing, but the wave was building faster. It was outrunning them! Out the corner of his left eye the Gimp could see the curve of the crest racing up to grab them.

Now for the final sprint! His right thumb closed over a red toggle switch. He flipped the safety off and pressed the switch down hard. The engine broke into a frenzied scream as underneath him a specially installed fuel injector squirted pressurised nitrous oxide directly into the cylinders. The entire engine block's computer management system had been designed and tuned for these final two minutes; the fuel spiked to produce a 120-second burst of flaming thrust, red-lining every pressure and temperature gauge in a furious scramble for speed.

Howling like a demon, the jet sprang forward, white foam boiling in its wake, streaking upwards with awesome power. Behind him, the Gimp glimpsed the King swinging out and he pumped the red switch savagely again, squirting the last dregs of explosive fuel mix into the combustion chambers. He felt the machine shaking under the shattering power output. It was literally hammering itself apart! Onwards and upwards . . .!

The King crouched, knees braced, the spray battering him like solid icicles, the slipstream tearing at him as the board raced over the water. Fifty, sixty knots, seventy! Unbelievable speed. At the last moment he dropped the tow, flinging it from him defiantly. The wind whipped him on. He was airborne! White water! He was on the crest! He was flying!

Valhalla!

The Coastguard dispatcher came back on air for the last time.

'What should I do?' the helicopter pilot yelled. He was angry now. They were making him look callous. 'There are people dying down there.'

'Back here and all,' Carly yapped at him.

Natalie felt the fist in her chest again where her heart should have been. Rick is calling for help. I should be with him.

'Do it!' she ordered. 'Make the overfly!'

'Screw that!' Zamos raged. 'Stay with our man. He needs us now more than ever.'

'My charter,' Natalie snapped back. 'You heard. Take us over the tanker!'

'I'm buying out the charter. I'll double what you make. I'll put ten thousand in your pocket. Twenty thousand! Just stay on the shot!'

Natalie pushed him out the way. 'Bitch!' Carly clawed at her face. Natalie balled a fist and punched her on the cheek. The other girl fell back. Natalie felt clear-headed with fury. She crawled forward to the cockpit.

'Take us over that tanker,' she ordered. 'Do it now and don't listen to anyone else.'

Rick Larsen stood on the foredeck of the *Marie-Sainte* and watched the great wave swinging in towards him. He estimated he had maybe a couple of minutes' existence left to him and was surprised that his only regret should be that he would never be able to tell anyone what a magnificent, awe-inspiring sight it was. Perhaps this was how death always seemed. Magnificent and terrible and beautiful. It almost made dying seem worthwhile. It made him feel beyond caring or fearing, just filled with wonder, wonder and curiosity as to what it would be like afterwards, on the other side.

That was when he heard the helicopter. Its shadow swung overhead and the downdraught of the rotor was like a storm beating on him. The pilot held a ten-foot hover just over the forepeak and there was Natalie in the hatchway screaming at him. He couldn't make out her words, but he guessed she was telling him to get a move on. The wave was behind them now, towering like a mountain.

And something else.

Something was catching in his throat. He was choking. His lungs were struggling for air even as his chest heaved, fighting for breath. Gas! It could only be gas leaking from a damaged tank or section of pipe, the freezing liquid warming and expanding, boiling off into a deadly unseen vapour, spreading and growing with every passing second. A deadly cloud waiting only for the least spark to touch off a fireball.

'Is he crazy? What's wrong with him? What's he trying to tell us?'

A buzzer sounded in the cockpit, an urgent sound that made them jump.

'That's our fuel warning!' The co-pilot was edgy. 'Switching to reserve. We need to head back in.'

'No!' Natalie shouted above the engine noise. 'Get lower. He needs our help!'

Half naked and grease-smeared on the tanker's forepeak deck, Rick waved frantically at the pilot, whose helmeted face was gaping at him through the Perspex of the cockpit. Natalie was screaming soundlessly from the hatch, her words lost in the thunder of the rotor. Behind her another man was making ready to throw out a rope.

'No!' Rick screamed to them. 'Get away!'

Helicopters, they had taught him in the navy, carried a static charge that could be earthed when any part of a hovering aircraft touched a vessel, often releasing sufficient energy to blow a man off his feet or detonate an inflammable vapour cloud.

'Go back!' he screamed again, waving his arms to warn them off. 'It's not safe!'

'Take us lower! Take us lower! He can't reach the rope from this height.'

'Are you crazy? That's a gas tanker down there. A floating bomb!'

The pilot had cut his teeth down in the Gulf of Mexico. He had worked oil platforms and tanker vessels and knew the risks. He sat in the right-hand seat, his feet on the yaw pedals, right hand gripping the pistol grip on the cyclic stick between his legs that controlled the aircraft's altitude. His left hand rested nervously on a large lever between the two seats. This was the collective used to control the pitch of the rotor blades moving the aircraft up or down in hover. With the helicopter in hover as it was at the moment, a simple tug upwards on the collective would set the aircraft into a vertical climb out of danger.

'Take us down! Take us down!'

'Okay, okay!' the pilot yelled angrily over his shoulder. Foot by foot he eased the aircraft lower till he was holding the hover alongside the prow of the stranded vessel and at barely head height.

'Closer! Get closer. We're too far for him to jump across!' Natalie was shouting from the hatch.

By the rail of the foredeck, Rick watched tensely as the helicopter edged nearer. The gap was barely six feet now. He could almost risk it.

And then disaster struck. With a hideous groaning sound and screech of twisting steel the tanker shuddered all along her length and canted sharply over, listing to her port side. Caught off guard, the pilot's hand jerked at the cyclic. The helicopter's nose tilted and slid sideways and the left-hand wheel housing crashed into the deck railing with a burst of blue sparks.

The sudden lurch of the ship had almost pitched Rick over the rail. He leapt back as the static charge crackled and spat around him. He heard the dreaded *whoomp* of a gas ignition close behind and turning saw a ten-foot tongue of flame leap from the forest of pipes around the nearest of the main gas tanks.

The aircraft reeled drunkenly. Its rotors sliced the air murderously above Rick's head. Heat from the erupting gas flare seared his skin. Any minute now one of the main tanks would blow up, taking the whole ship with it. The helicopter was lifting off again, clawing away for safety, the downwash of the rotors beating thunderously about him, its shadow dark against the sky. Rick took three running steps at the gap torn in the railings and launched himself outward and upward, jumping with every ounce of strength left in him.

Chapter 48

Rick's outstretched straining hand touched the sill of the hatch, scrabbling for a purchase on the bare metal, but his fingers were thick with grease and he felt himself slipping back. He flailed out desperately with his other hand, his left, and struck the nearside wheel housing. He clenched his fist convulsively and his hold closed around a steel strut. His body swung down with a jerk, the weight on his arm almost tearing him loose, but he clung on, twisting in the downdraught of the helicopter's wake, and looking down saw the deck of the tanker disappearing below his dangling feet.

Inside the helicopter, Natalie was on her knees in the hatch, trying vainly to reach him. One of the cameramen pulled her out of the way and took her place. Leaning out, he caught a hold of Rick's free right hand. Together they heaved him up towards the edge of the hatch.

'Let go the wheel!' the cameraman shouted.

'Let go your other hand or we can't pull you in.'

Rick's legs scrabbled in the empty air. Terror of falling coursed though him. He must, must release his hold of the wheel strut to allow himself to be pulled to safety, but if he did and their grip on his other arm slipped then he would no longer be able to save himself.

'Rick,' Natalie cried, her hair whipping around her mouth. 'Rick, let go your other hand!'

With a huge effort Rick forced himself to ease his hold on the strut. Closing his mind to the fear, with a convulsive movement he whipped his left hand across, straining for the edge of the hatch.

'Okay, we've got you now!' he heard Natalie call and with another desperate heave he brought his chest up to the edge of the sill. Relief flooded through him, he was almost home.

At that precise moment the helicopter banked round to the left, the nose lifting sharply as it climbed away. The cabin tilted, swinging Rick's weight against Natalie. With a cry she fell against the side of the hatch, clawing at the cameraman's shoulder to save herself. Caught off balance, the man slackened his grip momentarily. Rick's wrist slid through his hand. Rick clutched frantically at the hatch edge with his left hand, but there was no purchase for his scrabbling fingers. There was a dreadful moment of realisation that he was lost and then he felt himself toppling outwards into the void.

'Rick! Rick!' Natalie flung herself at the hatch. Sick with horror, she stared out at the figure dropping away below. A white splash blossomed briefly on the surface of the water. 'Rick, no!' she screamed.

'Come away!' The cameraman dragged her back from the edge. 'There's nothing you can do!'

'But we have to save him!' Scrambling to her feet, she shouldered her way back into the cockpit. 'Take us back down!' she screamed to the pilot.

But the pilots were silent. Both crewmen were staring in paralysed horror at the monstrous breaker building beyond the mouth of the Sound. Like a mountain pushing up out of the ocean, as one observer onshore put it later. Already the crest looked to be foaming level with the helicopter. All the men's training, every instinct of experience and personal survival was telling them to pull the collective and scramble to safe height.

That meant leaving the man down there to die.

This was no rescue aircraft with a winch to haul him off with. A rescue meant going right in low, holding the hover just above sea level, risking all their lives. And this while that hideous thing was charging down upon them, growing more massive with every passing second.

'We can't risk it!' the pilot shouted back. 'I'm taking us up!'

'Cowards!' Natalie flung herself into the cockpit. She pounced on the pilot's hand, forcing the lever downward with all her weight. With heart-stopping suddenness the aircraft's nose pitched upward and they dropped like a stone towards the deck of the ship.

Rick had once taken a parachute jump for charity. This was different. It took him a little over two seconds to cover the distance from the helicopter to the surface of the Sound, by which time his speed of falling had had become thirty-four miles per hour. In that fraction of time the most he could do was straighten his legs and extend his arms to try and hit cleanly. Even so the impact felt like hitting a wall. He plunged deep and as he came to the cold closed in around him, leaving him only one thought which was somehow to make his way back up to the air.

'You crazy bitch! What are you trying to do? Kill us all?' The pilot flung Natalie off with a sweep of his shoulder. 'Get her out of here!' he yelled to the others. Desperately he heaved the lever back up, applying full power to the already straining engine.

'Ditch alert! Ditch alert!' the co-pilot was yelling over the noise of the turbine as he watched the radar altimeter unwind like a broken spring. 'We're going down! We're going to hit!'

'Brace! Brace! Brace!' the pilot shouted as he

pulled maximum torque, hauling on the collect-ive. Flattened against the bulkhead, Natalie heard the turbine note change to a deafening howl. The aircraft shook as the rotors flailed the air for lift under full emergency power. Squirming around, Natalie gazed out the hatch at the giant wave thundering down towards the beached ship. Between the two lay a rapidly diminishing pool of eerily calm water trapped behind the edge of the undersea cliff. But where was Rick?

Seconds later the aircraft's belly smacked down on the water with an impact that jarred every bone in her body. Spray shot up higher than the roof and a torrent of water surged in through the open hatch. Screams erupted from the film crew. The helicopter was wallowing in the trough of the approaching tsunami, straining to lift off again under the load of water it had shipped. Natalie fought her way past the others to the hatch. The whirling blades were sucking up curtains of spray. At first she could see nothing and her heart sank, then suddenly a head broke the surface not a dozen yards away.

'Rick!' she called frantically. 'Rick, over here!'

He twisted round, screwing up his face to see through the spray. Then he started to swim towards them with slow, heavy strokes. 'Hurry, Rick!' she urged. 'Hurry! There isn't much time.'

Behind in the cockpit alarms were sounding. The pilots were yelling to one another.

'Low level abort!'

'Give her the gun, for God's sake!'

'Up! Up! Up!'

Storms of spray blotted out the windows as the rotor raced up in an effort to tear them free from the ocean's grip. Rick was ten feet away, ploughing through the water like a tired dog. He had realised the danger and was swimming for his life. 'Wait!' Natalie screamed to the pilots. 'Wait, you bastards! He's still out there.'

The helicopter's turbine howled afresh, shaking the cabin. The pilots hadn't heard her. 'We're too heavy!' the co-pilot yelled back. 'Throw stuff out!' Water surged knee-deep back and forth across the cabin floor as the hull lurched. The cameramen were cursing and fighting to save their equipment. Rick was still swimming. He reached the lip of the hatch and collapsed, too exhausted to climb in. Natalie caught him by the arms, trying to drag him inboard. 'Help me, someone!'

The aircraft nose lifted, momentarily breaking free of the suction. 'Give me a hand!' Natalie was crying. Rick was a dead weight. Someone else heard her and waded over. It was Zamos; he took an arm and together they hauled the gasping Rick inboard.

The helicopter gave another lurch, righted itself and began to climb, water draining out from the open hatch. Natalie felt light-headed with relief.

Zamos turned triumphantly to a cameraman.

'Did you get that?' he crowed. 'I saved this guy's life! Did you film me? I want the footage for the networks!'

But the man was paying no attention. 'Jeez,' he croaked, staring beyond them out the hatch. 'Jeez, will you look at that thing out there!'

The wave was almost on them. The pilot had pulled a vertical lift on full power. It was like being on an elevator. From 10 feet to 220 in 20 seconds. The engines were screaming, people were shouting. Everyone in the cabin was shouting at everyone else. All Rick could do was lie there and catch his breath. Where was *Pequod?* a part of his brain wondered. Then he caught a glimpse of Natalie's strained face and he knew it wasn't over yet.

The crest of the tsunami had reached the far edge of Goodwill Bank at the mouth of the Sound and was rearing up, swelling and growing to an insane height. There was the King, breasting the summit, riding the giant into the jaws of death. Natalie leaned out the port hatch over the cameraman's shoulder, her face a mask as she screamed into the slipstream.

Ahead of the King loomed the arms of the Sound, Indian Point on one side, the cliffs of Curtain Bluff to the north. Once inside he would be trapped with no way out to run. He must have an angle, an escape route planned, Rick was sure. That was what the Gimp had been searching for on the chart.

The King was skimming the wave from left to right, his board leaping fearlessly along the crest like a bird, glorying in his own skill. Behind him, the jet ski driven by the Gimp was running at full tilt to keep up. The sun had broken through the clouds and was shining on him. The camera team were screaming; Natalie was screaming. The King couldn't hear them, but he knew. The whole world was watching him racing into legend. He was the myth-maker and this was his birthright. Immortality was in his grasp. Till the end of time wherever surfers gathered they would tell his story.

And now all at once as he lay there coughing up seawater on the floor of the helicopter, Rick understood their plan. From the exact tip of Curtain Bluff a spit of rock ran out like a blackened spine. There was a spur there that mariners knew of and avoided. The right-hand end of the wave would catch there and start to break early. That was the exit point the King was aiming for. It was risky; great God it was a risk. A single error of balance or timing and thousands of tons of raging water would pound him to shreds against the cliffs. It might just be possible though if a man had superhuman strength, the raw courage, the will and nerve to hold on, to ride the mountain of death to the very last instant.

He was beginning his descent now, skimming down that awesome wall of water. From up in the helicopter it seemed a sheer drop, a near-vertical face striped at intervals with ripples of white, racing towards the land with a mass and momentum that took the breath away. As he dropped, tearing sideways across the face of the wave at dizzying speed, the wave was breaking behind him, curling over and chasing him like a racing avalanche, fast, faster than anyone could imagine.

The left-hand edge of the wave had reached the tanker now. For an instant Rick glimpsed it poised over the ship's bow, curled over like a giant hand. The white crest towered over the mast as water buried the great tanks. Then it came: a flash like a sheet of scalding lightning as the world changed.

The explosion caught the curl of the breaking wave, blasting it into a vast cloud of boiling foam a thousand feet high that engulfed the Sound from side to side. In the space of a second the huge breaker was transformed into a maelstrom of churning water and leaping spray shot through with torrents of mud and shattered rock, sections of steel plate, and in its raging heart a ball of yellow fire brighter than the sun that seared the eyes. A fireball that swelled until it seemed it would consume the town and everything in it, bursting with a thunderclap of sound that echoed back among the hills like the crack of doom.

The shock wave reached out an invisible fist that punched the helicopter across the sky. The cabin spun crazily. Gear crashed, people were screaming. Rick was flung back against the starboard door; miraculously it held. He heard Natalie shrieking either in pain or fear. The helicopter spun wildly like a crippled bird, lurching across the sky in looping parabolas as the pilots fought for control. Rick slid down the cabin and back, caught in a welter of bodies. The rotors were screaming at full throttle, thrashing the air to stay aloft, and the hull was being hammered by air pockets that bounced them up and down like rats in a cage. The cabin filled with smoke and fumes. Rick could hear the crew shouting above the cries of the others. He figured any moment they were about to crash into the cliffs or go down into raging water. Either way they stood no chance. The main rotor was making a noise like a cement mixer filled with gravel.

The co-pilot was yelling over the intercom and jabbing his finger at the crew alert panel. Warnings lights were flashing red on all three fuel gauges. Both tanks and the reserve were sucking dry. The pumps must have shorted out. Red hydraulic fluid was dripping from the ceiling. Once the fuel supply choked to its last gasp, the engine would flare out and die. The only hope then for the pilot was to go immediately into autorotation, lowering the collective to force down the angle of the rotating blades and use the inertia of the rotor to maintain a barely controllable descent.

The turbine was screaming overhead. Any

moment now a thrust bearing in the rotor gearbox would shatter, converting the entire assembly instantaneously into metal salad. The pilot had witnessed such an event during his time in the military when a Sikorsky H-60 shed its main rotor on take off. The twenty-five-foot titanium and carbon-fibre blades had scythed across the apron, cutting a T-38 trainer in half and decapitating the pilot.

The pilot had only seconds left to decide. If the aircraft went down with the rotors still engaged and spinning, the blades would shatter on impact, hurling shards of flying steel and carbon fibre through the thin skin of the cabin. Injuries to passengers and crew would be horrific. But the alternative, cutting power and lowering the collective, reducing the angle of attack on the blades, meant certain death for everyone.

At all costs therefore he must keep the aircraft airborne long enough to reach solid ground.

Thirty seconds later the engine flamed out. Abruptly a chilling silence descended on the wrecked aircraft. A silence broken only by whimpers of fear from among the passengers. Red-headed Carly was praying out loud. Through the hatch Rick glimpsed tumbled water breaking over Greenstone Island. But the peak sheltering the house was still visible, standing firm against the flood. The explosion must have disrupted the main body of the tsunami. The Sound below was churned with furious waves surging this way and that, clashing up into angry crests, then pulling back to create holes in the ocean big enough to drop a house into. If we go down in that, Rick thought, we're dead. We're dead, but the town is saved.

The inertia weight of the heavy rotor blades still circling without power was holding the helicopter in the air for a few vital seconds, long enough perhaps to bring them down without killing everybody onboard. Up in front the two pilots had pulled the straps of their safety-belts and checked the quick-release catches to reassure themselves they could exit fast in the event of fire. The tanks might be dry but they would still contain inflammable vapour that would detonate with a spark and touch off any spilled oil and lubricants. Also the fuselage comprised aluminium and magnesium alloys, both of which burned with very high temperatures.

Right now there was another and more immediate fear. 'I can't hold the course!' the pilot gasped. Instinctively both men checked the rear-view mirrors. The tail rudder was twisted out of alignment. The co-pilot screwed up his face in dismay. If the rudder or tail rotor became detached the helicopter would lose all stability and veer across the sky in freefall.

'Three two five feet. Losing height at one hundred a minute.'

At the present rate they had three minutes of flying time left. Except that the radar altimeter was reading that height off the ocean and the land coming up ahead was a cliff that looked to be a good two hundred feet high. Which cut the margin of safety, if you could call it that, to just sixty seconds.

Back in the cabin Rick had an impression of cliffs rushing towards them. On instinct he pulled Natalie down beside him, cradling her head against his chest to shield her face. There was a spare seat nearby and he wedged the pair of them into the foot well. The cabin was swinging from side to side and any protection afforded was probably illusory, but he did it anyway.

The town had been saved by the detonation of the *Marie-Sainte*, but one section of the tsunami had escaped the blast. The right-hand edge of the giant wave, its northernmost section, was still intact. The southern and middle sectors might have been shattered, torn apart by the explosion, but the outlying portion, a quarter of a mile wide, 120 feet from trough to crest, was still thundering landwards with undiminished energy and heading straight for the cliffs of Curtain Bluff.

In the cockpit, the co-pilot gazed at the radar altimeter in helpless panic. The rate of descent was accelerating. From 100 feet a minute it had jumped to 120 and now 150. He risked a single glance back and down and the sight left him cold with dread. Behind the dropping aircraft, racing in pursuit, growing with every second and now rapidly overhauling them, was the rearing crest of a mountain. In a few more moments its gaping maw would snatch them from the sky as they fell and hammer them to pieces against the face of the cliff.

In the final few seconds they seemed to be toppling out of the sky. Rick glimpsed a headland, rocks, a church spire looming up.

He prayed.

Down in Maple Cove, Doc Southwell was pushing the Landcruiser to its limit, racing the surge across the sand, bouncing over rocks, bursting through lakes of water, charging onto the beach, hearing the roar of the returning ocean at their backs. Doc was trying to blot out the pictures in his mind of what would happen if they struck a hole or a rock, images of the car being bowled over by huge breakers, rolled along the beach, water and sand pouring in through smashed windows, choking and crushing. And he and Donna would be dead and he'd never see Tab again and life would be over, over . . .

The breakers were hammering at the rear door as they hit the ramp of sand at the base of the track. Without thinking, knowing that this was their last chance ever, Doc set the Toyota at the vertical ledge of shale that he and Martin had toppled down minutes earlier and either the tyres gripped phenomenally at the slope or else the water rising gave them a boost because incredibly they scrambled on up somehow and onto the track and up the track, still with the arms of the ocean surging at them, trying to drag them back.

And then they were on the road, looking down at the ocean surging back and forth and crying hysterically because they were alive.

Out on Curtain Bluff, the tsunami rammed the base of the cliffs full on and the entire headland trembled with the shock of the blow. Cliff and rock cracked and tumbled under the charging energy of tens of thousands of tons of ocean. A surge of water shot up, arcing over the cliffs like a giant claw. For a second it hung there suspended, defying the laws of gravity and time. A sight so vivid it stamped itself on Rick's mental retina for ever after. Then it fell, cascading out of the sky like an avalanche.

But the immense force of water smashing into the rocks had one unexpected result. It drove a pulse of air before it across the top of the cliff, a gale strong enough to rip the branches from the apple trees around the old graveyard and dense enough to provide a few vital seconds of upward lift to the rotor blades of the falling helicopter. It was as though, people declared afterwards, the aircraft had actually ridden the final few hundred yards in from the ocean on the crest of the wave itself to crash-land right next to the graveyard, gliding down on a carpet of foaming water.

For those inside the experience was anything but gentle. A jarring, bone-shattering, smashing impact that bounced and battered them like being shaken inside a drum. The helicopter hit the ground in a burst of spray, bounced and flipped over on its side. The main rotor, its spinning blades checked violently and broken off, tore free from its roof mounting. A section of rotor blade embedded itself like a spear in the wall of the church. The mutilated hull of the aircraft slid thirty yards on its side on a carpet of grass and water and turned a complete circle, finishing up facing back out towards the ocean.

Inside the cabin, the passengers were turned upside down, thrown on their faces, on their backs. Bits of the cabin broke off and flew about. Everything was a mad jumble of equipment and limbs and people screaming and a noise that went on and on.

When it stopped the silence was worse. Rick was dazed and bleeding about the face and head. It took him several moments to collect his wits, but by then instinct was starting to take over. He saw an eddy of steam somewhere out the corner of his eye that urged him to get out quickly. Natalie was lying in a bundle with her head under a seat, her limbs moving, and he scooped her up and carried her across to where the hatch now faced the sky. The opening was stoved in where the chopper had somersaulted, crushing in the roof. Rick had to squeeze out, pulling her up after him and helping her down onto the sodden turf. Supporting one another, they stared around them, dazed by their own survival. Rick gazed out eastwards, half expecting to see another wave rising up beyond the mouth of the Sound.

But there was nothing. The threat had passed. Against all the odds, somehow between them all they had vanquished the monster, turned back the tide and saved their town.

Up on the Green the flash of the fireball from the tanker was like the rising of the sun. Don Egan heard the thunder. He saw the mighty cloud spouting up over the Sound and asked himself, Is this the end? Is this the end of Goodwill? Then the blast wave swept over, ripping off slates, cracking windows, bending trees and branches, and a biblical phrase about the breath of the Lord sprang to mind. He braced himself for the rush of the water carrying everything before it.

The remnants of the great wave that had been blown apart pounded the Sound, raging and destroying where they could. Huge breakers surged back and forth, battering, smashing, tearing apart buildings, sucking stones from walls and pavements. The Neck was swept clear again and again. Bay Road took repeated hammerings. Floods ripped through the alleys, destroying, sucking back and returning unsated to wreak more vengeance on the dry land that had defied them, just as others had done 200 years before.

The waters surged up across the Green to the foot of the memorial to the victims of the Great Storm, soaking the hallowed ground where the bodies of the dead from that terrible day lay sleeping. The waters surged to the stone – and no further. The gas tanker that had seemingly posed such a deadly threat had ultimately saved the town. Twenty thousand tons of fuel detonating beneath the wave had turned the ocean back as if with a giant hand.

As the waters receded a cool breeze rose. It blew away the cloud of darkness and smoke and the sun shone through again. Don Egan thought, Somebody up there loves us, loves Goodwill.

On the Dead River, the raft floated level and upright on calm water. The families were breathing normally again. Ted was counting heads. The girls' teeth were chattering. They looked like drowned rats, Lloyd thought and was on the point of telling them so when Mr Van Buren said, 'Where's Sandy?' And they all thought, Oh no!

'I'm over here!' called a voice. And they looked round and there was Sandy, swimming beside them, grinning.

'I'm fine,' she said when they had hauled her in. 'I got flipped out right early on when the raft started to go up. I figured I might never see you guys again and then when I come up there you all are a couple of feet away. Funny, huh?'

'What was that thing?' Lloyd wanted to know.

'That was a bore, a tidal bore.' Sandy patted his head. 'When the tide runs up the river real strong it makes a wave sometimes. That was a big one; you were lucky to see it.'

'That was a tide?' Lloyd said, delighted. 'There, didn't I tell you, Dad, back at the cottage I saw the creek come up?'

At Curtain Bluff, the survivors from the helicopter gathered in the church. 'Is that the last wave?' a bewildered voice shouted in the gloom.

'Sure hope so,' Rick answered weakly. 'I don't know that I could handle another trip.'

Natalic choked and laughed. Someone else joined in and then incredibly everybody – film crew, townspeople, pilots – was laughing, wildly, hysterically. Laughing because they were all still alive, laughing till the church nave rang because it was the only thing to do in the face of death and destruction.

Epilogue

Of course that was not the last wave. There were three more, some said four, but they were minor events compared to those that went before. The third wave was the greatest of all. The video footage of the King's mad ride was shown and studied endlessly in the days and months that followed. The tide gauges in the Sound were all knocked out, but height comparisons with the cliffs of Curtain Bluff, with the lighthouse, plus the known dimensions of the tanker put the tsunami's crest at 123 feet, a record for a ridden wave that looked as if it would stand a long while. The King's body was never recovered. In death, though, he achieved the immortality he craved. His fame would live for ever in surfers' annals.

K. Zamos's blockbuster *Doomed Youth*, shot on location and featuring live footage of the King's final moments, was rushed into production for the first anniversary of the eruption.

His cell in the jail had already become a place of pilgrimage for hundreds of young and not so young. It got so that the town had to build a new cellblock, allowing them to declare the old one a shrine to the sport and its new hero.

Even without the film the publicity generated by the tsunami and the events leading up to it ensured that Goodwill's economic recovery would be swift. The image of plucky inhabitants fighting to save their town caught the public imagination. Coupled with the tale of the lone surf rider and his quest for the ultimate wave it made an unbeatable combination. By spring, with rebuilding proceeding apace thanks to generous federal relief and insurance payouts, it was apparent that the coming year would be a record.

Wave measurements are notoriously fickle and open to dispute. The collapse of Cumbre Vieja's western flank was afterwards shown to have kicked up a splash wave that topped out at 496 metres. Within fifteen minutes it had radiated outward by 50 kilometres and reduced in height to 100 metres. By the time it reached the USS *Tarp* at 100 kilometres out decay was setting in rapidly and it was down to 30 metres, 100 feet. Unusually the wave at this point seems to have been breaking, which was what overwhelmed *Tarp*. Non-breaking waves only rarely sink ships, but a breaking wave, if it is higher than the ship is long, will either flip the boat over end on end or else break across it. Either way the result is the same: however big the ship is, however strongly built, the wave is bigger and stronger and the weight of the sea will literally drive the decks under. Water floods down through the stacks, bursts open steel hatches and the vessel founders. With that weight of water inside the hull it just goes straight on down to the bottom, taking everything with it. Understandably survivors are few.

Tarp's crew had one thing going for them: the weather was calm. Once the splash wave had done its worst the ocean returned rapidly to normal. Subsequent waves, the killer follow-ups that would go to commit destruction on coasts far away, passed almost unnoticed.

Mary Sennett, who had struggled into her survival suit with such difficulty, almost didn't make it out through the hatchway as the ship went down. Some piece of the suit snagged on a latch handle and for several seconds, which to her seemed like minutes, she kicked and scrabbled blindly to free herself while the water closed over her head and her lungs squeezed. When finally by a miracle she broke free the boat must have righted itself on its way down for she shot to the surface, gasping and alive. The wave had passed and left her utterly alone. She blew her whistle and shouted, but of the *Tarp* and all her comrades there was no trace. The next two waves that followed were small by comparison, but they carried her a long way out into mid-Atlantic. As darkness fell she switched on the light on her suit and prayed.

Next morning she was still alive, floating in a sea of pumice. Several aircraft passed overhead, evidently searching for survivors, but Mary was too weak to attract their attention. Then early in the evening as the light was starting to fade again and Mary was bracing herself for another night, it was the fear of sharks that got to her most; there was a hissing and a spouting some way off. She swung herself round expecting to see a whale only to find herself gaping at an enormous submarine that was surfacing a quarter-mile upwind of her. It was the USS *Thresher*, still limping from her noisy pump and somewhat battered from her close proximity to the eruption, but otherwise undamaged. She had been vectored onto Mary's position by an observer in one of the planes.

Mary was not alone in being lucky. Derek Wanless survived along with two thirds of the *Tarp*'s complement. Those survival suits worked. Malcolm Mackenzie and Concha lived to make it down off the mountain on an island that had lost fully a third of its land mass. Between them they were able to confirm the sequence of events that had propelled Cumbre Vieja from a modest level three eruption into a level six super-Krakatoa blast.

The total destruction of the western flank of the fire mountain including the port of Charco Verde made it impossible to verify claims of a deliberately induced fuel–coolant interaction. That Carlos, the hotel owner, had acquired explosives was admitted, but since he and all

689

other alleged participants were now dead no more could be said.

The worst predictions of the doomsayers proved unfounded however. Although terrible damage was done in the Bahamas and other low-lying islands, with particular havoc wrought on Bermuda, in general the focus of the waves' impact appeared to have been directed northwards, away from the vulnerable Caribbean basin and Florida and towards New England. By the time the waves reached the continental shelf, however, much of their force was spent. Topography played a large part. Some waves broke on the shelf, dumping their remaining energy. Others swept on to batter coastal communities. As Professor Ballister had forecast the worst hit were south-west-facing bays and inlets with deep-water anchorages. Fine natural harbours, in short, and a description that fit Goodwill perfectly.

In town the Neck was swept clean. The Larsen Chandlery, the Lobsterman diner, Jack Pearl's office were all pulverised by the ocean. The Seafarers Motel was washed away, luckily after everyone evacuated. The waves gutted Chance Greene's new marina, crushing yachts and boats to matchwood and depositing others in Bay Road or on the Green itself. There was much damage to buildings along the harbour front and in the streets and lanes leading off. The retreating waters sucked the paving off the sidewalks and pulled down several of the fine old brick residences on Washington Street. Even so, many more survived including the Ice Factory. The water rushed in from the harbourside, bursting open the main doors, then retreated back the way it had come, leaving the structure still standing. It became a national icon, a symbol of Maine's defiance. A fund was got up for its restoration and Chance Greene presented the building to the town; he really had no choice.

Pequod survived by being out at sea along with the Maxwell yacht and a bunch of other craft. The hospital was wrecked when the Causeway washed away, but no lives were lost there, though elsewhere there were individual tragedies. Rick's sister Rebecca spent a month in Portland being pieced together and was back running the rebuilt Chandlery. Hannah Morrissey had died, but the Whale remained and was more popular than ever. Hannah's body was recovered, but the satchel of gold and valuables was never found and that too passed into legend: the crock of gold lying somewhere at the bottom of the harbour.

A year on the survivors gathered at the memorial service for the victims of the flood and the unveiling of a statue. The bronze figure was the work of Natalie Maxwell. A life-sized surfer leaping on his board, seemingly almost airborne from a mighty breaker, arms outstretched for balance, his right hand straining upward as if reaching for a star.

Natalie by then was ambivalent about her role. She declined K. Zamos's invitation to star in his

movie. She and Rick were together again, taking
it one day at a time. At the unveiling she chose to
read a poem that felt appropriate to the sculpture.

I have a rendezvous with Death
At some disputed barricade,
When spring comes back with rustling shade
And apple blossom fill the air –
I have a rendezvous with Death.

But I've a rendezvous with Death
At midnight in some flaming town;
When spring trips north again this year,
And I to my pledged word am true,
I shall not fail that rendezvous.

The statue had been erected on the cliff at
Curtain Bluff overlooking the Sound where the
King had lived his finest hour and died. As she
finished reading, a low murmur arose from the
crowd that had gathered to listen. A murmur
that swelled into glad cries. People were pointing
and crying out excitedly.

Down in the water dark shapes were moving,
gliding with effortless grace among the waves.

The whales had returned.

'A voyage around the world.'

'You've decided?'

He nodded. 'West to east this time, the hard
way.' If it was going to be a challenge it might as
well be for broke.

692

'Single-handed?' she asked.

He shrugged. 'That was how I always saw it. It's not a trip I could expect anyone to share.'

Her eyes fixed on him. Those gypsy eyes filled with shattered light. 'You could try,' she suggested lightly.

He grinned, happy suddenly. 'A year in a small boat. It would have to be someone I got along with real well.'

'Or we might wind up killing one another, you mean? Better than going on with the same old story.'

'That's the way I look at it.'

She hooked an arm through his. The wind blew in her hair. It was as if the weight of the past year had dropped away from the both of them.

Natalie tugged his arm. 'Let's go, whale finder,' she said.

Flood

Richard Doyle

Flood is a devastating and compulsive thriller that reads like fact. The country has suffered floods on an unprecedented scale in recent years, but have we seen the worst, an inundation that threatens millions of lives? Flood is the disaster novel of today.

A storm rages over the north of Britain, a troop carrier founders in the Irish Sea, flood indicators go off the scale, the seas are mountainous and a spring tide is about to strike the East Coast. Air sea rescue and military personnel struggle to save lives all down the coast. The worst is yet to come. When the storm reaches the south the two forces of wind and tide will combine and send a huge tidal surge up the Thames.

But surely London is safe: the Thames Barrier will save the capital from disaster as it was intended to do? The river is a titanic presence by now, higher than anyone has known it, and the surge thunders towards the Barrier. Scientists begin to talk of the possibility of overtopping. Can fifty feet high gates be overwhelmed by a wave? Then there is an explosion the size of a small Hiroshima: a supertanker is ablaze in the estuary and most of the Essex petrochemical works are going up with it. The Thames catches fire and the wall of fire and water thunders towards Britain's capital. This is the story of what happens next, and the desperate attempts to save the capital from destruction.

arrow books

Executive Action

Richard Doyle

Jack Meade wakes in a hospital bed. The doctors tell him he has been in the sea for two days - that he is lucky to be alive. His face is so salt ravaged he barely recognises himself. He has lost nearly all his memory. All he can remember is his name. And that is when the nightmare begins. For Jack Meade is the name of the President Elect of the United States.

In Washington an exact double of Meade is preparing to take the Oath of Office, a man who thought he had killed Jack, a man who has taken his wife and fooled everyone in the country including Jack's closest associates. Meade realises he has only one option: to escape from the hospital, go to Washington and convince his wife and colleagues that he is the President. But the Usurper is now surrounded by the might of the Secret Service and America's armed forces. He has already tried to kill Jack once. Now with all the power of the Presidency behind him, he will try to silence forever the one man who knows about the deception that has tricked the world.

arrow books

Airframe

Michael Crichton

The twin jet plane en route to Denver from Hong Kong is merely a green radar blip half an hour off the California coast when the call comes through to air traffic control:

'Social Approach, this is TransPacific 545. We have an emergency.' The pilot requests priority clearance to land – then comes the bombshell – he needs forty ambulances on the runway.

But nothing prepares the rescue workers for the carnage they witness when they enter the plane. Ninety-four passengers are injured. Three dead. The interior cabin virtually destroyed.

What happened on board Flight TPA 545?

'A compulsive page-turner . . . Crichton dazzles the reader'
Financial Times

'This is the first book in ages which I can honestly say I read at a single sitting'
The Times

'A deftly-woven tale of corporate skulduggery, media deceit and sleuthing that culminates in a genuinely gripping and surprising ending . . . an engrossing yarn'
Express

arrow books

Congo
Michael Crichton

Deep in the darkest region of the Congo, near the legendary ruins of the Lost City of Zinj, an eight-person field expedition dies mysteriously and brutally in a matter of minutes . . .

'Ingenious, imaginative'
Los Angeles Times

'Thrilling'
New York Times Book Review

'Dazzling'
People

arrow books

ALSO AVAILABLE IN ARROW

Jurassic Park
Michael Crichton

The phenomenal worldwide bestseller

On a remote jungle island, genetic engineers have created a dinosaur game park.

An astonishing technique for recovering and cloning dinosaur DNA has been discovered. Now one of mankind's most thrilling fantasies has come true . . .

'Crichton's most compulsive novel to date'
Sunday Telegraph

'Breathtaking adventure . . . a book that is as hard to put down as it is to forget'
Time Out

'Wonderful . . . powerful'
Washington Post

'Full of suspense'
New York Times

arrow books

Order further Arrow titles
from your local bookshop, or have them delivered
direct to your door by Bookpost

Flood Richard Doyle	0 09 942969 1	£6.99
Executive Action Richard Doyle	0 09 926994 5	£5.00
Airframe Michael Crichton	0 09 955631 6	£6.99
Congo Michael Crichton	0 09 954431 8	£6.99
Jurassic Park Michael Crichton	0 09 928291 7	£6.99

Free post and packing
Overseas customers allow £2 per paperback

Phone: 01624 677237

Post: Random House Books
c/o Bookpost, PO Box 29, Douglas, Isle of Man IM99 1BQ

Fax: 01624 670923

email: bookshop@enterprise.net

Cheques (payable to Bookpost) and credit cards accepted

Prices and availability subject to change without notice.
Allow 28 days for delivery.
When placing your order, please state if you do not wish to receive any
additional information.

www.randomhouse.co.uk/arrowbooks

arrow books